Perfect

By Rachel Joyce

The Unlikely Pilgrimage of Harold Fry

Perfect

Perfect

A Novel

Rachel Joyce

RANDOM HOUSE ☖ NEW YORK

A Random House International Edition

Copyright © 2013 by Rachel Joyce

Published by Random House, an imprint and division of Random House LLC, a Penguin Random House Company, New York.

RANDOM HOUSE and the HOUSE colophon are registered trademarks of Random House LLC.

Originally published in the United Kingdom by Doubleday, an imprint of Transworld Publishers, London, and in the United States by Random House, an imprint and division of Random House LLC, in 2013.

ISBN 978-0-8129-9900-6
eBook ISBN 978-0-679-64512-2

Cover design: Greg Mollica
Cover illustration: Don Farrall/Getty Images

Printed in the United States of America

www.atrandom.com

1 2 3 4 5 6 7 8 9

Book design by Caroline Cunningham

For my mother and my son, Jo (without an e)

Only when the clock stops does time come to life.

—William Faulkner, *The Sound and the Fury*

Perfect

The Addition of Time

In 1972, two seconds were added to time. Britain agreed to join the Common Market, and "Beg, Steal or Borrow" by the New Seekers was the entry for Eurovision. The seconds were added because it was a leap year and time was out of joint with the movement of the Earth. The New Seekers did not win the Eurovision Song Contest but that had nothing to do with the Earth's movement and nothing to do with the two seconds either.

The addition of time terrified Byron Hemmings. At eleven years old he was an imaginative boy. He lay awake, picturing it happen, and his heart flapped like a bird. He watched the clocks, trying to catch them at it. "When will they do it?" he asked his mother.

She stood at the new breakfast counter, dicing quarters of apple. The morning sun spilled through the glass doors in such clean squares that he could stand in them.

"Probably when we're asleep," she said.

"Asleep?" Things were even worse than he thought.

"Or maybe when we're awake."

He got the impression she didn't actually know. "Two seconds are nothing," she smiled. "Please drink up your Sunquick." Her eyes were bright, her skirt pressed, her hair blow-dried.

Byron had heard about the extra seconds from his friend James Lowe. James was the cleverest boy Byron knew, and every day James read *The Times*. The addition of two seconds was extremely exciting, said James. First, man had put a man on the moon. Now they were going to alter time. But how could two seconds exist where two seconds had not existed before? It was like adding something that wasn't there. It wasn't safe. When Byron pointed this out, James smiled. That was progress, he said.

Byron wrote four letters, one to his local MP, one to NASA, one to the editors of *The Guinness Book of Records*, and the last to Mr. Roy Castle, care of the BBC. He gave them to his mother to post, assuring her they were important.

He received a signed photograph of Roy Castle and a fully illustrated brochure about the Apollo 15 moon landing, but there was no reference to the two seconds.

Within months everything had changed, and the changes could never be put right. Nothing could atone for his mother's mistake. All over the house, clocks that his mother had once meticulously wound now marked different hours. The children slept when they were tired and ate when they were hungry and whole days might pass, each looking the same. So if two seconds had been added to a year in which a mistake was made—a mistake so unexpected that without the added seconds it might not have happened at all—how could his mother be to blame? Was the addition of time not the bigger wrong?

"It wasn't your fault," he would say to his mother. By late summer she was often by the pond, down in the meadow. These days it was Byron making the breakfast, maybe a foil triangle of cheese squished between two slices of bread. His mother sat in a chair, clinking the ice in her glass and slipping the seeds from a plume of grass. In the distance the moor glowed beneath a veil of lemon-sherbet light; the meadow was threaded with flowers. "Did you hear?" he would repeat, because she was inclined to forget she was not alone. "It was because they added time. It was an accident."

She would put up her chin. She would smile. "You're a good boy. Thank you."

It was all because of a small slip in time, the whole story. The repercussions were felt for years and years. Of the two boys, James and Byron, only one kept on course. Sometimes Byron gazed at the sky above the moor, pulsing so heavily with stars that the darkness seemed alive, and he would ache—ache for the removal of those two extra seconds. Ache for the sanctity of time as it should be.

If only James had never told him.

PART ONE

Inside

Something Terrible

James Lowe and Byron Hemmings attended Winston House School because it was private. There was another junior school that was closer but it was not private; it was for everyone. The children who went there came from the council estate on Digby Road. They flicked orange peels and cigarette butts at the caps of the Winston House boys from the top windows of the bus. The Winston House boys did not travel on the bus. They had lifts with their mothers because they had so far to travel.

The future for the Winston House boys was mapped out. Theirs was a story with a beginning, a middle, and an end. The following year, they would take the Common Entrance exam for the college. The cleverest boys would win scholarships, and at thirteen they would board. They would speak with the right accent and learn the right things and meet the right people. After that it would be Oxford or Cambridge. James's parents were thinking St. Peter's; Byron's were thinking Oriel. They would pursue careers in law or the City, the Church or the armed forces, like their fathers. One day they would have private rooms in

London and large houses in the country where they would spend weekends with their wives and children.

It was the beginning of June in 1972. A trim of morning light slid beneath Byron's blue curtains and picked out his neatly ordered possessions. There were his *Look and Learn* annuals, his stamp album, his torch, his new Abracadabra magic box, and the biology set with its own magnifying glass that he had received for Christmas. His school uniform had been washed and pressed by his mother the night before and was arranged in a flattened boy shape on a chair. Byron checked both his watch and his alarm clock. The second hands were moving steadily. Crossing the hall in silence, he eased open the door of his mother's room and took up his place on the edge of her bed.

She lay very still. Her hair was a gold frill on the pillow and her face trembled with each breath as if she were made of water. Through her skin he could see the purple of her veins. Byron's hands were soft and plump like the flesh of a peach, but James already had veins, faint threads that ran from his knuckles and would one day become ridges like a man's.

At half past six, the alarm clock rang into the silence and his mother's eyes flashed open, a shimmer of blue.

"Hello, sweetheart."

"I'm worried," said Byron.

"It isn't time again?" She reached for her glass and her pill and took a sip of water.

"Suppose they are going to add the extra seconds today?"

"Is James worried too?"

"He seems to have forgotten."

She wiped her mouth and he saw that she was smiling. Two dimples had appeared like tiny punctures in her cheeks. "We've been through this. We keep doing it. When they add the seconds, they'll say something about it first in *The Times*. They'll talk about it on *Nationwide*."

"It's giving me a headache," he said.

"When it happens you won't notice. Two seconds are nothing."

Byron felt his blood heat. He almost stood but sat back again. "That's what nobody realizes. Two seconds are huge. It's the difference between something happening and something not happening. You could take one step too many and fall over the edge of a cliff. It's very dangerous." The words came out in a rush.

She gazed back at him with her face crumpled the way it got when she was trying to work out a sum. "We really must get up," she said.

His mother pulled back the curtains at the bay window and stared out. A summer mist was pouring in from Cranham Moor, so thick that the hills beyond the garden looked in danger of being washed away. She glanced at her wrist.

"Twenty-four minutes to seven," she said, as if she were informing her watch of the correct time. Lifting her pink dressing gown from its hook, she went to wake Lucy.

When Byron pictured the inside of his mother's head, he imagined a series of tiny inlaid drawers with jeweled handles so delicate that his fingers would struggle to get a grip. The other mothers were not like her. They wore crocheted tank tops and layered skirts and some of them even had the new wedge shoes. Byron's father preferred his wife to dress more formally. With her slim skirts and pointy heels, her matching handbag and her notebook, Diana made other women look both oversize and underprepared. Andrea Lowe, James's mother, towered over Diana

Hemmings like a dark-haired giant. Diana's notebook contained articles she had snipped and glued from the pages of *Good House-keeping* and *Family Circle*. She wrote down birthdays she had to remember, important dates for the school term, as well as recipes, needlecraft instructions, planting ideas, hairstyling tips, and words she had not heard before. Her notebook bulged with sug-gestions for improvement: "22 new hairdos to make you even prettier this summer." "Tissue paper gifts for every occasion." "Cooking with offal." "i before e except after c."

"Elle est la plus belle mère," James sometimes said. And when he did he blushed and fell silent, as if in contemplation of some-thing sacred.

Byron dressed in his gray flannel shorts and summer T-shirt. His school shirt was almost new, and he had to tug to fasten the buttons. Having secured his knee-length socks with homemade garters, he headed downstairs. The wood-paneled walls shone dark as conkers.

"I'm not talking to anyone but you, darling," sang his mother's voice.

She stood at the opposite end of the hallway at her telephone table, already dressed. Beside her, Lucy waited for her plaits to be tied with ribbon. The air was thick with Vim and Pledge polish, and it was a reassuring smell in the way that fresh air was reassur-ing. As Byron passed, his mother kissed her fingertips and pressed them to his forehead. She was only a fraction taller than he.

"It's just me and the children," she said into the mouthpiece. The windows behind her were opaque white.

In the kitchen Byron sat at the breakfast bar and unfolded a clean napkin. His mother was talking to his father. He rang at the same time every morning, and every morning she told him she was listening.

"Oh, today I'll do the usual. The house, the weeding. Tidying after the weekend. It's supposed to get hot."

Released from her mother's hands, Lucy skipped to the kitchen and hoicked herself up onto her stool. She tipped the box of Sugar Stars over her Peter Rabbit bowl. "Steady," said Byron as she reached for the blue jug. He watched the splashy flow of milk in the rough vicinity of her cereal. "You might spill, Lucy," he said, although he was being polite. She already had.

"I know what I'm doing, Byron. I don't need help." Every word of Lucy's sounded like a neat little attack on the air. She replaced the jug on the table. It was vast in her hands. Then she slotted a wall of cereal boxes around her bowl. Byron could see only the flaxen crest of her head.

From the hall came their mother's voice. "Yes, Seymour. She's all polished." Byron assumed that they were discussing the new Jaguar.

"Please could I have the Sugar Stars, Lucy?"

"You are not supposed to have Sugar Stars. You must have your fruit salad and your healthy Alpen."

"I'd like to read the box. I'd like to look at the picture of Sooty."

"I am reading the boxes."

"You don't need all of them at once," he said gently. "And anyway you can't read, Luce."

"Everything's as it should be," came their mother's voice from the hallway. She gave a fluttery laugh.

Byron felt a notch of something hot in his stomach. He tried to remove a cereal box, just one, before Lucy could stop him, but her hand flew up as he was sliding it away. The milk jug shot sideways, there was a resounding smash, and the new floor was suddenly a wash of white milk and blue pins of china. The children stared, aghast. It was almost time to clean their teeth.

Their mother was in the room within moments. "No one move!" she called. She held up her hands as if she were halting traffic. "You could get hurt!" Byron sat so still his neck felt stiff. As she made her way to the cleaning cupboard, balancing on tiptoes, her arms stretched out, her fingers pointed, the floor swished and snapped beneath her feet.

"That was your fault, Byron," said Lucy.

Diana rushed back with the mop and bucket, and the dustpan and brush. She twisted the mop in soapy water and dragged it through the pool of liquid. With a glance at her watch, she swept the broken bits of china into a dry patch and scooped them into the dustpan. The last splinters she scraped up with her fingers and shook out over the bin. "All done," she said brightly. It was then that she noticed her left palm. It was cut with crimson, like spilling stripes.

"Now you've got blood," said Lucy, who was both appalled and delighted by physical injury.

"It's nothing," insisted their mother, but the blood was slithering down her wrist and, despite her bib apron, had made several spots on the hem of her skirt. "Nobody move!" she called again, turning on her heels and rushing out of the room.

"We'll be late," said Lucy.

"We're never late," said Byron. It was a rule of their father's. An Englishman should always be punctual.

When Diana reappeared she had changed into a mint-green dress and matching lambswool cardigan. She had wound her hand with a bandage so that it looked like a small paw and had applied her strawberry-red lipstick.

"Why are you still sitting there?" she cried.

"You told us not to move," said Lucy.

Clip, clip, echoed her heels across the hallway as the children raced after her. Their blazers and school hats hung from hooks above their school shoes. Diana scooped their satchels and PE bags into her arms.

"Come along," she called.

"But we haven't cleaned our teeth."

Their mother failed to answer. Swinging open the front door, she darted into the shroud of mist. Byron and Lucy had to rush outside to find her.

There she stood, a slight silhouette against the garage door. She studied her watch, her left wrist clamped between the thumb and fingers of her right hand, as if time were a small cell and she was examining it through a microscope.

"It's going to be all right," she said. "If we hurry, we can make up time."

Cranham House was a Georgian residence of pale stone that shone bone-white in full summer sun and pink as flesh on a winter morning. There was no village. There was only the house and the garden and then the moor. The building sat with its back resolutely set against the mass of wind, sky, and earth that loomed behind, and made Byron think of a home that wished it had been built elsewhere, in acres of flat English parkland, for instance, or on the gentle banks of a stream. The advantage of the setting, his father said, was that it was private. This was what James called an understatement. You had to drive at least three miles to find a neighbor. Between the gardens and the first slopes of the moor was a meadow with a large pond, and then a belt of ash trees. A year ago the water had been fenced in and the children were forbidden to play there.

The gravel drive popped beneath the wheels of the Jaguar. The mist was like a hood over Byron's eyes. It stole the color and edges from even the closest things. The top lawn, the herbaceous borders and rose pagodas, the fruit trees, the beech hedging, the vegetable plot, the cutting beds and picket gate, they were all gone. The car turned left and carved its path toward the upper peaks. No one spoke. Diana sat straining forward over the wheel.

Up on the moor, conditions were even worse. That morning there was no dividing line between hills and sky. The car headlamps bored shallow holes into the blanket of white. Occasionally a watery group of cattle or a protruding branch took shape, and Byron's heart gave a bounce as his mother swerved to avoid them. Once Byron had told James that the trees were so scary on the moor they could be ghosts, and James had frowned. That was like poetry, James had said, but it was not real, just as a talking detective dog was not real on the television. They passed the iron gates to Besley Hill, where the mad people lived. As the wheels of the Jaguar rumbled over the cattle grid, Byron breathed a sigh of relief. Then, approaching the town, they turned a corner and braked hard.

"Oh no," he said, sitting tall. "What's happened now?"

"I don't know. A traffic jam." It was the last thing they needed.

His mother lifted her fingers to her teeth and ripped off a shred of her nail.

"Is it because of the mist?"

Again: "I don't know." She pulled at the handbrake.

"I think the sun is up there somewhere," he said helpfully. "It will burn this off soon."

There were cars blocking the road as far as they could see, all the way into the veil of cloud. To their left the dull silhouette of a burned-out vehicle marked the entrance to the Digby Road Estate. They never went that way. Byron saw his mother glance over.

"We're going to be late," wailed Lucy.

Snapping down the handbrake, Diana pushed the car into first gear with a crunch, yanked at the wheel, and accelerated toward the left. They were heading straight for Digby Road. She didn't even mirror, signal, maneuver.

At first the children were too stunned to speak. They passed the burned-out car. The glass of the windows was smashed, and the wheels, doors, and engine were gone so that the car was like a charred skeleton. Byron hummed gently because he didn't want to think about that.

"Father says we must never go this way," said Lucy. She smothered her face with her hands.

"It's a shortcut through council housing," Diana said. "I've been this way before." She eased her foot down on the accelerator.

There was no time to consider what she had said: that, despite their father's rule, she had been this way before. Digby Road was worse than Byron had imagined. In places it wasn't even tarmacked. The mist was glued to the rows of houses so that they reached ahead, dull and indistinct, and then appeared to disintegrate. Pieces of rubbish choked the gutters: rubble, bags, blankets, boxes, it was hard to tell what it was. Occasionally washing lines appeared, strung with sheets and clothes that held no color.

"I'm not looking," said Lucy, sliding down her seat to hide.

Byron tried to find something to look at that wouldn't cause alarm. Something that he might recognize and feel good about in Digby Road. He worried too much, his mother had told him so many times. And then suddenly there it was. One beautiful thing: a tree that glowed through the fog. It presented wide arching branches that appeared festooned with bubblegum-pink flowers, although the fruit blossom season at Cranham House was long since over. Byron felt a surge of relief as if he had witnessed a small miracle, or an act of kindness, at the moment he least believed in the existence of either. Beneath the tree came a moving silhouette. It was small, the size of a child. It was spinning toward the road and had wheels. It was a girl on a red bicycle.

"What time is it?" said Lucy. "Are we late?"

Byron glanced at his watch and then he froze. The second hand was moving backward. His voice sliced at his throat and he realized it was a scream.

"Mummy, it's happening. Stop." He grabbed her shoulder. He pulled hard.

He couldn't make sense of what came next. It was so fast. While he tried to poke his watch—or, more specifically, the adjusted second hand—in front of his mother's face, he was also aware of the miracle tree and the little girl bicycling into the road. They were all part of the same thing. All of them shooting out of nowhere, out of the dense mist, out of time. The Jaguar swerved, and Byron's hands smacked into the mahogany dashboard to brace himself. As the car slammed to a halt there was a sound like a metallic whisper, and then there was silence.

In the beats that followed, that were smaller than seconds, smaller even than flickers, where Byron sought with his eyes for the child at the roadside and did not find her, he knew that something terrible had happened and that life would never be the same. He knew it before he even had the words.

Above the moor shone a dazzling circle of white light. Byron had been right about the sun. It would burn through at any moment.

Jim

Jim lives in a campervan, on the edge of the new housing estate. Every dawn he walks across the moor and every night he walks back. He has a job at the refurbished supermarket café. There is wifi access and a facility to charge mobile phones although Jim has no use for either. When he started six months ago he worked in the hot beverages section, but after serving cappuccinos with a raspberry twirl topping and a Flake he was relegated to tables. If he messes this job up, there's nothing. There isn't even Besley Hill.

The black sky is combed with trails of cloud like silver hair and the air is so cold it pares his skin. Beneath his feet the ground has frozen hard and his boots crash over the brittle stumps of grass. Already he can make out the neon glow that is Cranham Village, while far behind car headlamps make their way across the moor and they are a necklace of tiny moving lights, red and silver, stringing the dark.

In his late teens, he was found up there in only underpants and shoes. He had given his clothes to the trees; for days he had been sleeping wild. He was sectioned on the spot. "Hello again, Jim," the doctor said, as if they were old friends, as if Jim was dressed, like him, in suit and tie. "Hello again, Doctor," Jim had said to show he was not trouble. The doctor prescribed electroconvulsive therapy. It brought on a stammer and later a tingling in his fingers that even now Jim still feels.

Pain is like that, he knows. Somewhere in his brain what happened to him then has got mixed up. It has become something else, not simply the hurt he felt at the time but another, more complicated one that is to do with more than forty years ago, and all he's lost.

He follows the road to the estate. There is a sign, welcoming visitors to Cranham Village and asking them to drive carefully. Recently the sign has been vandalized, along with the bus shelter and the children's swings, and now reads WELCOME TO CRAPHAM VILLAGE. Fortunately Cranham is the sort of place people visit only if their satnav has made a mistake. Jim wipes the sign because it is a shame, to see it humiliated like that, but the *n* will not come back.

The new houses are packed tight as teeth. Each has a front garden, no bigger than a parking space, and a plastic window box where nothing grows. Over the weekend many residents have strung their guttering with Christmas lights, and Jim stops to admire them. He especially likes the ones that are flashing icicles. On the top of one roof, an inflatable Santa appears to be dismantling the satellite dish. He is possibly not the sort of man you want coming down your chimney. Jim passes the square of mud that residents call "the Green" and the fenced-off ditch in the middle. He picks up some empty beer cans and carries them to the bin.

Entering the cul-de-sac, he looks at the house rented by foreign students, and the one where an old man sits every day at a window. He passes the gate with the DANGEROUS DOG sign, and the garden with the laundry that is never taken down. Ahead his van shines in the moonlight, pale as milk.

A couple of young boys whizz past on a bicycle, shrieking with excitement, one on the seat, the other balanced on the handlebars. He calls, Be c-careful, but they don't hear.

How did I get here?, Jim asks himself. There were two of us once.

The wind blows and says nothing.

Lucky Talismans

When James had first mentioned the addition of seconds to Byron, he had presented it as just another interesting fact. The boys liked to sit outside the chapel during their lunch break while the others ran about on the field. They showed their Brooke Bond tea cards—they were both collecting the History of Aviation set—and James told Byron stories from his newspaper. It had not been a leading article, he explained, and he had been obliged to read quickly because his boiled egg was ready, but the gist of it was that due to the leap year, recorded time was out of kilter with the natural movement of the Earth. In order to change it, he said wisely, scientists would have to look at things like the expansion of the Earth's crust, and also how it juddered on its axis. Byron felt his face flatten. The idea appalled him. And even though James talked about how exciting this was, and then went on to discuss something entirely different, the thought of tampering with the natural order of things grew and grew in Byron's mind. Time was what held the world together. It kept life as it should be.

Unlike James, Byron was a substantial boy. They made an odd

pairing. James was slight and pale, his fringe sliding into his eyes, nibbling his mouth as he thought something through, while Byron sat tall and stolid beside him, waiting for James to finish. Sometimes Byron would pinch at the folds of flesh at his waist and ask his mother why James didn't have them, and she'd say he did, of course he did, but Byron knew she was being kind. His body frequently burst through buttons and seams. His father said it straight out. Byron was overweight, he was lazy. And then his mother would say this was puppy fat, there was a difference. They would speak as if Byron was not there, which was strange when they were discussing the fact that there was too much of him.

In the beats that followed the accident, Byron felt suddenly made of nothing. He wondered if he was hurt. He sat waiting for his mother to realize what she had done, waiting for her to scream or get out of the car, only she didn't. He sat waiting for the little girl to scream or get up off the road, and that didn't happen either. His mother remained very still in her driving seat and the little girl lay very still beneath her red bicycle. Then suddenly, with a snap, things started to happen. His mother glanced over her right shoulder and adjusted her mirror; Lucy asked why they had stopped. It was only the little girl who stayed not moving.

Starting up the engine, Diana placed her hands on the steering wheel in the exact position her husband had taught her. She reversed the car to straighten it and pushed the gearstick into first. Byron couldn't believe she was driving away, that they were leaving the little girl where they had knocked into her, and then he realized it was because his mother didn't know. She hadn't seen what she had done. His heart thumped so hard it hurt his throat.

"Go, go, go!" he shouted.

In answer, his mother bit her lip to show she was concentrating and pressed her foot on the accelerator. She went to angle her mirror, twitching it a little to the left, a little to the right—

"Hurry up!" he shouted. They had to get away before anyone saw them.

Steadily they made their way down Digby Road. Byron kept twisting from left to right, craning his neck to see out of the rear window. If they didn't hurry, the mist would be gone. They turned onto the High Street and passed the new Wimpy Bar. The Digby Road children made shadowy queues at the bus stop. There was the grocer, the butcher, the music shop, and then the Conservative Party local headquarters. Farther along, uniformed assistants from the department store were polishing windows and unwinding the striped awnings. A doorman with a top hat was smoking outside the hotel, and a delivery van had arrived with flowers. It was only Byron who sat clutching his seat, waiting for someone to run out and stop the car.

Yet this did not happen.

Diana parked in the tree-lined street, where the mothers always parked, and lifted the school satchels from the boot. She helped the children from their seats and locked the Jaguar. Lucy skipped ahead. Other mothers waved good morning and asked about the weekend. One said something about the heavy traffic, while another wiped the sole of her son's school shoe with paper tissue. The mist was thinning fast. Already the blue sky shone through in patches and drops of sunlight pricked the sycamore leaves like tiny eyes. In the distance, the moor trembled pale as the sea. Only a trail of smoke lingered over the lower foothills.

Byron walked beside Diana, expecting his knees to give way. He felt like a glass that had too much water inside, and that if he rushed or stopped abruptly he might spill. He couldn't understand. He couldn't understand how they were still going to school. He couldn't understand how everything was continuing as before. It was an ordinary morning except that it wasn't. Time had been splintered and everything was different.

In the playground he stood wedged at his mother's side, listening so hard that his eyes became ears. Yet no one said, "I saw your silver Jaguar, registration number KJX 216K, in Digby Road." No one said that a little girl had been hurt, just as no one mentioned the extra seconds. He accompanied his mother to the girls' school entrance, and Lucy seemed so carefree she didn't even remember to wave.

Diana squeezed his hand. "Are you all right?"

Byron nodded because his voice wouldn't work.

"Time to go now, sweetheart," she said. He sensed her watching as he walked across the playground, and it was so hard to go that even his spine ached. The elastic of his cap cut into his throat.

He needed to find James. He needed to find him urgently. James understood things in ways that Byron couldn't; James was like the logical piece of Byron that was missing. The first time Mr. Roper had explained about relativity, for instance, James had nodded enthusiastically as if magnetic forces were a truth he had suspected all along, whereas for Byron the new idea was like tangles in his head. Maybe it was because James was such a careful boy. Byron watched him sometimes, aligning the zip fastening on his pencil case or wiping the fringe out of his eyes, and there was such precision in it that Byron was filled with awe. Sometimes he tried to be the same. He would walk carefully or arrange his felt-tip pens in order of color. But then he would find that his shoelaces were undone, or his shirt had got untucked, and he was back to being Byron again.

Byron knelt at James's side in chapel, only it was hard to get his attention. As far as Byron knew, James did not believe in God ("There is no proof," he said), but once he was engaged, as with most things, James took the business of praying very seriously. Head forced down, eyes screwed tight, he hissed the words with such intensity that it would be blasphemous to interrupt. Then Byron tried to linger beside James in the queue for the refectory, but Samuel Watkins asked what he thought about Glasgow Rangers and James got held up. The problem was, everyone wanted to know James's opinion. He thought things before you were even aware that there was anything to think about them, and by the time you had realized there was, James was off thinking about something else. At last Byron's opportunity came, during games.

James was outside the cricket pavilion. By now the day was so hot, it hurt to move. There was not a cloud in the sky, and the sun was almost shouting. Byron had already been to bat, and James was waiting his turn on a bench. He liked to concentrate before a game and preferred to be alone. Byron perched at the other end, but James did not look up or move. His fringe hung over his eyes, and his luminous skin had begun to burn below the sleeves.

Byron got as far as "James?" when something stopped him.

Counting. A steady stream of it. James was whispering, as if someone very small was tucked between his knees and he needed to teach this small person their prime numbers. Byron was used to James's muttering, he had witnessed it many times, but normally James did it under his breath, so that you could easily miss it. "Two, four, eight, sixteen, thirty-two." Above Cranham Moor the air shimmered as if the upper peaks would melt into the sky. Byron felt himself overheating inside his cricket whites. "Why do you do that?" he said. He was only trying to start the conversation.

James jumped as if he had not realized he had company, and Byron laughed to show he meant no harm. "Are you practicing your times tables?" he said. "Because you know them better than anyone. Take me. I'm useless. I get my nines wrong. Aussi my sevens. Those are très difficile for me as well." The boys voiced in French the things that were either too dull or difficult to explain in English. It was like having a secret language, except that it wasn't really because anyone could join in.

James dug the tip of his bat into the grass at his feet. "I am checking that I can double numbers. To keep me safe."

"Safe?" Byron swallowed hard. "How will that keep you safe?" James had never spoken in this way before. It was completely unlike him.

"It is like running to your bedroom before the lavatory stops flushing. If I don't do it, things might go wrong."

"But that's not logical, James,"

"Actually it is very logical, Byron. I am not leaving anything to chance. The pressure is on, with the scholarship exam. Sometimes I look for a four-leaf clover. And now I have a lucky beetle too." James pulled something from his pocket and it flashed briefly between his fingers. It was a bit of brass, slim and dark, the size of Byron's thumb, and shaped like an insect with closed wings. There was a silver ring onto which you might attach a key.

"I didn't know you had a lucky beetle," said Byron.

"My aunt sent it to me. It comes from Africa. I can't afford to make silly mistakes."

Byron felt an ache behind his eyes and inside the roof of his nose and he realized with a stab of shame that he was going to cry. Fortunately there was a shout of "Out" and a round of applause from the cricket field. "My turn to bat," said James with a gulp. Games was his least successful subject. Byron didn't like to mention it, but James tended to blink when the ball came toward him. "I have to go now," he said. He stood.

"Did you see, ce matin?"

"See what, Byron?"

"The two seconds. They added them today. At a quarter past eight."

There was a tiny hiatus where nothing happened, where Byron waited for James to say something and James didn't. He simply stared down at Byron in his intense, waxy-pale way, with the beetle tight in his hand. The sun was right behind him, and Byron had to squint to keep looking. James's ears shone like prawns.

"Are you sure?" said James.

"My second hand went backward. I saw it. Then when I looked again at my watch it started going the right way. It definitely happened."

"There was nothing about it in *The Times*."

"There was nothing about it on *Nationwide*. I saw the whole thing last night and no one mentioned it."

James glanced at his watch. It was Swiss-made with a thick leather strap and had belonged to his father. There were no digits to show the minutes, only a small window for the date. "You're sure? You're sure you saw?"

"I'm positive."

"Why, though? Why would they add the seconds and not tell us?"

Byron screwed up his face to stop the tears. "I don't know." He wished he had a beetle key ring. He wished he had an aunt who sent him lucky talismans from Africa.

"Are you all right?" said James.

Byron gave a vigorous nod that shook his eyeballs up and down inside his head. "Dépêchez-vous. Les autres are waiting."

James turned toward the pitch and took a deep breath. He ran with his knees high and his arms going like pistons. If he carried on at that speed he would pass out before he got there. Byron rubbed his eyes in case anyone was looking, and then he sneezed several times so that, if they were still looking, they might think he had hay fever or some sort of sudden summer cold.

The key for the new Jaguar had been a gift to Diana after she passed her driving test. Seymour rarely indulged in surprises. Diana, on the other hand, was more spontaneous. She bought a present because she wanted you to have it and wrapped it in tissue and ribbon, even if it was not your birthday. Seymour had not wrapped the key. He had placed it in a box beneath a white lace handkerchief. "Oh my goodness," she'd said. "What a surprise." She didn't seem to realize about the key at first. She just kept touching the handkerchief and looking confused. It was embroidered with her initial, D, and small pink roses.

At last Seymour said, "For God's sake, darling," only the word came out wrong and sounded less like a term of endearment and more like a threat. That was when she lifted the handkerchief and found the key with its special Jaguar emblem embossed on the leather tag.

"Oh, Seymour," she said over and over. "You shouldn't. You haven't. I can't."

Seymour nodded in that formal way of his, as if his body was dying to leap about but his clothes wouldn't make room. Now people would sit up and take notice, he said. No one would look down on the Hemmingses now. Diana said yes, darling, everyone would be so envious. She really was the luckiest woman. She reached out her hand to stroke his head, and, closing his eyes, he rested his brow on her shoulder as if he was suddenly tired.

When they kissed, Seymour groaned, and the children slid away.

Diana had been right about the mothers. They had crowded around the new car. They had touched the mahogany dashboard and the leather upholstery and practiced sitting in the driving seat. Deirdre Watkins said she would never be satisfied with her Mini Cooper again. The Jaguar even smelled expensive, said the new mother. (No one had quite got her name.) And all the while, Diana had flapped after them with her handkerchief, rubbing off finger marks and smiling uncomfortably.

Each weekend Seymour asked the same questions: Were the children wiping their shoes? Was she polishing the chrome grille? Did everyone know? Of course, of course, she said. All the mothers were green. Had they told the fathers? Yes, yes, she smiled again. "They talk about it all the time. You're so good to me, Seymour." Seymour would try to hide his happiness behind his napkin.

Thinking of the Jaguar and his mother, Byron's heart bounced so hard inside his chest he was afraid it would wear a hole. He had to press his hand to his chest in case he was having a heart attack.

"Daydreaming, Hemmings?" In class Mr. Roper pulled him to his feet and told the boys this was what you looked like if you were an ignoramus.

It made no difference. Whatever Byron did, staring at his books or out of the window, the words and hills floated out of focus. All he could see was the little girl. The curled-up shape of her, just beyond the passenger window, caught beneath her red bicycle, its wheels whisking the air. She lay so still it was as if she had stopped suddenly where she was and decided to fall asleep. Byron stared at his wristwatch and the relentless progress of its second hand, and it was like being eaten.

Things That Have to Be Done

Jim unlocks the door to his van and slides it open. He has to stoop to step inside. White winter moonlight falls in a cold shaft through the window and shines on the laminated surfaces. There is a small two-ring hob, a sink, a foldout table, and, to his right, a bench seat that pulls out to form a bed. Sliding the door shut, Jim locks it, and the rituals begin.

"Door, hello," he says. "Taps, hello." He greets each of his possessions. "Kettle, hello. Roll-up Mattress, hello. Small Cactus Plant, hello. Jubilee Tea Towel, hello." Nothing must be left out. When everything has been greeted, he unlocks the door, opens it, steps back outside, and relocks it. His breath blooms into the dark. There is music from the house with the foreign students, and already the old man who sits all day at his window has gone to bed. To the west, the last of the rush-hour traffic makes its way across the upper peaks of the moor. Then a dog barks and someone yells at it to shut up. Jim unlocks the door to the van and steps inside.

He performs the ritual twenty-one times. That's the number of times it has to be done. He steps into the van. He greets his things. He steps out of the van. In, hello, out. In, hello, out. Locking and unlocking the door every time.

Twenty-one is safe. Nothing will happen if he does it twenty-one times. Twenty is not safe and neither is twenty-two. If something else swings into his mind—an image or a different word—the whole process must begin again.

No one has any idea about this part of Jim's life. On the estate, he straightens the wheelie bins or picks up small items of litter. He says H-hello, how are you? to the boys at the skate ramp, and he carries the recycling boxes sometimes to help the refuse collectors, and no one would know what he must go through when he is alone. There is a lady with a dog who sometimes asks where he lives, if he would like to join her one day for bingo in the community center. They have lovely prizes, she says: sometimes a meal for two at the pub in town. But Jim makes his excuses.

Once he has finished stepping in and out of the van, there is more. There will be lying on his stomach to seal the doorframe with duct tape and then the windows, in case of intruders. There will be checking the cupboards and under the pull-out bed and behind the curtains, over and over. Sometimes, even when it is finished, he still doesn't feel safe and the whole process must begin again, not just with the duct tape but also with the key. Giddy with tiredness, he steps in and out, locking the door, unlocking it again. Saying Foot Mat, hello. Taps, hello.

He has had no real friends since he was at school. He has never been with a woman. Since the closure of Besley Hill, he has wished for both, for friends, for love—for knowing and being known—but if you are stepping in and out of doors, and greeting inanimate objects, as well as securing openings with duct tape, there isn't much leftover time. Besides, he's often so nervous he can't say the words.

Jim surveys the inside of the van. The windows. The cupboards. Every crack has been sealed, even around the pop-up roof, and it is like being inside a tightly wrapped parcel. Suddenly he knows he has done everything and relief swamps him. It is as good as being freshly scrubbed. Across Cranham Moor the church clock strikes two. He has no watch. He hasn't had one in years.

There are four hours left to sleep.

5

The Lady Contortionist

James Lowe once told Byron that magic wasn't a lie; it was about playing with the truth. What people saw, he said, depended largely on what they were looking for. When a woman was sawed in half at Billy Smart's Circus, for instance, this was not real. It was an illusion of reality. It was a trick to make you see the truth in a different way.

"I don't understand," said Byron.

James neatened the flop of his fringe and explained some more. He even sharpened his pencil and drew a diagram. The assistant, he said, would step into the box, and the magician would close the lid so that her head would stick out one end and her feet at the other. But then the magician would spin the box, and when her shoes were pointing away from the audience the assistant would tuck in her real feet and replace them with two fake ones. The lady would be a contortionist, so she would fold her legs into the upper part of the box and the magician would saw her down the middle.

"You see?" said James.

"I still can't watch him doing it. I don't like to think of her feet coming off."

James agreed that this was a significant problem. "Maybe you should eat your candyfloss during that part," he said.

Byron's mother was not a contortionist. Sometimes he caught her listening to her music on the record player and swaying. Once he even saw her lift her arms as if she were placing them on the shoulders of someone who was not there, then swirl in circles as if they were dancing, but that did not make her a magician's assistant either. And yet after school she stood waiting with Lucy, and there was nothing different about her. She wore her pink summer coat with matching handbag and shoes. Other women mentioned dates and she smiled at each of them and fetched out her notebook. No one would have guessed that only hours beforehand she had hurt a small child and driven away without stopping.

"Mothers' coffee next Wednesday," she said, writing the date carefully. "I will be there."

"What have you done to your hand, Diana?" said someone. Andrea Lowe, maybe.

"Oh, it's nothing."

Once again, no one mentioned the accident. No one mentioned the extra seconds.

"Au revoir, Hemmings," said James.

"Au revoir, Lowe," said Byron.

Walking the children to the car, Diana unlocked the doors without flinching. Byron watched her carefully, waiting for her to betray some small sign of anxiety, but she asked him about his day and checked the position of her seat, and there was still no hint of anything different. When they drove past Digby Road, with the burned-out vehicle on the corner, he was so anxious he had to sing. His mother merely adjusted her sunglasses and faced straight ahead.

"Yes, we've had another lovely day," she said on the telephone to his father later that afternoon. She poked the plastic coils of the cord around her forefinger so that they looked like a batch of white rings. "It was hot. I tidied the rose beds. I did the washing. I made a few things for the freezer. The weatherman says more sun." Byron kept wanting to ask about the accident and it was like having to sit on himself in order to remain quiet. He took a stool at the breakfast bar while she prepared the evening meal, wondering if he stayed silent how long it would take his mother to turn to him and say something. He counted each second, each minute, that she said nothing, and then he remembered again that the reason his mother said nothing was because she had no idea what she had done.

"You should get some fresh air," she said. "You look worn down, sweetheart."

Byron took the opportunity to slip into the garage. He pulled down the door behind him, leaving just a crack of daylight, then he removed his torch from his blazer pocket in order to examine the Jaguar. There was no sign of damage. Slowly he moved the beam of light from left to right, scanning the car more carefully now, but there was not a scratch. He touched the paintwork with his fingertips. The doors. The bonnet. The silver frame felt smooth beneath his fingertips. Still he found nothing.

The garage was dark and cold and smelled of oil. Byron had to keep checking over his shoulder in case anyone was watching. Along the back wall loomed the profile of Diana's old furniture, draped with sheets; it had been sent from her mother's house after she died. He had lifted the covers once with James and found a floor lamp with a deep red tasseled shade, as well as a set of tables and an old armchair. James said that someone had probably died in that chair, maybe even the woman who was Diana's mother. (Byron could not call her "Grandma" because he had never met her.) It was a relief to slide the garage door down and leave all this behind.

Outside, the sky was as open as a blue dish, the air was thick and scented with heat. Lupins stood tall like colored pokers, and the roses and peonies were in bloom. Everything in the garden had a place; nothing hurt the eye. The pink beds seeped into white ones and then into blue, the smaller shapes became bigger ones. Already the fruit trees bore small green buds like marbles, where only weeks ago there had been a scrambling of white blossom. Byron smelled the sweetness of the air, and it was so substantial it was like walking into the hall and hearing his mother's record player music before he found her. The smells, the flowers, the house, these things were surely bigger than what she had done that morning. Besides, even though his mother had committed a crime, it was not her fault. The accident had happened because of the two extra seconds. He dreaded what his father would say if he knew. It was lucky nothing had happened to the Jaguar.

"Lamb cutlets for tea," said his mother. She served them with frilled white paper crowns and gravy.

He couldn't eat. He could only carve his meat into small pieces and blend it with his potato. When his mother asked why he wasn't hungry, he told her he had an ache and she rushed to fetch the thermometer. "What about your Sunquick?" she said. "Don't you want that either?"

He wondered what had happened to the little girl, whether her parents had found her, or neighbors. How badly she was hurt.

"I will have Byron's Sunquick," said Lucy.

Byron had always liked the way his mother referred to an item by its brand name. It implied a specificity he found reassuring. It was like the small reminders she left for herself on the telephone pad: Polish Lucy's Clarks shoes. Buy Turtle Wax polish. A label suggested that there was one correct name for each thing and no room for mistakes. Now, as Byron watched her tidying the kitchen and singing under her breath, the irony of it brought a lump to his throat. He must do everything in his power to keep her safe.

While his mother ran water for the washing up, Byron went outside to speak to Lucy. He found her hunkered on the stone slabs of the terrace in front of a bed of jewel-colored wallflowers. She was arranging four garden snails in order of shell size and also speed. He asked in a casual way how she was and she said she was very well, except that he was kneeling on her snails' finishing line. Byron shifted to another spot.

"Are you all right about this morning?" He cleared his throat. "About the thing that happened?"

"*What* happened?" said Lucy. She still had a smear of Angel Delight custard around her mouth.

"When we went—to you know where." Byron winked expansively. Lucy lifted her hands to her face.

"Oh," she said. "I didn't like that."

"Did you—? Did you see anything?"

Lucy realigned one of her snails with the starting line because it seemed to be racing backward. "I wasn't looking. I was like this,

Byron." Smothering her eyes with her hands, she demonstrated how frightened she had been.

The situation required all Byron's skill. He twisted his fringe, the way James did when he was thinking something through. It might upset their father, Byron explained slowly, if he found out they had gone down Digby Road. It was important not to say it when he came for his weekend visit. It was important to act as if they had never been there.

"Supposing I forget?" Suddenly Lucy's mouth wobbled and Byron was afraid she might cry. "Supposing I forget we wasn't there?" She often got her words confused. It was worse when she was upset or tired.

Overwhelmed, Byron stooped to embrace her. She smelled of sugar and pink and he understood in that moment that they had become different, that she was still a child while he knew something bigger. The realization gave him a bubbling in his stomach that was like Christmas morning, only without the presents. He glanced toward his mother in the kitchen, drying plates by the window and caught in the crimson glow of aureole light. He was aware that he had reached a landmark in his life, a defining moment, and even though he had not been expecting a landmark or a defining moment it was part of becoming a man, just as passing his scholarship exam would be part of that. He must rise to both.

"Everything will be all right. I promise you." He nodded the way his father did when he was stating a fact, as if he was so correct even his own head had to agree. "You just need to put this morning out of your mind." Byron leaned to plant a kiss on her cheek. This was not manly but it was what his mother would do.

Lucy pulled back, her nose wrinkled. He was afraid she would cry so he reached for his handkerchief. "You have stinky breath,

Byron," she said. She skipped back into the house, her pigtails thumping her shoulder blades, her knees tucked high, and crunching at least two of her snails beneath her shiny school shoes.

That night Byron watched both the six o'clock news and *Nationwide*. There was more fighting in Ireland but no mention of the accident and no mention of the two extra seconds. He felt clammy and sick.

What would James do? It was hard to imagine Andrea Lowe making a mistake. If the situations were reversed, James would be logical. He would draw a diagram to explain things. Despite the fact that the children were not allowed, Byron carefully unclicked the door to his father's study.

Beyond the window, the garden was bathed in warm light, the spires of red-hot poker glowing in the evening sun, but the room was still and cool. The wooden desk and chair were polished like museum furniture. Even the tin of fudge sweets and decanter of whisky were things you must not touch. It was the same with his father. If Byron ever tried to hug him, and sometimes he wished he could, the embrace ran away at the last minute and became a handshake.

Perching on the very edge of his father's chair, so as to cause the least offense, Byron took a sheet of thick white paper and his father's pen. He drew a careful map, plotting with arrows the progress of the Jaguar along Digby Road. He marked the washing lines and the flowery tree. Then, with a change in the direction of the arrows, he showed how the car had swung to the left and rammed to a halt against the curb. He drew a circle where they had left the little girl. She was just to the side of the car, where only he could see.

Byron folded the map into his pocket and replaced the pen, dusting the chair with his shirt so that his father would not know he had trespassed. He was about to leave when an idea for a further experiment occurred to him.

Kneeling on the rug, he lowered his upper body to the floor. He practiced lying exactly as the little girl had done beneath her bicycle, on his side, with his knees tucked toward his chin and his arms curled around. If she had been all right the little girl would have got up. She would have made a noise. Lucy made an awful noise if you so much as scratched her by mistake. Supposing the police were searching for his mother even now?

"What are you doing in here?"

Startled, he turned to the door. His mother hovered at the threshold, as if she didn't dare tread any farther. He had no idea how long she'd been there.

Byron flipped himself over and over, up and down the rug, to suggest he was a perfectly ordinary boy, albeit on the large side, who was playing a game. He went so fast that it burned the bare flesh of his arms and legs, and made his head spin. His mother laughed and the ice cubes in her drink tinkled like shards of glass. Because she seemed happy, he rolypoly'd some more. Then he knelt up and said, "I think we should go to school by bus tomorrow."

His mother seemed to be swooping to the left and right for a few moments because he had slightly overdone it with the rolling.

"The bus?" she said, landing upright again. "Whatever for?"

"Or maybe a taxi. Like we used to do before you could drive."

"But there's no need. Not since your father taught me."

"I just thought the change would be nice."

"We have the Jaguar, love." She didn't even flinch. "He bought it so that I could take you to school."

"Exactly. The car is so new, we shouldn't use it. Besides, he says women can't drive."

At this she openly laughed. "Well, that's clearly not true. Although your father is a very clever man, of course. Much more clever than me. I've never read a book from start to finish."

"You read magazines. You read cookery books."

"Yes, but they have pictures. Clever books only have words."

In the silence that followed she studied her injured hand, twisting it palm up, palm down. There was nothing but the stream of light from the window, swirling with silver dust mites, and the insistent ticking of the mantelpiece clock.

"We had a little swerve this morning," she said quietly. "That's all." Then, glancing at her bracelet watch, she gave a gasp. "Goodness, it's time for your bath." She snapped into being a mother again, like an umbrella shooting into the right shape, and smiled. "If you like, you can have Crazy Foam. Are you sure you didn't touch anything of your father's?"

That was the most she said about the accident.

The week continued and everything went on as before. No one came to arrest his mother. The sun rose, climbed in a wide arc, and set over the other side of the moor. Clouds passed. Sometimes they poked bony fingers across the flanks of the hills and sometimes they grew and darkened like a stain. At night came the moon, a pale copy of the sun, spilling over the hills in shades of silvery blue. His mother left the bedroom windows open for air. The geese cried out from the pond. Foxes yelped through the dark.

Diana continued to do the small things she had always done.

She woke to her half-past-six alarm. She swallowed her pill with water and examined her wristwatch in order not to be late. She dressed in her old-fashioned skirts, the way her husband liked, and prepared Byron's healthy breakfasts. By Wednesday the bandage had disappeared from her hand and there was no longer anything to link her to the morning in Digby Road. Even James seemed to forget about the two seconds.

Only Byron kept remembering. Time had been changed. His mother had hit a child. Byron had seen and she had not. Like a splinter in his heel, the truth was always there, and even though he tried to avoid it by being careful, sometimes he forgot to be careful and there it was. He tried to do other things, playing with his soldiers, or practicing a magic trick to show James, but the images kept bobbing back, small details, as if they belonged to him now. The little girl's striped school dress, her black plaits like licorice, her socks at her ankles, the spinning wheels of her red bicycle. You could not do a thing without consequences. It was like Mr. Roper giving you lines for being an ignoramus, or Byron throwing a stone over the fence at the pond to watch the rings of water as they opened like flowers. Nothing happened by itself. And even though it was not his mother's fault, even though no one knew about the accident, there must be repercussions. He listened to the clocks all over the house, ticking and tocking and chiming their passage through time.

One day—if not now, then in the future—someone would have to pay.

6

The Orange Hat

Jim sprays a table beside the window. Once. Twice. He wipes. Once. Twice. He has his own bottle of antibacterial multipurpose spray and also his own blue cloth.

The early December sky is thick with snow that does not fall. Maybe there will be a white Christmas. It would be something to have snow for his first time in the van. Customers dart across the car park, carrying recyclable bags and small children, their bodies pinched against the cold as if the air is made of pepper. Some of them have Christmas-themed scarves and hats, and one little girl is wearing a set of antlers that keeps slipping sideways. Beyond all this, the upper peaks of Cranham Moor jut toward the sky. The greens, yellows, pinks, and purples that were brackens, heather, wild orchids, and grasses have been burned by the cold to brown. In the distance he can make out Besley Hill and the construction vehicles that circle it. Rumors are, it will be an estate of fifteen five-star luxury homes. Since the building of Cranham Village, there have been new developments all over the moor. They emerge from the earth like fragments of exposed bone.

"Haven't you got a job to do?" says Mr. Meade, appearing from behind. He is a small, neatly mustached man who keeps his own set of parking cones in case of emergency.

"I'm s-s—"

But Mr. Meade interrupts. Everyone does. They don't want to see a man stuttering so hard over words that they look painful. "And by the way, Jim, your hat is skew-whiff."

Jim's hat is skew-whiff because it is too small. It is also not technically a hat, at least not a serious one. It is orange, like his staff T-shirt, his staff apron, and also his staff socks, and it is made of meshed plastic in the approximate shape of a trilby. The only person who does not wear the hat is Mr. Meade, because he is the manager. After all, you wouldn't expect royalty to wave flags or hang up bunting; it is up to everyone else to look patriotic on their behalf.

Jim straightens his hat, and Mr. Meade goes to serve a female customer. The new cook is late again.

It is not as if the café is busy. Despite the recent refurbishment, there are only two men with coffees and they sit so still they could be frozen solid. The most alive thing here is the fiber-optic Christmas tree, positioned at the top of the stairs to greet shoppers as they arrive from the supermarket below, and blinking a festive passage from green to red to blue. Jim squirts and he wipes. Twice. Once. It is acceptable to do it like this at work. It is like using a magic plaster until he returns to the van and can perform the rituals properly, the full twenty-one times.

A slim hand tugs at his sleeve. "You missed my table," a female voice is saying. It's the woman Mr. Meade has just served. Jim recoils from her fingers as if burned. He can't even look her in the eye.

The inpatients used to walk side by side at Besley Hill. Never touching. If the nurses helped them dress, they took it steadily, not wanting to cause alarm.

"Can you see?" The female customer asks the question as if he is stupid. She points toward a table in the middle of the café, positioned exactly halfway between the window and the servery counter at the opposite end. Her new coat is already draped on the back of a chair and she has left her coffee on the table, beside the condiments and paper sachets of sugar. He follows her and she lifts her cup so that he can clean. If only she wouldn't stand so close; Jim's hands tremble. She sighs impatiently.

"Quite frankly, I'm shocked at the state of this place," she says. "They may have spent all that money refurbishing, but it's still a rubbish heap. No wonder no one comes."

Jim squirts. Twice. Once. He wipes. Twice. Once. In order to relax he empties his mind, just as the nurses used to tell him. He thinks of white light, of floating, until he is yanked to the present by a further disruption: "Fucking steps. Oh. Oh. Oh. Fuck this."

He can't continue. He steals a sideways glance at the rude woman, but she wears an appalled look and so do the two male customers who previously appeared refrigerated. They all stare at the Christmas tree at the top of the stairs.

"Bugger me," it says.

Jim is wondering if Mr. Meade knows that as well as flashing the tree both talks and swears when the face of the new cook, Eileen, emerges over the steps. She hauls herself to the top as if she has climbed a bare rock face to get here.

"Fuck this," she says.

Flash, flash, flash, goes the Christmas tree.

She is not supposed to use the customer stairs. She is supposed to use the staff stairs. It is enough to give Jim the jitters. And she

has also interrupted the rituals. He must squirt again. Wipe
again—

"I don't have all day," says the female customer. "Would you
please get a move on?"

He tries not to think about Eileen, but she is like the approach
of a bad-weather front. It's hard to pretend she isn't happening.
Sometimes he hears her laugh with the two young girls in the
kitchen and there is something so chaotic about the noise, so joy-
ous and unequivocal, that he has to cover his ears, waiting for it
to pass. Eileen is a tall, big-boned woman with a stiff shower of
titian hair—a darker shade than the regulation hat—that shoots
from a shocked-white parting in the center of her head. She
wears a holly-green coat that puckers at the seams in its effort to
contain her.

"For heaven's sakes," the female customer almost shouts. "I'm
only asking you to wipe my table. What's wrong with you?
Where's the manager?"

Eileen frowns as if she has heard. Then she begins her approach to the kitchen. She will have to pass right next to him. Jim
begins again. He squirts and he wipes. He must empty his
mind—

"Hurry, hurry, will you?" repeats the rude woman.

Despite the solidity of Eileen she is surprisingly nimble, and
the rude woman is directly in her path. Why doesn't she get out
of the way? Why doesn't Eileen go a different route? At this rate,
she will ramrod the rude woman. Jim's breathing comes faster.
His head bangs. If the woman doesn't move, if he doesn't do this
right, something terrible will happen.

Left, right, left, right. Left, right. His arm jerks so fast, the
muscles feel on fire. His fingers tingle.

Eileen is almost at his side. "T-table," he mouths, because the wiping is clearly not working, so he needs to do the words as well. "Hello—"

"What *are* you talking about?" says the rude woman, stepping closer in order to hear. As if through an opened sluice gate, Eileen lumbers past. The crisis is over.

Whether Eileen hits the chair by accident or design is unclear, but as she passes it rocks and sends the woman's coat slithering in a silk puddle to the floor. "Fuck it," says Eileen, not stopping. It rhymes with bucket.

This is a disaster. The crisis is not over at all.

"Excuse me," says the rude woman, only in a shrill way so that the two words take on their opposite meaning. "Excuse me, madam, aren't you going to pick that up?"

Eileen does not stop. She keeps walking toward the kitchen.

"Pick up my coat," orders the woman.

"Why don't you do it yourself?" says Eileen, over her shoulder.

Jim's heart gallops. The coat lies at his feet. "I will not have this," says the woman. "I will call the manager. I will lodge a complaint."

"You do that," says Eileen. And here—oh no—she stops walking away. She turns. Eileen is looking at the rude woman and the rude woman is looking at Eileen and here, in the middle, is Jim, squirting and wiping and whispering Salt Pot, hello, Canderel, hello, to make things right. If only the coat would magic itself onto the chair. He closes his eyes and gropes in his pocket for his key ring. He thinks of duct tape and being calm but none of it works. The woman will be hurt. Eileen will be hurt. The supermarket customers and Mr. Meade and the girls in the kitchen will be hurt and it is all Jim's fault.

He stoops for the coat. It is like water in his fingers. He folds it over the back of the chair, only his hands are shaking so hard the coat slips off, and he has to stoop again and lift the coat again and hang it again. He can feel the women watching, both Eileen and the customer with her metallic voice. It is like being peeled. He is more them than himself. Then the rude woman sits. She folds her knees but she doesn't say thank you.

At the kitchen, Eileen pauses. She turns her face toward Jim and gives a broad smile that lights up her face. Then she thumps open the door and disappears. Jim is so shaken he needs fresh air but he mustn't. He must wipe another table and this time he must get it right.

"Why do you have to do the rituals?" a psychiatric nurse asked once. "What do you think will happen if you don't?" She was a pleasant-looking girl, fresh from training. She said he was over-catastrophizing, he must confront his fears. "Then you will see them for what they are. You will see that the rituals make no difference." She spoke so kindly about his fears, as if they were a piece of furniture he could move into another room and forget, that he wanted her to be right. She obtained permission from the doctors to take Jim to a railway station where people freely came and went, where there was no opportunity to check the hidden spaces and secure exits and entrances. "It's all in your mind, you see," she said as they stepped off the bus and crossed the station forecourt.

But here she was wrong. There were so many people, there was so much chaos—there were fast trains, and busy platforms, there were pigeons missing feet, broken windows and cavernous air vents—that what he learned that morning was that life was even more hazardous than he had previously realized. If anything, he had not been worrying enough and neither had anyone else. He had been *under*catastrophizing. He must do something. He must do it immediately. Racing to the restroom to perform the rituals in private, he narrowly missed colliding with a steam urn in the station tearoom, thereby causing major injury to a roomful of commuters. It was too much. Jim pressed the station alarm. An hour later—after the arrival of so many fire engines that there were delays to all southwest services—he was found in a tight ball under a bench. He never saw the fresh-faced nurse again. She lost her job and that was another thing that was his fault.

Later, Jim is fetching a new roll of blue paper towels for the lavatories when he overhears Eileen again. Now she is in the kitchen, next to the supplies cupboard, talking to the two young women who are responsible for the dispatching of hot food.

"So what's with Jim?" he hears her ask. It's a shock to hear her use his name. It suggests they have a connection and they clearly don't.

He stands very still, with the roll of blue hand towels clutched to his stomach. It isn't that he wants to eavesdrop; it is more that he doesn't want to be here and acting as if he isn't appears to be the best alternative.

"He lives in a van," says one of the girls. "Over on the new estate."

"He doesn't have a house or anything," says her friend. "He's just parked there."

"He's a bit . . ."

"A bit what?" says Eileen impatiently, because whatever it is that Jim is, no one seems prepared to voice it.

"You know," says the first girl.

"Backward," says the other.

"Jim has tissues," corrects the first girl. And then he realizes he has misheard. *Issues* are what she has said he has. "He's been up at Besley Hill most of his life. When they closed it, he had nowhere to go. You have to feel sorry for him. It's not as if he'd hurt you or anything." He had no idea she knew all this.

The second girl says, "He plants things. Bulbs and seeds and that. He buys them cut-price in the supermarket. Sometimes he gets manure and stuff. It smells like shit."

Eileen makes a noise that is so ragged, so colossal, it takes him a moment to realize what it is. It's her laugh. It isn't unkind, though. This is what strikes him. It is as if she is laughing *with* Jim, and this is strange because he isn't laughing. He is crushed to the wall against a blue roll with his heart beating like an explosion.

"Oh, for fuck's sake," says Eileen. "How the fuck is this hat supposed to work?"

"We use hairgrips," says the first girl. "You have to stick them right through the rim."

"Stuff it. I'm not wearing the fucker."

"You have to. It's regulations. And the net cap. You have to wear that too."

Jim fails to hear what happens next. The door shuts and their voices snap out of hearing; they are a sound but without distinction, just as the rest of the world disappears when he is planting. He waits a little longer, and when it is safe, he delivers the roll of blue paper to the lavatories and disinfects the sinks and taps. For the remainder of the morning, Jim wipes tables and carries trays to the young girls in the kitchen who have described him as backward. The customers come and go, but they are few. Beyond the windows, the snow cloud is so heavy it can barely move.

He has spent his adult life in and out of care. Years have passed, and some of them he can't even remember. After treatment he could lose whole days; time was merely a selection of unconnected empty spaces. Sometimes he had to ask the nurses what he had eaten that day and if he had been for a walk. When he complained about memory loss, the doctors told him it was his depression. The truth is, he found it easier to forget.

All the same, it was terrible to leave Besley Hill for the final time. It was terrible to watch the other residents go, with their suitcases and their coats, driven away in minibuses and relatives' cars. Some wept. One patient even tried to make a getaway across the moor. They did not want to go to family members who had long since abandoned them. They did not want to live in hostels or supported housing. After his reassessment, it was a social worker who found Jim his job at the supermarket. She was friendly with Mr. Meade; they were in the same amateur dramatics group. And after all, she pointed out, Jim could live in his van. One day, if he wanted, he could get a mobile phone. He could make new friends. He could text them and meet up.

"But I'm frightened," he had said. "I'm not like normal people. I don't know what to do."

The social worker had smiled. She did not touch him, but she placed her hands beside his on the table. "No one knows how to be normal, Jim. We're all just trying our best. Sometimes we don't have to think about it and other times it's like running after a bus that's already halfway down the street. But it's not too late for you. You're only in your fifties. You can start again."

The next time Jim passes Eileen, he averts his eyes and goes to wheel around her when she pauses and says, "Watcha, Jim. How's things?" She is delivering a toasted sandwich to another customer.

It is open and easy, her question. Nevertheless he can't answer. He looks at his shoes. They are long and narrow. His trousers do not even reach his ankles. In the years since he was a boy, his body seems to have set its sights on the sky rather than on the suits and chairs that other bodies aim to fill. He buys boots and trainers a size too large because he is afraid his body will take him unawares and notch up a further inch overnight.

Jim continues to stare pointedly at his feet as if they are very interesting. He wonders how long he can keep this up and whether Eileen will go soon.

"Don't mind me," she says.

Even without looking at her he can see the way she stands, one hand on her hip, her feet squarely on the ground. The silence is unbearable.

"See you around," she says at last.

She is about to go when Jim lifts his head. It is too much to look her in the eye but he wants her to know—what? He tries to smile. Eileen is holding a seasonal sandwich with trimmings; he has his antibacterial spray. So it isn't a big smile. It's a minor exercising of his facial muscles. All he wants is for her to understand, though what he would like her to understand, it is hard to say. It's a bit like waving a flag, his smile. Or shining a light through the dark. It's like saying, Here I am. There you are. That's all.

She frowns at him as if he's hurt.

He will have to work on the smile.

7

A Close Shave

"I think there has been a conspiracy," whispered James Lowe on Friday afternoon. The boys were bent over their desks, learning about cell reproduction and amoeba.

"A conspiracy?" repeated Byron.

"I think this is why there was no mention of the two seconds. We weren't supposed to know the truth. It is like the moon landings."

"What about the moon landings?"

"I read it was all made up. The astronauts never went there. They made a pretend moon in a studio and took photographs."

"But why were we not supposed to know about the seconds?" whispered Byron. "I don't understand." He didn't understand either about the moon landings because he had his photographs from NASA of the astronauts and Apollo 15. They could not be fakes. His head reeled.

The heat did not help. The air in the classroom was so hot and stiff it stood like something solid. As the week progressed, the temperature had soared. The sun torched the land from a color-

bleached sky. At home the lawn was dull and scratchy under Byron's bare feet, and the paving stones on the terrace scorched like
hot dinner plates. His mother's roses drooped their heads as if
they were too heavy; leaves withered from their stems and the
petals on the poppies hung limp. Even the bees looked too hot to
buzz. Beyond the garden, the moor was a patchwork haze of
green and purple and yellow.

"Why didn't the government want us to know about the seconds?" repeated Byron, because James was drawing a diagram
and appeared to have forgotten them again.

Mr. Roper glanced up from his desk on the wooden dais at the
front of the class. He studied the sea of small heads as if he was
deciding which one to eat. James waited. When Mr. Roper looked
away, he explained: "In case people mount a protest. It's bad
enough with the miners. If things carry on like this, there'll be
another three-day week. The government don't want any more
trouble so they put the seconds in and hoped no one would notice."

Byron tried to return to his biology book, but the diagrams
meant nothing. They were merely shapes in the same way that
words could become meaningless when he repeated them in his
bedroom over and over. He kept seeing the little girl in Digby
Road. Her picture was plastered over everything. Her dress
caught over her knees, her socks gathered at her ankles, her feet
under the wheel. He couldn't keep quiet any longer. "James?" he
whispered. "I've got a problem."

James aligned his pencil with his rubber. He waited. When
Byron said nothing, he asked, "Is it by any chance to do with the
amoeba?"

No, whispered Byron. It wasn't. Although now they were on the subject, he had to admit he was still confused as to how a single cell could decide to become two.

"It's very complicated. It's a mistake."

"What is a mistake?"

"It's to do with the two seconds—"

At this point something hard thwacked Byron's ear. He found Mr. Roper looming over with him a dictionary, his face shiny with an anger that seemed to blacken his eyes and shorten his breath. Byron was given a hundred lines for talking during a lesson and another hundred for disturbing a classmate. ("I must endeavor to be no more stupid than God has intended.")

"I could do your lines for you," James offered later. "It's very quiet at the weekend. All I have is my scholarship work. Also," and here he leaned so close, Byron could see his tonsils, "I would not make any mistakes."

Byron thanked him but said Mr. Roper would spot the difference. James was not the sort of boy who splodged ink or whose letters dangled at perilous angles, in the way that Byron's were inclined to.

"Are you seeing votre père au weekend?"

"Oui, James."

"Moi aussi. Does he—?"

"Does he what?"

"Does he play games with you et choses comme ça? Does he talk?"

"To me?"

"Yes, Byron."

"Well, he is tired. He has to relax. He has to think about the week ahead."

"Mine too," said James. "I suppose it will be égal pour nous one day." Contemplating their futures, the boys fell silent.

Byron had visited James's house only once. The Lowe family home was a cold new house on a small estate with electric gates. It had paving stones instead of a garden, and inside there were plastic mats to protect the cream carpet. The boys had eaten in the dining room in silence. Afterward they had played in the private road outside, but it was a halfhearted game, almost solemn.

The boys left school with no further reference to the two seconds or Byron's secret. On reflection, Byron was relieved. He was afraid of burdening his friend with too much. Sometimes James stood with his thin shoulders hunched and his head low, as if his intelligence was all crammed into his satchel and it was a heavy thing to bear.

Besides, Byron had other concerns. Now that school was over for the week, there was nothing standing between himself and his father's visit. The slightest mistake, and his father would surely guess about Digby Road. At home Byron watched his mother arrange fresh roses from the garden and set her hair, and his heart thumped. She rang the speaking clock to confirm that her watch was punctual, and while she swept from room to room, checking that the hand towels were clean in the bathroom and straightening copies of *Reader's Digest* on the coffee table, Byron slipped to the garage. Once again he scanned the Jaguar with his torch, but there was no sign of the accident.

They waited for his father at the station, along with the rest of the Friday night families. It was still too hot to stand in the sun, and they hid in the shade of the fence at the end of the platform, a little apart. After all, his father dealt with people every day at the bank; he didn't want to get off the train and find his mother chatting with strangers. While they waited she kept tugging her compact mirror out of her handbag and angling it toward her face, as if to check that everything was in the right place. Byron taught Lucy how to tell the time by blowing the seedheads from a dandelion, but the air was so thick and still they couldn't seem to get them very far.

"It is thirteen o'clocks," sang Lucy. "It is fifteen o'clocks."

"Shh now, you two," said their mother. "Here comes the train."

Car doors flew open from the station forecourt, and mothers and children burst onto the platform. Where before there had been white heat and stillness and silence, there was now color and movement and laughter.

There was an occasion when they had been late, back in the days before Diana could drive. Seymour had said nothing in the taxi because it was not polite to air grievances in front of strangers, but at Cranham House he had railed. Did Diana not know how humiliating it was to be the only man left standing on the platform? As if she didn't care? No, no, she kept saying; it was a mistake. Seymour wouldn't stop. A mistake? Could she not tell the time? Was that another thing her mother had failed to teach her? Byron had hidden beneath his bedcovers, hands jammed over his ears, in order not to hear. Every time he listened he could hear his mother's cries, his father's roaring, and then later another sound, an altogether quieter one from the bedroom, as if his father was fighting for air. It often went like this.

The train stopped at the platform. Lucy and Byron watched carefully while the other fathers greeted their children. Some did it with shoulder pats, some with embraces. Lucy laughed out loud when one father slammed his briefcase to the ground and scooped his daughter into his arms.

Seymour was the last. He moved the length of the platform with the sun behind him so that it was like watching a shadow advance, and all three of them fell silent. He made a moist shape with his mouth against his wife's cheek. "Children," he said. He didn't kiss them.

"Hello, Father."

"Hello, darling." Diana touched her face as if to repair the skin.

Seymour took his place in the passenger seat with his briefcase parked on his lap. He watched Diana hard—the way she twisted the key in the ignition, and adjusted her seat, and released the handbrake—and all the time he watched, her tongue slipped in and out of her mouth, licking her lower lip and hiding again.

"Mirror, signal, maneuver," he said as she pulled out of the station forecourt.

"Yes, darling." Her fingers were trembling on the wheel and she kept tucking her hair behind her ears.

"You might like to get into the left lane now, Diana."

The air seemed to chill at weekends. Byron noticed that his mother often fingered the neckline of her cardigan when his father came home.

Despite Byron's fears, the visit began smoothly. Lucy said nothing about Digby Road. His mother said nothing about the Jaguar. She parked it where it belonged in the garage and there was no mention of the way it had skidded to a halt. There was no mention of the two seconds. Byron's father hung his business suit in the wardrobe and dressed in the selection of corduroy trousers,

Harris Tweed jackets, and silk cravats that were his country garments. Clothes on his father were always stiff, even when he was supposed to be relaxing. They looked less like clothes and more like cardboard. He read his newspapers in his study and, accompanied by Byron's mother, took a Saturday afternoon stroll down to the pond to watch her throw corn for the ducks and geese. She in turn laundered his shirts and smalls, and it was like knowing the Queen was in residence, except it was his father's underpants hanging in the sunshine instead of the Union Jack. It was over Sunday lunch that things went wrong.

Seymour was watching Diana serve vegetables onto his plate. He asked how Byron was progressing with his scholarship work, only he was still staring at Diana's hands, the way she spooned the potatoes one by one, so it took Byron a moment to realize that his father was waiting for him to reply. Byron said he was doing well. His mother smiled.

"As well as the Lowe boy?"

"Yes, Father." The windows were open in the dining room but it felt unbearably close. The heat was like soup.

Byron couldn't understand why his father disliked James so much. He knew there had been a telephone call after the incident with the bridge, that Andrea Lowe had complained, and that his father had promised to fence in the pond, but everything was resolved after that. The two fathers had shaken hands at the Christmas party and agreed there were no hard feelings. Since then, Seymour said Byron should make other friends; the Lowe boy was full of inflated ideas, he said, even if his father was a college man and a QC.

Diana untied her apron. She sat. Seymour sprinkled salt over his roast chicken. He spoke about the troubles in Ireland and the miners, how they both had it coming, and Diana said yes, yes, and then what he said was "Tell me about the new Jaguar."

Byron's stomach lurched. His insides flew away.

"I beg your pardon?" said Diana.

"Do the mothers still notice?"

"They all wish they were as lucky as me. Sit up straight, please, Byron."

Byron stole a glance at Lucy. Her mouth was clamped so tight her lips looked in danger of shooting toward her ear.

"I thought we might take her for a spin after lunch."

"Do you mean Lucy?" said his mother.

"I mean the new Jaguar," said his father.

His mother cleared her throat. It was the smallest noise, but his father's head shot up. Setting down his knife and fork, he waited, eyeing her carefully. "Has something happened?" he said at last. "Has something happened to the car?"

Diana reached for her glass, and maybe her hand gave the slightest tremble, because the ice cubes tinkled. "I just wish—" Then, whatever she wished, she appeared to think better of it and braked midsentence.

"You wish what, Diana?"

"That you would stop calling the Jaguar a she."

"I beg your pardon?"

She smiled. She reached for her husband's hand. "It's a car, Seymour. It isn't a woman."

Byron laughed because he wanted his father to see that the remark was not personal. In fact it was ha ha so hilarious you had to grip your stomach and howl. And considering the potential seriousness of the situation, it was also extremely clever. For someone who claimed to be uneducated, his mother was full of surprises. Byron caught Lucy's eye and nodded, encouraging her to join in. Relief at not speaking the secret possibly got the better of both of them; Lucy was laughing so hard she appeared screwed up with it, and her plaits were tipped with gravy. When Byron stole a sideways glance, he found his father's upper lip had congealed. It was beaded with small drops of perspiration.

"Are they laughing at me?"

"Of course not," Diana said. "It really isn't funny, children."

"I work all week." Seymour spoke carefully, enunciating the words as if they were difficult shapes between his teeth. "I do it all for you. I bought you a Jaguar. None of the other men buy their wives a Jaguar. The chap at the garage couldn't believe his ears."

The more he said, the older he seemed. Diana nodded her head and kept saying, "I know, darling, I know." There was an age gap of fifteen years between Diana and Seymour, but at that moment he seemed to be the only adult in the room. "Please. Can't we do this after lunch?" She threw a look at the children. "Black Forest gâteau for sweet. Your favorite, darling."

Seymour tried not to look pleased but it came out anyway, forcing his mouth into an infantile shape that looked pasted upside down. Thankfully here he picked up his knife and fork and they finished the meal in silence.

This was how it was with Seymour. Sometimes a child seemed to leap into his face and Seymour would grimace in order to push the child away. In the drawing room there were two framed photographs of him when he was a boy. The first was taken in his family's garden in Rangoon. He was dressed in a sailor suit, holding a bow and arrow. Behind him were palm trees and large flowers, with petals the size of hands, but from the way he held his toys, away from his body, it looked as if he did not play with them. The second had been taken just after his parents had stepped off the boat in England. Seymour looked cold and frightened. He was staring at his feet and his sailor suit was all wrong. Even Seymour's mother was not smiling. "You don't know how lucky you are," his father sometimes said to Byron. "For me, it was fighting all the way. We had nothing when we came back to England. Nothing."

There were no photographs of Diana. She never spoke of her childhood. It was impossible to imagine her being anything except a mother.

In his bedroom, Byron reexamined his secret map of Digby Road. He wished that his mother had not commented on his father's habit of referring to the car as female. He wished he had not laughed. Of all the times to disagree with his father, this was surely the worst. It gave Byron a low, loose feeling in the stomach that reminded him of the way he felt about the cocktail party his parents had given for the Winston House parents the previous Christmas. From downstairs he could hear voices in the kitchen. He tried not to listen, because his father had raised his voice, but Byron found that even when he hummed he was still hearing. The lines on his map began to swim and the trees beyond his window were a scribble of green against the blue. Then suddenly the house fell so silent it was as if everyone had melted into dust. He tiptoed to the hall. He couldn't even hear Lucy.

When he discovered his mother alone in the kitchen, Byron had to pretend he'd run a long way, he was so frightened. "Where's Father?"

"He went back to London. He had work to do."

"He didn't examine the Jaguar?"

She made a face as if she didn't understand. "Why would he do that? He took a taxi to the station."

"Why didn't you drive him?"

"I don't know. There wasn't time. You're asking a lot of questions, sweetheart."

She fell silent, and he was afraid she was upset until she turned to sprinkle the air with a flutter of soap bubbles. Laughing, Byron caught them in his fingers, and she slipped another, like a white button, onto the end of his nose. Without his father, the house felt soft again.

The Christmas party had been Seymour's idea. It came several months after the incident with the pond. It was time to show those school parents a thing or two, he'd said. There were special invitations on white card. Diana had bought a tree so tall it touched the plaster ceiling of the hallway. She strung up paper chains, polished the wood paneling, piped fillings into vol-au-vent cases, and skewered maraschino cherries with cocktail sticks. Everyone had come, even Andrea Lowe and her QC husband.

He was a taciturn man in a velvet jacket and a dicky bow who trailed his wife with her glass and her canapé in a paper napkin.

Diana handed out glasses from her hostess trolley, and all the guests admired the new under-floor heating, the kitchen units, the avocado bathroom suites, the fitted bedroom cupboards, the electric fireplaces, and the double-glazed windows. It was Byron's job to take coats.

"New money," he heard a mother say. And Byron supposed that was a good thing now that there was decimal coinage. His father was passing as the woman made her remark, and Byron wondered if he would be happy too, only he seemed to discover something unpleasant in his mushroom vol-au-vent. Seymour's face collapsed; but he had never liked vegetables without meat.

Later in the evening, Deirdre Watkins had suggested a party game; Byron remembered this too, although his witnessing of the event was now restricted to a vantage point at the top of the stairs. "Oh yes, a party game," his mother had laughed. She was kind like that. And despite the fact that Byron's father was not a gamey sort of person, not unless you counted solitaire or a very difficult crossword, the guests had agreed that a party game would be tremendous fun and he had been forced to concur. He was the host, after all.

His father had blindfolded Diana a little roughly, Byron felt, but she didn't complain. The game was, his father said, that she should find him. "My wife likes games. Don't you, Diana?" Sometimes Byron felt that his father overshot being a jolly person. You had a better sense of him if he was giving his views about the Common Market or the Channel Tunnel. (He was against both.) But by now the drawing room was heaving with grown-ups, all laughing and drinking and calling to Diana as she groped and flapped and tripped her way after them.

"Seymour?" she kept calling. "Where are you?"

She touched the cheeks and hair and shoulders of men who were not her husband. "Oh no," she'd say. "Goodness, you're not Seymour." And the crowd would laugh. Even Andrea Lowe managed a smile.

Shaking his head as if tired, or hurt, or maybe even bored, it was hard to tell which, his father had left. No one saw, only Byron. But still Diana kept searching, sometimes crushed against the crowd, sometimes passed from one to another by it, like a ball, or a doll, everyone laughing and jeering, almost knocking her into the Christmas tree once, while she kept looking for her husband with her fluttering, outstretched hands.

It was the last party his parents had held. His father said if there was ever another, it would be over his dead body. This did not seem to Byron an altogether inviting place to hold a party. But remembering it, and the feeling of sickness, of confusion, that had swamped him as he watched his mother carried like driftwood, he wished again she had kept quiet about the new Jaguar.

On Sunday night, Byron moved his sheet and quilt onto the floor. He set his torch and magnifying glass at his side, in case of emergencies. He saw there was hardship ahead, and even though it would not involve death or starvation, it was important to know that he could endure and make the best of things. At first the quilt seemed surprisingly thick and soft; he was delighted that enduring was so easy. It just didn't seem very easy to sleep at the same time.

The heat didn't help. Byron lay on top of the covers and unbuttoned his pajama top. He was beginning to doze when the bells struck ten across Cranham Moor and he was awake again. He heard his mother switch off her music in the living room and her slight footsteps on the stairs, the click of her bedroom door, and then the stillness that followed. No matter which way he turned, or plumped up his covers, his soft flesh found the hard surfaces. The silence was so loud, he couldn't imagine how people ever slept. He heard the foxes on the moor. He heard the owl, the crickets, and sometimes the house gave a creak, or even a thump. Byron fumbled for his torch and snapped it on and off, on and off, casting its light up and down the walls and curtains, in case there were burglars outside. The familiar shapes of his bedroom leapt in and out of the dark. No matter how hard he tried to close his eyes, all he could think about was danger. He would be bruised all over in the morning.

It was then that Byron understood. In order to save his mother, it wasn't enough to keep quiet about the Jaguar. It wasn't enough to endure. He must think what James would do. He must be logical. What he needed was a plan.

8

An Exit

Beyond the supermarket window, the snow cloud looks so heavy it's a wonder it's still up in the sky. Jim imagines it collapsing to the moor with a thud. He pictures it punctured open, spilling white over the hills, and he smiles. And then almost as soon as he has that thought, another follows, and he doesn't know why but this second one is like a jab in the solar plexus. He can hardly breathe.

Despite the years he has lost, sometimes a memory flies back. It can be very small, the detail that sparks a piece of his past. Glancing at it, another person might not look twice. And yet an insignificant detail can zoom out of its ordinary setting and induce such sorrow he feels twisted inside.

It was a winter afternoon like this, long ago, when they discharged him from Besley Hill the first time. He was nineteen. There was a powdery capping of snow on the moor. He stood watching it from the window while the duty nurse fetched his suitcase and then his blue gabardine coat. He had to wrestle to fit the coat around his shoulders. When he tried to find the sleeves, it caught his arms behind his back like a strap and bit into his armpits.

"It looks as if you're going to need a bigger size," said the nurse, looking up at him. And that was when it occurred to him how long he had been there. She told him to go to the waiting room. He sat alone with the coat on his lap. He folded it into the shape of a small pet and stroked the soft lining. He hadn't been in the waiting room since they'd carried him through on the day he'd arrived and it confused him because he didn't know anymore what he was. He wasn't a patient; he was better. But he didn't know yet what that meant exactly. When the nurse reappeared, she looked surprised. "How come you're still here?" she said.

"I'm waiting for someone to fetch me."

She said she was sure his parents would be there soon. She offered Jim a cup of tea.

He was thirsty and he would have liked tea, but he was thinking about his parents and he couldn't speak. He could hear the nurse singing from the kitchen while she boiled the kettle for herself. It was an easy sound, as if everything in her life was all right. He could even hear the little clink of a teaspoon in her mug. He tried to practice things he might talk about with other people. Fishing, for instance. He had overheard the doctors talk about that, just as he had overheard the nurses talk about going to a dance or dating a new boyfriend. He wished he knew about those things. But he could learn. Now that he was better, he could do those things. Fishing and dating and going to a dance. It was not too late. He was starting again.

At the window the light had begun to fade. The thin showing of snow on the moor glowed a fragile pewter. When the nurse reappeared, she almost jumped. "Are you still here?" she said. "I thought you'd gone ages ago." She asked if he was cold and he was, the room was ice, but he reassured her he was comfortable.

"Let me at least make you that cup of tea," she said. "I'm sure they'll be here for you any minute."

While she sang in the kitchen, the truth dawned on him. No one was coming. Of course they weren't. No one was going to teach him about fishing or inviting a girl to a dance. He didn't know if it was the room that made him tremble or the new knowledge in his head. He got up and slipped out the front door. He didn't want to insult the nurse with his sudden disappearance so he left the coat, neatly folded, in the chair, to show that the cup of tea was not for nothing. He kept expecting someone to run out, to take his arm and steer him back inside, but no one did. He walked the length of the drive, and as the gates were locked and he didn't want to trouble the nurse again, he found his way over the wall. After that he walked toward the moor, because he had no idea where else to go. He spent days up there, and he didn't know what he felt, only that he was wrong, a misfit, he was not cured, he was full of blame, he was not like everyone else, until the police found him in his underpants and drove him straight back to Besley Hill.

"You like those hills," says his right ear.

Turning swiftly, Jim finds Eileen behind him. He jumps as if she is contagious. Her orange hat is perched at such a precarious angle to her head it looks on the verge of flying off. She holds a ham sandwich on a plate.

Eileen gives a big frank smile that lifts her whole face. "I didn't mean to shock you," she says. "It's an effect I have. Even when I think I'm being not shocking, I still shock people." She laughs.

After his previous experience with the smiling, Jim would like to try something different. Maybe he should laugh, although he doesn't want to suggest that he's mocking Eileen or that he agrees she's shocking. He wants to laugh in the way that she does: a throaty, generous roar. He makes a smile shape and then does a noise.

"Do you need a glass of water?" she says.

He tries a bigger laugh. It actually twists his tonsils. This one sounds even worse. He stops laughing and looks at his feet.

"The girls tell me you're a gardener," she says.

A gardener. No one has ever called him that before. They have called him other things. Frog mouth, loony, weirdo, spaz, but never *gardener*. He feels a rush of pleasure, but it might be a mistake to do the laugh again so he attempts instead to appear casual. He tries digging his hands into his trouser pockets in an easygoing sort of manner, only his apron is in the way and his hands get stuck.

She says, "Someone gave me a bonsai tree once. Biggest mistake of my life, accepting that gift. And the thing is, I really wanted to look after it. I read the brochure. I put it in the right spot by the window. I watered it with this thimble. I even bought a pair of mini clippers. And then, guess what? The fucker withered up and died on me. I came down one morning and it had dropped its piddly leaves all over the floor. It was actually hanging sideways." She gives an impression of a tiny dead tree. He wants to laugh.

"Maybe you watered it too much?"

"I cared for it too much. That was the problem."

Jim is not quite sure what to do with her story about the bonsai tree. He nods, as if he is caught up with thinking about something else. He yanks his hands free of his pockets.

"You have nice fingers," says Eileen. "Artist's fingers. I guess that's why you're good at gardening." She glances back at the café, and he realizes she must be looking for an excuse to get away.

He would like to say something else. He would like to stay a little while longer with this woman who stands with her feet wide. Whose hair is the color of flame. But he has no idea how you do small talk. It's easy, a nurse at Besley Hill told him once. You just say what's on your mind. A compliment is always nice, she told him.

"I l-l-like your sandwich," says Jim.

Eileen frowns. She looks at the sandwich and then she looks back at him.

Jim's mouth is like sandpaper. Maybe the sandwich was not a good starting point. "I like the way you have set out the crisps," he says. "On the side."

"Oh," she says.

"And the—and the—lettuce. I like the way you have cut the tomato like a s-s-star."

Eileen nods as if she has not considered that before. "I'll make you one, if you like."

Jim replies that he would like that very much and watches her deliver the sandwich. She says something to the customer that makes him roar with laughter. Jim wonders what it might be. As she strides back to the kitchen, her orange hat jumps about in her hair and she lifts her hand to bat it in the way other people might swat a fly. He feels something inside, like a tiny light switch going on. He doesn't want to think anymore about the day nobody came to meet him.

Despite the fact that he was cured again when he was twenty-one, and released again, Jim was back at Besley Hill within six months. In that time he had tried to get it right. He had tried to be like everyone else. He enrolled at night school to catch up on his education. He tried to make conversation with his landlady and the other men who rented bedsits. But he found it hard to concentrate. Since the second round of electric shock treatment, he seemed to forget things. Not just the facts he had learned that day, but the most basic things, like his name, for instance, or the street where he was living. He failed to sign on one day because he couldn't remember where to get off the bus. He tried to take a job on the rubbish trucks but the other men laughed when he kept arranging the bins in order of size. They called him queer when he said he had no girlfriend. They never hurt him, though, and by the time he lost the job he felt he had begun to belong. Sometimes he watched the dustbin men from his bedsit window, carrying the bins on their backs, and he wondered if they were his team or a different one. In working with them, he had begun to understand a little more about what it was to be strong, and part of a group. It was like looking inside another person's window and seeing life from a different perspective.

There was a downside. For months afterward he could still smell the rubbish bins in his clothes. He took to visiting the laundrette every day. The woman behind the counter lit one cigarette after another; she held the smoldering stub of one to the fresh tip of the next. After a while he couldn't tell if it was the smoke in his clothes or the bins, but whatever it was, he had to keep going back to wash them because they were never fully clean. And eventually she said, "You're funny in the head, you are." So he couldn't go back there either.

It was wearing dirty clothing that upset him the most. Some days he couldn't even get dressed. From here came thoughts he didn't want. And when he tried to do other things to get rid of the thoughts, like saying no to them or going for a walk, the other tenants began to notice and steer clear of him. Then, opening his door one day, he happened to call hello to the Baby Belling. It wasn't even meaningful. It was simply to be kind because it occurred to him that the miniature oven looked lonely. But he noticed something happened afterward, or rather that nothing happened, not once all day. He had no bad thoughts. A little while later his landlady got wind of his stays at Besley Hill and the room was no longer available.

After several nights on the streets, Jim handed himself in to the police. He was a danger to other people, he said. And even though he knew he would never willingly hurt anyone, he began to shout and kick things as if he might. They drove him straight to Besley Hill. They even put the sirens on, although by that point he wasn't shouting or kicking. He was only sitting very still.

It wasn't clinical depression as such that took him back the third time. It wasn't schizophrenia or multiple personality disorder or psychosis or any of the other names people gave it. It was more like habit. It was easier to be his troubled self, he found, than to be the reformed one. And even though he had begun doing the rituals now, his return to Besley Hill was like putting on old clothes and finding that people recognized him. It felt safe.

Someone is making a noise from the café kitchen, a woman. Someone else is trying to calm her, and this is a man. The door flies open and Eileen bursts through it with her flaming-red hair wide on her head. There is no hint of her orange hat and she has her coat flung over her shoulder, like a thing she has killed. The door crashes back on itself and produces a yelp. When Mr. Meade emerges seconds later he has his hand to his nose.

"Mrs. Hill!" he shouts between his fingers. "Eileen!" He darts after her as she marches past tables. Customers are beginning to put down their hot beverages.

"It's me or the fucking hat," says Eileen, over her shoulder.

Mr. Meade shakes his head while still cupping it, as if he is afraid that vigorous movement may cause his nose to fall off. Shoppers queuing for their Festive Snack Deal (one hot drink with free mince pie; flapjacks/muffins not included) stare with open mouths.

Eileen stops so suddenly, Mr. Meade collides with a trolley of Christmas groceries. "Look at us," she says, addressing not only him but the whole room, the shoppers, the staff with their orange hats, even the plastic tables and chairs. "Look at our lives."

No one moves. No one answers. There is a moment of stillness as if everything has been stopped, or turned off, as if everything and everyone has mislaid what should come next. Only the Christmas tree appears to remember and continues its happy transformation from green to red to blue. Then Eileen's face creases with disbelief and she makes that wild honking noise that is in fact a laugh. But once again, it is as if she is not laughing *at* them but *with* them. As if she is looking down over the scene, herself included, and suddenly seeing the outrageous joke.

Eileen turns, revealing two white-gray legs where her skirt has pitched itself into the gusset of her underwear. "Oh, fuck it," she snorts, as she gropes for the handrail and throws out her foot for the first of the customer-only stairs.

Without Eileen, there is a fresh silence. Something unspecific has occurred and no one is prepared to move until they understand the full extent of the damage. Someone speaks in a low voice, and when nothing happens, nothing splits open or crashes down, someone else laughs. Gradually, softly, voices thread into the density of silence until the café is once more itself.

"That woman is fired," says Mr. Meade, although it could be argued that Eileen has already fired herself. "Back to work, team." Then: "Jim? Hat?"

Jim straightens his hat. It is probably best he will not see Eileen again; she carries such chaos in her wake. And yet her parting words resound in his head, as does her generous laugh. He can't help wondering what sort of sandwich she would have brought him. Whether she would have served it with crisps and lettuce and a star-shaped tomato. He remembers a time long ago when there were cut sandwiches on a lawn, when there was hot tea. He has to hold his head so that while he shakes he will not lose his orange hat.

The first flakes of snow begin to fall, silent and twisting, like feathers through the air, but he does not look.

9

Pond

The sun was up, and already the dawn sky was pasted with copper-tipped clouds. Gold light trickled over the moor like honey. Six days, twenty-one hours, and forty-five minutes had passed since the accident. At last Byron had a plan.

He made his way purposefully through the garden and toward the meadow. His mother and sister were still sleeping. Equipped with essential tools and a packet of Garibaldi biscuits in case the work was difficult, he clicked the picket gate shut. Heavy dew had fallen overnight, and fat drops clung to the wild grass like pendants. His slippers, his pajamas, and the hem of his terrycloth dressing gown were soaked within minutes. When he stopped briefly to glance back at the house he could see the dark path his feet had made, and sunlight growing like flames at the bedroom windows. Both his mother and Lucy were asleep. Far away, a farm dog barked across the hills.

James Lowe had once said that a dog was not necessarily a dog. It was only a name, in the same way that *hat* was just a name, or *chest freezer*. Maybe, he had said, a dog was really a hat.

"But how could a dog be a hat?" Byron had asked. He was getting a picture in his mind of his father's deerstalker on a lead, and it was confusing.

"I am only saying that *hat* and *dog* are words that someone has chosen. And if they are only words someone has chosen, it stands to reason they may have got the wrong ones. Also, maybe not all dogs are dogs. Maybe they are different. Just because we have given them all one name doesn't mean all dogs are actually dogs."

"But they are still not hats," said Byron. "And they are not chest freezers either."

"You have to think bigger than what you know," James said.

Using the magnifying glass from his biology set, as well as a torch and his mother's silver tweezers, Byron began his search. He found a yellow-striped stone, a tiny spider with a big blue ball of eggs, wild thyme, and two white feathers but not the important thing he needed. Maybe he was looking in the wrong place. Resting a foot on the lowest rung of the fencing around the pond, he hauled himself over. It was strange to be on the forbidden side of the fence after all this time. It was like being in his father's study, where the air grew sharp edges. The geese hissed and stuck their necks forward, but they didn't run at him. Losing interest, they swaggered toward the water's edge.

The remains of the bridge still crossed the pond, still stretched, like a shiny black spine, from the bank to the small island in the middle. He could see too where the fragile structure left the island and then disappeared halfway before reaching the farthest side. Kneeling in the grass, he tried to resume his search with his torch and magnifying glass, but it was no good, he couldn't concentrate. His head kept walking off and remembering things.

The bridge had been all James's idea. Byron was really only manual labor. James had thought about it for weeks. He had drawn up plans. At school he had talked about it constantly. On the day of construction, the boys had sat side by side on the bank, the two of them viewing the expanse of water through their splayed fingers in order to get a professional perspective. It was Byron who had lifted stones to the pond and dragged the larger of the branches from the ash trees at the end of the meadow.

"Very good, very good," James had called out, without actually getting up.

Byron had piled the stones one on top of the other in the shallows, using them as supports for the thicker branches. After several hours an irregular structure had spanned the skin of water. "Do you want to test it?" Byron asked.

James consulted his diagram. "I think we need to look at the load bearing." Byron insisted it was only a pond. He stepped out.

He remembered how his heart had swung like the structure beneath his feet. The wood was dark and oily; his toes could gain no purchase. With each step he was waiting to fall, and the more he expected failure the more inevitable it seemed. He remembered too how James had mouthed numbers and insisted it wasn't because he was worried, it was because he was calculating.

The memory of that day was so clear it was like watching two ghost children beside the water. Then something else began to happen.

The more Byron gazed at the water, the more he found not only the bridge but also the sky's reflection, as if beneath the surface lay a second, more refracted world that was also pasted with copper clouds and flickering sunshine. If a boy did not go to Winston House he might be forgiven for believing there were two skies that morning, one above his head and another below the water. And supposing, after all, the scientists were wrong?

They had clearly made a mess of time. Supposing there really *were* two skies? Until the accident, Byron had assumed that everything was the thing it appeared to be. Now, as he stared at the pond, and the sky within its shining circumference, it occurred to him that people knew things only because they had been told they were true. James was right. It didn't seem a very good basis for believing.

This was so much to think about, Byron thought he might eat a Garibaldi. A slight wind rustled the water and sent tiny jewels of light darting all over the grass. It was already quarter past six. He shook the crumbs from his dressing gown and returned to his task. The magnifying glass and the torch made no significant difference; the sun was sailing higher by the minute. They just made him feel more like a boy who found things. There would be no need for either if James were at his side.

"Goodness, you're soaked," said his mother when the alarm went off and her eyes flicked open. She reached for her pill and her water. "You haven't been down by the pond?"

"I think it's going to be another hot day," he said. "Do I have to go to school?"

Diana pulled him close and wound her arms around him. He couldn't wait to show her what he had found.

She said: "Your education is very important. If you don't have a proper beginning, you end up like me."

"I'd rather be like you than anyone else."

"No, you wouldn't. People like me will never get it right." She rested the point of her chin on his shoulder so that her voice seemed to come from inside his bones. "Besides, your father wants you to have the best. He wants you to make a success of your life. He's very definite about that."

For a while they remained bound together by her arms, her face close to his. Then she kissed his hair and threw back the covers. "I'm going to draw you a bath, sweetheart. You don't want to catch a cold."

He didn't know what she meant. Why would he not want to become like his mother? What did she mean when she said she never got it right? She surely hadn't guessed about Digby Road. As soon as she was gone, he eased the stem of clover from his dressing-gown pocket. It was a little rumpled, a little soggy, and it didn't really have four leaves, it was technically three, but he knew it would save her because James said clover was lucky. Byron tucked it deep beneath her pillow so that it would be there to protect her, even without her knowing.

Humming softly, he followed his mother to the bathroom. The light from the windows was like white stepping-stones across the hall carpet and he jumped from one to the next. He thought of his mother *drawing a bath*. It was not a phrase she'd used before. Sometimes she said things like that, or the remark about not wanting him to become like her, and they were so sideways it was as if there was another person inside her, just as there was a boy inside his father, and another world inside the pond.

He wished he hadn't eaten all those Garibaldis. It was not the sort of thing that James would do.

10

Planting

The snow falls on and off for three more days. It whitens even the night. Just as it begins to thaw, there is another blizzard and the land is hidden all over again. Silence pads the air and the earth is one and soon it is only by staring into the dusk that Jim can make out the movement of swarming flakes. The sky is of a piece with the ground.

On the estate, cars are abandoned at angles into the curb. The old man who never smiles watches from his window. Jim's neighbor with the dangerous dog shovels a path to the door, and within hours there is no path again. Bare branches are showered with snow as if they are in blossom, the leaves of the evergreens droop under the weight. The foreign students head out in Puffa jackets and wool hats with plastic bags on which to sledge. They climb over the fencing and try to skate on the iced-over ditch in the middle of the Green. Jim watches, a little apart, as they laugh and shout to one another in words he does not understand. He hopes they won't disturb anything. Sometimes he checks the window boxes when no one is looking, but there is no sign of life.

At work, the girls from the kitchen complain that there is nothing to do and Mr. Meade says the supermarket is already reducing its Christmas grocery prices. Jim cleans the tables and no one sits at them, he just squirts and wipes. At dusk the new snow creaks soft beneath his feet and the moor sleeps pale beneath the moonlight. Needlepoints of ice trim the streetlamps and hedgerows.

Late one night, Jim scrapes the snow from a bed of winter bulbs. This is his latest project. No need for rituals here. No need for duct tape or greetings. When he is planting there is nothing but himself and the earth. He remembers Eileen and her bonsai tree, how she called him a gardener, and despite the biting cold, he feels warm inside. He wishes she could see what he has done.

It was one of the nurses at Besley Hill who first noticed that he was happier outside. She suggested he might help in the garden. After all, it was a wreck, she said. He began slowly, a little raking, a little pruning. The gray square building was behind him, the barred windows were forgotten, as were the lime-green walls, the smells of gravy and disinfectant, the endless faces. He learned as he went. He saw how the plants changed over the seasons. He discovered what they needed. Within a few years, he had borders of his own. There were splashes of marigolds, spikes of delphinium, foxglove, and hollyhock. There were clumps of thyme, sage, mint, and rosemary, the butterflies hovering over them like petals. He grew them all. He even managed asparagus, as well as gooseberry, blackcurrant, and loganberry bushes. The nurses let him sow apple pips too, although the home was closed before he saw them flourish. Sometimes they told him about their own gardens. They showed him seed catalogs and asked what they should choose. Once, when he was released, a doctor gave him a small potted cactus for good luck. Jim was back within months, but the doctor said he could keep the plant.

There have been so many years in and out of Besley Hill, Jim has lost count. There have been so many doctors and nurses and inpatients, they all seem to share one face, one voice, one coat. Sometimes he notices a customer stop at the café, stare a little, and he has no idea if it is because they know him or because he is strange. There are gaps in what he remembers, gaps that span weeks, months, and sometimes more. Recalling the past is like traveling to a place he visited once and discovering that everything has lifted up and blown away.

What he cannot forget is the first time. He was only sixteen. He can still see himself in the passenger seat, scared and refusing to get out. He can see the doctors and nurses who rushed down the stone steps to the car, shouting, "Thank you, Mrs. Lowe. We will take over now." He remembers how they pried his fingertips from the lip of the leather seat and how he was already so tall they had to press down his neck so as not to knock the top of his head. He even has a picture in his mind of the nurse who showed him around once they had given him something and he had slept. He was assigned to a ward with five men who were old enough to be his grandfather. They cried at night for their mothers and Jim cried too but it made no difference and no one ever came.

After the first job on the rubbish trucks, he tried others. Nothing strenuous. He mowed lawns, stacked wood, swept leaves, delivered pamphlets. Between the stays at Besley Hill, there have been single rooms in flats and bedsits. There has been sheltered housing. None of it lasts. He has been given further shock treatment for depression and cocktails of drugs. After morphine shots he has seen spiders spill out of lightbulbs and nurses with razor blades instead of teeth. For most of his mid-thirties he was so undernourished that his stomach sank between his hip bones like a grave. In the occupational therapy department he learned pottery and drawing, as well as rudimentary woodwork skills and French for beginners. None of it prevented him from breaking down again and again, sometimes weeks or months after being discharged. The last time he returned to Besley Hill, he resigned himself to never leaving. And then they went and closed it.

Snow laces the hedgerows and the coils of old man's beard. The whitened branches of the trees sway as if there is music in the air only they can hear. Cars crawl over the frozen ridges of the moor, and the light on the lower foothills is a polished blue.

It is too soon for signs of life. The cold would kill new growth, and the earth is hard as stone. Jim lies on the snow beside his bulbs and stretches out his arms to send them warmth. Sometimes caring for something already growing is more perilous than planting something new.

11

Mothers and Psychology

"I don't understand," said James. "Why do you think we need to tell the police?"

"In case they don't know about the two seconds," said Byron. "In case you are right about the conspiracy. Innocent people may be in danger and it's not their fault."

"But if there is a conspiracy, the police probably know. And so do the government. We need to think of someone else. Someone we can trust."

Until the accident, Byron had no idea that keeping a secret could be so difficult. All he could think about was what his mother had done and what would happen if she knew. He told himself not to think about the accident, but not thinking took so much space it was the same as thinking about it all the time. Every time he began a sentence he was afraid the wrong words would escape from his mouth. Consequently he had to keep examining them on their way out, as if he was checking their hands for cleanliness. It was exhausting.

"Est-ce qu'il faut parler avec quelqu'un d'autre?" James said. "Monsieur Roper, peut-être?"

Byron shook his head in a nodding sort of way. He wasn't clear what James had said and he was waiting for further clues.

"It needs to be someone who would understand," James said. "Votre mère? Elle est très sympathique." At the mention of Diana, James's skin stained. "She wasn't cross with us about the pond. She made us hot tea and those little sandwiches. Also, she doesn't make you sit outside if you are muddy, for example."

Even though James was right about Byron's mother, even though she had not shouted like Seymour after the pond incident, or been tight-lipped, like James's mother, even though Diana had insisted all along that Byron's fall into the water was an accident, Byron suggested they should not tell her about the two seconds. "Do you think a person could be guilty if they didn't know they had made a mistake?" he said.

"Is this to do with the extra seconds as well?"

Byron said it was more of a general inquiry and slipped his Brooke Bond tea cards from his blazer pocket to lighten the conversation. He now had the full series, even the number one.

"I don't see how someone could be guilty if they didn't know about it," said James, transfixed by the cards. He stretched out his fingers but didn't touch them. "You can only be guilty if you have deliberately committed a crime. If you murder someone, for example."

Byron said he wasn't thinking of a murder. He was only thinking of an accident.

"What sort of accident? Do you mean cutting off someone's hand in the workplace?"

Sometimes Byron thought James read too many newspapers. "No," he said. "Just doing something you didn't mean to."

"I think if you said sorry for your mistake," said James, "and if you showed you really meant it, that would be all right. It's what I do."

"You never do wrong things," Byron reminded him.

"I get my *h*'s confused. I say *haitch* when I am tired. And once I trod in something outside school and brought it into the car. My mother had to scrub the foot mats. I sat on the wall all afternoon."

"Because of your shoes?"

"Because she wouldn't let me in. When she cleans, I have to stay outside. Sometimes I am not sure my mother wants me." With this confession, James studied his fingertips and fell quiet again. Then: "Do you have the Montgolfier Balloon card?" he said. "It's actually number one in the set."

Byron knew that the card was number one. It showed a blue hot-air balloon, festooned with gold, and it was his favorite; not even Samuel Watkins had it. Nevertheless there was something so compact and alone about the way his friend sat that Byron slipped the balloon card into James's hands. He offered it for keeps. And when James said, "No, no, you can't give me this. You won't have the full set anymore," Byron tickled him to show there was no problem. James bent double and shrieked with laughter while Byron's fingers found the hard little spaces in his armpits and beneath his chin. "Please s-stop," howled James. "You're giving me hiccups." When James laughed, he was like a child.

That night was no easier. Sleep came in fits, and when it did, Byron saw things that frightened him and woke tangled in wet sheets. When he looked in the bathroom mirror the next morning, he was shocked to discover a big, pale boy with shadows hanging beneath his eyes like bruises.

His mother was equally shocked. Catching sight of him, she

said he must stay at home. Byron pointed out that he had his important scholarship work, but she merely smiled. A day would make no difference. There was the mothers' coffee morning too, she said. "At least I won't have to go to that now." This troubled Bryon. If she did anything unusual, the other mothers would grow suspicious. He agreed to take the day off school but only because he planned to ensure that she attended the coffee morning.

"I would like a day at home," said Lucy.

"You are not ill," said their mother.

"Byron is not ill neither," said Lucy. "He has no spots."

Once a month the Winston House mothers met for morning coffee in the only department store in town. There were other cafés, but they were the type of new establishment at the lower end of the High Street that served American hamburgers and flavored milkshakes. The department store tearoom opened at eleven. It had wooden-framed gilt chairs with blue velveteen cushions. The waitresses wore lace-trimmed aprons and brought teacakes on plates with paper doilies. If you ordered coffee, it came with a choice of milk or cream, and also a slim mint chocolate in a black wrapper.

There were fifteen mothers present that morning. "What a marvelous turnout," said Andrea Lowe, batting at the air with her menu. She had bright eyes that appeared to stay open to their widest extent, as if she was permanently seeing things that shocked her. Deirdre Watkins, who had arrived last, was perched on a low stool she had requisitioned from the lavatories because all the gilt chairs were taken. Her face was filmy with the heat and she had to keep dabbing at it. "I don't know why we don't meet like this more often," said Andrea. "Are you sure you can see us down there, Deirdre?"

Deirdre said she was just splendid but would someone mind passing her the sugar.

"Not for me," said the new mother. Her husband was something to do with sales, but not door-to-door. She held up her hands as if merely touching sugar would fatten up her fingers.

"Is Byron ill?" said Andrea, nodding at him from the other end of the table.

"He has a headache," said Diana. "He's not infectious. He doesn't have lumps or spots."

"Goodness no," chorused the mothers. Who would bring an infectious child to a department store?

"No more accidents, then?" said Andrea.

Byron swallowed hard as his mother said no, there had been no more accidents. The pond was fenced in now. Andrea explained to the new mother that James and Byron had tried to build a bridge at Cranham House the previous summer. "They almost drowned," she laughed. She added that there were no hard feelings.

"It was only Byron who fell in," said Diana under her breath. "The water's not much deeper than my knees. And James didn't even get wet."

It was the wrong thing to say. Andrea Lowe battered her coffee with a teaspoon. "Still, you don't want Byron to miss his scholarship work. If I were you, I'd get him looked at. My husband knows a very good fellow in town. Howards, he's called. They were at the college together. This man is an expert on children."

"Thank you, Andrea," said Diana. "I'll remember that." She reached for her notebook and folded it open on an empty page.

"He is actually a psychologist."

The word hit the air like a small slap. Without looking, Byron saw his mother stall over her book. He knew the problem. She wouldn't know how to spell psychologist.

"Not that I've ever needed his services personally," said Andrea.

Scribble, scribble, scribble, went Diana's pen. She slammed her notebook shut and tossed it into her handbag.

"But there are people who do need him. There are some sick people out there."

Byron offered the women a wide smile to show the mothers he wasn't one of those people, that he was normal, just a bit achy.

"Take my mother-in-law," piped up Deirdre. "She writes love letters to that DJ on Radio 2. What's his name?"

Andrea said she had no idea. She wasn't a DJ person, she said. Beethoven was more her thing.

"I keep telling her, Mother, you can't write to him every day. She has that thing—what's it called?" The mothers shook their heads, but this time Deirdre got there. "Schizophrenia. That's it. She says he talks to her on the radio."

"I like writing letters," said Byron. "Once I wrote to the Queen. She wrote back. Didn't she, Mummy? Or rather, her lady-in-waiting wrote back."

Andrea studied him with her mouth pinched as if she was sucking on a throat lozenge. He regretted mentioning the Queen, even though privately he was proud of her correspondence. He kept it in a special Jacob's Crackers tin along with those from NASA and Mr. Roy Castle. He felt he had the knack of letter writing.

"But I don't suppose you wrote to the Queen on your underwear," said Deirdre. "That's what my mother-in-law does."

The women erupted with laughter, and Byron wished he could disappear. Even his ears were embarrassed. He hadn't meant anything to do with underwear and now there was a picture in his mind of all the mothers in peach corsets and he didn't know what to do with it. He felt his mother's soft hand close around his beneath the table. Meanwhile, Andrea Lowe said that mental illness was a disease. You had to put people like that in Besley Hill. It was the kindest thing in the long run, she said. It was like homosexuals. They had to be helped to get better.

From here the women discussed other things. A recipe for chicken escalopes. The Olympic Games in the summer, and who still had a black-and-white set. Deirdre Watkins said that every time she bent over the new chest freezer she worried her husband would stuff her inside it. Wasn't Andrea worried for Anthony's safety, asked the new mother, after the recent spate of IRA bombings? Andrea said that in her view the terrorists should be strung up, they were fanatics. Fortunately her husband's area was domestic crime.

"Gosh," said the women.

"I'm afraid he even gets women in front of him. Sometimes mothers."

"Mothers?" said Deirdre.

Byron's heart tossed itself upward like a pancake and fell flat onto his bowels.

"They think that just because they have children they can get away with it. Anthony takes the tough line. If there is a crime, someone must pay. Even if she's a woman. Even if she's a mother."

"Quite right," said the new mother. "An eye for an eye."

"Sometimes they shout the most appalling abuse as they get taken down. Anthony won't tell me the words sometimes."

"Goodness," caroled the women.

Byron couldn't look at Diana. He heard her gasping and purling like the others. He heard the pop of her lips as they met her cup, the chink of her pink fingernails against the china, and the small wet click of air as she swallowed her drink. Her innocence was clear, so palpable he felt he could touch it, and yet, without even knowing, she had been guilty for nine days. The pity of it was cruel beyond words.

"This is the price of feminism," said Andrea. "The country's going to the dogs."

"Yes, yes," agreed the women, dipping their mouths like little beaks toward their coffees.

Byron whispered to his mother that he would like to go, but she shook her head. Her face was a sheet of glass.

Andrea said, "This is what happens when women go to work. We can't be men. We are females. We have to behave like females." She gave extra stress to the *fe* so that this part of the word shot out of the sentence, sounding long and important. "The first duty of a married woman is to have babies. We shouldn't ask for more."

"Yes, yes," said the women.

Plonk, plonk, went two more sugar cubes into Deirdre's tea.

"Why not?" asked a small voice.

"I beg your pardon?" Andrea's coffee cup froze to her mouth.

"Why can't we ask for more?" said the small voice again.

Fifteen faces shot in Byron's direction. He shook his head, signifying that he meant no harm, when, to his horror, he realized that the small voice was his mother's. She had tucked her hair behind her ears and sat tall, the way she did in the driving seat to show his father she was concentrating.

She said, "I don't want to spend my whole life at home. I want to see things. When the children are older, I might take another job."

"You mean you had one before?" said Andrea.

His mother bowed her head. "It might be interesting. That's all I meant."

What was she doing? Byron mopped the sweat from his upper lip and sank into his chair. More than anything, he wanted her to be like the others. But here she was, talking about being different when already she was marked apart in ways she couldn't imagine. He wanted to get up, flap his arms, yell at her, just to cause a distraction.

Meanwhile, Deirdre asked again for the sugar. The new mother held up her hands as it passed. Several women became very busy with loose strands of cotton on their sleeves.

"Oh, *interesting*," laughed Andrea.

They drifted along the High Street in silence, Byron and his mother. The sun was a blinding hole, and a buzzard hung above the moor, waiting to swoop. The air was so stale and close it was like a fist pressing into the land. Even when a cloud popped up, the sky seemed to drink the moisture before the cloud could spill it. Byron wondered how much longer such heat could last.

After what his mother had said in the tearoom about taking a job, conversation between the women had faltered, as if it were unwell or overtired. Byron held his mother's hand and concentrated on stepping between the cracks in the paving stones. There were so many things he wanted to ask. Diana moved in her lemon dress past the windows of the Conservative Party shop, and her puff of hair glowed in the sunlight.

"They have no idea," she said. She seemed to be staring ahead.

"Who has no idea?"

"Those women. They haven't a clue."

He wasn't sure what to do with that piece of information so he said, "I think I will look at my letter from the Queen when we get home."

His mother smiled at him as if he were clever. It felt like her hand on his. "That's a fine idea, sweetheart. You're so good at letters."

"Then I might design a new *Blue Peter* badge."

"I thought they already had one."

"They do. They have silver and gold too. But you have to do something like rescuing a person in distress to get the gold. Do you think that's realistic?"

She nodded, but as if she were no longer listening, or at least not to him. They were stopped outside the off-license. His mother glanced over her shoulder. *Tap, tap, tap,* went her pointed toe on the pavement.

"Wait here a moment, like a good boy," she said. "I need tonic water for the weekend."

The weather broke that night. Byron woke when a gust of wind slammed open his window, causing his bedroom curtains to fill like sails. A fork of lightning sliced the sky, and the moor flashed like a blue photograph framed by his window. He lay very still and counted, waiting for the crack of thunder. Needles of rain began to fall. They shot through his open curtains. If he didn't get up and close them there would be a wet patch on the carpet. He lay on top of his covers, unable to sleep and unable to move. All he could hear was the rain, the splashing of it on the roof and the trees and the terrace. He couldn't imagine how it would ever stop.

Byron thought of what Mrs. Lowe had said about women not getting away with a crime. He didn't know how he was going to keep his mother safe. The job seemed too big for one boy alone. Take the way she had spoken out about taking a job, and the way she had objected at the weekend when his father called the car female. It wasn't simply what she had done in Digby Road that marked Diana apart. There was something about her, something pure and fluid that would not be contained. If she discovered what she had done, the truth would spill out. She wouldn't be able to stop it. He pictured again those tiny jeweled drawers inside her mind, and maybe it was to do with the rain, but all he could see was them brimming with water. He shouted out.

Suddenly the silver outline of her was at his doorway, shining in the light from the hall. "What is it, love?" He told her he was frightened and she rushed to close his window. She rearranged his curtains into neat blue folds.

"You're such a worrier," she smiled. "Things are never so bad as we think." Sitting on the edge of his bed, she stroked her fingers over his forehead. She sang a quiet song he didn't know and he closed his eyes.

Whatever happened, he must never tell his mother what she had done. Of all the people to know, she was surely the most dangerous. He told himself this over and over while her fingers crept through his hair and the rain pattered on the leaves and the thunder grew tame. Byron faltered toward sleep as if pulled on strings.

12

Another Accident

Five days after Eileen's exit from the café, Jim encounters her again. The snow has begun to thaw. During the day it slides from the trees and everywhere there is the pattering of water, the *tap, tap* of melting ice. As the land reappears, its muted colors—the greens, the browns, the purples—look too startling, too full of themselves. It is only up on the moor that there remains a white shawl of snow.

Jim is leaving the entrance to the car park after work. The street is dark. Commuters are going home. Lamps spill orange light over the wet pavements, and ice mounts in dirty ridges at the curb. He is heading toward the roundabout in order to cross safely when a maroon Ford Escort rattles past. A sticker is pasted on the back window—MY OTHER CAR IS A PORSCHE. With a screech and a metallic smell of fireworks, the car slams to a halt at the give way markings on the road. Jim steps out behind it.

There is no obvious reason why a car that is stationary should change its mind and reverse, but this one does both. With a roar and a sudden shot of smoke, the Ford jumps backward, then brakes with another jolt right against Jim. He realizes that something significant has happened and then that it is pain. It bolts up through him, starting from his toe and flashing the length of his leg into his spine.

"Whoa," a male voice shouts from across the road.

The passenger door flies open and there she is. Or rather, there her face is, at a slanted angle. She must have jumped across from the driver's seat. Blaze of sticking-out orange hair. Wide eyes. There is only her car between them.

"What the—?" There is no mistaking her.

Jim raises his hands. If he had a white flag, he would wave that too. "I-I-I. Your car— Your car—" He has much on his mind and 1,105 kilograms of Ford Escort on the end of his boot.

Eileen stares at him and the look she sends is one of bewilderment. He doesn't know why, but as he stares back at Eileen an image pops into his mind of a hydrangea he found in flower only that morning, so pink it was vulgar. He remembers how he wanted to cup its head and hold it safe until spring.

Eileen and Jim continue to stare at each other without moving, him thinking of hydrangeas, her mouthing "Fuck," until the voice from across the road shouts again: "Stop! Stop! There's been an accident!"

For a moment the words mean nothing. Then, realizing what they signify, Jim feels a flood of panic. He doesn't want any of this. It must stop happening. He calls out, "Nothing wrong." People are beginning to notice. He flaps his arms as if Eileen is wedged in his path and that with vigorous hand movements he can waft her free. "Go away!" he shouts, or something close to that. "Go away! Go on!" It is almost rude.

Eileen's head withdraws, the door is slammed shut, and she

drives forward. Her passenger wheel cuffs the curb as she takes the turning.

The man who shouted dashes across the road, dodging cars. He is young, dark-haired, leather jacket, face like a skeleton. His breath hits the cold in small plumes of smoke. "I got the registration number," he says. "Can you walk?"

Jim says he is sure he can. Now that Eileen's back wheel has parted from his shoe, he feels surprisingly light, as if his foot is made of air.

"Do you want me to call the police?"

"I-I—"

"An ambulance?"

"N-n—"

"Here." The young man hands Jim a scrap of notepaper on which he has apparently scribbled the car's details. His writing is childlike.

Jim folds the paper and pockets it. His thoughts are struggling to connect with one another. He has been hit and he is hurt. All he wants is to remove his boot in the privacy of the van and examine his toe, without anyone else running him over or threatening to fetch people who terrify him. And then he realizes that he has folded the young man's note only once. It should be twice, and then once. After all, there has been an accident. He should be performing the rituals, even here on the pavement. But he has done it now, he has done a wrong thing. Despite the cold, a rush of sweat showers his skin. He starts to tremble.

"Are you sure you're OK?" says the young man.

Jim tries to refold the piece of paper in his pocket, only somehow it is caught around his key ring.

The young man stares. He says, "Did the car knock your hip as well?"

There, it is done. The paper is folded twice. "Y-yes," he tells himself, because it is safe now.

"It did?" says the man. "Shit."

It is safe but Jim still doesn't feel it. Bad thoughts are clamoring at his back. He can hear and feel them. Further rituals are needed. He will know everything is safe only if he sees a 2 and a 1. He has to find the numbers. He has to find them right now, otherwise it will all get worse. "H-h-help," he says, scanning car registration plates as they pass.

The young man glances over his shoulder. "Help! Help!" he shouts.

Traffic is beginning to slow, but none of it has the right numbers.

If Jim hurries he can go back to the supermarket. The café is closed but the store will still be open. He can visit the personal hygiene aisle, where they stock 2-in-1 shampoo. This has worked before. It is like another sticking plaster for emergencies. As he turns from the young man, a hot flash shoots all the way up his leg. He wonders if his foot is still attached to the rest of him. He has to grip his hands into balls so that the young man won't see, but unfortunately Jim is right in the path of someone else. She sees everything.

"Jim? What happened?" Without her hairnet and her orange hat, it takes a moment for him to place her. It is one of the young girls from the supermarket café who described him as backward. She has a mane of bright pink hair and so many studs in her ears they look upholstered.

"You know this guy?" says the young man.

"I work with him. Up at the café. He does tables. I do food."

"He's been hit by a car."

"An accident?" Her eyes widen.

"The driver didn't even stop."

Her eyes pop. "A hit-and-run? You're joking."

"He says he's OK but he's in shock. He needs to go to hospital. He needs an X-ray and shit."

The girl's mouth lifts into a smile as if she is tasting something delicious that she hadn't expected. "Jim? Shall we get you to hospital?" There is no need for her to loom very close, or exaggerate the words, or indeed shout, as if he is deaf or slow of understanding, but she does all three.

Jim shakes his head to show a no. "I-I-I—"

"I know him. I understand his language. He's saying yes."

And so this is how Jim finds himself in a minicab, squashed between two young people who seem to like talking. He needs to see the numbers 2 and 1 or the girl will be hurt. The young man will be hurt. So will the minicab driver, and all the pedestrians hunched inside their winter clothes. Jim tries to breathe deeply. He tries to empty his mind. But all he can see is devastation.

"Look at the poor guy shaking," says the young woman, dipping her head to address the young man. And a little later: "By the way, my name's Paula."

"Cool," says the young man.

There will be ambulances, there will be doctors, there will be injuries everywhere. A coil of pain twists through Jim as the car turns in to the hospital car park and he remembers.

She says, "My parents named me after that singer. The one who died."

The young man nods as if everything is clear now and watches her, grinning.

When they took patients for treatment, the nurses used to tell them to wear loose clothing. This was not difficult. They were often wearing one another's things anyway. "Who's frying tonight?" he heard one of the older patients ask the first time. They walked the corridors in silence. There was one set of doors for entry and another for exit so that those who were about to receive treatment did not meet those who had already had it.

In the operating theater the staff smiled at him reassuringly, the psychiatrist, the nurses, the anesthetist. They asked him to remove his slippers and sit up on the bed. Bare feet were necessary, explained his nurse, so that they could see the movement in his toes when the fit took hold. Jim stooped to remove his slippers but he was shaking so much he almost fell. He wanted them to laugh because he wanted them to be kind and not hurt him so he made a joke about his feet, about the length of them, and they all laughed. Everyone, it seemed, was on best behavior. And that frightened him even more. The nurse stowed his slippers beneath the bed.

It wouldn't take long, they said. He must relax. "Don't fight it, Jim. Remember to breathe deeply, like we showed you."

The nurse took one of his hands and the anesthetist took the other. He was lucky, a voice said, he was lucky to have such good veins. There was a prick to his hand and emptiness trickled into his knuckles, his arm, his head. Briefly he heard female laughter from a dormitory, the yelling of crows in the garden, and then women were flying and the noises were nothing.

He came round in another room. There were other patients beside him and they were sitting quietly. One man was being sick into a bucket. Jim's head pounded as if it had grown too big for his skull. There were mugs of tea and a family assortment tin of biscuits.

"You must eat," said the nurse. "It will make you feel better if you eat." She offered him a pink wafer on a plate. The smell of it was like an assault. He could smell the vomit too and the violet scent of the nurse. Everything seemed to smell too big and that made him feel even worse. "All the others are eating," said the nurse.

She was right. They were sitting with their nurses and taking their tea and biscuits and each of them had two red marks on his forehead, as if the burns had been there all along. No one spoke. He saw this and it was terrible to witness and then somehow he didn't see. He wondered if he had marks too, but by the time he remembered to look several nights had passed, or maybe longer. This was how it went. Time was something altogether more fragmented than it had been before. It was like throwing a handful of feathers into the air and watching them drift. Moments no longer flowed from one to the other.

The waiting room at Accident and Emergency is so full there is standing room only. It's because it's the weekend, says Paula; her dad was always in A&E on a Saturday night. There are men with bloodied faces and closed-up eyes, and an ashen-faced boy with his chin high in the air. ("I bet that kid's got beans up his nose," says Paula.) There is a woman crying onto the shoulders of another woman, and several people with makeshift bandages and slings. Whenever the ambulance crew rush in with a patient on a trolley, everyone turns away. It is only Paula who stares long and hard.

She explains to the nurse in the reception kiosk that Jim has been hit by a car. It's a hit-and-run, she says. The receptionist replies that she will need a few simple details. His name, post-code, phone number, and also the address of his GP.

"Jim?" says Paula. She gives him a nudge because everyone is waiting and he isn't saying anything, he is only shaking.

"Proof of ID," repeats the woman.

But Jim can barely hear. The question is like being hit by a fresh barrage of memories that are so deep, so wild, he struggles to keep standing. His foot feels sliced in two; the intense pain seems to answer the pain in his head. It is too much to think about so many things. He grips the ledge of the nurse's window, mouthing, *Telephone, h-hello. Pen, hello.*

Paula's voice rings through the silence. "It's OK, he's with us. Can you put my address?" His records would all have been at Besley Hill, she suggests. "He was up there for years but he's completely harmless." She pulls a face to suggest that her mouth is about to voice something for which the rest of her is not responsible. "He talks to plants and stuff."

"Take a seat," says the receptionist.

When a blue plastic bench comes free, Jim offers it to Paula, but she laughs and says cheerfully, "You're the one with the injury. You're the one who got run over." She has a way of talking up her sentences, as if the conclusion of every one of them hangs at a point high in the air. It is like being repeatedly led up a precipice and left there, and it makes him dizzy. Meanwhile, the young man slots loose change from his pocket into a vending machine.

He snaps the tab from a can of fizzy drink and offers the opened can to Jim and Paula.

"Not for me," says Jim. He can barely swallow. He can't see the numbers 1 or 2 anywhere.

"I'm gasping," says Paula. It's stress, she adds. Stress does funny things to people. "I know someone who lost all her hair overnight."

"No way," says the young man.

"And I know someone else who ate a mussel and had a heart attack. Then there was this other woman, she choked to death on a cough sweet."

A nurse calls Jim's name and beckons him toward a cubicle. She wears a coat, a white coat, and it looks like all the other white coats, and briefly he wonders if this is a trick to give him treatment again. He almost falls.

"He should be in a wheelchair," says Paula. "It's outrageous."

The nurse explains that there is no wheelchair available until after the X-ray, and Paula takes Jim's arm. She holds too tight and he wants to scream but she is being kind and he mustn't. The nurse has rubber shoes that squeak on the green linoleum floor as if she has something half alive trapped on the sole. She studies her clipboard and signals for Jim to step up to the bed. He is shaking so hard they have to take his arms and help him. When the nurse tugs the plastic curtain around the cubicle, the chrome rings scream on the pole. Paula and the young man move to the far end, where Jim's boots poke over the end of the bed. They look concerned but eager. Every time he moves, the young man's bomber jacket creaks like a plastic chair.

"I gather there has been an accident," says the nurse. Again she asks for Jim's name.

This time Paula is taking no chances. She supplies it.

"And my name's Darren," adds the young man, although no one has asked.

"No way," says Paula.

"It is," says Darren, and even he sounds surprised.

The nurse rolls her eyes. "Can we get back to the accident? Have the police been informed?"

Darren pulls a sensible face. He describes at length how the driver reversed without warning while Jim, in turn, ceases to listen. He thinks instead of the bewildered look Eileen sent him, as if she were something else, not the person she appeared to be but another person locked inside that one, a fragile, small version of herself, like the last in a set of Russian dolls.

"He doesn't want to press charges," says Paula. "By the way, I knew this woman who had a car crash. She lost both her legs. She had to have plastic ones. She kept them under the bed at night."

"No way," says Darren.

The nurse asks to see Jim's foot and finally there is enraptured silence.

It is half past ten by the time they are ready to leave the hospital. The X-rays have revealed that there is no break in the toe bones, but the junior doctor on duty suspects damage to the ligaments. As a precautionary measure, Jim has a blue plaster cast set as far as his knee, a bottle of painkillers, and a borrowed set of NHS crutches.

"I always wanted crutches," Paula tells Darren.

"I bet you'd look lovely," says Darren. They blush like baubles.

Jim is lucky, adds the nurse, and she sounds confused: Due to the unaccountable length of his footwear, the damage is minimal.

She gives him a leaflet about looking after a plaster cast and a checkup appointment in two weeks' time. When she asks if he would recognize the driver, Jim stammers so hard over the word *n-n-no*, she rearranges her hair. She advises Paula that Jim should contact the police once he is over the shock. Even if he doesn't wish to press charges, there is Victim Support as well as telephone counseling. It's not like the old days when psychology was a dirty word. There are all sorts of strategies in place to help.

The young couple insist on taking another minicab and dropping Jim at the estate. They refuse to accept his money. Paula tells Darren about a number of accidents she has witnessed, including a real-life pileup on the motorway and the burning of her friend's ear with hair tongs. Jim is so tired he can think of nothing but sleep. His foldout bed seems to take shape in the dark, along with his blankets and pillow. He can hear the squeak of its hinges.

Once they have passed the sign welcoming careful drivers, the Green, and the skate ramps, he asks to get out.

"But where's your van?" says Paula, peering at the tightly packed houses and the Christmas lights pulsing all over Cranham Village like fast blue headaches. Jim points toward the cul-de-sac. He lives right at the end, he says, where the road stops and the moor takes over. Beyond his van, the black branches of the trees tremble as a gust of wind takes up.

Paula says, "We could take you inside. We could put the kettle on."

"You might need help," says Darren.

But Jim declines. No one has ever been inside his van. It is the deepest part of himself, the part that no one must see. And thinking this, he is aware of a searing pain that is like a fresh rift between him and the rest of the world.

"Sure you'll be OK?" calls Darren.

Jim nods because he cannot move his mouth to speak. He waves to the minicab driver to show that he is all right, that he is happy.

Beyond the estate, the moor looms dark and solid. Timeless layers of earth and grass have been ground to stone. An old moon shines over the land and a thousand million stars send points of light across the years. If the land stretched now, opened right up and swallowed the houses, the roads, the pylons, the lights, there would be no memory of anything human. There would be only the dark sleeping hills and the ancient sky.

The minicab makes its way past the Green, its tail lamps glowing. Turning the corner, it is gone with a snap and there is only Jim, watching the dark.

13

The Mistake

When the secret came out it was by mistake. It spoke itself. It was like having a dog that ran into other people's gardens before you could do anything about it, except that they had no dog, of course, because pet hair made his father sneeze.

His mother had only come to Byron's room to take his temperature before bed. Lucy was already asleep and he had been waiting for his mother a long time, but there had been a telephone call from his father. He couldn't hear what she was saying because her voice was slow and quiet. There was no fluttery laughter. When she entered his room she had stood for a moment, with her face lowered to the floor, as if she was somewhere else, not his bedroom, not even seeing him, and that was when he had mentioned his tummy ache. It was like reminding her who he was.

On studying the thermometer Diana sighed and said she couldn't understand what was wrong. "You don't seem to have any real symptoms," she said.

"I was fine before it happened." The words flew out and then he realized what they were and smacked his hand to his mouth.

"What do you mean?" said his mother. At this point she was busy wiping the thermometer with a cloth. She replaced it in its slim silver case. "You were fine before *what* happened?" She cocked her head. She waited.

Byron studied his nails. He hoped that if he kept quiet, if he acted as if he wasn't there, the conversation might go away. It might lose interest in Byron and saunter off to become an entirely different set of words about an entirely different set of problems. "Nothing," he said. Once again all he could picture was the red bicycle and the little girl.

His mother stooped and pressed a kiss to his forehead. She smelled sweet, like flowers, and her soft hair tickled his forehead. "She shouldn't have been running into the road," he said. This sentence too shot out so fast it was hot and fluid.

His mother gave a laugh. "What are you talking about?"

"It wasn't your fault."

"My fault? What wasn't?" Again she laughed, or at least she gave a smile with a noise attached to it.

"You haven't done anything wrong, because you didn't know. There was the mist and the extra seconds. You're not to blame."

"I'm not to blame for what?"

"The little girl. The little girl in Digby Road."

His mother's face pleated. "What little girl? I don't know what you mean."

Byron felt that solid ground had been suddenly swept away, that he was stepping once more on stones and branches while water swelled at his feet. He only went forward with the conversation because the option of going backward seemed to have sailed out of reach. Twisting the corner of his sheet, he described how he had seen the little girl shoot from her garden gate on her red bicycle and how he had seen her again, after the car stopped, not moving. He found he had only a small number of words at his disposal and so he kept repeating them. Digby Road. Mist. Two seconds. Not your fault. Then, because his mother was not speaking, only listening with her hands pressed over her mouth, he said: "I told you to drive on because I didn't want you to be scared."

"No," she said suddenly. It was a small sound and it was also the answer he was least expecting. "No. That can't be true."

"But I saw. I saw the whole accident."

"Accident? There wasn't an accident." Her voice grew with each phrase. "I didn't hit a little girl. I'm a careful driver. I'm very careful. I drive exactly as your father taught me. If there was a little girl, I'd know. I'd have seen. I'd have stopped the car." She kept her eyes fixed to the floor. It looked as if she were replying to a patch of the carpet. "I'd have got out."

Byron felt his head spin. He took shallow gasps, more and more of them, that yanked at his chest and throat muscles. He had thought about having this conversation so many times, or rather about not having it, and now that it was finally happening, everything seemed wrong. It was too much. It was too much to deliver his mother the truth and discover that, after all this, she could not see it. He wanted to fall to the floor and not think. Not feel.

"Are you all right?" she said. "What's happening, sweetheart?"

When he had nothing else to say—when all the words were used up and the room was wheeling on its axis, walls sliding and floors tipping—he said, "Excuse me. I'm going to be sick."

He wasn't. He gripped hold of the toilet bowl and shoved his head down. He even tried to push out with his stomach muscles and constrict those of his throat. His body retched but nothing came. When his mother knocked at the door and asked if she could come in, if she could fetch something, he repeated that he was all right. He still couldn't understand why she didn't believe him. He turned on the taps and sat very still on the floor, waiting for her to go, and when at last he heard her heels on the stairs, slow, as if she were not in a hurry but drifting, or deep in thought, he unlocked the door and returned swiftly to his room.

Byron missed James very much that night. It wasn't even that Byron had anything specific to say, it was more that James was in his head and so was the memory of the bridge they had built on the pond. If he knew about the accident James would know what to do, just as he had understood about load bearing and gravity.

Byron remembered how it felt to fall, the moment between losing his balance and landing in the cold water. The shock of that. The mud bed had pulled at his feet, and even though he knew the pond was shallow he had thrashed about, fearing suddenly he might drown. The water had swamped in at his ears and mouth and nose. "Mrs. Hemmings, Mrs. Hemmings!" James had screamed from the banks. He couldn't seem to do anything. He just flapped his arms. Byron saw his mother running so fast to his rescue that her arms and legs flew out and she appeared to be falling. She waded into the water without even throwing off her shoes. She walked the two boys back to the house with her arms around their shoulders, and despite the fact that James was dry she cocooned them both in towels. "It was my fault, it was my fault," James kept saying. But Diana stopped and held him by the shoulders. She told him he had saved Byron and that he should be proud. Afterward she made sandwiches and sweet tea for them to have on the lawn and James said through chattering teeth, "She is so kind, she is so kind, your mother."

Byron unfolded the map he had drawn in his father's study. With the aid of his torch, he studied it under the sheet. He traced the path of arrows with his fingertip, and his heart pounded when he reached the red mark where the Jaguar had pulled to a sudden halt. He knew he was right about the accident. After all, he had seen everything. From downstairs he heard the clunk of the fridge door as his mother opened it, and the slamming of the ice cube tray on the draining board. A little later he heard her music from the record player and it was so sad, this song, he wondered if she was crying. He thought again of the little girl in Digby Road and the trouble his mother was in. More than anything he wanted to go to her but he couldn't move. He told himself he would go in a minute and yet a minute passed, and another and another, and he was still lying there. In telling his mother what she had done, he felt he had become part of the accident too. If only he'd kept quiet, the whole thing might have disappeared. It might have remained not real.

Later, when his mother eased open his door, bringing a sharp arc of light into the room that hurt his head, and when she whispered "Byron, are you awake?" he lay still, with his eyes pressed tight. He tried to make his breathing heavy like someone who was asleep. He heard her footsteps creak on the carpet and he caught the sweet smell of her, and then the room flicked to dark.

"Are you all right?" she asked the next morning. It was Friday again and he was cleaning his teeth in the bathroom. He had no idea his mother was behind him until he felt her fingers on his shoulder. He must have jumped, because she laughed. Her hair was a golden cloud around her face, and her skin was soft like ice cream.

"You didn't come and wait for my alarm this morning. I missed you."

"I overslept." He couldn't turn and look at her. The mirror son was talking to the mirror mother.

She smiled. "Well, it's good that you slept."

"Yes," he said. "Did you?"

"Did I—?"

"Sleep."

"Oh yes," she said. "I slept well. Thank you."

For a moment, they fell silent. He felt they were searching for the most acceptable words, in the way that his mother tried on clothes before his father's arrival, slipping them on and sighing and slipping them off again. Then Lucy called for her school uniform and they both laughed. They did it long and hard as if it was a relief to have something that wasn't talking.

"You look pale," she said when the laughter had drained away and there was nothing left.

"You won't go to the police?"

"The police? Why would I do that?"

"Because of the little girl in Digby Road."

His mother shook her head as if she couldn't understand why he would say these things all over again. "We went through this last night. There was no little girl. You made a mistake."

"But I saw." He was beginning to shout. "I was sitting right beside the window. I saw the whole thing. I saw the extra seconds and then I saw the little girl. You couldn't see because you were driving. You couldn't see because of the mist."

His mother placed her forehead in her hands and then raked

her fingers through her hair as if she was clearing a space through which to see. She said slowly, "I was in the car, too. And nothing happened. I know it. Nothing happened, Byron."

He waited for her to say something else but his mother simply looked across at him, without speaking. And so all there was between them was the thing she had already said. Her words flapped over their heads and beat through his ears like an echo; even in the silence they found a voice. Nothing happened. Nothing happened, Byron.

It did, though. He knew it.

His father visited at the weekend and so there was no opportunity to speak to his mother again about the accident. The only time he found her alone was when his father checked the monthly accounts in his study. She was pacing the floor of the drawing room. She kept picking things up and putting them back down again without looking. When his father appeared at the door and said he had a query, her hands flew to her neck and her eyes widened. There was a blank, he said.

"A blank?" She repeated the word as if she did not know what it meant.

It was not the first time, said his father. He remained still, but his mother went back to straightening things that were already straight and lifting her fingers to her mouth. She couldn't think why there would be a blank, she said. She promised to be more careful in future.

"I wish you wouldn't do that."

"I said it was a mistake, Seymour."

"I mean, your nails. I wish you wouldn't bite them."

"Oh, darling, there are so many things you wish I wouldn't do."

She laughed and went to tidy the garden. Once again his father left on Sunday morning.

As the third week began, Byron trailed his mother like a shadow. He watched her washing up at the sink. He watched her digging over the rose beds. Their blooms were so full now he could barely see the stems, the petals all floppy and pink; they covered the pagoda like a skyful of stars. At night he listened to his mother playing her music downstairs on the record player. The only thing in his mind was Digby Road. He couldn't believe he had gone and told her. For the first time, there was something between them, like the fence separating the pond from the meadow, and it was to do with the fact that she believed one thing and he knew another. It even carried the implication that he was in some terrible way accusing her.

He wished he could tell James. At lunchtime on Tuesday he even ventured so far as to ask, "Do you have secrets?"

James gulped on a forkful of meat pie and said, "Yes, I do, Byron." He glanced both ways to check that none of the boys were listening, but Watkins had a new rubber balloon that made a fart noise and the others were busy placing it on the bench, squashing down on it, and laughing. "Why? Do you?" There was something alive about the way James watched, waiting for Byron's reply and not chewing his meat pie.

"I'm not sure." Byron felt a rush of adrenaline as if he were about to jump from a wall.

"For instance," said James, "sometimes I dip my finger in my mother's pot of Pond's cream."

This did not seem much of a secret to Byron but James continued, slowly and deliberately, and Byron assumed that worse was to come. "I only use a tiny bit. I do it when she's not looking. It's so that I won't get wrinkles." James returned to chewing his meat pie and washed it down with water. It was only when he failed to say anything else, and helped himself to salt, that Byron realized he had finished.

"But I don't understand. You don't have wrinkles, James."

"That is because I use Pond's cream, Byron."

This was a further example of how James planned ahead.

Byron decided to make amends for telling his mother what she had done. After school he followed her into the utility room where she was sorting dirty clothes for the washing machine. He told her he was wrong. It was his mistake, he said. She had done nothing in Digby Road.

"Would you stop going on about it?" she said. This was definitely strange, because it was the first time in five days he had referred to it.

Byron balanced with one foot on top of the other, as if by taking up less floor space he might also become less of an inconvenience. "You see, there is no evidence," he said. "No damage to the car."

"Please would you pass me the starch?"

"If we had hit the little girl there would be a dent on the Jaguar." He passed her the starch and she sprinkled it liberally over the whites. "And there is no dent," he said. "I have checked. I have checked several times, actually."

"Well, there we are."

"Also no one saw us in Digby Road."

"It's a free country, Byron. We can drive wherever we like."

He would have liked to say, Well, actually, Father says we are not supposed to go down Digby Road and we should bring back hanging and neither of those seems all that free to me, but it was a long sentence and he sensed it wasn't the time. His mother shoved the laundry into the drum of the washing machine and then slammed the door shut. He repeated that he was probably wrong, but she was already halfway toward the kitchen.

And yet, that afternoon he began to realize that she was thinking about what he had said. Despite her protestations, he caught her staring several times out of the French windows, glass in hand, with a preoccupied look. When his father rang to check that she was listening and that everything was as it should be, she said, "I'm sorry, what was that?" And when he repeated himself she even raised her voice: "Darling, what do you think happens? I never see anyone. No one has a clue where I live." She finished with her fluttery laugh, but from the way it cut midair, it didn't sound as if she found any of this very funny.

Why would she forget the truth like that? After all, there had been the Christmas party at Cranham House; all the mothers knew where Diana lived. He put the mistake down to further evidence of her anxiety.

"I'm sorry, I'm sorry, Seymour," said his mother to the telephone. She hung up and failed to move.

So once again Byron tried to reassure his mother. Even though what he had said earlier was not true, he explained, even though she had actually hit the little girl and driven away, the accident was not her fault. "What?" said his mother, as if she didn't speak his language. Then she shook her head and asked him to move from under her feet, she had things to do.

"The thing is," he said, "it wasn't proper time. It was added time. It was time that shouldn't have been there. It wouldn't have been there if they hadn't stopped the clocks to add two seconds.

So no one can blame you, because it wasn't your fault. There may have been a conspiracy like President Kennedy or the moon landings." Repeating James gave Byron's words extra weight, although he had no idea what he was talking about.

His mother appeared to be less impressed. "Of course they landed on the moon. Of course time didn't stop. That's the whole point of time. It keeps going forward."

He tried to explain that maybe time was not so reliable, but she was no longer listening. While the children ate tea, she thumbed through the pages of her magazine, so fast she couldn't possibly be reading. She bathed the children but forgot to fetch Crazy Foam. And when Lucy asked, as she did every evening, could she read with the funny voices, his mother sighed and said wasn't one voice enough?

Byron lay awake most of the night, trying to work out how to help his mother. The following morning he felt so punched he could barely move. His father rang and as usual his mother reassured him that no one was there. "Not even the milkman," she laughed. Then she said quickly, "No, I'm not being rude, darling." While she listened to his reply she stabbed the carpet with the point of her shoe, over and over. "Of course I care. Of course we want to see you." Again she replaced the receiver on its hook and stared at it.

Byron accompanied Lucy to school and walked with his mother back to the car. Diana kept sighing, and not saying anything, only sighing again. He was certain she was dwelling on something that caused her pain and that this must be the accident.

"No one knows," he said.

"I beg your pardon?"

"They would have arrested you by now and they haven't. There has been no mention of it in *The Times*. There has been nothing about it on *Nationwide*."

Diana threw up her hands and gave an impatient sigh. "Do you never stop?" And saying that, almost to the pavement, it seemed, she broke into a walk that was so fast Byron had to canter at a sideways angle in order to keep up.

At the car, his mother threw her handbag to the pavement. "Look," she said, pointing her finger at the silver bodywork. "There's nothing there. There's nothing there because there was no accident in Digby Road. You've got it wrong. You imagined it."

Wriggling her skirt up over her knees, she even knelt on the pavement. She pointed to the bonnet, the doors, the engine. Other mothers were beginning to approach, on their way back to their cars. Diana didn't look up at them or say hello; she kept her eyes fixed on Byron, as if none of the others was important. "You see, you see?" she kept saying. He had to smile at the mothers to show there was nothing wrong, and it was such effort to keep doing it, his face hurt. All he wanted was to get into the car.

Byron stooped closer. "Shouldn't we do this at home?"

"No," she said. "I've had enough. You don't stop. I walk into the garden, I go to do the washing, and you're still talking about it. I want you to see that everything's all right." She smoothed her fingers over the paintwork, showing him how clear it was. And she was right; it shone bright as a knife blade, shimmering with heat and light. Against it her nails were small pearly shells. "There's not a scratch. There's nothing. You see?" She craned her neck beneath the bodywork of the car. "You see? You see, sweetheart?"

Byron felt his eyes bud with tears. He understood now. He

understood that he must have been mistaken, that there had been no accident, that he had been wrong about what he had witnessed. Shame filled him like heat. Then his mother let out a gasp. She pulled back from the car with her face clutched in her hands.

"What is it?" he said.

She was trying to stand but her skirt was too narrow and wouldn't make room for her legs. Her hands were still over her mouth, pressing something inside.

Byron peered at the car but he could see nothing. He helped his mother to her feet and she stood with her back to the Jaguar, as if she couldn't bear to look. Her face was blanched, her eyes terrified. He didn't know whether she was about to be ill.

Byron lowered himself to his knees. He pressed his fingers into the grit and peered at the spot she had been indicating. There was a heated-up smell of oil but he could see nothing. And then just as he was about to laugh and say, Don't worry, he found it. He found the evidence. His heart went so fast it was like someone at a door. It was as if they were actually inside him, banging all over his insides. He bent closer to the hubcap.

"Get inside the car," moaned his mother. "Get in right now."

There it was. A tiny nick just above the engraved Jaguar emblem. No bigger than a graze. He couldn't think how he had missed it. It was red. Bicycle red.

14

Jim's Sorrow

A scrap of fast-moving cloud splinters the china plate of a moon. The evergreen leaves rattle like plastic. Rain is coming. Carefully Jim makes his way to the van. His footsteps do not sound like ones he recognizes. He hears the click of crutches on the pavement. The slow pulling forward of a plaster cast. He feels the bottle of painkillers weighted in his pocket. His foot is not a foot. It is a brick. A blue brick.

The curtains of the houses are drawn against the dark and the moor and the outsiders such as Jim.

Something has happened tonight. Not just the accident. It has sliced open the space between past and present. He wishes for his bed at Besley Hill and the patients who wore one another's pajamas. He wishes for the food that arrived every mealtime and the nurses who brought his pills. He wishes for the emptying of his mind. For sleep.

But he knows that none of these things will come. Fragments of memories flash through his mind and it is like being struck. Beyond Cranham Village, beyond the moor, there are lost years, there are lost people, there is all that. He recalls Eileen's look of confusion and the boy who was once his friend. He thinks about the bridge over the pond and the two seconds that started everything.

The pain in his foot is as nothing compared to this other wound that is deep inside. There is no atoning for the past. There are only the mistakes that have been made.

The rituals will go on all night. And even when he finally believes he has done enough, there will be tomorrow, and the whole process must begin again. There will be the day after that. The next day, and the next. He pulls the key from his pocket, and briefly the brass key ring catches the light.

Black rain begins to fall. It explodes on the paving stones of Cranham Village, the wheelie bins, the slate rooftops, and the van. Slowly Jim moves forward. Anything, he thinks, anything would be better than what lies ahead.

15

The Burning of the Past

"It was a terrible mistake."

When Byron confessed the truth, James's face lost the little color it had. He listened to the story of how the girl had run toward the road at the exact moment the seconds were added, and a knot emerged between his eyebrows, so deep it looked cut with a knife. He twisted his fringe until it made a loop when Byron described how he had tried to keep the secret and failed. For a long time James sat with his head in his hands. Byron began to fear it had been a mistake to ask James's help.

"But, Byron, what were you doing in Digby Road?" James said at last. "Doesn't your mother know it's dangerous? Once a person had their knees shot off. And some of the houses have no lavatories."

"I don't think my mother was thinking about things like that. She told us she had been there before."

"I don't understand how this could happen. She drives very carefully. I have watched. Some of the other mothers are not good drivers. Mrs. Watkins, for instance. She is actually dangerous. But your mother is not like that. Is she all right?"

"She isn't saying anything. She washed the car twice yesterday. If my father finds out, there will be trouble. I don't know what will happen at the weekend."

"But it isn't her fault. The accident only happened because of the two seconds."

Byron said it was lucky James had read about the addition of time. It was such a relief to have him on board.

"You are sure you saw the little girl?" said James.

"Yes."

"You can say 'Correct' if you like."

"Correct, James."

"And your mother did not?"

"Correct. Yes."

"We do not want her to go to prison."

(Even though this was correct as well, Byron's throat constricted and the word got stuck.)

"If the little girl was dead, we would have heard. It would have been in my newspaper. So we must rule that out. And if she was in hospital, I would have heard that too. My mother does not read *The Times* but she knows all sorts of information like that because she talks to the volunteers at the Conservative Party shop. Also, even though your mother drove off, she didn't know what she had done. That is important."

"But I don't think she's very good at lying. She's bound to tell in the end. She won't be able to help it."

"So we have to think what to do." James slid his brass beetle from his blazer pocket and clenched it tight. He closed his eyes and his mouth began to move. Byron waited patiently, knowing that his friend was forming an idea. They had to think in a scientific way, James said slowly. They must be very logical and precise.

"In order to save your mother," he said, "we must form a plan of action."

Byron could have hugged him, apart from the fact they were boys from Winston House. He knew everything would be all right now that his friend was involved.

"Why are you doing that funny face?" said James.

"I am smiling at you," said Byron.

As it turned out, Byron had no need to worry about his father. That weekend his mother was in bed with a headache. She came downstairs only to cook and do the laundry. She was too ill to join them in the dining room. The Jaguar remained in the garage and Seymour remained in his study. Byron and Lucy played quietly in the garden.

On Monday their mother drove the car to school, but Byron had to remind her twice to check her wing mirror and keep in the left lane. She had changed her clothing several times before they left the house. It was as if, now that she had this new piece of information about herself, she was trying to work out who she was and what she looked like. She wore her sunglasses too, even though the sky that morning was pleated with cloud. They took a different route to school across the hills in order to avoid the turning to Digby Road. Byron told Lucy it was because the new route was scenic. Their mother liked the moor.

"But I don't," said Lucy. "It has nothing for me to look at."

James's plan of action was extensive. He had spent all weekend working on it. It involved checking the newspapers for further news of Digby Road, and also any other accidents that were related to the two seconds. He had found none. He had made a list of Diana's attributes in case they were needed as a point of reference, along with a duplicate copy for Byron. The handwriting was precise. There were separate lines for each point.

Numéro un: The accident was not her fault.

Numéro deux: DH is a good mother.

Numéro trois: DH does not look or think like a criminal.

Numéro quatre: When her son, Byron, started school, DH was the ONLY parent who visited the classroom.

Numéro cinq: DH has a driving license and fully paid tax disc.

Numéro six: When her son's friend (James Lowe Esq) was stung by a wasp, DH removed the wasp to another part of the garden but refused to kill it on humanitarian grounds.

Numéro sept. DH is beautiful. (This last was crossed out.)

"But what are we going to do about the evidence?" said Byron. James had thought this through too. The boys would raise funds to replace the hubcap, but until they had enough money, Byron must hide the red nick with silver Airfix paint. James had a good supply, he said: "My parents keep giving me models for Christmas and the glue gives me a headache." He produced from his blazer pocket a small pot of paint, along with a special brush. He instructed Byron how to dip the point of the brush in the paint, how to wipe off the residue on the lip of the pot, and how to apply the color in light strokes, without rushing. He wished he could do it himself but there was no opportunity for him to visit Cranham House. "You must do it when no one is watching," he said.

Byron produced from his pocket the map he had drawn of Digby Road, and James nodded approvingly. But when Byron asked if it was time to get the police involved, James's eyes stretched so wide, Byron had to turn and check there was no one behind him. James whispered violently, "We must definitely not tell the police. We must never betray your mother. Besides, she saved our skins at the pond, remember? She pulled you out and she said I was not to blame. She was kind to us. In future we need a secret code whenever we are discussing the case. Il faut que le mot est quelque chose au sujet de ta mère. So that we remember."

"Please could it not be in French?" said Byron.

James chose "Perfect."

The next day James invented a clever reason to walk past the Jaguar. At the point where it was parked, he stopped and knelt on the pavement, apparently tying his shoelace. Afterward he reported to Byron that he had done a good job. You really couldn't see, he said, unless you knew to look.

There were times that week when Diana appeared to forget about Digby Road. She played Snakes and Ladders with the children, or made fairy cakes, but then she suddenly stopped shaking the dice, or sieving flour, and walked away. Minutes later she was filling a bucket with soapy water. She sponged the bodywork of the Jaguar all over and then she rinsed it with further buckets of cold. She polished it with a chamois leather, in slow deliberate circles, exactly as Seymour liked her to. Only when it came to the hubcap did she falter. She approached it with her head slightly drawn back, her arm outstretched. From the look of things, she could barely touch it.

In the school playground, Diana said little. When a mother asked on Thursday how she was, she simply shrugged and looked away and Byron realized she was doing everything she could to hide her real feelings. The mother didn't seem to understand. She said, "I bet you worry about that new Jaguar. I'd be terrified of driving it." She was only being polite.

But Diana's face turned hollow. "I wish I'd never set eyes on the thing," she said. Byron had only glimpsed that expression once before, when she had received the news of her mother's death. The woman was evidently surprised by the sharpness of the reply and tried to laugh and make light of it, but Diana turned on her heels and walked away. Byron knew that his mother wasn't being rude. He knew she was going to cry. He was so appalled and concerned that instead of following he remained with the woman, making small talk and waiting for his mother to come back. He mentioned the weather several times and the fact that the Jaguar was in perfect working order. There was absolutely nothing wrong with it, he added. His mother was such a careful driver. They never had accidents. He wished his mouth would stop.

"Goodness," said the woman, glancing about. Diana was no-where to be seen. In the end the woman gave a tight smile and said it was lovely talking to him but she had a thousand things to do and she must hurry.

That night a strange, cracking noise woke Byron and brought him to his bedroom window. Looking out, he saw that the garden was dark apart from an orange light flickering at the corner, just inside the picket gate. Fetching his dressing gown and torch, he went to his mother's room and found it empty. He checked the bathroom and Lucy's room, but there was no sign of her. Beginning to grow anxious, he went downstairs, but none of the lamps were lit. Byron put on his outdoor shoes and set off to find her.

There was a shade of afterglow on the moor's upper slopes, while in the lower foothills the darkness was broken only by sheep, and they were pale as stones. The flowers stood tall and still, the evening primrose flowers were like yellow lamps. He passed the top lawn, the rose pagoda, the fruit trees, the vegetable garden, all the time following the snapping of the fire and the orange halo of its light. Even though the fruit was not yet fully ripe, the air was sweetly heavy with the promise of it. A pink moon hung low, so slight it was no more than a smile nestling on the cheeks of the moor.

It did not surprise him to discover his mother warming her hands over the flames. After all, she often made a bonfire. What surprised him was to find that she had both a drink and a cigarette. He had never seen her smoke, though from the way she pressed it to her mouth and tugged hard, it looked as if she liked it. Deep shadows were carved into her face, and her hair and skin glowed. She stooped to pull something out of a bag at her feet. Then she seemed to pause a moment, smoking and drinking, before tossing whatever it was into the fire. Briefly the flames cowered under the weight, and then spat out a tongue of heat.

Again his mother lifted the glass to her mouth. She drank in an efficient way, suggesting that the glass wanted her to empty it, as opposed to the other way around. Finishing her cigarette, she threw it down and wriggled over it with the pointed toe of her shoe as if it were a mistake.

"What are you doing out here?" he said.

Her face shot toward his. She looked terrified.

"It's only me." Byron laughed and shone his torch on himself to show he meant no harm. He was blinded by a sharp cone of light. Suddenly everything had a blue hole burned through it, even his mother. He had to keep peering at her in case he had gone blind. "I couldn't sleep," he said, because he didn't want her to think he was spying. The blue holes began to fade.

"Do you often come outside when you can't sleep?" she said.

"Not really."

She smiled sadly, and he felt that if he had replied differently, if he had said yes, I am out here all the time, she too would have said something else, and that whatever that was it would have led the conversation in a different direction and somehow explained things.

His mother tugged another item out of her bag. It looked like a shoe with a pointed toe and a slim heel. This too she threw at the fire. The air cracked as the fingers of flame flew up to snatch it.

"Are you burning your clothes?" he said with alarm. He wasn't sure how he would explain this development to James.

His mother couldn't seem to find a reply.

He said, "Are they the ones you wore that day?"

"They were old-fashioned. I never liked them."

"Father liked them. He bought you those."

She gave a shrug and drank some more. "Yes, well," she said. "It's too late now." She lifted the whole bag and stretched it open over the flames like a yawn. Two stockings snaked out, along with her other shoe, and her lambswool cardigan. Once again the flames reached up and he watched the clothes turn black and disintegrate. A halo of heat melted the dark. "I don't know what I'm going to do," she said.

It was as if she was talking to someone else, not him, and he watched, afraid of what would come next.

But she said no more. Instead she began to tremble. She hunched her shoulders to stop but still it came, like a movement all through her body, a no, no, no, even into her clothes. Slipping off his dressing gown, he arranged it carefully over her shoulders. He couldn't say how but he felt in that moment that he was actually taller, that he had grown in the time they were standing beside the fire. She caught his hand in hers.

"You need sleep, love," she said. "There's school tomorrow."

As they walked back to the house, through the meadow and then the garden, its square profile stood against the blacker shoulder of the moor. The windows shone like glass jewels, spilling into the dark. They passed the pond where the geese waited, dim against the water's edge. His mother slipped over on her heel, as if there was something unhooked inside her ankle joints, and he held out his arm to steady her.

Byron thought of his friend. He thought of James's lucky beetle and his plan of action. He thought of the fund for the hubcap. Together he and James would be like the dressing gown that covered her shoulders. They would protect her. He said, "Everything will be all right. You don't need to be afraid." He guided her into the house and up the stairs.

When Byron checked the next morning, her clothes were nothing but a pool of ash.

PART TWO

Outside

1

A Very Good Idea

"I think we need to do something," said Byron.

Diana glanced up from the counter where she was chopping apple and failed to speak. Emptying her glass, she placed it alongside all her other empty glasses, and gave him a distant look as if she was so lost in thought she could not trace her way back to the present. Then she gave a small smile and returned to her chopping.

It was early July. Twenty-nine days had passed since the accident, and twelve since the discovery of evidence on the hubcap. All over the kitchen units were precariously balanced stacks of dirty plates and bowls. If Lucy wanted a clean spoon, Byron had to find a dirty one and rinse it. There was also such a fusty smell lodged in the utility room that he kept closing the door. Diana no longer parked in the tree-lined street with all the other mothers. She left the car where no one would spot it and they walked the rest of the way. Lucy's school shoes were scuffed at the toe. Byron had popped through another button on his school shirt. His mother's cardigans kept slipping from her shoulders. It was as if everything had begun to forget what it was.

When Byron had reported this development to James, he said they must come up with a new plan of action.

"But what?" Byron had asked.

"I'm still thinking about it," said James.

There was also his mother's behavior at the weekend to consider. Diana couldn't seem to get things right. She had been so frightened of being late for Seymour that they had waited nearly an hour on the station platform. She painted her mouth over and over until it began to look like someone else's. Byron tried to distract Lucy with a game of I Spy but had only upset her by failing to guess what began with *Ch*. ("Chrees," she sobbed. She was still crying when the train drew in.) Afterward his mother had dashed to the car, talking nervously about things that didn't connect, the heat, Seymour's week, something nice for supper. She might as well have been shouting, Hubcap, hubcap, hubcap. On the way back she kept stalling the car.

It had been no better at home. Over Saturday dinner Byron had tried to lighten the tension by asking his father his views on the European Economic Community, but his father merely wiped his mouth. Was there no salt, please? he asked.

"Salt?" his mother replied.

"Yes," he said. "Salt."

"What about salt?"

"You seem preoccupied, Diana."

"Not at all, Seymour. You were saying something. About salt."

"I was saying I don't taste any. On my dinner."

"Salt is all I can taste." She pushed her plate to one side. "I actually can't eat this food."

It was as if the words meant something else, something that was not to do with salt, please, but another thing entirely. Byron listened out for his parents afterward and they remained in different rooms. Whenever his father walked in, his mother seemed to fly out. Once again, Seymour left early Sunday morning.

"It sounds as if she is worrying," James had concluded.

"What can we do?"

"We have to help her. We have to prove there is no reason for concern."

"But there is," said Byron. "There are actually lots of reasons."

"You have to keep looking at the facts." James slid something from the inside pocket of his school blazer and unfolded it twice; he had clearly made another of his lists over the weekend. "Operation Perfect," he read out. "One: We do not think the little girl was seriously hurt. Two: The police have not come to arrest your mother. Three: It was not her fault, because of the extra seconds. Four." Here he paused.

"What is four?" Byron asked.

"Four is what we must do next," said James. And he explained his plan in detail.

The morning light at the glass doors showed up the smudges and stains as if the sun preferred not to come inside anymore. It gathered in secret dust-filled pockets and showed up the dirty trail of Lucy's footprints from the French windows.

Byron said, "Did you hear me, Mummy? We have to do something. About the thing that happened in Digby Road." His heart was beating hard.

Chop, chop, chop, went his mother's knife through apple. If she wasn't careful she would hurt her fingers.

He said, "What we have to do is go back. We have to explain that it was an accident."

The knife stopped. His mother raised her head and stared. "Are you joking?" Already tears were springing to her eyes and she did nothing to stop them, she just let them slide down her face and jump toward the floor. "I can't go back now. It happened a whole month ago. What am I going to say? And anyway, if your father found out—" She failed to finish that sentence and took up another one instead: "There's no way I can go back."

It was like hurting someone and not wanting to. He couldn't look. He simply kept repeating James, word for word: "But I will come with you. The little girl's mother will see how kind you are. She will see you're a mother. She will understand it wasn't your fault. And then we will replace the hubcap and all this will be over."

Diana gripped her temples as if there was something so heavy inside her head she could barely move. Then a new thought seemed to snap her awake. She broke across the kitchen and placed the chopped fruit decisively on the table. "Of course," she almost yelled. "What on earth have I been doing all this time? Of course I have to go back." She plucked her apron from its hook and wrenched it around her waist.

"We could wait a bit," he said. "I didn't mean we had to do this today."

But his mother failed to hear. She kissed the mop of his hair, then ran upstairs to wake Lucy.

There was no opportunity to alert James. Byron scoured the pavements from the front seat of the car, but since they were not even parked by the school he knew it was hopeless. He knew he would not find him. The sky that morning was so flat and new it looked ironed. Sunlight splintered the leaves of the trees, and the far-

away peaks of Cranham Moor melted into lilac. As Diana set off
to walk the last few streets with Lucy a mother called out hello,
but Diana went fast with her arms tight around her waist as if she
were holding herself in one piece. Byron realized that he was very
frightened and that the last place he wanted to visit was Digby
Road. He didn't know what they were going to say when they
arrived; James had not got that far with his plan. Everything was
moving much faster than either boy had intended.

When his mother swung open her car door and sat beside
him, Byron jumped. Her eyes shone hard, almost the color of tin.

She said, "I have to do this on my own."

"But what about me?"

"It isn't right to take you. It isn't right for you to miss school."

In a rush Byron tried to think of what his friend would say. It
was bad enough that the plan was progressing without James,
who had been very clear that both boys would accompany Diana
in order to take notes. Byron said, "You can't. You don't know the
spot. You can't go alone. You need me to come."

"Sweetheart, they will be angry. You're a child. It will be difficult."

"I want to come. It will be worse for me if I don't. I'll worry
and worry. And everything will be all right when they see us. I
know it will."

And so it was settled. Back at home Byron and his mother
avoided eye contact and spoke briefly, mentioning only the smallest of things. Digby Road had already become a presence in the
room, like a sofa, and they moved carefully around it. "I need to
change before we go," she said at last.

"You look nice."

"No. I need the right costume."

He followed his mother upstairs and checked his reflection in her mirror. He wished he wasn't in school uniform. James had a grown-up black two-piece suit that his mother made him wear for church despite his failure to believe in God. Meanwhile, Diana took a long time to choose her clothes and she did so with scrupulous care, standing in front of the mirror and holding up dress after dress. In the end she settled on a peach-colored fitted tunic. It was one of Seymour's favorites, displaying the pallor of her bare arms and the ridges of her collarbone. Sometimes she wore it for dinner when her husband was home and he guided her down the stairs with his hand on the small of her back as if she were an extension of his arm. "Aren't you going to wear a hat?" Byron said.

"A hat? Why would I do that?"

"To show it's a serious occasion."

She chewed her lip, thinking this through, and pulled her arms around her shoulder blades. There were goose bumps popping all over her skin; she probably needed a cardigan as well. Then she dragged the upholstered armchair to the wardrobe and stood on it while she rummaged through a selection of boxes on the top shelf. A number of hats came floating to the floor, along with the odd feather and scrap of netting—berets, pillboxes, stiff wide-brimmed hats and a Russian sable hat, as well as a white silk turban and a jeweled headdress with a plume of feathers. "Oh my goodness," said his mother, chasing after them and shoving them out of the way. She perched at her dressing table, pulling on the more sensible models, one after another, and tossing them to the floor. Her hair flew out slightly static from her face so that she looked pressed against a window. "No, I don't think I will wear a hat," she said at last.

She dusted powder on her nose and pressed her lips together to paint them red. It was like watching her disappear, and he was filled with such sadness he had to blow his nose.

"Maybe I should wear something of Father's?"

"I wouldn't," she said, barely moving her mouth. "He'd know if you did."

"I was thinking something small like a cravat. He wouldn't know about that."

Byron eased open the double doors of Seymour's wardrobe. The jackets and shirts were lined up on wooden hangers like headless versions of his father. Byron slid out a silk cravat as well as his father's deerstalker, then he slammed the doors before the jackets and shirts could shout at him. He wrapped the plum cravat around his neck. He kept the hat in his hands because you were not supposed to wear a hat inside the house. James would call that bad luck.

"There," he said. "All sorted."

She gave a backward glance over the room. "Are you sure about this?" she asked, not of him but of the furniture, the upholstered chair and the matching chintz curtains and bedspread.

He gulped. It made a splashy noise all over the bedroom. "It will be over soon. Off we jolly well trot."

She smiled as if nothing could be simpler and they left.

Diana did her most careful driving. Her hands were exactly at the 10-to-2 position on the steering wheel. Over the moor, the sun blazed through the vast sky like a searchlight. The cattle stood anchored in swarms of black flies, flapping their tails but not shifting, only waiting for the heat to go away. The grass was bleached to straw. Byron wanted to say something but didn't know where to begin, and the longer he failed to speak the harder it was to touch the silence. Besides, every time the car moved to the left or right, his father's deerstalker shot down over his nose. It seemed to have a life of its own.

"Are you all right?" said his mother. "You look very red under there."

She chose to park at the end of Digby Road, just beyond the burned-out car. When she asked if he would remember the house he produced the map from his pocket and unfolded it for her benefit.

"I see," said Diana, though she didn't pause to look. Now that she had made up her mind about returning here, there was no stalling her. All she said was "Maybe you should take the hat off now, sweetheart."

Byron's hair was pasted in wet spikes to his forehead. He heard his mother's heels hitting the pavement like sharp hammer blows, and he wished she would go more quietly, because people were beginning to notice. A woman in an overall stared from over her washing basket. A line of young men perched on a wall whistled. Byron felt squashy inside, and he was finding it harder and harder to breathe. The estate was even worse than he remembered. The sun bit down on the stone houses and cracked their paintwork. Many were sprayed with words like PIGS OUT or IRA SCUM. Every time he looked he felt a whip of fear and wished he would stop doing it but he couldn't. He remembered what James had told him about the kneecapping in Digby Road and then he remembered the remark his mother had made about driving that way before. Again he asked himself why she would do that.

"Are we nearly there?" she said.

"There will be a flowery tree. The gate comes right afterward."

But when Byron saw the tree, there was a further shock. In the four weeks since their last visit to Digby Road, it had been assaulted: its wide branches snapped off, the blossom scattered all over the pavement. It was not a tree anymore, it was only a stunted trunk without limbs. Everything was so wrong. His mother paused at the gate belonging to the girl and asked if this was the one. She held her handbag with both hands and suddenly she looked too little.

The gate gave a screech as she lifted the latch. Inside his head, he prayed.

"Is that hers?" Diana pointed to a red bicycle leaning against a dustbin beside the house. He nodded.

She made her way toward the door and he followed closely. The garden was small enough to fit inside one of the main borders at Cranham House, but the path was clean and there were rocks on either side dotted with peeping flowers. At the upstairs windows the curtains were drawn. It was the same downstairs.

Maybe James had been wrong? Maybe the little girl was dead? Maybe her parents were at her funeral or visiting the grave? It was an insane idea to come back to Digby Road. Byron thought with longing of his bedroom with the blue curtains. The white-tiled floors in the hall. The new double-glazed windows.

"I think they're out," he said. "Shall we go home now?"

But Diana tugged her fingers, one by one, from her gloves and knocked at the door. Byron stole another look at the red bicycle. There was no sign of damage. Diana knocked a second time, a little more more urgently. When there was still no answer, she took a few steps backward, her heels pinning the hard turf. "There's someone in," she said, pointing at an upstairs window. "Hello?" she called out.

The window swung open to reveal a man's face. It was hard to get a real picture of him but he seemed to be wearing only an undershirt. "What do you want?" He didn't sound friendly.

She broke the silence with a small click of her tongue against the roof of her mouth. "I'm sorry to trouble you. May I have a word?"

Byron took hold of his mother's fingers and gripped hard. An image had come into his head and he couldn't shift it. No matter how hard he tried, he could only picture his mother lifting above the ground, light as a feather or a wisp of cloud, and drifting clean away.

When the front door opened, the man stood staring down at them. He filled the threshold. Clearly he had combed his hair on the way downstairs and put on a shirt, but there were bloodstains at the collar the size of tomato pips and some of his buttons were missing. Byron's father would never leave his shirt open; his mother would never fail to sew on buttons. The skin of the man's face was gray and hung in oily folds, shadowed at the jaw where it was unshaven. He remained blocking the door.

"If you're selling stuff," he said, "you can clear off."

Diana looked appalled. "No, no," she cried. "We're here on a private matter."

Byron nodded to show how private it was.

Diana said, "It's about your daughter."

"Jeanie?" The man's eyes flashed. "Is she all right?"

Diana glanced over her shoulder. A small group had assembled at the gate, the woman in the overall and the youths from the wall, as well as several others. They watched with stony faces. "It would be much easier to explain inside."

The man stood aside to let them pass. He closed the door, and the smell was so wet and old Byron had to breathe through his mouth. The walls were not papered with stripes or flowers like at Cranham House but instead a yellowing floral pattern that made him think of old ladies. Toward the ceiling the paper curled loose.

"Beverley," the man called up the stairs.

A thin voice answered. "What now, Walt?"

"Visitors, Bev."

"What do you mean, visitors?"

"People to see us. They want to talk about Jeanie." Turning to Diana he said softly, "She's all right, isn't she? I know she gets in trouble and everything but she's a good girl."

Diana couldn't speak.

"We'll wait for Beverley," Walt said.

Pointing to a room to the left, he apologized. They got lots of women calling with those cosmetics, he said. "And women like nice things." Diana nodded to show she understood. Byron nodded too but he didn't.

After the gloom of the narrow hall, the small sitting room was surprisingly clean and light. A selection of china ornaments was set at the window, kittens in baskets and baby koala bears on branches. The carpet was a floral pattern and the walls were papered with wood chip. There was no television set but there was an empty space where there had once been one, above which three plaster ducks took flight. To the left there was a boxed record player with a selection of 45s in paper sleeves. Byron smiled at the women's magazines on the coffee table, at the Whimsies figurines on the windowsill, at the flying ducks and the frilled lampshade, feeling an overwhelming rush of kindness toward the items of furniture as well as their owners. A row of soft toys lined the leatherette sofa, some that he recognized, like Snoopy, others with hats or T-shirts that said I LOVE YOU! or HUG ME!

"Please take a seat," said Walt. He looked too big for the room.

Byron eased himself into a position between the soft toys, taking care not to squish any of their limbs or small accessories. His mother sat at the other end of the sofa, next to a blue giant thing that was maybe a bear or possibly a dinosaur. It almost reached her shoulders. Walt stood in front of the fireplace. No one spoke. They each studied the swirly brown carpet as if they had never seen anything so interesting.

When the door flew open, they turned. The woman who entered was slight, like Diana, and short black hair tasseled her face. She wore a T-shirt with a shapeless brown skirt and a pair of cork wedge sandals. "What's going on, Walt?" she said. Then, catching sight of her guests, she gave a start as if she had received a current of energy.

"They've come about something private, Beverley."

She raked back her hair. It lay flat on either side of her ears like two blackbird wings. Her skin was pale, almost without color, her features pointed. Her eyes darted from her husband to her guests and back again. "Not the bailiffs?"

No, no, they all chorused, nothing to do with the bailiffs.

"Did you offer them a drink?"

Walt shrugged apologetically. Diana assured her they were not thirsty.

"It's to do with Jeanie," said Walt.

Beverley drew up a plastic chair and sat opposite Diana. She raked her visitor up and down with her fast green eyes. With her thin hands and her pale skin, her pinched mouth and her cheekbones like pencils, she had an altogether hungry look, as if she survived on scraps of things.

"Well?" she said.

Diana remained very still with her knees together and her pink shoes side by side.

"I like your daughter's bears," said Byron, trying to sound grown-up, like James.

"The bears are Beverley's," said Walt. "So are the china knick-knacks. She collects. Don't you, Beverley?"

"I do," said Beverley. She did not move her eyes from Diana.

There was no sign of the little girl, except for a school photograph on the mantelpiece. She appeared to be scowling at the camera with screwed-up eyes. It was not like Lucy's school photograph, where the flash had clearly taken her by surprise. This little girl looked as if someone had called out at her to smile at the dicky-bird and she had chosen not to. She had Beverley's small, tight features.

Walt said, "Beverley wants the Robertson's Gollywog Band. She likes their little instruments and everything."

"My mother likes little things," said Byron.

"But Robertson's is too pricey."

Byron slid another glance at his mother. She held her body braced as if she were peering over a cliff edge and hoping not to fall.

"Listen here," said Walt. "Jeanie hasn't done anything wrong, has she?"

At last Diana opened her mouth. In a fragile voice she began the story about the accident. Listening to her, Byron's mouth was so dry it felt stripped. He could barely look. Instead he watched

Beverley and the way she in turn watched Diana. She seemed to be fixed on his mother's rings.

Diana explained how four weeks ago they had used the road as a shortcut and how she had lost control of the car just as their daughter came out on her bicycle. Diana blew her nose while she cried. "I'm so sorry, I didn't see," she kept saying. In the silence that followed, she plucked up the stuffed blue toy at her side. She drew it to her lap and clasped its middle.

"Are you saying you knocked over Jeanie in your car?" said Walt at last. His face was all creased with not understanding. "Is that why you're here?"

The blue animal in Diana's arms began to shake as if it had acquired a nervous life of its own. "I should have stopped. I don't know why I didn't. I don't know why I didn't get out. Is your daughter—is she all right?"

Byron's pulse thudded in his eardrums.

Walt stared at Beverley with a questioning look. She stared too. "There must be a mistake," he said at last. "Are you sure it was Jeanie?"

Byron stood to check her school photograph. He was certain, he said. He added that, as the chief and sole witness, he had seen everything. There was evidence too, he went on, because no one was saying anything; they were only staring at him. It was like being under hot lights. He explained about the nick on the hub-cap. The proof was incontrovertible, he said. It was a James sort of word.

But Walt still looked confused. "It's nice of you to come, but Jeanie's all right. She never mentioned a car. She never mentioned an accident. Did she, Beverley?"

Beverley shrugged as if to say she wasn't sure.

"She's running about same as usual. Sometimes I can't keep up with her, can I?"

"You can't, Walt."

Diana let out a cry of relief. Byron wanted to stroke all the soft toys and pat their heads. He couldn't wait to tell James. She said how worried she had been, how she had not slept for days; Byron reminded her that she had been frightened too of his father finding out. It was a private aside but everyone heard.

"And I thought you were selling that makeup," smiled Walt. They laughed.

There came a sound so sharp it was like a scissor snip through the air. Everyone turned to Beverley. Her forehead was puckered as if she had received a blow, and her green eyes twitched up and down the carpet. Walt reached for her hand, and she whipped it away before he could find it. "What on earth are you talking about? She had a cut. She had a cut on her knee."

Byron turned to Diana, and Diana turned to Walt. He blew out his cheeks.

"It would have been four weeks ago," Beverley continued. "Now I think about it, it must have been that day. Four weeks is a long time, of course. But there was blood on her sock. It wasn't a deep cut. I had to find a new pair of socks, remember? I had to fetch a plaster."

Walt hung his head, apparently trying to get the past into focus.

"He hasn't a clue," Beverley said to Diana, as if they were friends now. "You know what men are like." She smiled. Byron could see inside her mouth, the sharp tips of her molars.

"What sort of cut?" There was barely anything to Diana's voice. "Was it serious?"

"It was small. It was nothing, really. On her kneecap." Beverley lifted the hem of her skirt and indicated her own. It was white and small, more like an elbow than a knee, and Diana stared. "She didn't need a stitch or anything. As you said, it was an accident."

At the door, they all shook hands. Walt kept nodding at Diana. "Don't you worry," he kept saying, and she kept saying, "Thank you, thank you." She was so glad everything was all right, she kept saying. Was the bicycle damaged? Was it a present? She mustn't even think about that, said Walt.

"Cheerio!" called Beverley, waving from her front door. "See you again!" It was the first time she'd looked happy.

Driving from Digby Road, Byron felt a flush of excitement. His mother wound down the car windows so that they could feel the breeze on their skin.

"I'd say that went terribly well," he said at last.

"Do you think?" She looked unsure.

"They seemed nice to me. Even Father would like them. It just goes to show there are kind people on Digby Road."

"The little girl had a cut. Her mother had to throw away her sock."

"But it was an accident. They understood that. And the little girl is all right. That's the main thing."

A truck rumbled past, and Diana's hair blew up in her face like a spume of foam. She drummed her fingers on the steering wheel.

"She didn't like me," she said.

"She did. And she reads the same magazines as you. I saw. The little girl's father definitely liked you. He kept smiling."

Suddenly Diana slammed so hard on her brakes, Byron was afraid they were having another accident. She pulled over to the curb without indicating, and a passing motorist beeped his horn. When she turned to Byron he saw that she was laughing. She didn't seem to have a clue about the other car.

"I know what we're going to do." Waiting for a gap in the traffic, Diana made a swift U-turn and headed back toward town.

They parked near the department store. His mother was invigorated in a way that Byron had not seen since she found the evidence. Wouldn't it be wonderful, she said in a rush, if they could get Beverley the entire Robertson's Gollywog Band? As the doorman opened the glass doors for his mother, they were greeted with excited chatter and the chords of an electric piano. A new model of the Wurlitzer was being demonstrated to customers by a musician in a tuxedo who showed how at the press of a button you could get different forms of accompaniment: drums, strings, samba. It was the new age of music, he said. Someone called out, "Not at that price." The customers laughed.

Byron whispered to his mother that they would have to eat a lot of jam and marmalade in order to acquire the Gollywog Band and his father might get suspicious. He suggested a soft toy instead.

The department store glittered with reflected light from the floors, the wide windows overlooking the street, the lamps on the counters, the jewelry, the colored bottles of perfume. Women gathered at the counters testing scent and lip color. Few were buying. His mother passed swiftly from one display to the next, her heels clicking the marble, tapping items lightly with her fingernail. If it weren't for James, Byron knew he would never want to go to school again. He felt he had stumbled onto something sweetly scented and forbidden, like the pictures in his book of the Arabian Nights that showed women with thin robes that barely covered their soft flesh. He wished it could always be like this, the worry over, and him alone with his mother, shopping for presents to make things good. In the gift department, they chose a blue lamb in a striped waistcoat with a pair of cymbals sewn to his velvet paws. It came in a box with a blue glossy ribbon.

"Don't you think we should get something for Jeanie as well?" his mother said.

Byron suggested clackers. Everyone liked those. His mother was already flying toward the lift for the toy department when he had to stop her. Clackers were dangerous, of course. A boy nearly lost his eye once. James had told him all about it.

"Well, we don't want that," she said. "She sounds quite a dangerous little girl." At this they almost smiled.

"And not a space hopper either," he said. "She might bounce into all sorts of trouble."

Now they actually laughed. They chose another lamb, this one with a small guitar. The instrument even had strings. It was only as they were queueing at the cash desk that his mother had another idea. She called to the assistant, and her voice was so breathless it rang out like laughter.

"Do you sell red bicycles?"

She already had the checkbook in her hand.

His mother offered to take Byron for something to eat. It was not quite lunchtime but he was ravenous. She chose the hotel in the middle of town. The tables were set with stiff white cloths, and the floor shone so hard it was like ice. The air was thick with smoke and soft chatter, the clinking of cutlery on china. The staff moved silently, examining the cutlery and polishing glasses. Many tables were empty. Byron had never been there before.

"Table for two?" said a waiter, sliding out from behind a potted palm. He wore sideburns that crossed his jaw like wool caterpillars and a dicky bow at the collar of a frilled mauve shirt. Byron thought that one day he would like to invest in one of those colored shirts. He wondered if bankers could have sideburns or whether it would only be for weekends.

The customers glanced up from their coffees as Byron and Diana passed. They took in Diana's slim heels and the way her body rustled inside her peach dress. They noticed her stiff band of gold hair and the rounded bump of her breasts. She moved like a wave, rippling its path over the glassy floor. Byron wished that people would glance away but he also hoped they would keep looking. His mother continued as if she didn't know. Maybe people thought she was a film star. If he were a stranger, seeing her for the first time, he would think that she was.

"Isn't this exciting?" she said as the waiter slid out a chair for her, again without noise.

Byron tucked his stiff napkin into his collar because that was what the gentleman at the next table had done. The man had oiled his hair across his scalp so that it looked like a plastic cap, and Byron thought he would ask his mother if he could buy some of that oil too and slick his hair.

"No school today, sonny?" said the waiter.

"We've been shopping." Diana didn't even flinch. Instead she glanced over the menu and tapped her mouth with her fingertip. "What would you like, Byron? Today you can have whatever you want. It's a celebration." When she smiled she looked lit up from inside.

Byron said he would very much like cream of tomato soup, but he would also like prawn cocktail, and he couldn't decide which.

To his amazement his mother ordered both, and as she did so the gentleman at the next table winked.

"And what can I get for you, madam?"

"Oh, nothing for me."

Byron didn't know why the gentleman had winked at him and so he winked back.

"Nothing?" said the waiter. "For a lovely lady like yourself?"

"Just water, please. With ice."

"A glass of champagne?"

She laughed. "It's not yet noon."

"Oh, you must," added Byron. He couldn't help catching the gentleman's eye again, because now the man seemed to be smiling. "After all, it's a special occasion."

While they waited for their drinks, Diana played with her hands. Byron thought of how Beverley had stared at his mother's fingers as if she were measuring the size of her rings. "Once I knew a man who drank nothing but champagne," she said. "I think he even had it for breakfast. You'd have liked him, Byron. He could make buttons come out of your ear. He was funny. Then one day—he was gone."

"Gone? Gone where?"

"I don't know. I never saw him again. He said the bubbles made him happy." She smiled, but in a sad, brave way. Byron had never heard his mother talk like this before. "I wonder what happened."

"Did he live in Digby Road? Is that why you went there?"

"Oh no," she said. "That was something else." Diana made a small flicking movement with her hands as if she had discovered a scattering of breadcrumbs on the tablecloth and needed to brush them away. "I'm talking about years ago. Before I met your father. Sit tall. Here come our drinks."

His mother curled her fingers around the slim flute and lifted it to her lips. Byron watched the way the bubbles clung to the glass. He fancied he heard them crack as the buttery yellow liquid slid toward her mouth. She took the smallest sip and smiled. "Here's to all that's gone."

The waiter laughed and so did the gentleman with the plastic hair. Byron didn't know what any of it meant. The men watching his mother, and her blushing, and toasting all that had gone. She had never talked before about people who could make buttons appear from your ear, just as she had never mentioned a time before she knew his father.

"I expect my soup will come soon," Byron said. He laughed too, not because the waiter's hand was close to his mother's, and not because the gentleman at the next table was staring at her, but because he was about to have soup and also prawn cocktail when it was not quite lunchtime. It was like jumping out of ordinary time and seeing the world from a fresh perspective. And unlike the adding of two seconds, this was his mother's decision. It was no accident.

That afternoon the gifts were delivered to Digby Road. His mother telephoned the garage to inquire about a new hubcap. She spoke to his father too and gave her fluttery laugh. It had been another good day, she said. James was right. If you thought in a logical way, there was a solution to everything.

When Byron checked the next morning, the glass by his mother's bed was empty and the lid was off her bottle of pills. She slept heavily. Even when the alarm went off she failed to stir. She had forgotten to close the curtains, and a shower of glittering light fell over the room; outside, a fragile mist like a spider's web clung to the moor. Everything was so still, so at peace with itself, it was a shame to have to wake her.

2

Angels

Sometimes, when the wind stops, the air carries music across the moor. Jim waits at the door of his van and he listens. He watches the last crack of gold light as it slips over the western rim of the hills. He does not know what the music is, and he does not know who is playing it. The sound is sad, songs with words he cannot hear. Somewhere out there someone is playing music to fill their loneliness, and if only they knew it, here is Jim, listening too. We are not alone; and even as he has that thought it occurs to him there is no one with whom he can share it. He closes the door of his van and pulls out his key, his duct tape. He performs the rituals smoothly and efficiently and then he sleeps.

He doesn't know if it is his injury or the pressure of work, but he finds that since the accident he is more tired. His stutter is bad and so is the pain in his hands. Things have got busier at the café too. Human Resources at Head Office have decided that in the run-up to Christmas, the general atmosphere in the building needs to become more festive. Due to the recent bad weather and also the recession, sales figures are down. Something must be done; a tree that flashes is apparently not enough. In response,

HR have hired the services of a youth brass band to play carols at the store entrance. The store manager, who is not generally known for her warmth or her creativity, has come up with a further idea. Every week a soft toy snowman will be hidden in the store, and the first lucky customer to find it will win a Christmas hamper. Meanwhile, all staff have been issued with flashing badges that read HI! MY NAME IS _____! SEASON'S GREETINGS! Paula has painted her nails in alternate shades of red and green and stuck sparkling motifs on them. Her friend Moira has a pair of reindeer earrings. Moira's flashing badge shouts from her left breast like an invitation, while Jim wears his as if the rest of him is an apology.

Word has flown around the supermarket café about Jim's accident. Initially Mr. Meade offered sick leave, but Jim begged to keep working. He insists he doesn't need the crutches. ("Can I have a go?" says Paula.) He has his special plastic sock from the hospital with which to protect the plaster cast. If he moves slowly, if he just wipes tables, he promises, he won't cause trouble.

It is the prospect of being alone in the van for nights and days on end that terrifies him. Since the hospital, he knows he wouldn't survive. The rituals would get worse and worse. He also knows that this is another of the things he can tell no one.

"Health and Safety won't be happy," says Mr. Meade. "They won't like you on the café floor with a broken foot."

"It's not exactly his fault," pipes up Paula, "if a lunatic woman reverses into him and drives off."

It is a source of pain to Jim that Paula has worked out Eileen's part in the accident. He had not intended to tell anyone; it was bad enough to have a plaster cast. Only when Darren described the car and remembered the registration number did she twig.

She had a photographic memory, she said. (In fact what she said she had was a photogenic memory, but they knew what she meant.) Since the trip to hospital, Paula wears an array of love bites like a necklace of purple and green stones. Jim sees Darren waiting for her after work in the car park. Spotting Jim, Darren waves.

Now the truth is out, everyone agrees. Eileen is the sort of person who should be put away. They cite her final exit from the café, her consistent lateness, her foul language. In the short space of time in which she worked as cook, it seems that three complaints were made against her. Paula says that the problem is people like Jim are too good. And he knows that the problem is not that. The problem is that people need other people—like Eileen—to be too bad.

"You have to report her to the police," she tells Jim every day. "It was a hit-and-run. She could have killed you."

Mr. Meade adds that Eileen is a danger to the community. She should not have a driving license.

"You have to press charges," says Moira. Her reindeer earrings keep getting caught in her hair, and Paula has to step in and unthread them. "These days they do witness protection and stuff. They put you in sheltered housing and give you a new name."

It's too much for Jim. It was an accident, he repeats. The girls fetch him lavatory paper to blow his nose.

The fact is, something has changed. It isn't that he has become more likeable or any less strange, but the accident has accentuated the fragility of things. If this could happen to Jim, it could happen to any one of them. Consequently the café staff have decided that Jim's strangeness is a part of themselves, and they must protect it. Mr. Meade picks Jim up by the sign welcoming careful drivers to Crapham Village and gives him a lift to work. Every morning he says it's shocking, what kids get up to. In turn, Jim looks out of the car window with his nose pressed to the glass. Sometimes he pretends to sleep, not because he is tired but because he needs to be quiet.

"You have to confront your assailant," Paula tells Jim. "Otherwise you can't heal. You heard what the nurse told you. You're the victim of a violent crime. You will never get over this unless you confront it head-on."

"But my f-foot is healing. I don't want to c-c—"

"It's the inner trauma I'm talking about. I knew someone who didn't confront his assailant. No, no, he kept saying, I'm cool with what happened. And guess what?"

Jim admits he has no idea, though he has a hunch the answer will involve personal injury and that it will be of a devastating nature.

"He ended up stabbing a man in the supermarket. Just because he queue-jumped."

"Who? The assail—?"

"No, the victim. He had unresolved issues."

That word again.

"The victim became an assailant," says Paula, "because of the trauma. It happens."

"I don't u-understand," says Jim. "You knew—"

"I didn't know him as such," she interrupts. "I knew someone who knew him. Or I knew someone who knew someone else." She shakes her head impatiently as if Jim is being deliberately obtuse. "The point is, you will never get over this if you don't confront it. And that is why we are going to get you some help."

The visit takes place on Wednesday after work. Paula has arranged everything and both she and Darren will accompany him. They help Jim on and off the bus and he feels like an old man. He watches them, shoulders touching in the seat in front, and the way Darren lifts the pink curl of her hair to whisper in her ear, and it is like being left behind.

For the last part of the journey, Darren and Paula walk on either side of Jim. There are no stars, and the sky is thick with cloud that shines sulfur orange. They enter the pedestrianized High Street, passing the Pound Shop, the amusement arcade, the closed-down electrics store, USA Chicken, and Café Max. The windows are brightly illuminated, some decorated with colored lanterns, some squirted with foam snow. A young woman is collecting for victims of cancer at Christmas and shakes her collection box at passersby. When she sees Jim, something about him unsettles her and she holds her box very still. She pretends to be studying a shop window, and this is hard because it is one of several that are available for letting. Bar several dead flies on the windowsill, and some ransacked units, it is empty.

"My mum had breast cancer," says Paula. "She died when I was eighteen." Hearing this, Darren stops a moment and wraps her inside his jacket.

At the end of the High Street they turn into a long road of terraced housing. Almost there, says Darren. The curb is packed with cars and vans. Many of the houses have roof conversions and front porches with frosted glass windows. All of them have satellite dishes and TV aerials. As they pass, Jim counts the Christmas trees in the front rooms. He wonders if he will find twenty-one.

Paula says, "You just have to talk to the woman. About how you feel. She won't bite."

Jim realizes he has lost his place with the counting, and he would like to go back to the beginning of the street to start again. He would feel better if he could do that, less exposed. He turns to head back.

"Where do you think you're going?" says Paula.

"I don't need a-a-a d-doctor—"

"She isn't a doctor. She is a person to help. She's fully trained."

Darren pulls out the address from his pocket. This is it, he says. He pushes open the gate to a garden. He steps to one side, allowing Jim and Paula to go first.

Wind chimes hang from the low black branches of three or four closely planted fruit trees. In single file, Jim and Paula follow Darren along the dark path to the door.

"How come we're at someone's house?" says Darren. "I thought this woman was professional."

"She is professional," says Paula. "She's a friend of a friend and she's going to give Jim an introductory session for free. Apparently she is awesome. She does all sorts of things, including phobia therapy. She even does parties. She's been fully trained online."

The psychic counselor is a sturdy woman with a thick gray bob that is held from her face by an Alice band. She wears sensible shoes, elasticated slacks, a loose-fitting blouse, and an optimistically colorful scarf. In the presence of the counselor both Paula and Darren become children, she twisting her pink hair, he mumbling into bundled hands.

"Who is the client?" says the counselor, casting her eyes over the three of them.

Paula and Darren quickly point at Jim and he in turn lowers his head.

The counselor invites the couple to sit in the kitchen, but Darren says they would prefer to wait outside.

Her house smells of something clean and sterile, like a disinfected lemon, and the narrow hallway is so dark Jim has to feel his way with his hands as he follows her. She points to an open door to her left and asks Jim to go first. The small room is tidy and brightly lit. There are no chairs, no pictures, simply a bookcase on top of which sits a plaster-cast Buddha.

"Please take a seat," says the woman.

She slips one foot behind the other, lowers her rear, and then plummets toward the floor with such speed it is like watching a lift go down. She hits what turns out to be a beanbag with a polystyrene pop. "Do you need a hand?" she says, looking up.

Carefully Jim attempts to do the same on the free beanbag opposite hers, although he has a problem with his legs. If he crosses them, as she is doing, he fears he will never walk again. He pushes his plaster-cast foot out ahead and lowers himself down on the other leg, but this gives way and he too crashes into his beanbag with a splash. His arms and legs stick out from his body. He is not sure if or how he will get up again.

"How can I help you, Jim?" says the counselor.

Short of fetching a chair, he has no idea. She has green socks. But not Eileen-green. Just sensible.

"Your colleague tells me you're the victim of a violent crime. I gather you do not wish to press charges against the assailant. We need to talk about that."

"It was an a-a-a—"

"Nothing is an accident. Everything happens for a reason and that reason is deep inside us. What we have to do today, Jim, is get that reason out. I know it frightens you but I'm here to help. I want you to know you are not alone. I am in this with you." Here she gives a small smile and her eyes narrow. "You have a good aura. Are you aware of that?"

He admits he isn't. He is more aware of a stinging sensation in his good foot.

"Why do you stammer?"

Jim blushes and it is like being burned all over his back, his face, his arms. She waits for him to answer but he can't and there is only the sound of her breathing, like small pinches at the air.

She says, "In my experience, people stammer for a reason. What is it you feel you can't say?"

There are lots of things Jim can't say. And it's not as if they didn't try to help at Besley Hill. They gave him exercises to focus his mind, they gave him tips to form words. He spoke into mirrors. He visualized sentences. He said *Grr* when he got stuck. None of it helped. ECT would not cause a stammer, the doctors agreed. Jim knew they must be right; they were professionals. It was just that a short while after his last session his mouth stopped remembering how to make words.

However, this is not the time for thinking back. The psychic counselor is still talking. She is pointing at herself and then raising her fists into unlikely punch shapes. "Imagine I am your assailant. What would you like to tell me? There is no need to hide. I can take it."

He would like to say, It was an accident. He would like to say, Hear me, Eileen.

"Jim, I'm a woman. I work with my instincts. And I look at you, and I know this accident has been very tough."

He slowly nods. He can't lie.

"Why do you think that is?"

Jim tries to say he doesn't know.

The counselor says she is going a little off-topic, Jim must bear with her. "Your assailant ran over your foot. She didn't stop. But as far as I understand, you shouted at her to go. You didn't want her help. Is that right?"

Jim tries to say yes but the word is not there.

"So why did you want her to go? Why did you choose to be the victim? You could have shouted at her. You could have let her know she'd hurt you. What happened, Jim? Why couldn't you say that?"

The silence seems to ring like glass. His mind races back over the years and it is like throwing open doors on things that have long been safely shut away. His throat locks. His pulse flaps. He tries not to think, tries to be empty. From outside he can hear Paula and Darren's laughter. He can hear the low playing of wind chimes. Slipping his hand inside his pocket, he grips his key ring for help.

The counselor smiles gently. "I'm sorry. Maybe we're going too fast."

Instead she asks Jim to imagine he is a letter. What would he like to say? She asks him to imagine he is an arrow. Where would he like to hit? He must picture himself as a receptacle, a tree with roots, a rubber ball. There are so many versions of himself, all bouncing, shooting, and posting themselves inside his head, he feels very tired. "We need to get everything out in the open," says the counselor with robust enthusiasm. "Now is not the time to be afraid."

He whispers, "Bookcase, hello. Buddha, hello."

"Think about all the things that you've hidden away, Jim. It is time to let them go." She makes a whooshing noise as if she has been punctured and is rapidly losing air. "You have to own the past and let it go."

It is like being grabbed by the mouth, the ears, the eyes, and wrenched open. The accident, the hospital, they were nothing compared to this. He does not know how he will piece himself back together again.

She says, "You don't have to be a victim, Jim. You can be a player." She shakes herself as if she has just woken. She smiles. "It's time to stop. Our introductory session is over."

Jim's psychic counselor pushes herself up from her beanbag and squints down. He bows his face so that she will not see the state of it.

"You should come for an angel reading," she says. "You know you can ask the angels for the simplest things? Finding a parking space, for instance. Nothing is too small."

Jim tries to explain that it is very kind but he already has a parking space. Also, he adds, there is a problem with the gearbox and the van won't drive. It was a gift, he says, many years ago from an employer who didn't want it. He adds that he used to stack logs for her and dispose of her sherry bottles. Words rise and spew out of his mouth. It is possible that half his sentences lack verbs. Anything rather than to speak the pictures surfacing in his mind. The things she says he must let go.

The counselor nods. Well, it was just a thought, she says.

She asks if he has been satisfied with the service, and Jim promises he has. If he does not feel he has been offered the service he needs, he is free to make a complaint. Jim reassures her he has no wish to complain. Maybe he would like to add a testimonial to her website? He explains that he has no laptop. She reaches into a notebook and hands him a form. She asks if he would be so good as to give her service a rating from 1 to 10 and return the form in the self-addressed envelope. "It's time to go home now," she says.

Jim tells her he can't.

She smiles as if she understands. "I know you feel you can't cope. You think you need me. But you will be OK, Jim. I am giving you permission to be OK."

Jim explains he actually can't get up. He has lost all feeling in both legs. It takes both Paula and Darren to lift him, and they do so by taking one arm each and hoicking him upward. Returned to his full height, he looks down on Paula, on Darren and the psychic counselor, and despite his extra inches he feels painfully small.

"Yes, we have done some very good work," says the counselor. "Jim is ready to let go. He can get on with his life now."

A flock of seagulls rise and swoop above the black profile of the moor, and they are so luminous, so fragile, it would be easy to mistake them for shreds of paper. Jim does not mention angel guides or parking spaces to Paula and Darren. He does not mention the counselor's questions. He is so shaken he can barely remember how to put one foot in front of the other. Several times he staggers and Darren has to catch him.

"There, there, Jimbo," says Paula. "It's been a big day."

Walking back to the High Street, past the dark houses with their front porches and loft conversions, she says, "This place used to be a real dump. Not fit for humans, some of it."

And he realizes they are in Digby Road.

Two Stitches

"It isn't that I am offended, Byron," said James. His voice was high and childlike. "It is just that I am surprised you went so suddenly. I thought the plan was that I would come too."

"But things went faster than you said they would."

James ignored this. He finished his milk and wiped the top of the bottle clean. "I have been before, you know."

"To Digby Road?"

"There is a doctor there. My mother took me when I had head lice. He is a private doctor. My mother didn't want people to know."

It occurred to Byron there were things about James Lowe that still surprised him.

James said, "It is difficult for me to help save Diana if I do not know the full situation. I would have liked to hear the conversation in order to make observations for my Operation Perfect notebook."

"I didn't know you had a notebook."

"I have diagrams, as well. Also, I would have liked to go to the hotel restaurant. Prawn cocktail is my favorite. Did she really let you have tomato soup before lunchtime? Did she really buy a red Chopper bicycle for the little girl?" Yes, a Tomahawk, Byron repeated. James's eyes widened like shiny blue buttons. "There is no one like her," he said. "Tout va bien."

It was true. The return to Digby Road, and the subsequent delivery of such generous gifts, had marked a turning point. Byron's mother became herself again. She went back to doing all those things she did so well, the tiny details that marked her above everyone else. She filled the vases with cut flowers, she weeded the grass between the paving stones, she sewed on loose buttons and darned small holes. His father came for his weekend visit and this time she did not cough or twitch her napkin when he asked how the Jaguar was driving.

"Beautifully. She is a wonderful vehicle," said Diana. She gave an immaculate smile.

The school mothers met for their last coffee of the summer term at the beginning of the second week in July. Byron was present only, Diana said, because he had a dental appointment. "We can't stay long," explained Diana. "We'll perch at the end." The new mother asked if Diana wasn't worrying about Byron's scholarship work, what with all the lessons he was missing. ("What *is* the woman's name?" said Andrea.) The women talked about holiday plans. Deirdre had booked a two-week foreign trip. The new mother was going to visit her sister-in-law in Tunbridge Wells. When they asked Diana, she said she had no plans. Her husband would be taking his annual holiday with work colleagues in Scotland and she would spend the summer at home with the children. Home was so much nicer than going away, said Andrea Lowe. There were none of those things to worry about, like water tablets and insect bites. Then someone else began to talk about economizing, and Andrea mentioned, by the bye, that she had been fortunate enough to purchase a marvelous new leather sofa in nigger brown.

Diana abruptly reached for her handbag and pushed back her chair. Byron thought they were about to leave and he didn't know why because the dental appointment was not for another thirty minutes. Then his mother appeared to catch sight of someone at the other side of the tearoom and she waved. Byron couldn't think who it was. And then, as the woman began to dart toward them, threading between tables and chairs, he realized that it was Beverley.

Dressed in a pair of black swing trousers and a cheesecloth smock top, she was also wearing a wide-brimmed purple hat. "Don't let me interrupt," said Beverley, glancing at all the mothers. She took off her hat and turned it around and around in her hands like a wheel. "I'm looking for the soft toys department. But I keep going wrong. I've been here ages." Her eyes traveled so fast over the women that she was tripping over words.

Diana smiled. "Everyone, this is Beverley."

"Hello, hello, hello," said Beverley. She offered a series of frantic waves, like polishing an invisible window. In return, the women gave tight smiles that appeared to stick to their mouths and hurt.

"I'm not interrupting you, am I?" said Beverley to Diana.

"No, no," said Andrea in a yes, yes sort of way.

"Byron, offer Beverley your chair," said Diana.

"Oh no, please. I won't stop."

But Diana insisted.

Byron carried his gilt chair to his mother's side, and Andrea shifted her own several feet to make a space. He lingered behind his mother's shoulder. It was a mistake to offer Beverley a chair. It was a mistake to introduce her to the Winston House mothers. He was sure James would agree.

Nevertheless Beverley took his chair. She sat very tensely, her spine not touching the back of it, and she clearly didn't know what to do with her hat. First she draped it on her lap, then she hooked it over her chair, but it slipped to the floor and that was where she left it. "Yes," she said, as if someone had asked her a question, though no one had, or showed any likelihood of doing so. "Jeanie loves the lamb you bought her." Still she addressed only Diana. "She plays with it all the time. But guess what?"

Diana gave the smallest shake of her head. "I don't know, Beverley."

"His little guitar broke. I told her to be careful. That's a collector's item, I said. But she is so sad. It just went snap in her hands. Like that. *Snap!*" She snapped her fingers.

Byron stood very still. If he so much as moved a muscle he was afraid he would push Beverley out of the way. He wanted to shout at her not to mention the bicycle. He wanted to shout at the mothers to get on and drink their coffees. They watched with stony, glazed smiles.

"I knew from the bag you had bought it here and so I promised. I said, You be a good girl, Jeanie, and don't go on, and Mother will fetch you another one. It's so nice to bump into you again." She cast a net of a glance over the other mothers. "Do you come here a lot?"

The mothers said they did. All the time, said Andrea. Beverley nodded.

"Would you like anything to drink?" asked Diana, offering the leather-bound menu.

"Do they do the hard stuff?" This was clearly meant to be a joke, but no one laughed or smiled or even, for that matter, said no, they don't, what about coffee. Beverley's face slid so fast into red, she looked on the verge of moving on to an altogether more violent shade, like blue.

"I won't stop," she said, failing to go. Then: "I suppose you all have kids like Diana?"

The women reached for their cups and muttered things like yes and one or two.

"I suppose they're all at Winston House?" She was clearly trying to be friendly.

Yes, yes, said the mothers, as if there was nowhere else.

"It's a very nice school," said Beverley. "If you can afford it. Very nice." Her eyes darted around, swallowing the cut-glass light fittings, the waitresses in their black-and-white uniforms, the starched tablecloths. "Shame they don't do Green Shield Stamps in this place," she said. "I'd be here all the time."

She laughed. There was something defiant about it, though, that suggested she did not find herself or her situation funny. Diana joined in, only hers was a generous, public laugh that said, Isn't she wonderful?

"But you can't always have what you want," said Beverley.

Andrea leaned toward Deirdre. She spoke behind the flat of her hand though Byron could hear and so, he was sure, could Beverley. "Is she from the House? Staff?"

In the silence Beverley dug her teeth into her lower lip until it lost all color. Her eyes blazed.

"Beverley is my friend," said Diana.

The remark seemed to invigorate Beverley. To Byron's relief, she swooped to her feet, only she seemed to have forgotten about the hat and her foot went straight through the brim. The new mother stifled a laugh. Beverley patted her hat onto her head, but the floppy hat didn't flop anymore. It hung. Catching the new mother's smile, Andrea smiled too, and so did Deirdre.

Beverley sang, "Well, goodbye, everyone. Nice to meet you."

Few replied.

"It was lovely to see you again," said Diana, shaking her hand.

Beverley was about to turn when she appeared to remember something else. "By the way," she said. "Good news. Jeanie's on the mend."

The women stared back at her in the way they might look at a broken pipe, as if something needed to be done about it but by paid help and not themselves.

"Yes. Jeanie's my daughter. She's in her first year at school. Not Winston House, just the local. But she was hurt in an accident. Involving a car. The driver didn't stop at the time but there's no hard feelings. They came back in the end. And nothing broken. That's the main thing. Nothing apart from skin. She had a stitch. Two, actually. Two stitches. That's all."

An almost palpable discomfort settled over the table. The mothers shifted in their seats, they exchanged small glances, they checked their watches. Byron couldn't believe what he was hearing. He thought he was going to be ill. He stole a glance at Diana and immediately he had to look away because her face was so devastated that she looked empty. When would Beverley stop? Words spilled out of her. "She has a limp but things are getting better. They get better every day. Be careful, I keep saying, but she doesn't listen. It's different, of course, when you're five. If it was me, I'd be lying down. I'd be in a wheelchair, knowing me. But you know what kids are like. They don't stop." Glancing at her watch, she said, "Is that the time?" It was a cheap Timex with a frayed fabric strap. "I must be off. See you soon, Diana." She walked so defiantly across the restaurant floor that when a waitress emerged with a tray there was almost a collision.

"What a character," said Andrea at last. "Where on earth did you meet her?"

For the first time Byron turned to face his mother. She sat erect, as if she had a pain somewhere deep inside and was afraid to move.

"In Digby Road," she said quietly.

He couldn't believe she had come out with it. She looked on the verge of confessing everything. Byron started to make a noise that was not exactly words, it was more like cramming the silence with indiscriminate sound. "Oo oo," he said, hopping from one foot to the other. "My teeth hurt. Ouch."

His mother plucked up her handbag and stood. "Come along, Byron. We'll pay on our way out. And by the way—" Yet again, she broke off from the path she was supposed to be on, and turned in the direction of Andrea: "Your sofa. It isn't nigger brown."

"My dear, it's a turn of phrase. It isn't offensive."

"It is, though. It's very offensive. You should be more careful."

Scooping Byron's hand in hers, Diana steered him away. Her heels rang against the marble floor. When he glanced back, he saw the shade of menace on Andrea's face, the look of mouth-parted shock from the others. He wished he had not fetched a chair for Beverley. He wished Diana had kept quiet about Andrea's sofa. Of all the women to upset, he couldn't help fearing that his mother had chosen the worst.

———

They searched throughout the gift department but there was no sign of Beverley. "Maybe she went straight home," Byron said. His mother kept looking. She took the stairs to the toy department and also the ladies' powder room, and when it was clear that Beverley had gone, she gave a long sigh.

"Two stitches. Two stitches, Byron." She held up two fingers, as if she had forgotten he could count. "Not one, but two. We need to go back."

"To the tearoom?" It didn't seem her best idea.

"To Digby Road." This was even worse.

"But why?" he said.

"We need to check that poor little girl is all right. We have to do it right now."

He tried to persuade her that he needed the lavatory and afterward that he had a stone in his shoe. He said they would be late for the dentist but there was no distracting her; she seemed to have forgotten his appointment entirely. They arrived in Digby Road with a jigsaw puzzle, a bottle of Bell's whisky for Walt, and two new dressed blue lambs in boxes for Beverley, sharing a selection of musical instruments, woodwind and string. This time his mother parked right outside the house. A passing young man asked if she wanted the Jaguar cleaned. He had no bucket and no cloth.

But "Thank you, thank you," she cried. It was as if she was flying above the surface of things. She ran down the garden path, *click, click,* and rapped with her bare hands at the door.

When Beverley appeared, Byron was shocked. Her face was so red it was swollen, and her eyes were tiny raw puffs. She wiped her nose repeatedly, pinching it between the folds of her handkerchief and apologizing for the state of her. She said it was a summer cold, but black lines slanted her face like drips where she had rubbed her nose and her cheeks.

"I should never have come over. I should never have said hello. You must think I'm such an idiot."

His mother proffered the new bag of gifts. She asked if Jeanie was at home. She asked if she might say hello. She was so sorry about the stitches, she said. If only she had known—

Beverley interrupted and took the handles of the bag. "You're too kind. You didn't need to do this." She peered inside and her eyes widened.

It was only when Diana explained that she had put in a note with her telephone number that Byron shared Beverley's surprise. He had no idea she'd done that. It was a decision she had made without telling him and he wondered when she had done it and how.

"But why didn't you tell me?" his mother was saying. "When I came before? Why didn't you say about the two stitches?"

"I didn't want to upset you. You seemed so nice. You're nothing like those other women."

"I feel terrible," said his mother.

"Jeanie's leg only got worse after your visit. I took her to the doctor and that was when he put in the stitches. He was very kind. She didn't cry with the needle or anything."

"Good. I'm glad." His mother looked wretched, keen to get away.

"At least there's one thing."

"Oh?"

"At least you came back this time."

"Yes," murmured Diana.

"I don't mean that in a horrible way," said Beverley, all in a rush.

"No, no, I know," said his mother, all in a rush back.

Beverley smiled and again Diana apologized. If there was anything she could do, "You have my telephone number. You must ring. Anytime."

To their astonishment, Beverley made a reply that was halfway between a laugh and a shout. "Oich!" she went. Byron couldn't think what the noise meant until he followed the path of her fast eyes and landed on the roadside. "You'd better run," she said. "That little sod is trying to break into your car."

They drove away and this time he and his mother did not share a word.

4

Father Christmas

The outfit is Mr. Meade's idea. He slides it carefully from its plastic packaging. Mrs. Meade has ordered it from the Internet. The velour suit comes with its own white beard, plastic belt, and sack.

"You can't be serious," says Paula.

But Mr. Meade says he is very serious. Health and Safety are on his case. If Jim wants to keep his job, he has to do it in a chair.

"Why can't he have a wheelchair?" says Paula.

Mr. Meade says Health and Safety will not allow a cleaner in a wheelchair on account of the further Health and Safety issues. Supposing, for instance, he runs over a customer?

"It's a café," says Paula. "It's not a racetrack."

Mr. Meade clears his throat. He is looking mulled-wine warm. "If Jim wants to stay, he's going to have to sit in a chair and wear the outfit. And that's the bottom line."

However, there are further complications. Despite the fact that Mrs. Meade has ordered the deluxe outfit in an X-Large size, the hems of the trousers do not reach Jim's ankles and the mock-fur-trimmed sleeves hang between his elbows and wrists. There is also the issue of the blue plaster cast on his foot and Jim's skeletal thinness inside the X-Large jacket.

When he hobbles from the staff changing room, they gawp at him as if he has crashed through the ceiling.

"He looks terrible," says Paula. "He looks like he hasn't eaten for a year."

"He'll scare everyone off," pipes up Darren, who has spent the entire day in the café. Paula brings him hot drinks when Mr. Meade isn't looking. "He'll have the kids in tears."

Paula rushes downstairs to the store. She returns with white gloves, as well as several square cushions from the home interiors department. She looks the other way as she slips the padding beneath Jim's jacket and secures it with festive ribbon.

"Maybe tinsel would help?" says Darren. "On his red hat or something?"

Paula fetches tinsel. She circles it carefully around Jim's head. She makes short humming noises as she goes.

"Now it looks like he's got an aerial," says Darren.

Jim is positioned beside the youth brass band at the foot of the stairs. His chair has been draped with plastic ivy that sparkles. A collection bucket is placed in front of his plaster cast in order to hide it. It is Jim's job to hand leaflets to shoppers, advertising cut-price Christmas gift ideas in the home department. These include leaf vacuums for the man in your life and foot massagers for women. Mr. Meade and Paula stand with their arms folded, surveying the scene. Jim actually looks quite sweet, she says.

"Just make sure he doesn't open his mouth," says the general manager, appearing through the automatic doors. Mr. Meade promises Jim won't.

"'Cause if I catch sight of him scaring customers," continues the general manager. She is an angular woman in a black suit. Her hair is pulled so hard into a ponytail that even her face looks scraped. "If I see any of that, he's out. You understand?" She swipes her finger across the white of her throat as if she is slicing it.

Both of them nod vigorously and head back upstairs. It is only Jim who sits very still.

Every Christmas there was a tree in the television room at Besley Hill. The nurses put it by the window with the chairs circled around it so that all the patients could see. There was even a visit from local schoolchildren. They brought wrapped presents and they sang carols. The residents were not allowed to touch the children or frighten them. In turn, the children stood in their school uniforms with their hands clasped tight and their eyes very wide, on best behavior. Afterward the nurses handed out the presents and told the residents to say thank you, only the children frequently misunderstood and clamored "Thank you" instead. One year, Jim's present was a tin of pineapple chunks. "Aren't you lucky?" said the nurse. She told the children Jim loved fruit and he was about to say yes, he did, only the words wouldn't come fast enough and the nurse said them instead. When it was time to go, the children pushed and jostled their way out, as if the door was too narrow, and the space beneath the Christmas tree was suddenly so empty it felt ransacked. Several of the patients cried.

Jim watched from an upper-floor window as the children boarded their bus. When three of the boys turned around and noticed him, he waved and then held up his tin of pineapple chunks so that they would remember who he was and that he liked his Christmas gift. The boys made a sign with two fingers.

"Loony!" they shouted. And they made startled faces, as if they were being fried.

The youth brass band, it turns out, have a repertoire that only really includes three songs. They can do "Jingle Bells" and "Away in a Manger," as well as "She'll Be Coming Round the Mountain." This last is clearly their favorite, and the pimply young man on cymbals shouts out "Yee-ha!" every time they collide with the chorus. A tall green-coated woman marches through the door and past Jim. She stops suddenly and does a double-take.

"Bloody hell," she says. "What have you come as?"

Jim is about to offer a leaflet when he realizes with a flood of panic who she is and with another flood of panic that he is dressed in red velour with mock-fur trimming.

Eileen undoes the big green buttons on her coat. The fabric shrinks back, revealing a purple skirt that puckers at her waist. "So how's things, Jim? Still here?"

He attempts to nod as if being here is the thing he most wants. A passing shopper throws money into his bucket, and Jim hides his large blue foot behind his more conventional trainer.

She says, "I was hoping I'd find you."

"Me?"

"I wanted to say sorry. About the other week."

He can't look at her he is shaking so hard.

"I didn't see you. You came out from fucking nowhere. You were lucky I didn't hit you."

Jim tries to pretend he is cold. He tries to pretend he is so chilled he cannot hear properly. "Brrr," he says, rubbing his hands, although the gesture is so frantic he looks like a man washing his hands with invisible soap.

"You all right?" she says.

Fortunately the band begins a lively rendering of "I Wish It Could Be Christmas Everyday" and she cannot hear his answer. This is not one of their rehearsed numbers. There are disagreements over tempo and also the length of the chorus so that one half of the band plays an entirely different set of notes from the other. Inside the supermarket, the general manager peers toward the foyer. She adjusts a mouthpiece and talks into it. Jim makes a swiping movement across his neck, only the white beard is in the way. "Can't t-talk."

"I'm not surprised," says Eileen. "You're covered in frigging tinsel." She glances in the direction of the manager and fetches a trolley. He admires the way she steers it, purposeful and fast. He admires the way she stops to examine a potted poinsettia and afterward pulls such a face at a toddler that he kicks his feet and laughs.

On her way out Eileen drops something into Jim's bucket. It is one of his leaflets. She has written all over it in capitals: I WILL WAIT 4 U IN CAR PARK AFTER WORK!!!

The capital letters shout themselves in his head. He studies the abundance of exclamation marks and wonders what they mean. Wonders if the message is in fact a joke.

5

The Afternoon Visit

James was deeply troubled by the news of Jeanie's two stitches. "This is not good," he said. "It does not reflect well on your mother."

"But the accident was not her fault."

"All the same," said James. "If there is evidence of an actual wound, it makes things more complicated. Supposing Beverley goes to the police?"

"She won't do that. Beverley likes my mother. My mother was the only one who was nice to her."

"You are going to have to watch closely."

"But we are not going to see Beverley again."

"Hm," said James, and he twiddled his fringe to show he was thinking. "We have to set up a further meeting."

The next morning Byron and his mother were walking up through the meadow after feeding the ducks. Lucy was still sleeping. Diana had climbed the fence to fetch eggs, and they carried them, one each, treading carefully through the grass. The sun was not yet fully risen, and caught in the low, weak shaft of light, the dew shone silver over the meadow although the crust of earth beneath was hard and cracked. The ox-eye daisies made white pools on the lower hills, while every tree sprang a black leak away from the sun's light. The air smelled new and green like mint.

They talked a little about the summer holidays and how much they were looking forward to them. Byron's mother suggested that he should invite a friend for tea. "It seems a shame James doesn't come anymore," she said. "It must be almost a year."

"Everyone is busy. We have the scholarship work." He didn't like to mention that since the pond episode, James was no longer allowed to visit.

"Friends are important. You need to look after them. I had lots once but I don't anymore."

"You do. You have all the mothers."

For a moment she said nothing. Then she went, "Yes." Her agreement was flat, though, as if she wasn't inside it. The rising sun threw stronger batches of light over the moor, and its purples, pinks, and greens began to shine so bright they looked as if Lucy had painted them. "If I have no friends it's my own fault," she said.

They walked on in silence. His mother's words made Byron sad. It was like discovering he had lost something important without noticing he had dropped it. He thought of James's insistence that there should be another meeting with Beverley. He remembered too what his friend had told him about magic: how you could make a person believe a thing by showing them only one part of the truth, and hiding the other pieces. His pulse began to rush. He said, "Maybe Beverley could be your friend."

His mother looked blank. Clearly she had no idea whom he

meant. When he explained he was thinking of the lady from Digby Road, she laughed.

"Oh no. I don't think so."

"Why not? She likes you."

"Because it's not that simple, Byron."

"I don't see why. It is for me and James."

Diana stooped to pick a stem of oat grass, running her nail along the tip and scattering a feathery trail of seedheads, but she said no more about friends. Byron felt that he had never seen her look so alone. He pointed out a pyramidal orchid and also a red admiral butterfly, but she didn't reply. She didn't even glance up.

It was then he realized how unhappy she was. It was not simply because of the accident in Digby Road and Jeanie's two stitches. There was another, deeper unhappiness that was to do with something else. He knew that grown-ups were sometimes unhappy with cause; when it came to certain things, there was no option. Death, for instance. There was no avoiding the pain of grief. His mother had not attended her own mother's funeral, but she had cried when the news came. She had stood with her arms wrapped around her shoulders and shaken. And when his father had said, "That is enough now, Diana," she had dropped her hands and given him a look of such undiluted pain, her eyes all red and rimmed, her nose all slippery, that it was uncomfortable. It was like seeing her without clothes.

So this was how it felt to lose a parent. It was natural to be unhappy like that. But to discover that his mother was also unhappy in a way that he sometimes was, because something to which he couldn't even give a name was not right—that had not occurred to him before. There was a clear way to remedy the situation.

In the privacy of his bedroom, Byron took out James's duplicate list of Diana's attributes. Copying the handwriting, because it was somewhat neater than his own or indeed his mother's, and flourishing the tails of the *y*'s and *g*'s with James-like loops, he began to write. He explained that he was Diana Hemmings, the kind lady who had been the driver of the Jaguar on that unfortunate morning in Digby Road. He hoped he was not inconveniencing dear Beverley, he wrote, but he wondered if she would be so good as to accept an invitation for tea at Cranham House. He enclosed the telephone number, address, and also a new decimal two-pence piece from his money box to cover her bus fare. He hoped it would be enough, he added, crossing out the childish word *enough* and replacing it with the more professional-sounding *sufficient*. He signed the letter in his mother's name. As a postscript he added an observation about the clemency of the weather. It was this sort of clever attention to detail, he felt, that marked him apart as a letter writer. In a further postscript he also asked her to destroy the message on reading. "This is a private matter," he wrote, "between ourselves."

He knew the address, of course. There was no forgetting. Telling his mother it was his *Blue Peter* design, Byron asked for a stamp and posted the envelope that same afternoon.

The letter was a lie and Byron knew it, but as lies went this was a kind one and could bring no harm. Besides, his experience of the truth had been stretched since Digby Road. It was difficult to discern the point where things strayed from one version of themselves into another. For the rest of the day he couldn't sit still. Would Beverley receive the letter? Would she telephone? Several times he asked his mother how long the post took and the exact hours of the first and second deliveries. That night he barely slept.

He watched the school clock all day, waiting for the hands to move. He was too nervous to confide in James. The telephone rang the following afternoon.

"Cranham 0612," said his mother from her glass table.

He couldn't hear the whole conversation; his mother sounded cautious to begin with. "I'm sorry?" she said. "Who are you?" But after a while he heard her exclaim, "Yes, of course. That would be lovely." There was even a little polite laughter. Afterward she put down the receiver and stood a few moments in the hall, deep in thought.

"Anyone interesting?" he said, sauntering casually down the stairs and following her to the kitchen.

"Beverley's coming tomorrow. She's coming for tea."

He didn't know what to say and he wanted to laugh, only that would betray his secret, so he had to do something else that was more of a cough. He couldn't wait to tell James.

She said, "Did you write a letter, Byron?"

"Me?"

"Beverley mentioned an invitation."

The heat flew to his face. "Maybe she was thinking of when we took her the presents. Maybe she got muddled because you gave her our telephone number. You told her to ring anytime, remember?"

His mother seemed satisfied. Ducking her head inside the loops of her apron, she began pulling flour, eggs, and sugar out of the cupboard. "You're right," she said. "I'm being silly. It can't do any harm inviting her for tea."

James was less sure. This bewildered Byron. While James admitted that Byron had acted shrewdly in writing to Beverley, and that he was glad there would be another meeting, he wished that Byron had suggested a neutral setting. "If you were meeting her in town, for instance, I could arrive as if by coincidence. I could wander in as if I was not expecting to find you and say, Oh, hello there, and join in."

"But you could come for tea tomorrow at my house."

"Due to circumstances beyond my control, that is sadly not possible."

Instead, James issued Byron a full set of instructions. He must take careful notes. Did he have a spare notebook? When Byron admitted he didn't, James slipped a lined exercise book from his satchel. He unscrewed the lid from his fountain pen and wrote OPERATION PERFECT on the cover. Notes should include observations about the conversation, most importantly references to Jeanie's injury, although the smallest and most seemingly insignificant details should also be recorded. Byron must be neat as possible and give references to dates and the time. "Also, do you have invisible ink at home? This must be confidential."

Byron said he didn't. He was saving Bazooka bubblegum wrappers for the X-ray ring but you needed a lot, he said. "And I am not allowed bubblegum."

"It doesn't matter," said James. "Over the holidays I will send you a code." He added again that Jeanie's stitches were a matter of concern; it was important to find out as much as possible about them. But he didn't sound anxious about the prospect. If anything, he looked excited. He wrote his telephone number carefully at the back of the exercise book and told Byron to ring as soon as there were developments. They must keep in regular contact over the summer, he said.

Byron noticed that his mother appeared nervous when she came to collect him. The boys in the years above were singing and throwing their caps into the air, the mothers were taking photographs, and some had set up trestle tables for a leavers' picnic, but Diana was in a hurry to get back to the car. At home she flew around the house, fetching clean napkins and making rounds of sandwiches that she wrapped tight in PVC film. She mentioned that she would give the Jaguar one quick wash before she parked it in the garage, but then she grew so busy straightening chairs and checking her reflection that the car slipped her mind and remained parked in the drive.

Their guests were half an hour late. It transpired that Beverley had got off the bus too soon and had to walk the rest of the way through the lower fields. She stood at the front door, her hair stiff as a wedge (she had possibly used too much hairspray), in a short, brightly colored dress that was patterned with large tropical flowers. She had painted her eyelids with turquoise, only the effect was of two thick rings above her eyes. Poking out from beneath the rim of her purple hat, her face looked top-heavy.

"It's so nice of you to invite us" was the first thing she said. "We've been excited all day. We've talked about nothing else." She apologized for the state of her pantyhose. They were slashed with ladders and stuck all over with tiny burrs. It was so nice of Diana to spare her precious time, she said again. She promised they wouldn't stay long. Byron thought she looked as nervous as his mother.

At Beverley's side hung a child, smaller than Lucy, in a gingham school dress, with thin black hair that hung toward her waist. She wore a large fabric plaster on her right knee to protect the two stitches. It was ten centimeters in diameter. Catching sight of the injury, Diana gave a start.

"You must be Jeanie," she said, bending to greet her. "I'm afraid my daughter is out today."

Jeanie slotted behind her mother. She looked a slithery child. "Don't worry about your knee," said Beverley. She used a loud, jolly voice as if people were watching from right across the moor and she needed them to hear. "You won't hurt it again. You're perfectly safe."

Diana twisted her hands so hard she looked in danger of turning them inside out. "Has she walked far? Does she need another dressing?"

Beverley assured her the dressing was clean. In the last few days you could barely notice Jeanie's limp, she said. "You're much better, aren't you?"

In agreement, Jeanie wriggled her mouth as if she was eating a large toffee and it had got stuck.

Diana suggested they should sit outside on the new sun loungers while she fetched drinks. After that she would show them the garden. But Beverley asked if they could possibly come inside. The sun gave her daughter a headache, she said. Beverley couldn't seem to keep her eyes still. They flew over Diana's shoulder and scurried up and down the hallway, taking in the polished woodwork, the vases of flowers, the Georgian-style wallpaper, the curtains in their theatrical swirls. "Nice house." She said it in the way Lucy said, "Nice custard. Nice biscuits."

"Come in, come in," said Diana. "We'll have tea in the drawing room."

"Nice," said Beverley again, stepping inside. "Come along, Jeanie."

"I say 'drawing room,' but it's not half as grand as it sounds." Diana led the way along the hallway, her slim heels going *clip, clip,* while Beverley's sandals followed with a *slap, slap.* "The only person who really calls it a drawing room is my husband, and of course he doesn't live here. Or rather, he does, but only at week-ends. He works for a bank in the City. So I don't know why I call it a drawing room. My mother would have called it 'the best room,' but Seymour never liked her." She was talking far too much and her sentences didn't seem to join up. "I'm a bit of a misfit, really."

Beverley said nothing. She merely followed, peering to the left and right. Diana offered a choice of tea or coffee or something stronger, and Beverley insisted she would have whatever Diana was having.

"But you're my guest."

Beverley shrugged. She admitted she wouldn't say no to a snowball or something fizzy like cherry cola.

"A snowball?" Diana looked perplexed. "I'm afraid we don't have those. We don't have fizzy drinks either. My husband enjoys a gin and tonic at the weekend. I always keep Gordon's and Schweppes in the house. Or there's whisky in his study. You could have that." She also offered Beverley a pair of her tights to replace her laddered ones. "Do you mind Pretty Polly?"

Beverley said that Pretty Polly would do very nicely and so would a glass of squash.

"Please put down your notebook, Byron, and take care of Beverley's hat."

Diana pushed open the drawing room door tentatively as if half expecting something to jump out at her. "Oh, but where's your daughter?"

She was right. In the short distance from the hallway to the drawing room, they had already lost her.

Beverley rushed back to the front door, shouting her daughter's name at the stairs and wood-paneled walls, at the glass telephone table and Seymour's ship paintings, as if Jeanie had made herself part of the fabric of the house and should materialize out of thin air. She looked mortified.

The search began gently. Diana called out for Jeanie, and so did Beverley, although it was only Diana who rushed purposefully from room to room. Then suddenly she began to worry. She ran out to the garden and called there too. When there was no reply, she asked Byron to fetch towels. She would go down to the pond. Beverley kept saying she was sorry. So sorry for the inconvenience. That child would be the death of her, she said.

Diana had already thrown off her shoes and was tearing down the lawn. "But how could she have got over the fence?" Byron called, running after her. "She has her bad knee, remember?" His mother's hair flew out like gold streamers. Clearly there was no sign of Jeanie down there. "She must be somewhere in the house," said Diana, returning through the garden.

Byron passed Beverley in the hall, studying the label on his mother's coat.

"Jaeger," she said to herself. "Nice."

He must have frightened her, because she darted him a nail of a look that softened afterward into a smile.

The search continued downstairs. Beverley opened every room and cast her eyes inside. It was only when Byron checked upstairs a second time that he noticed Lucy's door ajar, and stopped. He found Jeanie curled like a rag doll inside the bed. In the half hour in which they had searched for her, calling her name in the garden, in the meadow, and down by the pond, she had evidently fallen asleep. Her arms were thrown across the pillow, revealing two thick scabs like flattened cherries at her elbows. She was right under the top sheet.

"It's all right!" he called to the women. "You can relax now. I've found her."

With shaking fingers, Byron dialed James's telephone number from his mother's glass table. He had to whisper, because he had not asked permission. "Who is speaking, please?" said James's mother. It took three goes to make her understand and then he had to wait a further two minutes for her to fetch James. When Byron explained about the search for Jeanie and finding her asleep, James said, "Is she still in the bed?"

"Affirmative. Yes."

"You have to go back upstairs. You have to examine the injury while she is asleep. Bonne chance, Byron. You are doing very good work. Be sure you make a diagram."

Byron reentered the room on tiptoes. Very gently, he lifted the corner of the sheet. Jeanie breathed thickly through her mouth as if she had a cold. His heart was beating so hard he had to keep gulping so as not to wake her. The plaster looked stuck hard. Her legs were slim and dirty from the walk. He held his fingertip right over the thin point of her knee. There was no blood on the plaster. It looked new.

He was just slipping his nail under the corner when Jeanie woke with a start. She stared at him with dark, wide eyes. The shock sent him lurching backward into Lucy's doll's house, and

Jeanie found this so funny she gave herself a round of hiccups. They popped right through her. Some of her teeth were like cracked brown beads. "Do you want me to carry you?" he said. She nodded and threw out her arms but still she didn't speak. Lifting her up, he was shocked by the lightness of her. She was barely there. Her shoulder blades and ribs stuck out in points beneath her cotton school dress. He took care not to touch her injured knee, and as she clung to him she thrust her leg carefully forward to protect the plaster.

Downstairs, Beverley's anxiety seemed to have manifested itself in hunger. She sat in the drawing room helping herself to cucumber sandwiches and chattering freely. When Byron appeared with Jeanie, she nodded impatiently and went on. She asked Diana where she got her furnishings, did she prefer china plates or plastic, who was her hairdresser. She asked the make of her record player. Was Diana pleased with the quality? Did she know that not all electrical goods were manufactured in England? Diana smiled politely and said she didn't know that, no. The future was in imports, said Beverley, now that the economy was such a mess.

She commented on the quality of Diana's curtains. Her carpets. The electric fireplace. "It's a lovely house you've got," she said, indicating the new glass lamps with her sandwich. "But I couldn't live here. I'd be scared of people breaking in. You have such nice things. I'm a townie myself."

Diana smiled. She was a town girl too, she said. "But my husband likes country air. And anyway"—she reached for her glass and shook the ice cubes—"he has a shotgun. In case of emergencies. He keeps it under the bed."

Beverley looked alarmed. "Does he shoot things?"

"No. He just holds it, really. He has a special tweed jacket as well as a deerstalker hat. He goes shooting in Scotland every August with his work colleagues and he completely hates it. He gets bitten by midges. They seem to love him."

For a moment neither woman spoke. Beverley skinned the crust from another sandwich and Diana studied her glass.

"He sounds like a right banana," said Beverley.

An unexpected laugh seemed to shoot from Diana. Glancing at Byron, she had to hide her face.

"I shouldn't laugh, I shouldn't laugh," she kept laughing.

"You have to. Anyway, I think I'd rather beat a burglar over the head. With a mallet or something."

"Oh, that's so funny," said Diana, wiping her eyes.

Byron reached for his notebook. He reported that his father had a shotgun and that Beverley possibly had a mallet. He would have liked one of the tiny sandwiches carved into triangles no bigger than his thumb, but Beverley seemed to think they were all for her. She had the plate on her lap now, and she nibbled at one half of each sandwich before discarding it and starting on another. Even when Jeanie tugged at her arm and asked to go home, she kept eating. Byron drew a diagram for James showing the little girl's leg and the location of the plaster. He made exact references to the time, but he couldn't help feeling disappointed when he began to record the conversation. For a new friendship, it seemed to err on the morbid side, although he had to admit he had never seen his mother laugh the way she did when Beverley called Seymour a banana. He did not write that part down.

He put: "Beverley said three times that DH is lucky. At 5:15 pm she said, 'I wish I had done something with my life, like you.'"

Beverley also told Diana that in the future you would have to think big if you wanted to get on, but Byron's hand was getting tired so he drew a plan of the room instead.

Meanwhile, Beverley asked for an ashtray and plucked a packet of cigarettes from her pocket. When Diana placed a small varnished clay pot at Beverley's side, she turned it over. "Looks foreign," she said, examining the rough underside. "Interesting."

Diana explained that it had belonged to her husband's family. He was brought up in Burma, she said, before things went wrong. Beverley said something between her teeth about the old days of the Empire, but Diana failed to hear because she was fetching a slim gold-plated lighter. While she held it out, flicking at the flint, Beverley tugged on her filter tip and said with a smile, "You'll never guess what my dad was."

Before Diana could answer, Beverley shot out a coil of smoke and laughed. "A vicar. I'm a vicar's daughter and look what happened. Up the duff at twenty-three. Council house and not even a wedding."

At the end of the afternoon Diana offered them a lift to town, but Beverley declined. As they walked to the door, Beverley thanked Diana profusely for the drinks and the sandwiches. It was only when Diana said "But what about her leg?" that Jeanie faltered and began to swing it like a wooden one.

Fiddling with her hat, Beverley insisted they would take the bus. Diana had already done more than enough; Beverley wouldn't take up any more of her precious time. And when Diana said that her time was not precious, and now that they had the holidays she had no idea what she would do with herself, Beverley gave a laugh that was like one of Seymour's, as if she were trying to quell it but couldn't. Well, how about next week? she said. She thanked

Diana again for the tea and the Pretty Polly tights. She would wash and return them on Monday.

"Goodbye, goodbye!" called Diana, waving from the front step and turning inside.

Byron couldn't be sure but he thought he saw Beverley pause as she passed the Jaguar. She seemed to scan the bonnet, the doors, the wheels, as if she had seen something of interest and was committing it to memory.

After the visit Diana was in a light mood. Byron helped her to wash the plates and glasses, and she told him how much she'd enjoyed the afternoon. More than expected, she said.

"I knew a woman once who could dance the flamenco. She had the dress and everything. You should have seen her. She would put up her hands like this and bang her feet and it was the most beautiful thing." His mother held her hands in an arch over her head. She stamped several times and her heels rang out. He had never seen her dance like that.

"How did you know that woman?"

"Oh," she said, dropping her arms and taking up the tea towel, "that was in the past. I don't know why she came into my head."

She stowed the dried plates in the dresser and closed the door with a click, and it was as though the dancing version of his mother had been shut in the cupboard too. Maybe her new happiness was something to do with Beverley's visit. Now that James was involved, everything had taken a turn for the better. His mother went to fetch newspaper for a bonfire.

"You haven't seen my lighter, have you?" she said. "I can't think where I left it."

6

Looking for Small Things

Eileen's car is parked and waiting beneath the sign that reads NO PARKING. NO WAITING. It is only once he has stepped out of the staff door that Jim realizes it is hers. Panic prickles his neck and shimmies all the way to the backs of his knees. He tries to reverse but the door has already clunked shut behind him.

There is nothing for it but to pretend he is someone else. A person without a new plaster-cast foot, for instance. Eileen stares straight at him and her face erupts into an eager, happy smile of recognition. She waves. Clearly he needs a new tactic. He must pretend she is someone else instead and that he has never met her.

Jim peers carefully through the dark at other things—the stashed trolleys, the bus stop, the cashpoint. He studies each of them as if he is finding them so extremely interesting he cannot possibly register anything else and will need to keep this up for a good few hours. He hums to give his distracted appearance further authenticity. And all the while he is studying these extremely interesting inanimate objects, what he is in fact seeing is Eileen. Her image is branded over his vision. She is all there is. Her green coat. Her flame of hair. Her radiant smile. It is as if she is talking to him.

Jim finds a very interesting spot in the pavement. He stoops to take a closer look. Then he makes a show of seeing another interesting spot a few feet on. If he can keep this up, if he can follow a trail of interesting spots, he should make it to the other side of the car park.

Already he is right next to her car. Without looking he can feel all through his left side that she has noticed him and is watching. He is dizzy with the closeness of her. And then, just as he is almost safe, he forgets that the extremely interesting spot is purely ground-based and accidentally raises his head. His eyes bump straight into Eileen's.

Her car door swings open and she scrambles out of the passenger seat. "Have you lost something, Jim?"

"Oh, hello, Eileen," he says. "I didn't see you sitting next to me in your car."

He can't imagine why he has said that, since it is now clear he recognized her straightaway. He tries to make a dash toward the supermarket entrance and realizes he can only hobble. Unfortunately, Eileen realizes he can only hobble too. She sees everything. His plaster-cast foot. His plastic sock. "Jim," she cries. "What happened?"

"N-n-n—" He can't say it. He can't get the word out and it is so small. She stands and waits. And all the time he gropes for it, mouth poised, chin jabbing the air, he is wretched. It is like clawing for words his mouth can't make.

"How are you getting home?" she says. At least she has not connected his foot with her Ford. "Do you want a lift?"

"Mr.—Mr.—Mr. Meade."

Eileen nods. She says nothing and neither does Jim. The pause extends itself into something more solid.

"So do you want a hand?" she asks at last. "Looking for whatever it is you're looking for?" Caught in the glare of the car park security lighting, her eyes are the color of a hyacinth. The blue of them is almost shocking. How has he not noticed this before?

"Yes," he says. It is the wrong word. He means no. No, you mustn't help me. He shoots his gaze away from her eyes and back to the ground. It will surely be safer down there.

Oh, but her feet are so small. She wears patent-leather brown lace-up shoes with a square toe, and they shine under the streetlamp. She has tied the laces into bows like flower petals.

"How big is it?" she says.

He has no idea what she's talking about. He's thinking about her tiny feet. They are so perfect, they are heartbreaking.

"Sorry?"

"The thing we're looking for."

"Oh," he says. "Small." It's the first word his head comes out with, because it is still busy with her shoes. He must stop staring at them. He must look up.

Eileen gives a wide, uncomplicated grin. Her teeth are as beautiful as her feet.

This new knowledge so alarms him that he tries to fix on a different bit of her. A neutral upper bit. And then he realizes with another flip of horror that the bit of her he has alighted upon is her left bosom. Or the shape of it, like a firm, smooth hillock inside her rucked green coat.

"Are you sure you're all right, Jim?" says Eileen.

To Jim's relief, a middle-aged suited man with a trolley charges through the space between them. He's talking into his mobile.

Jim and Eileen step back hastily, as if they've been discovered doing something wrong.

"Excuse me, both," says the man. He says it as if they are an item. Jim feels a pulse of excitement.

It seems to take the man with the trolley a long time to pass. He has filled it to overflowing with bottles and Christmas groceries, on top of which he has balanced a bouquet of lilies in plastic wrapping. He keeps mistakenly ramming the trolley into the gaps between paving stones. Then his Christmas gift bouquet slides off the trolley, but the man walks on.

Seeing the lilies, Jim's heart bangs inside his chest. The petaled hoods are so white, so waxy, that they shine. He can smell them. He doesn't know if he is terribly happy or terribly sad. Maybe he is both. Sometimes things happen like that; they appear like a sign from another part of life, from another context, as if stray moments from past and present can join up and gain extra significance. He sees a church full of lilies, from long ago, and he also sees the coat that Eileen caused to fall from a chair only the other day. The unconnected memories are combined, newly blended, by the flowers lying just a few feet away. He doesn't even think; he stoops to pick them up.

"Here," he says, handing the man his bouquet. He would like to give it to Eileen.

When the man has gone, the newly empty space between Jim and Eileen feels so alive it seems as if it should make a noise.

"I hate flowers," says Eileen at last. "I mean, I like them in the ground. When they're growing. I just don't see why people give each other cut flowers. They're dying. I'd rather have something useful. Pens or something."

Jim tries to nod in a polite way to suggest that he is interested but not *that* interested. He doesn't know where to look. At her mouth. Her eyes. Her hair. He wonders if she prefers biros or rollerballs.

Eileen shrugs. "Not that people ever give me flowers," she says. "Or pens, for that matter."

"No." It is only once he says the word that he realizes it is not the one he means.

"I'm too mouthy."

"Yes." Again. Wrong word.

"So you're sure you don't want a lift? We could stop for a drink on the way."

"Thank you," he says. And then with a bang he realizes what she has said. She has asked him for a drink.

Only maybe he has misunderstood, maybe she has said something else, such as "I'm gasping for a drink," because now it is Eileen's turn to bow her head and scour the pavement. He wonders if she has lost something too and then he remembers that he hasn't lost anything, he is simply pretending. So they are now side by side, almost touching but not quite, both of them looking for things that may or may not be there.

"How big is yours?" he says.

"Mine?"

"Have you lost something too?"

"Oh," she says, blushing. "Yes, well. Mine's very small as well. It's teensy. We won't find it."

"A shame, though."

"I beg your pardon?" Suddenly it is Eileen who appears not to know where to look. Her blue eyes are everywhere. Smacking into his mouth. His hair. His jacket.

"It's a shame to lose something."

"Oh yes," she says. "Crap."

He doesn't know if the words they are using actually mean the things they purport to mean or whether the words have taken on a new significance. They are talking about nothing, after all. And yet these words, these nothings, are all they have, and he wishes there were whole dictionaries of them.

"The thing is, I lose things all the time," says Eileen. "My purse. My keys. Do you know what I really hate?"

"No." He is only smiling because she is smiling. It isn't funny yet. It is going to be.

"When people say, Where did you lose it?" Eileen's laugh rips forth, causing her shoulders to shake and her eyes to stream. She prods them with her finger. "Fuck me. That's a stupid question." She has no wedding ring. "But actually I've lost big things too."

Jim says, "Oh." He can't think of anything else.

"I don't mean small stuff like cars and money." He is aware of having to run in his mind to keep up. Cars and money do not strike him as small. Then she says suddenly, "To be honest, sometimes I don't know how to keep going. You know what I mean?"

He says yes, he does.

"I can't get up. I can't speak. I can't even clean my teeth. I hope you don't mind me saying that."

"No."

"It's a thin line. It's a thin line between the people in Besley Hill and the ones outside."

She laughs again but he doesn't know anymore if Eileen is being funny. They return to staring at the pavement. "So we might as well keep looking, then?" she says. "For whatever it is we're looking for. Hey, Jim?" And all the time they walk up and down, heads bowed, he is aware of the square-set woman beside him.

He wonders if their eyes are making contact on the ground, if his beam of vision and her beam of vision are meeting down there in one unifying point. The thought sends his pulse galloping. Beneath his long feet, and her small ones, the frozen paving stones shine as if sequined. He has never found a pavement so beautiful.

A shout interrupts and Paula approaches, with Darren galloping to keep up.

"I can't believe you," hollers Paula. "Haven't you done enough damage?"

Eileen turns. She stands solid inside her holly-green coat.

"First you run him over," shouts Paula. "Then you stalk him. He's in counseling because of you."

Eileen's jaw drops. Jim can almost hear the clunk of it. What surprises him most, however, is that she does not swear. She stares at Jim as if he has changed, as if bits of him have swapped place. "What do you mean, run him over?" she says slowly. "What do you mean, counseling?"

"After you reversed into him. He had to go to hospital. You're a disgrace. You're not fit to drive."

Eileen doesn't reply. She remains still, taking in Paula's words, and not retaliating, not even blinking. It is like watching a champion boxer on the television and waiting for him to make a devastating punch before realizing he is not going to do anything. It is like seeing the other side of the champion boxer, the frail, human one, who should be at home, sitting in an armchair beside yours, and it is uncomfortable.

"He could sue," yells Paula. "You should be locked up."

Eileen sends Jim a look of confusion that is so tender, so childlike, he can't bear to meet it. All of a sudden he would like not to be here. He would like to be in his van. But before he can move,

Eileen backs away from him, from Paula and Darren, and more or less flees to her car. She doesn't even shout goodbye. She starts up the ignition and her car retches forward.

"She's still got the handbrake on," says Darren.

As if she has heard, the car stops with a jolt and then passes smoothly out of the frosted car park. The moon is not full but shines in a half-circle, burning a yellowy-green nimbus of light into the dark. The moor glitters so hard it is like little whisperings.

He will not share a lift with Eileen. They will not go for a drink. He thinks briefly of how she fell still when she talked about losing things, how she watched and said nothing while Paula shouted. It was like meeting Eileen in completely different, slight summer clothes.

Jim wonders if she had mislaid something on the pavement after all. And then it occurs to him that if she had, he would like to spend forever finding it.

7

Friendship

"You have to show Beverley that you know she stole your mother's lighter," said James over the telephone.

"But I don't know that," said Byron. "And why is the lighter so important?"

"Because it tells us more about the sort of person Beverley is. This is why you have to do what I say. It is known as calling her bluff. If she has not stolen the lighter, she won't understand what you are talking about and you can cover your tracks. You can say, My mistake, my mistake. But if she is guilty she will show signs of guilt and we will know the truth." James dictated Signs of Guilt in alphabetical order. They included: Blushing. Nervous Hand Movements. Not Looking a Person in the Eye.

"But she does those things already," said Byron.

James confirmed that he was glad the two women had met again and that further meetings should be encouraged in order to get the full evidence about Jeanie's knee. He added that things were very quiet that weekend. His parents were attending a cheese and wine luncheon at the Rotary Club.

———

Beverley spent every afternoon the following week at Cranham House. The children often found her sitting at the kitchen table, flicking through the pages of Diana's magazines. But despite James's suspicions about Beverley and the lighter, the new friendship clearly made Diana happy. More than once she said it could do no harm. When Byron questioned what she meant by that, she shrugged as if she were throwing a cardigan from her shoulders. She only meant they shouldn't mention it to his father, she said.

He didn't know why his father would disapprove. Byron overheard the women's laughter from the plastic sun loungers, or a room inside the house if there was rain. It was true that the friendship had grown quickly and started in an unusual place, but he didn't see how there could be anything wrong with being happy. He felt proud of the part he and James had played in bringing the women together. Sometimes he idled past with James's notebook, and they were so lost in conversation his mother didn't even look up. Beverley told Diana frequently how kind she was, how beautiful, how different from the other Winston House mothers. These things were true; it seemed natural that Beverley should become his mother's confidante. He was careful to inquire after Jeanie, but Beverley never brought her. Walt could look after her, she said. The knee was almost healed; her two stitches would be out soon. "Everything turned out for the best in the end," she said, smiling at Diana.

Meanwhile, Diana was so taken up with her guest—fetching drinks, listening to her stories, providing her with small plates of canapé food, not to mention vacuuming after her visits, airing the rooms, plumping up cushions, putting away ashtrays and disposing of the empty bottles of advocaat she had begun to provide—

there was no time for her to think about the hubcap. It was as if every time Beverley came to visit, Diana was so busy tidying away one set of evidence, she forgot about the other. And maybe that was good for her too.

When Seymour rang in the mornings she repeated the usual phrases: that no one was there, that of course he had her full attention. In the evenings she said the day had been the same as always. The holidays were going well.

Since they were no longer at school, James and Byron wrote to each other and frequently telephoned. Diana didn't question this; after all, she knew they were friends. She knew that Byron liked to write letters. He sat on the front step every morning, waiting for the postman. When James's correspondence arrived, he rushed it straight to his room. He read it several times over and kept the letters in his Jacob's Crackers tin, along with those from the Queen and Mr. Roy Castle. Meanwhile, he filled pages and pages of the Operation Perfect notebook. He described on one occasion how the women laughed thirty-two times and his mother produced cigarettes from her handbag. "My mother used matches to light them," he read out on the telephone. "And my father does not like women smoking." (*When are you going to mention the issue of the lighter?* hissed James.) Another time, Byron noted that his mother had produced a plate of Tunnock's Tea Cakes. "Beverley ate all of them and did not share. She does not eat fruit. She does not drink tea. Yesterday she finished the Sunquick and we had none for breakfast." Again James repeated, "You still have to confront Beverley about your mother's lighter."

It was clear that Beverley liked Diana. She talked endlessly. She asked her about the other Winston House mothers; she had formed a shrewd picture of them, even in her difficult meeting with them in the tearoom. While Diana answered—explaining about Andrea's right-wing politics or Deirdre's difficult marriage—Beverley watched with a smile as if Diana were something out of a film or a book. When Diana coiled a lock of hair around her finger, for instance, Beverley's hand scampered to her own black hair and she did the same. She told Diana how much she had hated her C of E school when she was a teenager, how she had flunked all her exams. She described once how her father had found her with a boy in her room and thrown him out of the window. She talked about running away when she was sixteen, how she had plans to work in a bar, how none of that had happened. She talked about men and how they always let you down.

"But Walt seems a nice man," said Diana.

"Oh, Walt," said Beverley, rolling her eyes. "I'm not like you, Diana. I'm not a looker."

Diana went on to compliment Beverley's black hair, her cheekbones, her complexion, but Beverley laughed as if they both knew better.

"I have to take what I can get. One day, though. You watch me, Di. One day I'll move on."

Byron only wished she wouldn't abbreviate his mother's name. It was like cutting her in half.

When the women weren't sunbathing or talking in the drawing room, they sat in his mother's bedroom. It was more difficult to find excuses to follow them up there, and sometimes he was afraid Beverley was doing it deliberately to get him out of the way. He had to sit outside or pretend he needed something. Beverley sat in front of the mirror at the dressing table while Diana curled her hair and trimmed her nails. Once she drew black liquid lines around Beverley's eyes and painted the lids different shades of gold and green so that she looked like a queen. "It's like you're professional," said Beverley, staring into the mirror, while Diana merely wiped the brushes clean and said it was a thing she'd picked up. Then Diana commented that red was not Beverley's color, what did she think about pink for her lips, and Beverley said, "I looked a right mess, didn't I? That day I bumped into you at the department store. No wonder those women laughed."

Diana shook her head. No one had laughed, she said, but Beverley gave a look that was like sticking a knife through butter. "They did, Diana. They thought I was dirt. You don't forget a putdown like that."

By midweek it was clear that Lucy didn't like Beverley and it seemed possible that Beverley felt the same way about Lucy. Beverley told the children how lucky they were, growing up somewhere big and nice like Cranham House. They should appreciate it, she said; Jeanie would give her right arm to live somewhere like that. Lucy said very little, she simply stood at her mother's side with a scowl. "You should watch yourself," warned Beverley. "The wind will change and your face'll get stuck." Sometimes Byron forgot that Beverley was a mother. ("My face won't get stuck, will it?" he heard Lucy ask later in the bath. Beverley was being funny, said Diana.)

Byron overheard Beverley telling Diana she was too nice, she let the kids run rings around her, she was surprised Diana didn't get paid help. A gardener. A cook. People like that. And then the air almost gave a crack before she added, "Or a chauffeur, maybe. Because that's how accidents happen, you know. When people do too much."

———

The women were sitting in the drawing room when they began to talk about work.

"I always wanted to be one of those Avon ladies," said Beverley. "I wanted one of those red suitcases with all the brushes and pots. And that lovely red uniform. It was my hands, though. I couldn't because of my hands."

"Your hands are very pretty, Beverley." This wasn't strictly true, but his mother was like that. She saw the good things in other people and sometimes she saw them when they weren't there.

"It's nothing to do with how my hands look," said Beverley, a little impatiently. "It's my arthritis. Sometimes I can't move my fingers, the pain is so bad. Or they get locked. Like this." She held out her hands, and Byron had to glance up because she was showing them like stiff claws. He could understand why she would not want people to see them. "But you could've been an Avon lady, Diana. You'd have looked lovely in that red uniform. You could have been a manager, if you wanted. You'd have been perfect."

Diana shrugged and smiled. "I can't work."

"You can't work? What's wrong with you?"

"It's not because there's anything wrong with me. It's Seymour. His view is that women should stay at home with the children. I had a job before I met him but I couldn't do that now."

"What sort of job?"

"Oh," said Diana. She laughed and reached for her drink.

Beverley pulled a face, as if *she* would not be told by a man whether or not she could work. It was a strange look, and Byron couldn't tell whether it held sympathy for his mother and disdain for his father, or disdain for the two of them and sympathy only for herself. He tried to sketch her expression to show James, but drawing was not his strong point and she came out looking more like a small animal. Byron had to give the drawing ears and whiskers and pretend to James he had observed a stray cat.

James agreed on the telephone that Diana could be an Avon lady if she wished. He asked if there had been any further conversation about the two stitches, and Byron said there had not. He was still noting everything down, with dates and times and exact references to location; it was like doing history at school.

"History is not true, though," said James. "When you think about it, it is just what someone has told us."

Byron pointed out that if it was printed in your history book, it must be true. Again James disagreed: "Supposing the people who wrote our history books didn't see the whole picture? Supposing they lied?"

"Why would they lie to us?"

"To make it easier to understand. To make it look as if one thing leads to another."

"Are you saying history is the same as the lady at the circus with her feet falling off?"

James laughed so hard, Byron was afraid he had dropped the telephone. Byron had to keep whispering his name. Then James asked if he had mentioned the matter of the lighter yet, and Byron said he was building up to it, he just didn't know how to introduce the subject. James gave a small sigh to indicate he was about to be very sensible. "Have you got a pen in your hand?" He dictated the exact words Byron should use.

The opportunity finally came on Friday afternoon. The women were sunbathing on the loungers. Diana had set the table with drinks and cocktail sausages on sticks, as well as celery slices stuffed with soft cheese. She was wearing a blue swimsuit, but Beverley had simply rolled up her dress and sleeves to expose bony flesh so white that she shone in the sun. "I would like to travel," said Diana. "There are so many things I would like to see. The desert, for one. I saw it in a film once. I'd like to feel real heat on my skin, and feel real thirst."

"But you get heat in England," said Beverley, flapping at it with her hand. "Why would you want to go to the desert?"

"To be different. And I mean real heat. Blistering heat."

"You could go to Spain," said Beverley. "You could afford it. I know someone who went to Spain and she came back with a lovely tan. You have to take tablets before you go because the drinking water's filthy and there are no toilets out there, only holes. But my friend came back with a toy donkey. It was wearing one of those hats. What are they called? Those Spanish ones?"

Diana smiled but clearly she didn't know.

"There's a funny word for them," said Beverley.

"Do you mean a sombrero?" said Byron. Beverley continued talking as if he hadn't.

"It was the size of a kid. The donkey, not the hat. She has it in her front room. I'd love a donkey with a sombrero."

His mother bit her lip. Her eyes were glittering. He knew what she was thinking. He knew she was already wanting to find Beverley such a donkey.

"Anyway, your husband won't let you," said Beverley. "He won't let you go to the desert. Or Spain, for that matter. You know what he'd say." She puffed out her chest and flattened her chin into her neck. It wasn't a very accurate impersonation of his father—she had never met him, after all—but there was something suggestive of Seymour in the way she sat very upright and stiff. "I'm not mixing with wops," she bellowed. "Eating wop food." It was exactly what his father would say.

Diana smiled. "You are awful."

"But I like you."

"I'm sorry?"

"It's from the television. 'You're awful, but I like you.' *The Dick Emery Show*? Do you not watch television?"

"I sometimes watch the news on BBC1."

"My God. You're so posh you haven't a clue, Di." Beverley laughed, but there was an edge, in the same way there had been an edge when she told Walt he had forgotten Jeanie's injury the first time they visited Digby Road.

"I'm not posh at all," said Diana quietly. "You shouldn't judge people by appearances. And please don't call me Di. My mother used to, and I don't like it."

Beverley rolled her eyes. "Ooo," she sang. "Get her." She paused, apparently weighing up in her mind whether to say what she had in her mind. Then she gave a laugh as if she had thought better of her reticence: "You're so posh, you thought you didn't need to stop for my little girl. You thought you could get away with it for a whole month."

Diana sat up sharp. For a moment neither woman gave way. Diana held Beverley's gaze long enough for her to know that she understood the exact implication of the words. Beverley stared back as if she had no intention of unsaying them. There was almost violence in the air. And then Diana's head drooped. It was like seeing her knocked to the floor—although she wasn't, of course, she was side by side with Beverley on a new plastic sun lounger. Beverley continued to watch Diana and she didn't say anything or do anything, she simply fixed Diana with that unforgiving look.

Byron said in a rush, "I wonder where your lighter is." He didn't think about it. He simply wanted Beverley to let go of his mother.

"I beg your pardon?" said Diana.

"Would you like me to fetch it? Your lighter? Or is it—is it still lost?"

"But we're not smoking," said Beverley. He could hardly look at her. "Why would we want a lighter?"

It was only as the conversation progressed that Byron realized that James had failed to prescribe what everyone else should say. There was nothing for it but to keep going and hope for the best.

He said, "I haven't seen the lighter for a whole week."

"Well, it must be somewhere," said Diana vaguely. "Down the back of a chair or something."

"I have looked all over the house and it isn't. I wonder"—and here he spoke specifically to Beverley's toes—"if someone has stolen it."

"Stolen it?" repeated Diana.

"Put it in their handbag by mistake?"

There was a pause. The sun beat his head.

Beverley said slowly, "Is he talking to me?" Even without looking at her face, Byron knew that her eyes were right on him.

His mother almost yelped. "Of course he isn't!" She leapt up from her sun lounger and began smoothing her towel, though there was not a fold to be seen, it had been soft and blue beneath her. "Byron, go inside. Make another jug of Sunquick for Beverley." His sandals felt welded to the terrace. He couldn't move.

"I would never steal from you, Diana," said Beverley quietly. "I can't think why he would say that."

His mother kept saying, "I know, I know, I know," and "He isn't, he isn't, he isn't."

"Maybe I should go?"

"Of course you shouldn't go."

"No one has ever accused me of stealing."

"It wasn't what he meant. And anyway the lighter was nothing. It was cheap."

"Just because I live in Digby Road doesn't mean I steal things. I didn't even have my handbag when you lost your lighter. I left it in the hall."

His mother was dashing around the terrace, picking up bowls and putting them down, straightening the plastic chairs, plucking scraps of weed from between the paving stones. If anyone was showing Signs of Guilt, it was she.

"My mistake, my mistake, my mistake," he repeated miserably, but it was all too late.

"I'm off to the little girls' room," said Beverley, seizing her hat.

As Beverley left, Diana turned to Byron. She was so shocked, her face was pointed. She said nothing, she merely shook her head, as if she couldn't understand who he was anymore.

The terrace wobbled, and his eyes filled with tears. All over the garden, fruit trees and flowers sprang leaks and grew new edges. Even the moor spilled into the sky. Then Beverley appeared at the French windows with a laugh. "Found it!" She held the lighter between her fingers and it glinted in the sun. "You were right, Diana. It was down the back of your sofa."

She moved between Byron and Diana and picked up the sun

cream from the table. Squirting a button-size pool of it onto her palm, she offered to do Diana's shoulders. She mentioned something about her figure, how lucky Diana was, but she made no further reference to the lighter or what had happened in Digby Road. "You have such lovely, soft skin. But look, you need to be careful with your coloring. You're burning. If I ever get to Spain I'm going to get you one of those funny big Spanish hats."

This time Byron did not correct her.

That weekend, things got worse. His father was in a strange mood. He kept opening drawers, checking cupboards, hunting through papers. When Diana asked if he had lost something, he glared at her and said that she knew what he was looking for.

"But I don't," she stammered. "I haven't a clue."

He mentioned the word *gifts* and Byron's heart plummeted.

"Gifts?"

"There is a blank stub. In the checkbook. Have you been buying gifts again?"

Diana gave a broken-up laugh. Oh yes, that was her mistake, she said. Her fingers flew like frightened birds toward her teeth. It was Lucy's birthday present. The shop was keeping it until her birthday. She must have been so excited she had forgotten to fill in the checkbook again.

Remembering she was not supposed to bite her nails, she gripped one hand in the other. Seymour studied her as if she was a new acquaintance. She promised she would be more careful with the checkbook in future.

"Careful?" he repeated.

"You know what I mean," she said.

He said he didn't. He hadn't a clue.

Diana mentioned that the children were listening and he nodded and she nodded and they went their separate ways.

At least nothing could happen when Diana was in the garden and his father was in his study. Byron and Lucy played board games in the drawing room and he let her win because he liked to see her happy.

Then things took another turn for the worse on Sunday morning.

Emerging from his room, his father beckoned Byron to one side. After lunch he would like to talk man-to-man, he said, and as he did so a sad, sour smell rushed from his mouth. Byron was so terrified that his father had found out about the hubcap, he could barely swallow his roast dinner. It seemed he was not the only one who had no appetite. His mother barely touched her plate. His father kept clearing his throat. Only Lucy asked for extra potatoes and gravy.

His father began the man-to-man conversation by asking if Byron would like a fudge sweet. At first Byron wondered if it was a test and he said he wasn't hungry, but when his father lifted the lid and said go on, one wouldn't harm, Byron worried it was wrong to refuse the fudge, and so he took one. His father asked how he was progressing with his scholarship work, how his end-of-year report had compared with James Lowe's, and Byron tried to say everything was going well without dribbling from the fudge or talking with his mouth open. His father pulled the stopper from the decanter and poured a tumbler of whisky.

"I am wondering how things are at home," he said, examining his glass, as if he were reading the remark from inside it.

Byron said they were jolly good. He added that his mother was a careful driver and then there was such silence it was dark as water and he wished he had said nothing. He wished he could swallow the words, along with the fudge sweet.

"I suppose she is busy?" said his father. Above his shirt collar the skin had turned so mottled it was like shadow.

"Busy?" said Byron.

"Doing housework?"

"Very busy." He didn't know why, but his father's eyes were wet and laced with red veins like netting. It hurt to look at him.

"Seeing friends?"

"She doesn't have any friends."

"No one who comes to visit?"

Byron's pulse raced. "No."

Byron waited for the next sentence but it did not happen. In reply, his father looked back at his glass. For a few moments there was nothing but the steady ticking of the clock. Byron had never blatantly lied to his father before. He wondered when his father would see through him but he didn't, he kept staring into his drink, not guessing the truth. Byron realized he wasn't afraid of his father. They were men together. It was not too late to ask for his help. It was not too late to confess about the hubcap. After all, Byron had been out of his depth with Beverley and the lighter.

Seymour's drink gave a jolt and slopped over the rim of the glass, splashing onto his papers. He said, "Your mother is a very beautiful woman."

"Father?"

"It's not surprising if people want to visit."

"Something happened recently. It's to do with time—"

"It doesn't mean any harm if another man looks. I am lucky, after all. I am lucky that she chose me."

His father gazed at Byron with his sore eyes and Byron had to pretend he was having difficulty with the fudge sweet. "You were saying?" his father said.

Byron said he was saying nothing, really.

"Well. It's good to have a conversation. It's good to talk man-to-man."

It was, said Byron.

Seymour poured himself another measure. It sent rainbow glints of sunlight as he lifted the crystal tumbler toward his opened mouth. The amber liquid vanished in one go. He mopped his chin. "My own father never did. Talk, I mean. Not man-to-man. When my mother died, he died a week later. It was shortly before I met your mother." The words ran together. It was hard to understand, but Seymour kept stumbling through them. "When I was six he took me to a lake. He threw me in. Survivors swim, he said. I was afraid there were crocodiles. I still don't like water."

Byron remembered his father's face when he heard about the accident with the bridge and Andrea Lowe's complaint. The skin had turned so gray and stiff, Byron had feared a whipping. As if reading his thoughts, his father said, "Maybe I overreacted. About the pond. But you see, he was not an easy man, my father. He was not easy at all." He appeared to run out of words.

As Byron clicked open the door, he heard the clink of the glass stopper on the decanter. His father called, "So you will tell me? If your mother has a new friend?"

Byron promised he would and then he shut the door.

8

The Huddle

All morning Jim sits in his Father Christmas chair, hoping for Eileen, and all morning she does not come. Sometimes his mind plays tricks on him. He sees a strong figure in a green coat, pacing from the car park, and he briefly succumbs to the fantasy that it is she. He goes so far as to imagine their conversation. It resembles most of those he overhears beside the automatic doors to the supermarket. The only difference between the real conversations and the one inside his head is that the imagined one always ends with Eileen's invitation for a drink, and his unequivocal acceptance.

The coats that pass him, however, are never holly green. The women are never noisy. They are slim, they are tidy, they are all the same. It is only in seeing all these not-Eileens that Jim understands how truly Eileen she is. And in allowing himself to pretend she is here, he must also acknowledge that she isn't. It is like missing her twice over.

He imagines showing her the light across the moor on a moon-filled night. The beauty of an early morning. A wren flickering, slight as a thought, on air. There is an apple tree on the moor, and its fruit still clings to its leafless branches like frosted baubles; he would like to show her that too. He would like to show her the winter sunset, the underbelly of the clouds an electric pink, its final splashes of red light on her cheeks, her mouth, her hair.

But she will never find him attractive. Peering into the mirror in the men's urinals, he finds a mass of silvering hair and two deep eyes. He tries to do a smile and his skin is shot all over with lines. He tries not to do a smile and the skin hangs loose. He is past loving now. There were offers long ago and they came to nothing. He remembers a nurse who told him once he had a nice mouth. He was young then and so was she. There were female patients too who looked at him. They watched him in the garden and waved. Even in his life outside Besley Hill, there have been encounters. The woman for whom he raked leaves, for example, a very presentable middle-aged lady, invited him several times to join her for rabbit pie. He was in his thirties. He liked her. But it was like pretending to be a shiny new cup when he knew he had a hairline crack. There was no point getting close to anyone, because by then there were the rituals. Besides, he knew what happened when he loved people. He knew what happened when he intervened.

In the lunch break, Jim changes into his café uniform and visits the supermarket. He finds himself in the stationery aisle, where he stares at all the pens. Fiber-tipped, uni-ball, gel stick, retractable, jumbo highlighters. They come in every color. There is even one for corrections. Looking at them, shiny and purposeful, he sees Eileen's point. Why give a person something dying? He chooses a selection and pays for them at the checkout. He does not catch the assistant's eye, though recognizing his orange hat and T-shirt she asks him how things are upstairs. They're quiet in the store, she says. It's recession depression. Who's going to drive all the way over the moor to a supermarket, even if it's been refurbished? "We'll be lucky if we have our jobs next year."

He thinks of the neat bow of Eileen's shoelaces, and his stomach flutters.

"Why do you want to know her address?" says Paula when he asks if anyone knows where she lives. "Why do you want her phone number?"

Jim tries to assume the careless air of someone who doesn't.

"I hope you're reporting her to the police," says the small girl, Moira. She writes down Eileen's address and number.

Paula adds that she keeps getting text messages on her phone from those legal firms who waive costs.

"That's what you should do," says Moira. "You should sue."

"I knew someone once who knocked her head open in a furniture store," Paula says. "She got a sofa bed and free meal vouchers. She lived for a whole year on Scandinavian meatballs."

"Haven't you all got work to do?" shouts Mr. Meade from the servery.

The truth is, Mr. Meade is on a short fuse. Human Resources have reviewed sales figures before the year-end and sent out an urgent email. Trade is seriously down. Local regional managers will be required to take Saturday off work and attend a nearby Center of Excellence. They will spend the day with actors learning about Efficacy in the Workplace and Team Building. There will be demonstrations and role-play exercises. "Don't they realize it's the week before Christmas?" says Mr. Meade. "Don't they realize we have work to do? They can't just send us off with one day's notice. We're rushed off our feet."

Jim, Paula, and Moira survey the empty café. There is only one customer. "Hello there!" calls Darren. He gives a thumbs-up in case they have forgotten who he is.

It is a surprise to everyone that Mr. Meade returns from the Center of Excellence on Monday full of enthusiasm. He asks customers and staff how they are doing. When they reply that they are well, or so-so, he sings, "Good, good. Splendid stuff. Well done, you." It is about affirmation, he says. The power of now. This is the new beginning.

"He's probably about to get the sack," says Paula to Moira.

Mr. Meade laughs heartily, as if Paula is a scream.

The reason the café is not doing well, says Mr. Meade, is lack of confidence. The café does not believe in itself. It is not behaving like a successful café. Paula listens with her arms folded and one hip hitched higher than the other.

"Does that mean we get to ditch the orange hats?" she says. "Does that mean Jim stops dressing like a twat?"

"No, no," cries Mr. Meade. He laughs good-humoredly. "The orange hats work. They give us a sense of connection. And Jim's Father Christmas outfit is a marvelous gesture of goodwill. We need more things like that."

"More orange hats?" says Paula doubtfully.

"More joie de vivre," says Mr. Meade.

"More what de what?" says Moira.

"You could hand out free drinks and stuff," says Darren, who keeps forgetting he is a customer.

"That would upset Health and Safety," says Mr. Meade gravely. It is clear that he has an alternative idea up his sleeve. "What we are going to do, team, is huddle."

"Huddle?" repeats Paula flatly.

Mr. Meade is so excited, he skips his weight from one foot to the other. He opens his arms wide and wriggles his fingers, beckoning his few staff to draw close. Paula drifts toward him, followed by Darren. Moira twiddles her hair and takes one small step at a time. Jim limps, but actually the movement is more like treading water.

"Closer, closer!" laughs Mr. Meade. "I won't bite!"

Moira and Paula shuffle forward. Jim wonders if anyone would notice if he disappeared. Not immediately. Just in a shuffling backward sort of way.

Mr. Meade throws his arms wide enough to reach their shoulders. Around him stands his band of staff, stiff as boards. "Huddle!" cries Mr. Meade. "Come along, Jim! Huddle!" He waves at them to come closer. He does it with little hand movements, the way he helps female customers to park their Range Rovers.

Says Paula, "What about Darren?"

"What about him?" says Mr. Meade.

"Is he supposed to huddle as well?"

Mr. Meade looks at his three members of staff, one of whom is ripping out her split ends, another who is scowling like a thundercloud, and the last of whom appears to be moving almost imperceptibly backward. Mr. Meade makes a face that suggests compromise. "Huddle, Darren!" he calls.

Eagerly Darren darts forward and weaves one arm around Paula's waist. The other arm, the one nearest to Mr. Meade, wafts midair as if it doesn't quite belong to anyone.

"Make room for Jim!" says Mr. Meade.

Paula extends her hand to welcome Jim. He has no choice. He is suddenly hot, congested with the claustrophobia of it. He wonders if he will scream. Paula's left hand is on his right shoulder, resting there like a tiny bird. Mr. Meade's right hand thumps Jim's left shoulder.

"Huddle, huddle!" sings Mr. Meade. There is an overpowering smell of fabric conditioner. For an aroma that is supposed to be fragrant as a summer morning, it suggests something surprisingly unpleasant. "Closer, closer!"

In silence the group shuffles closer, closer. Their reluctant feet make small scraping sounds on the lino. They are so closer, closer, the faces in front of Jim's swim. He is overwhelmed by the intimacy of it, by the feeling of them sucking him in like a vacuum cleaner. He towers over the group. "Hug me, Jim!" says Mr. Meade.

Jim lifts his hand to Mr. Meade's shoulder. There it stays, aching up and down the muscles. "Isn't this good?" says Mr. Meade.

No one answers.

"Of course there were about twenty of us at the conference," says Mr. Meade. "Senior management and personnel. And the actors were professional, of course. It was a bit different."

"Have we finished yet?" says Paula.

Mr. Meade again laughs. "Finished? This is only stage one. What I want you to do now, team, is think about the person beside you."

"What, Darren?" says Paula.

"And Jim too," says Mr. Meade. "Think something positive. Think what you would really like to say about them."

There is a constipated silence. "Supposing we can't?" says Moira at last. Her hand is on Mr. Meade's shoulder.

Mr. Meade fails to answer. He closes his eyes, his lips twitching as if there are words hatching in his mouth and getting ready to burst free. Jim closes his eyes too, but the room lurches so fast he has to open them again. Darren has crumpled up his face like a piece of paper.

"I've done that," says Paula.

"Now can we stop?" says Moira.

"No, no," says Mr. Meade. "We have to say it."

"Say what we were thinking?" repeats Moira. She looks stricken.

But Mr. Meade laughs as if this is tremendous fun. "I'll go first, so you get the hang of it." He turns first to Paula. "Paula, I admire you. You are a very strong young lady. When I first interviewed you, I had my worries. It was because you had a nose ring and all those studs in your ears. I worried about Health and Safety issues. But you taught me not to be prejudiced."

Paula turns the color of her hair. Mr. Meade continues: "Jim, you are never late. You are a very reliable worker. Moira, you bring an air of creativity to the workplace and I hope your mother's rash clears up soon. And, Darren, I have come to like you."

"Aw, that's nice," croons Paula. "I knew this woman once. She wrote to all her friends to tell them she loved them, and next day, guess what?"

"I don't know," says Darren. He is the only one who still has his eyes closed.

"She had a heart attack."

"Back to the huddle," says Mr. Meade. "Who would like to go next?"

There is an uncomfortable silence as if all four are not in fact present. Moira is glued to a particularly interesting strand of her hair. Paula blows out her mouth, although she has no bubblegum in there. Darren might be asleep. Jim makes a series of small popping noises. Mr. Meade sighs, a little disappointed but not yet downhearted.

"Come on, team," he laughs. "Someone must have something positive to say."

A voice nudges its way into the silence. "Jim, you're a good man. You spray all the tables and you never miss one out. Mr. Meade, you have some weird ideas but you kind of want the world to be a better place, and I like your car. Moira, you have nice breasts."

"Thank you, Darren," says Mr. Meade, only Darren clearly hasn't finished.

"But Paula, oh, Paula. I love the way you sort of chew your fingers when you are thinking. I love the way your skin is like honey. I love the soft little bit of skin behind your ears. When you talk I just want to sit and watch you forever. You wear really nice skirts. You have eyes like Christmas nuts."

For a while no one speaks. But this is a different silence from the beginning. It is a childlike silence, where the lack of words is to do with wonder, as opposed to judgment.

"It's just as well that Eileen woman isn't here," says Paula. "There's some stuff I'd like to say to her." The group silence becomes a group laugh.

"Jim?" says Mr. Meade. "Your turn?"

But Jim is stunned. In his mind there is nothing but a woman with flaming hair, the smallest feet, and a coat that rucks in the effort to fit around her. He understands the truth with the wildness and urgency of an accident. The psychic counselor was right after all. He must come clean. He must own the past, whatever that means. And the sole place, he sees this so clearly it is like shouting in his head, the sole place that is big enough to contain his chaos is the one that is Eileen. She is his last and only chance.

"Excuse me?" calls a voice from the café floor.

The huddle springs open, like a multiheaded orange-hatted beast. A customer watches from the servery with a look of fear. She says, "Is it too late to order the Festive Snack Deal?"

9

A Surprise

In the second week of the summer holidays, Beverley spent every day at Cranham House. She was there from morning to evening. Sometimes when Byron went to bed, he could still hear the women talking on the terrace. Their voices filled the evening air like the thick, sweet perfume of night-scented stocks and white nicotiana. "You're right. You're right," his mother would howl as Beverley did one of her impressions or told a story. One morning Byron opened his bedroom curtains and she was already sunbathing in her purple hat with a drink in a glass tumbler. It was only the addition of Jeanie and a pair of white plastic boots that made it clear she had not been there all night. Jeanie stood balanced on the garden table. The stitches were gone from her knee. There was no need for a plaster. Nevertheless he preferred to avoid Jeanie.

Lucy refused point-blank to play with her. Jeanie smelled, she said. Jeanie had also ripped the heads from Lucy's Cindy dolls. Byron tried to snap them back, but it was tricky to fit the cavity of their necks over the bump of plastic that was the top of their spines. He put the dismantled parts in a shoebox with a lid. It alarmed him to see all those smiling faces without bodies.

Meanwhile, Byron continued to record observations in the notebook about the meetings between Beverley and his mother. James posted him a secret code, involving swapping letters of the alphabet, as well as new code names for Beverley and Diana ("Mrs. X" and "Mrs. Y"), but it was complicated and Byron frequently made mistakes.

The two women listened to music. They opened the French windows and set up the record player on the table so that they could dance on the terrace. Seymour's album collection was sober—("What century was he born in?" said Beverley)—and Beverley brought a box of her own records. They listened to the Carpenters and Bread. Beverley's favorites were two singles by Harry Nilsson and Donny Osmond. Byron stood at the drawing room window and watched. Beverley's movements were jerky and involved shaking her hair a lot, whereas Diana glided around the terrace as if she were carried on a current. When Diana offered to show her a step, they moved arm in arm, Diana's neck held high, her arms poised on air, while Beverley studied her own feet so that, even though they were the same height, Diana looked taller. Byron heard his mother offer to teach Beverley all she knew, but when Beverley asked what that was exactly, his mother broke away and said it was nothing. If "Puppy Love" came on, or a song by Gilbert O'Sullivan, Beverley clung to Diana and they moved in a slow shuffle around and around on the spot. At the end, Beverley would return to her drink, staring from beneath her floppy hat.

"You're so lucky, Diana," she would say. "You were just born beautiful."

Beverley said that your future is in your name. It's your ticket to success. How could a girl ever become someone if she was called Beverley? If only she'd been given a classy name, like Diana or Byron or Seymour. Things would have been different.

That week Beverley began to borrow clothes of Diana's. It was only a small thing to begin with, a pair of lace gloves to protect her hands from the sun. Then the outfits became more sizeable. When, for instance, Beverley spilled a glass of yellow drink down her front, Diana rushed to fetch her a blouse and pencil skirt. Beverley asked if she could borrow a pair of heels, because she couldn't exactly wear sandals with a skirt like that. She wore all these items to go home. The next day, Byron reported in his notebook, they were still missing.

"Those clothes are out of date," said Beverley. "You should get something more fashionable."

"Between you and me," Byron wrote, "I believe she has stolen them. I also now believe she had the lighter in her handbag all along."

The shopping trip was Beverley's idea. Diana drove them into town and they parked near the department store. They tried on matching dresses while Jeanie swung between the rails and Lucy scowled. They stopped for more advocaat at the off-license and a bottle of cherry cola for the children. When Lucy said they were not allowed sugary drinks, on account of their teeth, Beverley laughed heartily. "You lot need to live more," she said. The women paraded their new kaftan dresses on the terrace and it was like watching two contrasting halves of the same thing. Diana, blond and slim and graceful; Beverley, black-haired and undernourished, and altogether more glued to the spot.

After lunch, Byron was fetching lemonade for his mother and Beverley when he interrupted a conversation. He could tell it was important, because his mother and Beverley had their heads so close that Diana's blond hair appeared to grow out of Beverley's black parting. Beverley was painting Diana's nails. They didn't even look up as Byron tiptoed across the carpet. Carefully he removed the glasses from the tray and set them on coasters. And that was when he heard his mother say, "Of course I wasn't in love with him. I just thought I was."

Byron edged from the room as quietly as he had entered. He couldn't think what his mother was talking about. He was aware of not wanting to hear any more while also not being able to move away. Then Jeanie gave a wild laugh from the garden, and he hid on his knees, cramming himself against the hall side of the drawing room door, because he didn't want to play with Jeanie again. Now that her leg was healing, she seemed to like hiding in bushes and running out at him when he least expected her. It was dreadful. Crushing his eye to the crack between the door and its frame, he could see the two women as if they were caught in a shard of light. He reached for his notebook, and even as he opened it the binding creaked and his mother glanced up. "I heard something."

It was nothing, said Beverley. She told Diana to go on. She placed her hand on Diana's and he didn't know why but the longer it stayed there the more he wished she would take it away. He wished it very much.

His mother began to speak. Her voice was soft and he caught only unconnected phrases, words that at first made no sense. He had to flatten his ear to the crack. She was saying, ". . . an old friend. We bumped into— I didn't mean any harm. And one day— It all grew from there."

Byron's pencil stalled over the pages of his notebook. He didn't know what he was writing. When he pressed his eye back to the splinter of light, his mother had sat back in her chair and was emptying her glass. "It's a relief to say this," she sighed.

Beverley agreed that of course it was a relief. She asked for Diana's other hand so that she could finish her nails. She talked about how lonely it must be at Cranham House, and all the time Diana watched her hand in Beverley's and agreed that yes, it was. So lonely sometimes she could hardly bear it. "But the person I'm thinking of, I met before we moved here. Just after Seymour and I were married, in fact."

Beverley's eyebrows shot up and stayed there. She dipped her brush into the polish. Byron couldn't say how, but it felt as if she were somehow beckoning the words out of his mother's mouth simply by saying nothing.

"Seymour found out. He's a clever man and he sees straight through me. If I try to lie because I want to buy a little gift, or something secret, he's on to me like a hawk. Although at the time Ted didn't feel like a lie."

"Ted?"

"He just felt like a young friend."

"If Ted was only your young friend, I don't see the problem."

"Hm," said Diana, suggesting that—despite Beverley's inability to see the problem—there was one and it was of considerable size. "Seymour bought the house here after that. He said the country air would be good for me. I owe everything to him. You have to remember."

Finishing Diana's nails, Beverley passed her a cigarette and flicked at the retrieved lighter. She warned Diana to keep still or the color would be ruined. Diana pulled long drags from the cigarette and blew the smoke above Beverley's head, where it spread like opaque fingers and disappeared.

"Seymour needs me, you see," she said quietly. "It's frightening sometimes, how much he needs me."

Byron could barely move. It had never occurred to him that his mother might have loved anyone other than his father, that there might once have been a young man called Ted. His head was hot and spinning, dashing all around the things he could remember, overturning them like stones and trying to make sense, trying to see the underside of them. He thought of the man she had once mentioned who liked champagne, and her unexplained visits to Digby Road. Was that what she meant? Then she continued speaking, and he had to clasp his damp hands in a ball in order to concentrate. "When I met Seymour I'd had enough. Enough of those men who love you and then disappear. The theater was full of them. Or even the men who waited at the stage door and wrote letters and took us out for dinner. They all had wives. They all had families and they never—" She left the sentence as if she was afraid of finishing it or wasn't sure how to. "Seymour was persistent. He was traditional too. I liked that. He brought me roses. He took me to the cinema on my afternoons off. We were married within two months. It was a small wedding, but he didn't want the fuss. And my friends were not the sort of people you'd invite. We didn't want my past to come with me."

Beverley gave a splutter as if she had just choked on something in her drink. "Hang on. What was your job exactly?"

But Diana said nothing. She rubbed out her cigarette and reached straight for another. She laughed, but for once it was a hard sound as if she were looking at herself and not liking the person she saw. She pulled again on the cigarette and yawned out a wraith of her blue smoke. "Let's just say, I took after my mother."

For the first time, Byron could not write in the notebook. He could not telephone James. He did not want words. He wanted nothing to do with the meanings of things. He ran and ran across the lawn, trying to leave his thoughts behind, and when Jeanie called to him, laughing, to wait he ran faster. His breath cut his throat and his legs felt boned but he kept going. He crawled under the fruit cages, and the smell was so full, the raspberries so red, the prickles so sharp, he was dizzy. He sat there for a long time. Later he heard his mother call his name from the house but he still didn't move. He didn't want to know about Ted or his father or the job his mother couldn't mention, and now that he did, he didn't know how to stop knowing. If only James had not asked him to take notes. Byron stayed hidden until he glimpsed Beverley and Jeanie strolling down the drive, waving their good-byes. They were not hand in hand; Beverley stalked ahead, beneath her purple hat, while Jeanie ran large circles around her. Once he saw Beverley stop and shout, though he couldn't hear what she said. The house was a glaring white in the late-afternoon sun, and behind it the sharp rim of the moor sliced into the sky.

James telephoned first thing the next morning. He was very excited about a new Operation Perfect folder he was making. He explained that he had redrawn Byron's map of Digby Road because the scale of it was not right, and all the time that James spoke Byron felt he was on the opposite side of a window, looking in at his friend and unable to be heard.

"What happened yesterday?" said James. "Did you write everything down?"

Byron said that nothing had happened.

"Do you have a cold or something?" said James.

Byron blew his nose and replied that he had a stinker of a cold.

At the weekend there was rain. It flattened the nicotiana, the delphiniums, and the stocks. Diana and Seymour sat looking out of windows from different parts of the house. Sometimes they passed and one or the other of them made a remark that the other appeared to only half hear. Then Seymour observed that there was an odd smell in the house, a sweet one. Diana claimed that it must be her new perfume. Why was the smell in his study? Seymour asked. Where was his paperweight? And while he was on the subject of missing items, why was there another blank stub in the checkbook?

Diana emptied her glass as if it were medicinal. She must have moved the paperweight when she was dusting. She would look for it later. She sat down to serve dinner. She looked exhausted.

"What are you wearing?" said Seymour.

"This?" Diana sounded surprised, as if moments before she had been wearing something entirely different, a cocktail dress, for instance, or a two-piece suit from Jaeger. "Oh. It's a kaftan."

"It's a hippie garment."

"It's the fashion, darling."

"But you look like a hippie. You look like a feminist."

"More vegetables?" She ladled each plate with three extra boiled carrots and a golden pool of butter. Seymour's voice bulldozed the silence.

"Take it off."

"I'm sorry?"

"Go upstairs. Get rid of it."

Byron stared at his plate. He wanted to be able to eat as if everything was normal, but his mother was making small swallowing noises and his father was breathing like a bear. It was hard to want your buttered carrots with all that going on.

"Beverley has a kaftan too," said Lucy. "It is exac'ly the same."

Seymour paled. The little boy rushed into his face again and he looked for a moment as if he had no idea what to do.

"Beverley? Who is Beverley?"

"Mummy's friend," said Lucy. She took a large forkful of her lunch.

"A Winston House mother?"

"Jeanie doesn't go to Winston House. They live in Digby Road. She wants to go on my space hopper and I won't let her because she is dangerous. She has black bits on her teeth, here and here and here." Lucy pointed at her open mouth. There was quite a lot of carrot in there so it was hard to tell where precisely she was pointing.

His father turned to Byron. Byron didn't have to raise his eyes to know. "This woman comes to visit? Is that right? Does she bring anyone else?" Byron's head began to bang.

"Leave them alone." Diana threw down her fork with a clatter and pushed her plate away. "For God's sake, Seymour, I'm only wearing a bloody kaftan. I'll change after dinner."

She had never sworn like that before. Seymour moved back his chair and stood. He walked to Diana and stopped, looking like a black pillar behind a little fountain of color. Seymour's fingers tightened around the rim of her chair. They were not on her skin, but all the same it was like watching him touch a part of her and it was hard to tell if he was tickling or hurting. The children did not move. He said quietly, "You will not wear that dress. You will not see that woman again." Seymour's fingers kept squeezing her chair, while Diana's made tiny noises against the tablecloth like a bird flapping its wings in a cage.

Suddenly, Seymour left the room. Diana patted her neck with the backs of her hands, as if she were pressing everything into place, the veins and the skin and the muscle. Byron wanted to say how much he liked her new dress, but before he could she told the children to run outside and play.

That night Byron tried to read his *Look and Learn* annuals. He couldn't stop seeing his father with his fingers on his mother's chair. So much had happened, and for the first time he had no idea how to share any of it with James. At last he fell into a dream about people with heads that were too big for their bodies and whose voices were low but persistent, like cries without words.

Waking, he realized that the voices belonged to his parents. As he crossed the landing, the sounds grew louder. He pushed the door open a crack and stood stock-still, not believing what he was seeing. He could make out his father's torso, almost blue, and beneath him the profile of his mother. His father dug and dug at her body and her arm flailed at the pillow. Byron closed the door without clicking the handle.

He didn't even know he was going outside until he was there. The moon was pale, the sky bruised. There seemed to be nothing between himself and the moor. The night stole all the detail of foreground and middle spaces. He moved through the garden and opened the picket gate into the meadow. He wanted to throw something, stones, and he did, he aimed them right at the moon, but they merely scattered around his feet. They didn't even touch the dark. Of course James was right about the Apollo landings. How could a man get all the way up there? How could Byron have been so stupid as to believe in NASA and the photographs? He climbed over the fencing and made his way to the pond.

There he sat on a stone. The air was alive with tiny clickings and scrapings and patterings. He didn't know what to think anymore. He didn't know if his mother was good or bad, if his father was good or bad. He didn't know if Beverley was good or bad—if she had stolen the lighter, the paperweight, the clothes—or if there was another explanation. The night seemed to be so slow. Byron kept looking at the horizon, waiting for the crack of dawn light over the east and the first blaze of sun, but they didn't come. The night just went on and on. Slowly he returned to the house.

He wondered if his mother would be waiting, if she would be worrying, but the only sound came from his father's clocks, striking at the silence. Time was a different thing entirely inside his home, as if it were bigger than the silence, but it wasn't really. It was all made up. He wrote a brief letter for James: "Jeanie's leg now fully healed. Tout va bien. Yours sincerely, Byron Hemmings." That was the end of Operation Perfect, he thought. It was the end of many things.

Byron never saw the kaftan dress after that weekend. Maybe it found its way to the bonfire, like the mint-green dress and the matching cardigan and shoes; he did not ask. He put away his torch, his magnifying glass, his Brooke Bond tea cards, his annuals. They seemed to belong to someone else. And he was not the only one who appeared changed. After the weekend, his mother was more guarded too. She set up the plastic sun loungers on the terrace for Beverley, but she smiled less and did not fetch the record player. She did not offer drinks.

"You only need to say if I'm in the way," said Beverley.

"Of course you're not in the way."

"I know you have all those other mothers to see."

"I'm not seeing anyone."

"Or maybe you have other people you prefer to dance with?"

"I don't always feel like dancing," said Diana.

Here Beverley laughed and rolled her eyes, as if she had heard differently.

August 2 was Lucy's sixth birthday. Byron was woken by his mother's voice, and the flowery scent of her, tickling him out of sleep. She had an idea for a surprise, she whispered. It was going to be the happiest day. They must dress quickly. As they headed downstairs, she couldn't stop laughing. She was wearing a red summer dress, the color of a field poppy, and had already packed towels and a picnic.

The drive lasted several hours, and his mother hummed nearly all the way. Looking at her from the backseat of the Jaguar, he admired the wave of her hair and the softness of her skin and the pearliness of her fingernails, placed exactly right on the steering wheel. It seemed the first time in many weeks that she had driven the car without looking frightened. When Lucy needed a lavatory they stopped at a small roadside café and she told them they could have ice cream. The vendor asked if they would like flakes or sauce, and she said yes to both.

"They look like good kids," he said. And she laughed and said yes, they were.

They sat to eat at a metal table in the sun because she didn't want ice cream in the car, and while they ate she closed her eyes, tilting her face to the warmth. When Lucy whispered that she was asleep, Diana opened one eye and laughed. "I can hear every word," she said. Already her forehead and shoulder blades were tinged pink with the heat, and it was like little fingerprints all over her.

The sun was blazing by the time they arrived at the beach. Families had set up homes for themselves on the sand with wind-breaks and deckchairs. The sea crinkled silver, and Byron watched the sunlight, the way it landed on the moving waves like sparks. The children took off their sandals, and the sand burned beneath their toes. Diana showed them how to make castles and to bury their legs. There were still sugary smudges on their skin from the ice cream, and the sand glued to their knees and chafed when she rubbed it away. Afterward they visited the pier and she showed them the penny slot machines, the candyfloss stalls, the dodgem cars. She bought them each a stick of rock.

In the House of Mirrors, their mother swept them from one glass to another. "Look at me!" she kept laughing. Her happiness was like something in the air that day, something sweet they could taste on their tongues and swallow. Sidling close to her, Byron and Lucy held her hands and found shortened, fattened, or elongated versions of themselves in the mirrors. The children were sticky and red from the heat, their clothes creased, their hair tousled. It was only their mother in the middle with her poppy-red dress, her puff of hair, who looked beautiful.

She sat them on a bench to eat their sandwiches. While they ate, she strayed to the edge of the pier and looked out over the sea. She held her hand over her eyes to block the sun. When a passing gentleman stopped to say hello, she laughed. "Be off with you. I've got children."

Outside the theater at the end of the pier there were notices: STALLS FULL. GALLERY FULL. Diana licked the tip of her handkerchief and wiped the children's faces clean before pushing at the glass doors and leading them inside. She held her finger to her mouth, urging them to be silent.

The foyer was empty but they could hear laughter and applause beyond the velvet curtain. Diana asked a uniformed woman at the ticket kiosk if there were any seats left, and the woman said there was a box free, if that would suit them. While Diana counted the money from her purse, she told the woman that it was years since she'd seen a show. She asked if the woman had heard of the White Supremo and Pamela the Lady with a Beard, as well as a dancing group called Sally's Girls, and the ticket lady shook her head. "We get them all here," she said; and once again Diana laughed and took the children's hands. A young man with a box hat and a torch led the way up the darkened stairs and along a corridor. Diana asked for two programs and gave them to the children, one each.

A huge roar of laughter hit them as they stepped into their box. The stage was brilliantly illuminated, like a well of yellow. Byron couldn't make out what the people on stage were saying or what exactly the crowd was laughing about, because at first he wasn't listening, he was only watching. He thought the audience was laughing because of him, because they were late, but taking his velvet seat he realized that the crowd was pointing at the man on stage and gripping their stomachs, they were so amused.

The man was juggling plates. He ran between them, spinning china on wires that looked like stalks, and as the plates whipped around they caught the light. Every time a plate faltered to a halt, about to fall and crash, the man seemed to remember at the last moment and rush back to it. Diana watched with her fingers to her eyes, as if hiding. Behind the juggler was a painted scene of a terrace by a lake. The artist had even caught how the moon shone over the water in a single silver path toward the horizon. At the end of his act the juggler gave a bow, like a great flop from the waist. He blew kisses to the audience, and Byron was sure that one landed right on his mother.

When the curtain rose again, the moon-filled lake had vanished. In its place was a painted beach with palm trees. There were women with real grass skirts and flowers in their hair. A man sang about the sun and the women danced around him, bearing pineapples and jugs of wine but never stopping to eat. Then the curtain bounced down on them and once again the scene was whisked away.

There were several more acts, each with a new painted backdrop. There was a magician who kept making mistakes, a violinist in a glittering suit, the troupe of dancers again, dressed this time in sequins and feathers. Byron had never seen anything like it, not even at the circus. Diana clapped after each one and then sat very quietly, as if she were afraid that with too big a breath the whole thing might disappear. When a man in a tuxedo played an organ, and a small chorus of ladies in white dresses danced behind him, Diana's face shone with tears. It was only when a second magician came on, wearing a red fez and a suit that was too big, that she began to laugh. Once she had started, she couldn't stop. "Oh, this is funny," she screamed. She had to grip her stomach, she was laughing so hard. It was late afternoon by the time they left the pier and the seaside. Lucy was so tired, Diana carried her through the turnstile and back to the car.

Byron watched the sea growing fainter behind them until it

was no more than a silver trim on the horizon. His sister was asleep within moments. This time his mother did not sing but drove quietly; only once did she lift her eyes to catch his in the rearview mirror. "That was a happy day," she said with a smile.

Yes, he said, it was. She was so good at surprises.

As it turned out, there was a further surprise waiting for them when they arrived home, their skin sun-tingled and sticky. They arrived to find Beverley and Jeanie waiting at the back of the house on the sun chairs. Jeanie was stretched out asleep, but as soon as Beverley caught sight of them entering the kitchen she sprang up and began pointing at her watch. Diana unlocked the French windows and pinned them flat against the outside wall, asking if everything was all right, but Beverley was furious. She said that Diana had let her down. She had forgotten the visit.

"I didn't realize the visits were a daily thing." Diana explained that they had only been to the seaside to see a concert, but this made things worse. Beverley's mouth dropped open.

"There was a very good organist," said Byron. He offered to fetch the program to show Beverley the pictures, but she gave a terse shake of her head, with her mouth pursed so tight she looked as though she had a row of pins in there.

"Beverley, you mustn't be upset," said Diana.

"I would've liked to go to the seaside. I would've liked to see a concert. We're starving here. It's been a bad day for me. My arthritis is rotten. And I love hearing the organ. It's my favorite."

While Diana rushed to fetch one of Beverley's yellow drinks and began slicing a loaf for sandwiches, Beverley was rooting through her handbag. She kept tugging things out, her purse, her small diary, her handkerchief, and then shoving them back inside.

"I told you it would be like this," she said. She looked on the verge of tears. "I said you'd get bored." Jeanie crept up from the sun lounger and slipped through the French windows.

"I'm not bored, Beverley."

"You think you can invite me for tea and then have a better idea and drive off and forget all about me." Whatever she wanted to say next she couldn't manage, she was crying so much.

Diana handed her a handkerchief. Then she took her hand. Then she held her tight. "Please don't cry, Beverley. You're my friend. Of course you are. But I can't be here for you all the time. I've got the children—"

At this Beverley pulled back with her arm lifted as if she was about to lash out, then she was interrupted by a howl of laughter from the kitchen. Jeanie flew through the opened French windows on Lucy's space hopper. Hitting the threshold, she bounced too hard and was hurled over the top of the rubber handles, landing with a smack on the paving stones. She lay very still, her leg splayed, her hands pressed flat on either side of her head. She did not move.

Screaming, Beverley ran to her side. "There, there," she shrieked. "There, there." It didn't sound comforting. She shook her daughter roughly, as if Jeanie were asleep. She pulled at her arms. "Can you walk? Have the stitches opened?"

"She doesn't even have stitches," said Diana, but she looked terrified. "And why was she on a space hopper if her leg's so bad?"

It was the wrong thing to say, even though it was the truth. Beverley hoisted the child into her arms and staggered through the French windows into the kitchen. Diana fled after her with her handbag, but Beverley tripped and stumbled forward, as if she had forgotten how to stop.

"I'm sorry, I'm sorry," called Diana. "I didn't mean it."

But "It's too late, it's too late," shouted Beverley.

"Let me give you a lift home. Let me help." Diana was using her fluttery Seymour voice. For half a moment Byron was afraid his father was standing right behind.

Beverley stopped suddenly and turned. Her face was puce. Jeanie lay in her arms, frail as cloth, and Beverley's fingers were locked and outstretched as if it were too painful to use them as hands. There was no blood on Jeanie's knee; Byron looked carefully. However, Jeanie was pale and her eyes were only half open; he saw this too. "Do you think I'm here for your charity?" spat Beverley. "I'm as good as you, Diana. My mother was a vicar's wife, remember. Not a cheap showgirl. We'll get the bus."

It was Diana's turn to falter. She could barely speak. She got out a few words about the car and the bus stop, but no more.

To Byron's astonishment, Beverley laughed. "What? And watch you veer all over the place? You're so nervous of that car, you're not safe. You shouldn't even have a license."

She walked off toward the drive, still carrying Jeanie. Diana watched from the threshold and pulled her fingers through her hair over and over. "This is not good," she said at last. She went into the kitchen.

Byron heard her washing the dishes and shaking the sand from the beach towels. He remained at the door watching Beverley's profile growing smaller and fainter as she made her way toward the road until there was nothing but the garden and then the moor and then the enamel summer sky.

Like Beverley, James was very interested in the concert. Disappointed, perhaps, with the conclusion of Operation Perfect, he transferred all his energy to the surprise visit to the pier. He quizzed Byron about the different acts: what they wore, how long they lasted, what exactly they did. He asked him to describe the painted backdrops, the orchestra, the curtains that fell between each scene. It was the story about the organist and the white-dressed dancers that entranced him. "Did your mother really cry?" he kept asking.

There was no news from Digby Road for four days. During that time Diana said little. She grew busy in the garden, dead-heading roses and cutting back the sweet peas. Without Beverley, time seem to yawn open again. Lucy and Byron played close to their mother and sat beneath the fruit trees to eat. Byron showed his sister how to make perfume with crushed flower petals. When Seymour visited, Diana wore her slim skirt and blow-dried her hair. He talked about his imminent trip to Scotland and she made a list of things he required. They ate birthday cake for Lucy and he left early Sunday morning.

It was the afternoon when Beverley telephoned. The conversation was brief. Diana barely spoke, but she came away white as milk. She sat in a kitchen chair, her face in her hands, and for a long time she could not utter a word.

"There has been an appalling turn of events," Byron wrote to James that evening. "The little girl, Jeanie, CANNOT WALK. Please reply immediately. Situation VERY SERIOUS. OPERATION PERFECT IS NOT OVER. This is an EMERGENCY."

10

Moor

In a phone box, Jim explains to Eileen that he got her number from the girls in the kitchen. Could he see her after work? It's an emergency. He promises not to take much of her time but he needs to tell her something important. The line is bad. At first she doesn't appear to know who he is or what he's talking about. She says if he's trying to sell kitchen improvements, or household insurance, he can bug right off. "Eileen, it's m-me," he stammers.

"Jim?" She breaks into a laugh, as if she has just seen something happy. He asks again if she will meet him.

She says she can be there as soon as he wants. She needs to see him too, she says.

For the rest of the afternoon, Jim is terrified. He keeps forgetting to smile at customers. He neglects to hand them leaflets. Maybe he should phone Eileen back? Maybe he should say he has remembered he has a previous engagement? He doesn't even know what exactly he is going to tell her. This is an emergency insofar as by the time she arrives he will no longer be able to do it. How can he voice everything that is in his mind? It is filled with pictures, memories, things that happen in the flicker of time before there are words. In all the years at Besley Hill, and despite the encouragement of nurses, social workers, and doctors, he was never able to explain. His past is like the sounds that drift from the hills, made of air. How can he ever speak of it?

In the last group session at Besley Hill, the social worker promised the patients that this was a beginning, not an ending. Some of the staff were out of jobs too, she laughed, and from the way she kept laughing it was clear she was one of them. This was a strange, new time for everyone. She said she wanted them all to think of what they would like to be. Someone said Kylie Minogue, several patients cried, another said an astronaut and then they laughed. Afterward the social worker told Jim that Mr. Meade had agreed to take him on trial. She explained what that meant and that he could manage, she was sure of that. He wanted to tell her that the thing he wished he could be was a friend, but she was already on her mobile phone, sorting out his paperwork.

It is Eileen's idea that they head for the moor. Sensing his anxiety, she suggests they should get some space. She's always found it easier to talk in the dark. She drives at a steady forty miles an hour and he sits with his hands tight in his lap in the passenger seat. The seat belt cuts into his neck. He can hardly breathe.

They travel in the opposite direction from town, past the new drive-in food chains and the construction site where there will soon be a retail park. The floodlit billboards promise 1,430 free parking spaces, 20 eateries, major high street brands, and three levels of hassle-free shopping. Eileen says there won't be any moor left soon, and Jim makes no reply. He remembers standing at the barriers of a demolition site once. He watched the bull-dozers, the cranes, the diggers: a whole army to punch down a few bricks and walls. He couldn't believe how quick they were to fall.

Once they reach the cattle grid, the land takes over and darkness spills on either side of the car. House lights pepper the flanks of the hills; ahead of them there is nothing but night. When Eileen parks and asks if Jim would prefer to sit and talk, he says he'd like to get out. It's just over a week since he was last on the moor. He has missed it in the way he imagines other people miss family.

"We can do whatever you want," says Eileen.

Apart from the buffeting wind, the lack of sound up here is breathtaking. For a while neither of them speaks. They just push slowly against the wind. It charges at their bodies and whistles through the long grasses with the rage of the sea. There are many stars sprinkled like embers over the sky, but Jim can't find the moon. On the western ridge of the hills, the horizon is rimmed with orange light. It is streetlamps, but you might think it was a fire, somewhere very far away. It is sometimes bewildering: to look at a thing and know it could mean something else, if only you changed your perspective. The truth is inaccurate, he remembers suddenly. And then he shakes his head in order not to think that anymore.

"Cold?" says Eileen.

"A bit."

"Do you need my arm?"

"I'm OK."

"Foot OK?"

"Yes, Eileen."

"Are you sure you should be doing this?"

He takes short steps in order to be safe. He is so churned up he can barely swallow. He has to do small blowings of air, like the nurses showed him. He has to empty his mind and visualize the numbers 2 and 1. Briefly he wishes for the seeping away that came from the anesthetist's needle before the treatment, though it is years since they stopped doing that at Besley Hill.

It seems that Jim is not the only one with odd breathing. Eileen's too is coarse and fast, as if she is dragging it from her lungs. When at last she asks what the emergency phone call was about, he can only shake his head.

A night bird flies on the wind and it is so fast, so dark, it looks tossed, as if the moor is playing with it, as if the bird is not flying at all.

"If you don't want to talk, that's all right, Jim. I'll talk. Try stopping me. I could do with some of your silence." She laughs and then she says, "Why didn't you answer my calls? I rang the supermarket. I left messages. Didn't you get them?"

Again he shakes his head. She looks agitated. "Did I do this to you?" She stops. She points at his foot. She does not flinch.

He tries to say *accident* but he can't get near the word.

"Shit," she says.

"Please don't be upset."

"Why didn't you tell me? You could sue if you want. People sue all over the place. Children sue their own fucking parents. Not that I have much to give unless you would like my car and a buggered TV."

He is not sure if she is being serious. He is trying to hold on to the things he wants to tell her. The more she says, the more difficult it is to remember.

"You could at least have reported me to the police. Why didn't you do that?"

She watches him, waiting for the answer, and all the time she watches he opens and shuts his mouth and makes small relaxing noises that are so wired with tension, they actually hurt.

"You don't have to tell me right now," says Eileen. "We can talk about something else."

The wind blows so hard, the trees swing their branches like skirts. Jim tells her their names. Eileen pulls her collar to her ears, and sometimes he has to shout. "This is an ash. The bark is silver. The buds are black. You can always tell an ash because the tips point upward. Sometimes the old seedheads hang and they are like threads." He pulls down a branch, he shows her the pointing buds, the seedheads. He barely stammers at all.

When he glances at Eileen her smile is wide, but above the corners of her mouth spread two blushes like strawberries. She laughs as if he has handed her a present. "Well, I never knew that about trees." After that, she says nothing. She simply steals glances at him that seem to make her redder and redder. It is only when they are back at the car that she says, "There's nothing wrong with you. Jim. How come they kept you so long at Besley Hill?"

He begins trembling so hard he could almost fall. It is the question he most wants to answer. It carries everything he wants her to know. He sees himself as a young man, shouting at the constable, hitting at walls. He sees himself in clothes that were not his. The view from barred windows. The view of the moor. The sky.

"I made a mistake."

"We all make mistakes."

He keeps going. "There were two of us. Many years ago. There was me and a friend. Something happened. Something terrible. It was my fault. It was all my fault." He can manage no more.

Once it is clear he has finished and there is nothing else he can say, she hoists her bosom beneath her arms and gives a long sigh. "I'm sorry. About you and your friend. Do you see him now?"

"No."

"Did he visit you at Besley Hill?"

"No."

It is so hard to say these things, these fragments of truth, he has to stop. He can't tell anymore what is sky and what is land. He remembers how he longed for letters, how he waited and waited, certain that one would come. Occasionally patients got a Christmas card, maybe something for a birthday; for Jim there was nothing. Noticing his distress, Eileen reaches for his sleeve. She laughs, and it is a gentle laugh, as if she is trying to show him the way to join her. "Take it easy. You'll be back in hospital if we're not careful. And that'll be my fault as well."

It's no use. His head swims. He doesn't know if he is thinking about what she has said or Besley Hill or something else, something long ago. He says, "It was an accident. I forgive you. We must forgive."

At least that is what he wants to say. The words glue to his mouth. They are only sounds that do not amount to proper language.

"OK, Jim. It's OK, darlin'. Let's get you back."

He hopes, he prays, she has understood.

11

Beverley's Organ

"I understand the situation, Byron. But we must not panic. We must think in a logical way," said James in a breathless voice down the telephone. He had telephoned as soon as he read Byron's letter. "We must list the facts and work out what to do."

The facts were simple. Jeanie had not walked for five days, not since Lucy's birthday trip to the beach. According to Beverley, she could not put any weight on her leg. At first Walt had tried to encourage her with sweets; Beverley had cried. They had taken her to the hospital. Walt had begged the doctors to help. Beverley had shouted at the nursing staff. None of these things made any difference. There was no obvious sign of a wound, and yet the child appeared to be lame. If Jeanie tried to stand, she either hit the ground or screamed. Now she refused point-blank to move. She had a bandage wrapped all the way from her ankle to her upper thigh. She was refusing some days even to lift her hands and feed herself.

If Diana's initial response had been one of stupefaction, her second was one of frantic activity. On Monday morning she had bundled the children into the car. Parking outside the Digby Road house, she ran into the garden with a bag of magazines and comics she had bought on the way. For the first time, it was Diana who looked the slighter and smaller of the two women. She bit her nails and paced while Beverley watched with her arms folded. Diana suggested a man whose name she had in her notebook, but when Beverley heard he was a psychologist she hit the roof. "Do we think we're making this up?" she yelled. "Do you think we're nutters just because we live on Digby Road? What we need is proper *help*!"

Beverley said it would be easier for her to move Jeanie around if she had wheels; her hands were a problem. Diana rushed home and fetched Lucy's old pushchair. Again the children watched from the car as their mother showed how to clip the pushchair in place, all the while promising to drive Beverley wherever she needed. Beverley shrugged. People were very helpful when they saw you were dealing with a child's injury. They helped you get on the bus and let you go first in queues at the shops. Her manner remained guarded.

Diana had spent that entire evening poring over medical books from the library. The following morning Beverley telephoned with the news that the doctors had given Jeanie a buckled caliper.

Presented with all these facts, James replied in one sentence: "The situation is very serious."

"I know that," whispered Byron. He could hear his mother pacing upstairs; she couldn't seem to keep still, and he had not asked her permission to use the telephone.

James gave an anguished sigh. "I just wish there was a way I could examine the new evidence for myself."

For the rest of the week Jeanie sat on a blanket beneath the shade of the fruit trees at Cranham House. She had Lucy's coloring books and her dolls and Byron could hardly look. Every time he needed to pass he took a longer route. Lucy had tied a handkerchief around her knee. She wanted her pushchair back, she said. She needed it. She even cried.

"The thing is this, Diana," said Beverley from the terrace. "You ran into my daughter and then you drove off. You didn't own up to what you had done for a whole month. And now my daughter is lame, you see. This is what we are dealing with." It was the first time Beverley had threatened Diana, and even so, it wasn't said as such. She spoke softly, almost with embarrassment, fiddling with the buttons on her blouse, so that if anything it sounded like an apology. "We may have to get the police involved. Lawyers. You know."

"Lawyers?" Diana's voice was high-pitched.

"I don't mean this in a horrible way. You're my best friend. I just mean I have to think. I have to be practical."

"Of course you do," Diana said bravely.

"You're my best friend, but Jeanie is my daughter. You would do the same. You're a mother. You would put your kids before me."

"Do we really need to involve the police? And lawyers?"

"I'm thinking of Seymour. When you tell him, he'll probably want to do things in the proper way."

Diana hesitated. "I really don't think we need to tell Seymour," she said.

In one last slavish effort to avoid the truth, Diana seemed briefly to become more perfect. She appeared slimmer, neater, faster. She polished the kitchen floor every time the children crossed it, if only for a glass of Sunquick. But to be so perfect requires constant vigilance, and the effort took its toll. Frequently she listened as if she was not hearing, or as if what she was hearing was something different from what everybody else heard. She started making lists. They appeared everywhere, not only in her notebook. Torn pages appeared on the kitchen worktops. In the bathroom. Beneath her bedside lamp. And not just run-of-the-mill lists of food to be bought or phone calls to be made, but alarmingly fundamental ones. Among reminders like "White-washing" and "New blue button for Lucy's cardigan," there would also be "Make lunch" and "Clean teeth."

No matter what, every day when she was getting it right, when she was making the children their healthy breakfasts and washing their clothes, it seemed there was also the moment in the car when she had got it wrong. It was as if right from the beginning she had hit a child and not stopped the car, even before she had learned to drive, even before she had met Seymour. The accident was always in her life, and whatever she did to make amends, nothing she did would ever be enough. Besides, Beverley had now started her own motion. The two women were spinning in separate places.

"I don't understand," Diana said one time. She stared at the floor as if she were searching for physical clues to help her. "She had a cut on her knee. They said the first time we went to Digby Road that it was small. Nothing, they said. How can she not walk? How can that have happened?"

"I don't know," said Byron. "Maybe it is in her head."

"But it isn't in her head!" Diana was almost shouting. Her eyes were more light than color. "She can't walk. The doctors do test after test and no one can help her. I wish it *was* in her head. But she is lame, Byron. I don't understand what to do next!"

Sometimes he brought in little gifts from the meadow, a feather, a stone, something that might once have made her smile. He left them in places where she would come across them as a surprise. And sometimes the little gifts, when he checked, had vanished; sometimes he found them afterward, stowed, say, in her coat pocket. He felt he was bringing her luck without either of them having to say it.

The final straw came at the end of that second week in August. There had been a day of rain, and Beverley was fractious. She sat staring out the French windows, kneading her finger joints and sighing, while outside dirty curtains of rain splattered the terrace and upper lawn. Clearly she was in pain. She had already shouted at Lucy for snatching a doll from Jeanie.

"I'm going to need a few things, Diana," she said suddenly. "Now that Jeanie is lame."

Diana's face puckered and she took a sharp intake of breath.

"You needn't look so uptight," said Beverley. "I'm just being practical."

Diana nodded. She held her chest quite high. It was clear she wasn't breathing all the way down to her stomach. "So what things are you thinking of?"

Beverley poked in her handbag and produced a list. Glancing over his mother's shoulder, Byron saw that it was uncannily similar to something James might have written, except that Beverley's writing was tighter and less clear and the paper she had used was unevenly ripped from a "Love is . . ." jotter pad. It listed small items: Plasters. Headache tablets. Teabags. An extra rubber sheet for emergencies.

"Of course the other things I'm thinking of are more practical."

"What do you mean, the other things?" said Diana.

Beverley's eyes ran over Diana's kitchen units. "Things to make life easier. Like—I don't know—your chest freezer."

"You want my chest freezer?"

"I don't want yours, Diana. You need yours. But I would like one too. Everyone's getting them. Now that my hands are tied by Jeanie's injury, I have to cut corners. After all, she needs my help with the most basic things. She can't even get dressed. And there's my arthritis to think of. You know how hard it is for me some days to move my fingers." She held out her hands again as if Diana might need help remembering what fingers were, and from the way Diana was staring, mouth open, it was possible Beverley was right.

"I don't see how a chest freezer can help Jeanie," said Byron.

"Well, I could ask for a car, but your father might notice."

"A car?" said Diana. "I don't understand. You want a car?"

"No, no. I don't need a car. I can't drive. It was Walt who mentioned that idea. As I said to my neighbor the other day, what's wrong with the bus? Hundreds of injured people take the bus."

"But I drive you." Diana was speaking carefully again, as if the language they were speaking was not her natural one. "It's no problem."

"It's a problem for Jeanie. It brings back memories when she sits in your car. She has nightmares. This is why I am so exhausted. What I would like—" She paused. "No, no," she said. "I can't say it."

"Why don't you try?" said Diana weakly.

"What I would really like is an organ."

Byron gulped. Suddenly he had a picture of a bloodied heart in

Beverley's hands. As if reading his thoughts, she smiled. "A home needs music."

This time it was Diana who broke the silence. "So not a chest freezer?"

"No."

"And not a car?"

"No, no."

"But an organ?"

"A Wurlitzer. Like when you went to the concert without me. They have one now in the window of the department store."

Diana was lost for words. "But—how? I mean, I can manage the little things but . . ." Here she simply ran out. She sat in devastated silence. "What will I tell Seymour? And anyway, I didn't even know you could play the organ."

"I can't," said Beverley. "But I've got a feeling I would take to it. If I put my mind to learning. As for Seymour, I guess you'll have to play the blank stub trick. It's worked before, Di. You're an old hand."

The organ was delivered to Digby Road after the weekend. Diana had gone straight to the department store in town and written a check. According to Beverley, half the inhabitants of the street gathered to watch as the four deliverymen lifted the organ from the truck and tried to negotiate its passage through her gate and along the garden path. Most of the neighbors had never seen a delivery van before, she said, let alone a Wurlitzer organ. The gate had to be lifted from its hinges in order to get the organ into the garden. Beverley said that the marvelous thing was that the gate had not squeaked once since the delivery fellows put it back.

The organ was installed in the sitting room opposite the new saloon doors that led to the kitchen. It came with a double stool that had an upholstered leather cushion that lifted to provide storage space for her sheet music. When she plugged the organ into the socket, it gave a purring noise, and a rush of green and red lights shot high and low above the keys.

Over the next few days, Beverley's visits to Cranham House stopped altogether. Diana began to worry again. She drove twice past the house on Digby Road, though she didn't park the car or go inside. There was no sign, she said, of anyone, and the washing line was empty. Eventually, on Thursday, Beverley rang from a pay phone. Jeanie's leg had been particularly bad, she told Diana; this was why they had not visited. Byron sat at his mother's feet. He could hear every word.

"Jeanie's been in such pain I couldn't leave the house," said Beverley. "But there is good news."

"Oh?" Diana pressed the receiver closer to her ear. She actually crossed her fingers.

"My organ," came Beverley's voice, a little distorted by the line.

"I'm sorry?" said Diana.

"My Wurlitzer. I've taken to it like a duck to water."

"Oh. That's wonderful news." There were tears welling in Diana's eyes, but she spoke with a smile in her voice.

"Yes, Walt can't believe it. I'm at it all day and night. I know five pieces by heart already. Walt says I'm a natural."

She said she would pop around the next day.

The plan for Beverley's musical performance came the same evening, and it was entirely James's idea. He said it had presented itself to him as a whole; he could see the event from start to finish. He spoke so loud and fast, Byron had to lower the receiver away from his ear. There would be a concert at Cranham House, just like the one on the pier, and Beverley would play her new organ. There would be tickets to raise funds for Jeanie, as well as refreshments, and all the school mothers would be invited. James would accompany his mother, and this way he would finally be able to examine for himself the state of Jeanie's injury. Diana would make a speech, introducing Beverley and thanking the boys for their help.

"But I don't think this will work," argued Byron. "An organ is very heavy. They are difficult to lift. You need removal men. And the other mothers weren't nice to Beverley."

But James was adamant. He kept talking so fast, he trampled right over Byron. He would write the speech for Diana. In fact he had already written it. There would be a finger buffet on the terrace; all the mothers would bring something. The kitchen would serve as a stage; Byron would operate the curtains, while James would show guests to their seats. Maybe they should allow Lucy to help with the programs? James would do the handwriting. He spoke almost without gaps.

"But my mother can't do a finger buffet. Beverley can't do a concert. She's only just learned how to play."

James was not listening. Yes, he repeated, this was his best idea yet. It was a James Lowe special. Byron must tell Beverley as soon as she arrived.

"Trust me," said James.

12

Deodorant and Perfume

It was Eileen's idea that they should meet in town. Dropping him off the previous night after their walk on the moor, she suggested they might go out again. She mentioned a pub, near to the Pound Shop. "Only if you want to," she said. "You might be busy."

He said he wanted to very much.

After his shift, Jim heads straight to town. Arriving early, he looks at a selection of cut-price Christmas chocolates in the Pound Shop. He studies the shelf of deodorant spray, and it occurs to him that he would like to smell nice, although he can't tell which deodorant is best. In the end he picks up one that has a picture of what appears to be a green lion on the can.

He wonders what a green lion smells like.

The assistant says she will ring up those two items, and this is how Jim ends up with a plastic bag containing both the chocolates and the green lion deodorant.

The latter is a mistake. He finds this out as soon as he tries it, while he is waiting for Eileen. He lifts his shirt, just as he has seen other men do, not patients but Mr. Meade and Darren.

Holding the can toward his armpit, he feels a shot of ice-cold spray. Now that he knows what green lions smell like, he wishes he had picked something different. There was a can, for instance, with a picture of a mountain. He wishes he had chosen that instead.

Since he is still early, he limps as fast as he can up and down the street, trying to lose the smell, or at least dilute it. But it is like being followed by a particularly pungent shadow. The moment he stops, it is back with him. He tries to go faster. He is conscious of his elbows going up and down like pistons. People are diving out of the way, he is going at such speed.

When he stops, the smell seems to have got even worse. He wonders if he should go back to the van, if he can wash and change; but then he will be late for Eileen. He sets off again. Only now the smell seems to have grown more solid. It has grown paws. It is actually thumping along behind him, a green shape, getting faster. He runs. So does the lion.

"Hey!" It can even talk. "Hey!" it shouts. "Wait!"

It is only when Jim shoots a glance at a shop window, and sees his reflection, and the solid one chasing behind, that he realizes this last one is Eileen. He stops so suddenly that she comes flying straight into him. She actually lands in a crushed-up shape against his chest, and for a moment he wishes he could wrap his arms around her and hold tight. Then he remembers that even though she is not a green lion, he still smells like one, and he jumps backward.

"Shit! Did I stand on your foot?" Eileen talks in exclamation marks. Catching the scent of him, she takes a deep breath and makes a noise as if she is about to lose her balance. "Whoa!" she yelps.

The second meeting is a terrible idea. He should never have agreed to it. He would like to be in the van right now. Quickly he passes her the bag with the chocolates, only too late he realizes he has left the dreadful deodorant in there too. He says it is nice to see her and that he must dash. Eileen listens with her face opened up in confusion, and all he can see is the way he sometimes feels about the world, as if he has been stripped of layers of skin.

"It's me. Isn't it?" she says suddenly. She looks appalled. "I smell awful. Oh, fuck."

"N-n-n," he says. The word is hiding.

"I tried on this scent in a shop. I was early. I had nothing else to do. On the bottle it said it was called Scent of the Hills. I thought you would like that. So I gave it a go. I sprayed my wrists and my neck, the whole ruddy lot. And now I smell like a fucking toilet cleaner." She lifts the bag. "But thank you for the chocolates. Unless you want them back? For someone else?"

Jim shakes his head to show he doesn't. "You smell nice," he manages to say at last, although now that he is actually beside her, he can barely breathe. He doesn't know if it is his deodorant or her scent, or whether the two smells have already got together to produce something even more toxic, but either way the result is devastating. His eyes begin to water.

"So do you still want a beer?" she asks awkwardly, and he replies equally awkwardly that yes, he does.

They walk to the pub, Jim and Eileen, followed by two smells, deodorant and perfume, that are so noxious it is like spending Christmas with an unpleasant set of relatives.

Apart from the fact that he has none, of course.

They talk about many things. His gardening, the news at the supermarket café. When he describes the huddle she laughs out loud, and hearing her laugh he sees it too, the funny side, and he is no longer afraid. It occurs to him how much he would like to have that in his life, her laughter, her other way of seeing things, and he wonders if that is what people look for in a partner or a friend: the part of themselves that is missing. They talk about Eileen's life: how she's looking for another job, how she works part-time in the charity shop on the High Street. She asks again about Besley Hill, but sensing he cannot answer, her questions stop. He has a list of interesting things to talk about if conversation dries up, but it is difficult, he realizes, to refer to such a list when the person you would like to interest is sitting right opposite. He wishes he had thought of that before. He wonders if this is a date or just something friendly.

"So," says Eileen. She drums her fingers on the table.

Jim says in a rush, "Please, will you describe your house?" He says, "Do you have a dog?" He says, "What is your favorite food?" He says, "What do you wish you could be?"

It is as if his mouth is charging on despite the rest of him, determined to get the business of talking over and done with.

After their meeting, which may be a date but which may also just be something friendly, he opens the door to the van and it occurs to him they have lost an evening talking about the smallest things. She has told him she likes frost, not snow. The frost, according to Eileen, picks out each thing and marks it apart. "Whereas snow just dumps all over everything. And they don't lay off the buses when there's a frost."

From now on, he will always like frost.

It is indeed a small thing, that Eileen prefers frost to snow, but it is these, he realizes, these smallnesses, that make up the big things. Besides, the big things in life do not present themselves as such. They come in the quiet, ordinary moments—a phone call, a letter—they come when we are not looking, without clues, without warning, and that is why they floor us. And it can take a lifetime, a life of many years, to accept the incongruity of things: that a small moment can sit side by side with a big one, and become part of the same.

It is several hours after the meeting, when he is binding the van door with duct tape, that another picture of Eileen fills Jim's mind. They were sitting in her car and he was about to get out when she said, "You asked me some stuff earlier. About who I am. And I didn't answer. So—if you still want to know, here goes." She told him about her flat on the edge of town. She told him she had no dog, though she would like one. She talked a little about her parents: Her father was an army man in the seventies, her mother a society girl. They split when she was thirteen. She has traveled a lot in the last few years, not always to nice locations. She has found it hard to stay in one place. Then she smiled at him from her driving seat, and he had no idea why but it looked as if her eyes were filmed with tears. "I've done loads of things in my life. You have no idea how much I've fucked up. But if I could be anything—I'd ask to be a decent person. That's all that counts."

Jim stretches a strip of duct tape over the top of the door to the van. He cuts it with scissors to make an exact fit. Then he unpeels two more lengths and presses them down the sides. The rituals are performed swiftly, efficiently, and by the time the town clock rings eleven, Jim is already in his foldout bed.

13

The Catching of a Goose Egg
and the Losing of Time

James was right about the concert. When Byron suggested the idea, Beverley's eyes widened. "What? Just me?" she sang. "And in front of all the mothers?"

"I don't understand what you mean. What sort of concert?" said Diana warily.

Byron repeated James word for word. He explained about inviting the mothers to Cranham House; there would be tickets and programs to raise funds for Jeanie as well as a finger buffet. He showed how the boys would pin back the French windows and arrange dining room chairs for the audience in a semicircle on the terrace, and all the time he spoke Beverley watched him hard, nodding her head, and crooning "Hm, hm" as if she were snatching up the ends of his sentences. His mother listened in silence. It was only once he had finished that she shook her head, but Beverley leapt in and gasped, "Oh, I couldn't—could I? Do you think I could, Di?"

There was no choice for his mother but to insist that of course she could.

"I will need a costume and some more sheet music, but I think he's right. It will be good for Jeanie."

"How will this help her leg?" murmured his mother. "I don't understand." But Beverley was already fetching her handbag along with Jeanie's pushchair and blanket from the hallway. She had to get home and start practicing, she said.

Seymour's visit did not happen at the weekend. He had work to finish before his shooting trip to Scotland. Diana told him on the telephone that she was missing him. She promised to wash his country clothes, but she drifted in and out of the words as if she was thinking about something else.

Waking early on Sunday morning, Byron went to his mother's bedroom and discovered it was empty. He checked the kitchen, the bathroom, Lucy's room, and the drawing room, but there was no sign of her. He knew where to look.

She was crouched low in the grasses by the pond with her glass between her hands. The water was dark and still, hung with soft green rags of duckweed. Despite the mid-August heat, the hedges still foamed with white blossom and dog roses, their petals like pink hearts. He trod carefully, not wanting to frighten his mother. He hunkered at her side.

She didn't look up but she seemed to know he was there. "I'm waiting for the goose to lay her egg," she said. "The trick is to be patient."

Above the moor the clouds were beginning to collect like granite peaks. There might well be rain. "Don't you think we should go in for breakfast?" he said. "Beverley might be here soon."

His mother stared at the pond, as if Byron had not spoken. At last she said, "She'll be practicing. I doubt she'll come today. Anyway, the goose won't take much longer. She's been on her nest since dawn. And if I don't get her egg, the crows will."

She gestured with her glass toward the fencing. She was right. They were lined up all around them, smooth and velvet-black against the moor behind. "They look like executioners. Waiting for the end." She laughed.

"I don't think so," he said.

The goose ruffled her downy white feathers. She sat very still in her bed of nettles with her neck slightly erect and her blue eyes, rimmed with the same orange as her beak, blinking only now and then. From the ash trees at the meadow's edge came the hollow rattle of a cry and the flapping of leaves; the crows were everywhere, waiting for that egg. He could understand why his mother wanted to save it. The gander pecked at the water's edge.

Diana took another swig of her drink. "Do you think Jeanie will walk again?" she said suddenly.

"Of course I do. Don't you?"

"I can't see where this is going to end. You know it's nearly three months since it all began? It feels like years. Beverley is happy, though. That concert was a very good idea of yours." She returned to staring at the pond.

It occurred to Byron that over the summer holidays she had become someone else. She was not like a mother anymore. At least not one who told you to clean your teeth and wash behind your ears. She had become someone who was maybe more like a friend of your mother's or her sister, if only she'd had either of those. She had strayed into being someone who understood that it was not always pleasant or interesting to keep cleaning your teeth and washing behind your ears, and who turned a blind eye when you chose not to do them. It was a gift to have a mother like this. He was lucky. But it was also unsettling. It left him feeling slightly out in the wind, as if a wall had fallen down that was something to do with why things kept going. It meant he wanted to ask sometimes if she had remembered to clean her own teeth or wash behind her ears.

A slight wind took up. The lower feathers of the gander blew out around his haunches like soft white frills. Byron felt the first spots of rain.

"I've been thinking." Here his mother fell silent again, as if she had run out of energy.

"Oh yes?" he said. "What have you been thinking?"

"About what you said once. About time."

"I think it's going to pour in a minute."

"You said we shouldn't play with time. It isn't up to us, you said. You were right. It's playing with fire when we tamper with the gods."

"I don't remember mentioning the gods," he said, but she seemed to be thinking something all of her own.

"Who's to say time is real just because we have clocks for measuring it? Who knows if everything is going forward at the same rate? Maybe everything is going backward or sideways. You said something about that too once."

"Oh, dear," he said. "Did I?" The raindrops dimpled the water of the pond. The rain was surprisingly soft and warm and smelled of grass.

"Or we could take matters into our own hands. We could move the clocks. We could make them what we want."

Byron let slip a guffaw that reminded him uncomfortably of his father. "I don't think so."

"My point is, why are we slaves to something that is just a set of rules? Yes, we get up at six-thirty. We get to school for nine. We eat lunch at one. But why?"

"Because if we didn't there would be chaos. There would be people going to work and people eating lunch and people going to bed. Nobody would have a clue what was right and what was not."

Diana sucked the left corner of her lip, considering this. She said, "I'm beginning to think chaos is underrated."

Unclipping her watch, she slipped it over her wrist and into the ball of her palm. Before he could stop her she had lifted her hand and opened it. The watch twisted silver in the air and then cut through the dark skin of the water with a plop, sending a basket of ripples toward the bank. The gander looked up, but the goose didn't move. "There." Diana laughed. "Goodbye, time."

"I hope Father doesn't find out," he said. "He gave you that watch. It was probably expensive."

"Well, it's done now," she said quietly.

They were interrupted when the goose raised her lower haunches, tipping her neck forward. Her wings lifted and fell, lifted and fell, in the way that Byron might tense his shoulders and fingers. Then, where there had been no more than white feathers emerged a soft pink mouth of muscle, contracting and flexing. It peeped at them, like a wink, and then it was gone.

His mother sat up straight. "It's coming." She took a deep breath.

The crows knew it was coming too. They were dropping from the ash trees and then steering overhead on slanted wings like gloves.

Here it was, the goose egg: a tiny white eye blinking at the center of the goose's pink muscle. It disappeared and suddenly there it was again, only now the size and luminosity of a new ping-pong ball. They watched in silence as the goose lifted her tail feathers high, pushing and quivering, until the egg shot from her and lay on the bed of nettles. It was perfect. His mother stood slowly and took up a stick, poking at the bird until she lifted to her feet. The goose opened her beak and gave a hiss but trundled away. She seemed too exhausted to put up a fight.

"Quick!" Byron shouted, because, hearing her, the gander was crossing the water toward them and the crows were hopping closer. His mother bent to scoop up the egg and passed it to Byron. It was so warm and heavy, it was like holding a living thing. He needed two hands. The goose waded away from them down the bank, still hissing. Her underfeathers were streaked with mud from where she had pushed herself into the ground to force the passage of the egg. Afraid of dropping it, he returned the precious weight to his mother.

"I feel awful now," she said. "She wants it back. She's grieving."

"If you hadn't taken it, the crows would. And that's a lovely goose egg you got. You were right to make us wait for it." Rain filled the air and hung like tiny beads in his mother's hair. The leaves and grasses creaked under the soft weight of it. He said, "We should go inside now."

As she walked back to the house she stumbled once and he had to reach out a hand to straighten her. She bore the goose egg like a gift, staring at it as she went. She faltered again at the edge of the garden. He held her empty glass and the egg while she opened the picket gate.

From the trees beyond, the crows gave a rattling cry that hacked through the wet morning air. He wished she had not described them as executioners. He wished she had not talked about them waiting for the end.

"Don't drop them," she said.

He promised to take care.

In the end, the goose egg was never used. His mother stowed it in a dish on the windowsill. Byron saw the crows outside, flapping their wings for balance on branches that appeared too fragile. He clapped his hands to scare them and ran outside to chase them off. "Shoo, shoo," he shouted. But as soon as he turned his back they floated down and perched in the treetops, waiting.

It was the same with time, he thought, and also sorrow. They were both waiting to catch you. And no matter how much you shook your arms at them and hollered, they knew they were bigger. They knew they would get you in the end.

When Seymour came to fetch his country clothes and his shotgun, the visit lasted a matter of hours. He said little. ("It's because he's nervous," said Diana.) He checked in various rooms. He flicked through the pages of Diana's calendar. When he asked why the lawn was so overgrown, she said there had been difficulties with the mower, and this was possibly true: It was growing harder to tell what was real and what was imagined. Seymour said it was wrong not to keep up appearances, and she apologized and promised to have everything ready for his return.

"Have a wonderful holiday," she said. "Telephone us when you can." He asked for his sun cream and midge deterrent, and she clasped her head in her hands. She had clean forgotten, she said. When she kissed him, she touched the air.

Afterward the plans for Beverley's concert became more concrete. She was practicing every day; she now had ten pieces. James told Byron eagerly that he had enlisted his mother's help. She'd rung all the other mothers, encouraging them to attend and provide a plateful each of refreshments. James said he had made tickets to sell at the door and programs. He had designed a seating plan and was rewriting his speech for Diana. He telephoned every evening.

And when Byron said, as he sometimes did, "Are you sure this is a good idea?" or if he said, "My mother is sometimes sad," or even if he said, "But suppose Beverley tells everyone what my mother did?" James simply talked over him. The most important thing, James said, was that he got to see the evidence.

14

Dates

Jim and Eileen meet every evening. He folds up his Father Christmas suit and replaces it in its plastic wrapper and leaves via the staff stairs to meet her in the car park. She drives them into town and they do the things that everyone does, the everyday things. They go to the cinema, they meet for a drink, and if the sky is clear they head for a brief stroll on the moor. One evening they visit the small Italian restaurant for a bowl of pasta. She asks about his day and he tells her that Mr. Meade has offered Darren a job. He tells her about a child who gave him his Christmas list, and meanwhile Eileen laughs and sighs, as if these things are interesting. In turn he asks about her day, her flat, her search for a new job. He is always home by nine.

When she drops him off at the end of the cul-de-sac she says, "I'd have a tea, if you're offering," but he doesn't know why she would say that since he isn't. "See ya!" Eileen calls, waving, as he shuts the passenger door.

"You be careful," he tells her. She laughs and promises she will.

And even though, after these meetings, he is not like everyone else—he steps in and out, hello, Small Cactus Plant, he binds the doors and windows with duct tape—he is not troubled by the rituals. They are a thing he does before he gets on with a different thing, which is thinking about Eileen. His heart jumps as he pictures her. He laughs at her jokes, even when the evening is long since over. He can smell her. He can hear her. He feels bigger than the rituals; they are just a part of him, like his leg is a part of him, but not the whole person. Maybe one day he will even stop.

Paula corners him one afternoon on his way to the urinals. She asks how things are and he can't look her in the eye but he assures her they are good. She says he seems well. She likes the way he's done his hair and he says oh, that, because actually all he has done is comb it over his skull, more from left to right. He has seen Darren doing it this way. Maybe that is why Paula likes it.

"I've got this idea," she says. She tells Jim she is an instinct person. She is not erudite. Actually what she says is that she is not *araldite,* but he gets her drift. "Darren has this aunt. She's nice. You'd like her. She lives on her own. We were thinking you should go for a drink."

"With your aunt?"

"Me and Darren would come too."

Jim twists his hands. He tries to explain he would love to go for a drink with Paula and Darren but he already has a date. She makes a squashed face that suggests she is impressed. He says in a rush that his date is Eileen, because he can't help it, he is longing to tell someone, only now she looks struck.

"Eileen? The woman who ran you over?"

"It was an accident."

He laughs but Paula doesn't. She shrugs and begins to move away. She stoops to pick up a tin can someone has dropped and says as she aims it for the bin, "I hope you know what you're doing."

15

The Concert

It was a beautiful day for a concert. Rain had been forecast the previous night, but there was not a sign of it when Byron woke at dawn. There was blue sky and a soft rose-colored light over the moor. The meadow was already thick with clashing pockets of flowers. There were purple thistles, pink and white clover, orange trefoil, and yellow bundles of lady's bedstraw. Unfortunately the upper lawn was also deep in grass and spotted with daisies. The roses sprawled every which way over the pagoda and swung thorny branches across the path.

Byron reassured himself that James was right, that the concert was a good idea. His mother was still sleeping. It seemed wise to leave her like that as long as possible.

He wasn't sure how to go about cleaning a house, but now that he looked he saw that something needed to be done before the guests arrived. Not knowing where to put dirty linen and dishes, he decided to stow them in the kitchen drawers, where no one would notice. He retrieved the mop and a bucket and had a go at the kitchen floor. He didn't know why there was so much water. He tried to remember how his mother did it, and all he could picture was the day of the accident when she had rushed to clear the spilled milk and broken jug and cut her hand. His mother had been right. It seemed a very long time since that morning in early June when everything began.

There was considerable difficulty with the delivery of Beverley's organ. The van got stuck in one of the narrow steep lanes leading up to the house, and the driver had to go back to town and ring from a telephone box to ask for help.

"I want to speak to your mother," he said.

Byron said she was currently inconvenienced.

"I'm bloody inconvenienced as well," said the driver.

Four men carried it around to the back of the house so that they could heave it through the French windows. Their faces were red and shiny with effort. Byron didn't know whether he was supposed to give them anything and all he could think of was fruit. They asked if he knew his alphabet and he said he did, but when they asked what came after *s* he got confused and said *r*. He noticed the way the men looked around the kitchen, and he didn't know if it was because it looked right or because it looked wrong.

"Does the kitchen look like a kitchen?" he asked Lucy as he found and washed her Peter Rabbit bowl.

There was no time for her reply, because he had just noticed the state of her. Her hair was tangled, her socks didn't even match, and her dress had a big tear all the way from the pocket.

"Lucy, when did you last have a bath?"

"I don't know, Byron. Nobody has run me one."

There seemed to be so much to organize. There were no cereals in any of the boxes and so he made Lucy a sugar sandwich. Afterward he pinned open the French windows and carried the dining room chairs as well as the kitchen stools to the terrace to form a half-circle facing the kitchen. The organ sat in an arc of sunlight, just inside the French windows. Lucy slipped from the breakfast bar and poised her fingers over the glossed wood lid.

"I would like to play the organ," she said sadly.

Byron scooped her in his arms and carried her upstairs. And while he washed her hair with Pears soap he asked if she had any idea about sewing because he didn't seem to have enough buttons on his shirt.

When Andrea Lowe finally arrived with a tall young man in a suit, Byron thought for a moment that everything had gone wrong, that she had left James behind.

"Hello there," called a squeaky voice.

Byron was shocked. It was only six weeks since the end of term, but James had become a different person. He was taller. His soft gold hair was completely gone. Where he had once had a flopping fringe, there was only a short crop of mouse-brown hair and, below it, a pale stretch of forehead bursting with pimples. On his upper lip were tiny brushstrokes of a mustache. They shook hands and then Byron withdrew a few paces because it was like meeting someone he did not know.

"Everything set?" said James. He kept going to swipe his fringe and finding he hadn't got one and rubbing his forehead instead.

"All set," said Byron.

"But where is your mother?" said Mrs. Lowe. She cast her eyes over the house as if every time she looked it turned into a different shape.

Byron said she was fetching the performer and her daughter. He omitted to mention that, due to the lack of a wristwatch, she was late.

"Such a tragedy about the child," said Mrs. Lowe, shaking her head. "James told me the whole story."

To Byron's surprise, all the invited guests arrived. Not only that, they had clearly dressed for the occasion. The new mother had blow-dried her hair into flicks; Deirdre Watkins had gone so far as to have a perm. She kept touching the tight curls as if they might fall out, and crimping them up with her fingers.

"Well, of course it's a look that worked for Charles the First," said Andrea Lowe.

There was a pause in which no one knew what to say. Andrea gripped Deirdre's arm to show she meant no harm, she was only joking. The women laughed heartily. "You mustn't mind me," said Andrea.

They had come bearing gifts of Tupperware boxes of salad and cakes. There was coleslaw, Russian salad, deviled kidneys, cheese straws; stuffed grapes, olives, mushrooms, and prunes. The women produced flasks from their handbags whose contents they poured into glasses and passed around. As the food was unpacked onto the garden table, there was a high buzz of excitement. It was such a good idea to meet again, they agreed; so generous of Diana to suggest the concert. They talked as if they had been kept away from one another for years. They spoke of the summer holidays, the children, the lack of routine. They asked one another what they had heard about Jeanie's appalling injury, as they snapped off plastic lids and set out paper plates. They asked Byron what he knew about the poor little girl with the caliper. It was terrifying, they agreed, that something like that could happen to a child, simply because of a small accident. No one seemed to know about Diana's involvement in Jeanie's injury. No one mentioned Digby

Road, but it would only be a matter of time before they found out, he was sure of it. He could barely move for worry.

When his mother drew up in the drive with the performer and Jeanie, Byron led a small round of applause because he wasn't sure what else to do. Beverley and her daughter both sat in the back of the car in sunglasses. Beverley wore a new black maxi dress with a spangled motif of a rabbit that jumped slightly around her breasts. "I am so nervous," she kept saying. She lifted Jeanie out of the car and into her pushchair, and the women parted as they made their way to the house. Byron asked Jeanie how her leg was, and she nodded to show it was still the same.

"She may never walk again," said Beverley. Several of the mothers expressed their sympathy and offered help bringing Jeanie's pushchair inside the house.

"It's my hands," said Beverley. "I get terrible pains in my hands. Though my pain is nothing compared to hers. It's her future that bothers me. When I think of what that poor child is going to need."

Byron had expected Beverley to be nervous, to be sheepish with the women, especially after the coffee morning where they had talked right over her and laughed, but she was the opposite. She was in her element. She shook each of them by the hand and said how lovely it was to meet them. She took care to memorize everyone's name, repeating it as soon as they told her.

"Andrea, how nice. Deirdre, how nice. Sorry," she said to the new mother, "I didn't catch your name."

It was Diana who looked out of place. Now that Byron saw her in the context of the other Winston House women, he realized how far from them she had strayed. Her blue cotton dress hung from her shoulders as if it was someone else's, and her hair was so limp around her face it looked empty of color. She couldn't even seem to remember what to say. One of the mothers mentioned the Olympics, and another said that Olga Korbut was a darling, but his mother merely bit her lip. Then James announced, as a sort of prompt, that he had prepared a few words by way of introduction, but Beverley insisted it was Diana's place to speak.

"Oh no, please," said Diana faintly. "I couldn't."

She tried to take a seat in the audience, but the mothers insisted too. Just a few words, sang out Andrea. James ran to offer Diana his prepared speech.

"Oh," she said. "Goodness."

She took her place on the terrace. She stared down at the words. The piece of paper jigged in her hands.

"Friends, mothers, children. Good afternoon."

There were allusions to charity, music, and something about the future. Whatever it was she was saying, she could barely be heard. She had to keep stopping sentences and starting them afresh. She plucked at the skin of her wrist and then twisted her fingers through her hair. It was as if she couldn't even read. Unable to bear any more, Byron led another round of applause. Fortunately Lucy, who was busy scowling from her dining room chair at Jeanie, clearly thought the concert was over and shot to her feet shouting, "Hurrah! Hurrah! Now can we have tea?" It was humiliating for Lucy, not least because something funny had happened with her hair since Byron had washed it and it looked like flat ribbons, but at least her response broke the ice and everyone stopped staring at Diana.

So this was the first shock of the afternoon: that she was so publicly not herself. The second—and this was less of a shock and more of a surprise—was that Beverley could play. She could really play. What she maybe lacked in natural talent, she had more than made up for in application. Once Diana had crept to a stool in order to watch, Beverley waited for the applause to build, and then fade into silence. She walked efficiently to her place at the center of the stage, holding her sheet music under one arm and lifting the hem of her maxi dress with the other. She took her seat in front of the organ. She closed her eyes, she lifted her hands over the keyboard, and she began.

Beverley's fingers ran over the notes, and the colored dials danced in front of her, like a series of small fireworks. The women sat up sharp. They nodded approvingly and exchanged glances. Beverley followed her classical piece with a more popular film track, then she played a short piece by Bach, followed by a Carpenters medley. Byron pulled the curtains closed between each piece to allow her time to compose herself and arrange her sheet music, while outside James handed out plates of refreshments. The chatter was loud and there was laughter. At first Byron stood to one side while he waited for Beverley to prepare for her next piece, simply pretending he wasn't there. She was clearly nervous. As soon as the curtains were drawn she took deep breaths, she smoothed her hair, she whispered to herself little words of encouragement. But as she grew in confidence, as the applause grew more animated and excited, she too seemed to become less isolated, more aware of herself within the context of her audience. Once he had closed the curtains at the end of her sixth piece, she glanced at him and smiled. She asked if he would make her a jug of Sunquick. And when he poured her a glass, she said, "What a lovely group of women."

Glancing through a crack in the curtains, Byron saw James

offering Jeanie a biscuit. She sat right in the middle of the front row, with her leg buckled tight in its leather caliper. James was staring hard.

"I'm ready for my last piece, Byron," called Beverley.

He gave a *hrr-hrrm* for silence and pulled the curtains open.

Beverley waited too. And then, instead of playing, she twisted on her stool to face the audience. She opened her mouth and spoke.

She began by expressing how much she wanted to thank the women. Their support meant so much. Her voice was thin and high-pitched, and Byron had to dig his nails into his palms in order not to scream. It had been a hard summer, she continued, and without Di's kindness she didn't know how she would have survived. "Di has been here for me all the way through. She has stopped at nothing to help me. Because I must admit there were times when I ..." And here she trailed off and merely gave a brave smile. "This is not the time to be sad. This is a happy occasion. So my last piece is a favorite of me and Di's. It's by Donny Osmond. I don't know if any of you know him?"

The new mother called out, "Aren't you a bit old for Donny? What about Wayne?" But Beverley countered with "Oh, Di likes them young. Don't you, Di?"

The mothers were drinking from their flasks. Everyone laughed, even Beverley.

"Well, this is for you," Beverley said, "whatever your preference." Lifting her hands over the organ she encouraged the audience to sing along if they felt the inclination. "And why don't you come up to the front and dance for us, Di?"

Diana flinched as if she had been hit with a stone. "I couldn't. I can't."

Beverley stopped. She shared a confiding look with her audience. "True to form, she is being modest. But I have seen her dance, and you've got to believe me, she's the most beautiful mover. She was born to it. Weren't you, Di? She could make a man go weak."

"Please no," begged Diana.

But Beverley was having none of it. She walked to Diana's chair and took hold of her. As Diana rose to her feet, Beverley removed her hands to lead another round of applause, only somehow Diana must have already been leaning on her, and she gave a small lurch forward.

"Whoa there!" laughed Beverley. "Maybe we should put down that glass, Di?"

The women laughed, but Diana insisted on keeping it.

It was like watching a chained animal being brought out and poked with a stick. It should never have happened. Even as Beverley led Diana forward, Diana still tried to object, she tried to suggest she couldn't dance, but by now the women were curious and they insisted. Diana tripped as she moved past the chairs and made her way to the front. Byron tried to get James's attention. He made frantic movements with his hands and shook his head. He mouthed, "Stop, stop," but James had eyes for no one except Diana. He watched her with a face so crimson he looked burned. He barely moved. It was as if he had never seen anything so beautiful. He waited for her to dance.

Diana took up her place on the terrace, pale and small in her blue dress. She seemed to take up too little space. She still had her glass in her hand, but she had forgotten her shoes. Behind her sat Beverley, her black hair puffed out, her hands poised over the keys of her organ. Byron could not look. The music began.

It was Beverley's best piece. She brought in flourishes, she played a chord that was so sad she almost stopped, then she played the chorus with such enthusiasm that several of the mothers began to sing. Meanwhile, center stage, Diana drifted up and down the terrace like a rag caught on water. She lifted her hands and fluttered her fingers, but she kept tripping, and it was hard to tell what was dancing and what was a mistake. It was like watching something so private, so internal, it should not be watched. For Byron it was like looking right inside his mother and seeing only her terrible fragility. It was too much. As soon as the music stopped, Diana had the composure to stand and give a small bow before turning to Beverley and lifting her hands in brief applause. Beverley gave a swift curtsy and ran to clutch Diana.

There was no mention of the accident. There was no mention of Digby Road. Beverley simply held tight to Diana and moved her up and down in a shared bow and it was like watching a new act, one that involved a ventriloquist and a doll.

Diana made her excuses to get away. She needed a glass of water, she said, but overhearing her, Andrea Lowe offered to go to the kitchen and fetch it. Moments later, Andrea emerged, laughing good-humoredly.

"I've seen some funny things, Diana, but it's the first time I've opened a kitchen drawer and found socks in there."

Byron could barely breathe. Beverley talked animatedly with the mothers while Diana removed herself to the sidelines and sat with her hands in her lap. A few of the mothers asked if she needed anything, if she felt all right, but she gazed back at them as if she didn't understand. When Byron and James carried the chairs back to the dining room, Byron took the opportunity to ask James what he thought now that he had seen Jeanie's injury for himself, but James wasn't listening. He could talk only about the success of his concert. He had no idea Diana could dance like that, he said.

Outside, Beverley was sitting beside Jeanie in the middle of the mothers. She aired her views on politics, the state of the country, the prospect of strikes. She asked what they thought about Margaret Thatcher, and when several of the women lifted their hands to their mouths and hollered, "Milk snatcher," Beverley shook her head. "You mark my words, that woman's the future," she said. Byron had never seen her so sure of herself, so animated. She told them about her father, the vicar, and how she had been brought up in a beautiful country vicarage that was really like Cranham House, when she thought about it. Beverley and the mothers exchanged telephone numbers, they suggested visits. And when one of them—the new one, perhaps—offered Beverley a lift and help with Jeanie's pushchair, Beverley said that would be so lovely, if her new friend could spare the time.

"It's my hands. It's a wonder I can play, my hands get so bad. Look at poor Di. She's worn out."

Everyone agreed that the concert had been a tremendous success. "Goodbye, goodbye, Di!" they called as they took up their empty Tupperware and headed back to their cars. As soon as they were gone, Diana poured herself a glass of water and drifted upstairs. When Byron checked half an hour later, she was already asleep.

It was another fitful night for Byron. He put Lucy to bed and locked the doors. There were so many things to hide: the hubcap, the payment for Beverley's organ, Jeanie's injury, and now the party at Cranham House. He couldn't see how everything could keep going forward.

———

That night the telephone began to ring at nine o'clock, but his mother failed to waken. It rang again first thing the following morning. Byron answered, expecting his father.

"It's me," said James. He sounded as if he had run a long way.

Byron said hello and asked him how he was, but James merely replied, "Go and find the notebook."

"Why? What is it?"

"This is an emergency."

Byron's hands began to shake as he flicked through the pages. There was something in James's voice that had frightened him. "Hurry, hurry," said James.

"I don't understand. What am I looking for?"

"The diagram. The one you drew of Jeanie with her plaster. Have you got it?"

"Nearly." He opened to the page.

"Describe it."

"It isn't very good—"

"Just describe what you see."

Byron spoke slowly. He described her blue summer dress with short sleeves. Her sloppy socks because she had no elastic garters. Her hair in two black plaits. "Though they're not very good in the drawing. They look more like squiggles—"

James interrupted sharply. "Get to the plaster."

"It's on her right knee. It's a big square. I drew it carefully." There was a silence as if the air had swallowed James. Byron felt his skin creep with cold and panic. "What is it, James? What's happened?"

"That's not her damaged leg, Byron. Her caliper leg is on the left."

16

Words as Dogs

"Please lift your foot," says the nurse. She reassures Jim that none of this will hurt. Eileen stands beside him. The nurse uses scissors to cut the plaster cast open. Inside, Jim's foot looks surprisingly neat and soft. Above his ankle the skin has turned dry and pale; the toes are shadowed with moss-green bruising. The nails have slightly lost their pink.

A doctor examines his foot carefully. There is no damage to the ligaments. Eileen asks the doctor practical questions about whether or not Jim will need painkillers, and about exercises he should do to help his recovery. It is so new to him, that someone should be concerned like this, he has to keep looking at her. Then she makes a joke about her own state of health and everyone laughs, including the doctor. It has never occurred to Jim that doctors like jokes. Eileen's blue eyes sparkle, her teeth shine, even her hair seems to bounce. He realizes he might be falling in love and it is so happy, this feeling, that Jim laughs too. He doesn't even have to think about it.

Afterward the nurse replaces Jim's plaster cast with a bandage and a soft plastic boot to protect it. Good as new, she says.

—

Jim takes Eileen to the pub to celebrate. Without the plaster cast his foot feels made of nothing. He has to keep stopping to check it is still there. When he is paying for the drinks, he realizes he would like to tell the barman that he is here with Eileen, that she has agreed to come with him for a beer, that she does so every evening. He wants to ask the barman if he has a wife and what it is like to fall in love. A man at the bar is feeding his dog crisps. The dog sits on a stool next to the man and wears a spotted scarf round its neck. Jim wonders if the man is in love with his dog. There are many ways of loving, he sees.

Jim passes Eileen her drink. "Would you like crisps?" he says.

"Thank you."

The room spins. Jim remembers something like a dog, only as soon as he has the picture that precedes the formation of a word, it changes form to become another shape. He is light-headed with confusion. He doesn't know suddenly what words mean. He can't see the sense in them; they seem to slice things in half even as he thinks of them. Is he, when he says, "More crisps?," actually saying something else, something like "I love you, Eileen"? And is she, when she says, "Thank you," saying something else, something like "Yes, Jim. I love you too"?

The carpet at his feet swoops sideways. Nothing is what it seems. A person can offer crisps and mean *I love you*, just as a person can say *I love you* and presumably only mean they want the crisps.

His mouth clams up as if it is stuffed with wool.

"Do you want a glass of water?" says Eileen. "You look funny."

"I'm all right."

"A bit green. Maybe we should go?"

"Do you want to?"

"Well, I'm thinking of you. I'm easy."

"I'm easy too," he says.

They finish their drinks in silence. He doesn't know how they have got to this place. A moment ago they were possibly saying they loved each other and now they seem to be claiming they would rather be alone. It strikes him how careful you have to be with words.

He says in a rush, "You said something once. About losing things."

"Oh," she says. And then a little while later, "Yes."

"Will you tell me what you have lost?"

"Well," she says. "Where do I start? Husbands."

At least they are back exchanging words again, although he has no idea what she is talking about. She folds her arms.

"Two of them," she says. "The first was a telesales man. We were together thirteen years. Then one day he rang someone, got into a chat about this and that, sold her a timeshare apartment, and that was it. They ran off to the Costa del Sol. I was on my own for a long time after that. I didn't want to get hurt again. Then I gave in a few years ago. Got married. He was gone within six months. Apparently I am impossible to live with. I grind my teeth at night. I snore. He moved into the spare room, but I sleepwalk as well."

"That's a shame."

"That I sleepwalk?"

"That he left you."

"C'est la vie. My daughter."

Eileen's face compresses as if someone has placed a weight on her head and ordered her not to move. When Jim says nothing, she fixes him with her eyes. She asks if he heard what she just said. And when he says yes, he puts his hand next to hers on the table, just as the social worker did with him when she explained about being ordinary. About making friends.

She says, "Rea left the house one day. She was just seventeen. I'd bought her this bracelet for her birthday—it was one of those silver ones, you know, with charms. She said she was going to the corner shop. We'd had a row, but it was a silly one. About washing up. She didn't come back." Eileen reaches for her beer and she drinks and then she wipes her mouth slowly.

Jim doesn't understand. He doesn't see how these pictures in his head of Eileen's daughter and a corner shop and a bracelet fit with the other detail about her never coming back. Eileen takes her cardboard coaster and places it on an exact line with the table edge, and all the time she shifts it and realigns it, she talks. She tells Jim how she has not seen her daughter since that day. She has looked for her and never found her. Sometimes she gets a hunch, it can be in the middle of the night, that she knows where Rea is and she gets in the car, she drives there, but she is wrong. She never finds her. Eileen takes up the coaster, which she has made so straight against the table, and she rips it into tiny pieces.

"All I want is to know that she's safe and I can't have that, Jim."

Eileen grips the table. She apologizes but she is going to cry. He asks if he can fetch her something, a glass of water or something stronger, but she says no to both. She just wants him to sit with her.

At first he can't bear to look. He hears the sharp intakes of breath that precede sorrow and he wants to jump up. He saw people crying at Besley Hill. Sometimes they simply lay on the floor like children and you had to walk around them. But it is different witnessing the onslaught of Eileen's pain. He twists on his stool, trying to search for the barman and the man with his dog, but both have disappeared. He wishes he had something to give Eileen but he has nothing, not even a clean paper tissue. He can only sit. She keeps a wide grip on the table; she spreads her feet wide, as if bracing herself for the worst. Tears overflow her eyes and wash down her cheeks and she does not try to stop them, she simply sits, bearing her sadness, waiting for it to pass. Watching her, Jim feels his eyes prickle, though it is many years since he has cried.

When it is over, she wipes her face. She smiles. "Can I show you her picture?"

Eileen becomes very busy with the contents of her drawstring handbag. She plonks on the table a leather purse, her car keys, her house keys, a hairbrush. "Here." Her fingers are trembling as she opens a torn blue plastic wallet with a bus pass behind the transparent window. The pass is years out of date, and the fading image shows a pinched white face, doe eyes, a mane of thick red hair. This girl is unmistakably a part of Eileen, only she is a fragile, youthful part. The part he has guessed at sometimes and never seen. "You see. We all fuck up," she says.

Eileen reaches for Jim's fingers, but he can't do it. He can't take hers. She puts her hand back where it was. "So what happened to your friend? The one you told me about? What did you do, Jim, that was so terrible?"

He opens his mouth but he cannot voice it.

"I've got all the time you need," says Eileen. "I'll keep waiting."

17

The Outsider

Once James's suspicions were confirmed about Jeanie's leg, he wouldn't let the subject go. He asked when Byron was going to confront Beverley. He even wrote the scenario. Why didn't Byron at least unbuckle the caliper while Jeanie was asleep? Did he not want to save his mother? James kept telephoning.

But Diana was a different person now. In the last few days of the summer holiday, after she had thrown away her watch, and after the disastrous concert, there came a final abandonment of time. She seemed to grow less substantial. She spent long periods doing nothing. Byron tried to tell her about the caliper, about Jeanie's original injury being on a different leg, but she gazed back at him as if he were heartless. "She still can't walk," she said.

Throughout Cranham House, clocks had either fallen into silence or were keeping their own versions of the hour. Byron could walk into the kitchen, where it might be ten to eight, only to enter the drawing room and discover that it was half past eleven. The children went to bed when the sky drew dark, and ate when their mother remembered. The notion too of a certain order of meals—breakfast, lunch, tea—seemed to escape her, or at least strike her as no longer relevant. Every morning there were silver snail trails crisscrossing the hall. There were cobwebs like soft clouds and pepperings of mold at the windowsills. The moor was coming inside.

"It was always going to happen," she said. "This is my destiny."

"What is your destiny?"

She merely shrugged as if she knew a secret he was too young to understand. "The accident was just waiting for me."

"But it was an accident," he reminded her. "It was a mistake."

She gave a laugh that was more of a huff of air. "This is where I was heading right from the start. All those years of trying to get it right—they meant nothing. You can run and run, but in the end you won't get away from the gods."

The gods, he wanted to say, who exactly are they? She had never to his knowledge been a religious woman. He had never seen her enter a church; he had never even seen her pray. And yet she referred to them increasingly. She lit small candles in the windows at night. After swearing, sometimes she looked at the air above her head and asked its forgiveness.

"In a strange way, it's a relief," she said. This time they were eating burgers in the new Wimpy Bar in town because they were hungry. Lucy was drawing a picture of mothers in pink dresses and removing her gherkins into an ashtray.

"What's a relief?" he said.

"The accident. Everything falling apart. I have been afraid of it for years. At least there isn't that anymore."

"I don't think you should talk as if everything is over."

She pursed her lips around her straw, and when she had finished her water she said, "We don't know what to do with sadness. That's the problem. We want to put it out of the way and we can't."

The effort of being the woman she had tried so long to be was finally too much for Diana. It took everything she had merely to talk to Seymour and Beverley. Without them, she seemed to become diaphanous. It was like blowing the seeds from a dandelion and watching them drift. She started to become the naked thing she really was.

Directly after the conversation in the Wimpy Bar, Diana carried her mother's furniture out of the garage. Byron watched her crossing the lawn with it toward the meadow, and he assumed it would be burned, just as she had done with her clothes. But to his surprise he found her a few hours later down by the pond, sitting on her mother's chair, with the small wooden hostess table at her feet and several magazines. She had even set up the floor lamp with its fringed shade, although it wasn't plugged in. It was like a living room with flowers for a carpet, with the belt of ash trees for faraway walls, and the flickering leaves and new elderberries for wallpaper. The cloudless sky was her ceiling.

Spotting Byron, she waved. "Over here!" She had set out colored glasses and a jug of something that looked like lemonade. She had even brought tiny paper umbrellas and a round of cucumber sandwiches. It was like the old days—except for the meadow part.

"Would you like to join me?" She pointed to a low upholstered hassock. He hunkered down, and it gave a squelch.

"Is Beverley not coming today?" he said. "With Jeanie?"

His mother scanned the trees. "Maybe they won't today." She

sat back in the chair, nestling into the headrest and spreading out her fingertips, as if her nails were wet and required drying. "My mother used to sit in this chair. It was her favorite place. Sometimes she sang. She was a beautiful singer."

Byron swallowed hard. He had never heard her speak of her mother before. He spoke gently, hoping that a question would not tip his mother back into silence. He very much wanted to know about her past.

"Did your mother sit outside?"

Diana laughed. "No. She sat inside. For years and years she sat inside. She never went anywhere."

"Was she all right?" Byron wasn't quite sure what he meant by the question but felt compelled to ask it.

"She was unhappy. If that's what you mean. But that's the price you pay."

"The price you pay for what?"

She looked at him briefly and then glanced back to the trees. A small wind passed through them so that the leaves lifted and rustled like water. The sky was such a deep shade of blue, it looked freshly minted. "It's the price you pay for a mistake," she said. "An eye for an eye. A tooth for a tooth. What goes around comes around."

"I don't understand. Why was it an eye for an eye? What was her mistake?"

She closed her eyes, as if she were drifting into sleep. "Me," she said quietly. And then she kept so still, he had to prod her briefly to check she hadn't died or anything.

He wanted to ask more. He wanted to know why his mother's mother spent her life inside, and what his mother meant when she described herself as a mistake, but she had begun to hum, very quietly, as if to herself and no one else, and she looked so at peace with that, he didn't have it in him to interrupt. He helped himself to several of her miniature sandwiches and poured himself a little of her lemonade. It was so sweet he felt his teeth zing.

Clusters of red poppies were still out in the lower fields of the moor, as if the earth were bleeding. Byron didn't want to think of the poppies like that, but he had now, and there was no seeing them otherwise.

"I could sleep out here." His mother's voice surprised him.

"I think you just were."

"No, I could bring a bed and a cover. I could sleep under the stars."

"You wouldn't be safe," he said. "The foxes might get you. Or snakes."

She laughed. "Oh, I don't think they'd want me." She picked up one of her sandwiches and unpeeled the crust between her pinched thumb and forefinger. "The truth is, I don't think I am a very housey sort of person. Maybe I belong outside. Maybe that's my whole problem."

Byron surveyed the field of moving grass, threaded with pink campion, vetch, spears of lady's bedstraw, scabious, and the deeply cut purple petals of meadow cranesbill. Beneath the blue of the sky, the pond was a deep green and thick with velvety strings of duckweed. A small pink petal was tucked into his mother's hair, and a picture came to his mind of her covered in meadow flowers. It wasn't frightening. It was beautiful. "All the same," he said, "I don't think you should tell Father when he telephones that you want to sleep outside."

"You're probably right." She nodded and then, much to his

surprise, she winked—as if they had shared a joke or a secret except that they hadn't because he had no idea what it was.

"When I was just a little girl," she sang, "I asked my mother, What will I be? Will I be pretty? Will I be rich?"

He quietly rose from the hassock and made his way back to the house. With every step he seemed to send grasshoppers springing out of the grass. They burst up like firecrackers. When he stopped to look back, he could still see his mother down at the pond. A cloud of summer flies billowed around her head.

In the kitchen, Byron poured milk into glasses and offered Lucy what was left of the biscuits. He thought of his mother sitting outside, maybe sleeping or singing or maybe a little of both, and he felt like crying, although he didn't know why. She had not seemed unhappy. He wondered if she would really sleep all night out there. Maybe he should take her blankets? A pillow?

She was right, though; he could see it. She was not a housey person. When he pictured her, the tiny jeweled drawers had completely gone, and she was not within the confines of walls or even a car. He felt he had lost her even without seeing her go. That she was part of something he did not understand and did not know. There was no pulling her out of it, though. Maybe she was right not to be a housey person? Maybe that was where the trouble started? People tried to tame themselves within walls and windows, and they tried to find knickknacks to make the walls and windows their own, when maybe what they needed was to be free of those constraints. Byron asked himself again how such a person could call herself a mistake.

"Where is Mummy?" said Lucy.

"She's outside. She's gone for a walk, sweetheart."

The telephone was ringing again, and whoever it was, James or his father, Byron could no longer answer either of them. Instead he chased Lucy upstairs to make it fun and then he ran her a bath and found the Crazy Foam. Afterward he wrapped her in a towel and rubbed her dry, just as his mother would. He even stroked the tiny spaces between her toes. "You're tickling," she said, but she didn't laugh. She looked sad.

"Mummy will be back soon," he said.

"She used to make tea and read us stories and she looked pretty. And another thing, she smells."

"Of what?" He hadn't noticed his mother smelling.

"Stinky sprouts."

He laughed. "You don't know what stinky sprouts smell like."

"I do. They smell like her."

"Well, I don't know how," he said. "She hasn't even eaten sprouts. It's summer."

Lucy curled into the space beneath his arm. She drew up her legs and folded them beneath her like a small fawn. "She used to be like a proper mummy. She used to hold our hands and say nice things."

"Mummy will be back soon," he repeated. "Now, why don't I read you a story?"

"Will you do the funny voices?"

"I will do really funny ones."

After he had read to Lucy he held her hand. It was small and warm inside his.

"Mummy sings," she said, opening one eye and snapping it shut again.

He sang the song he had heard his mother sing in the field, although he didn't know the words or the tune. Lucy lay very still, her head tucked into her pillow. The light was dimming. Outside, the clouds were swept across the sky in drifts that shone the color of tinned peaches.

He found his mother by the pond, curled into her chair. He led her back to the house, inch by inch, in the same way he had coaxed Lucy toward sleep. He felt he had to be very careful with her. Obediently Diana climbed the stairs and slipped between her sheets. She was still wearing her shoes and her skirt, but it wouldn't matter this once.

"There, there, dear," he said softly, but there was no need. She was already fast asleep.

18

Goodbye, Eileen

Jim has been looking forward to his date all day. Since the initial experience with the deodorant he has avoided scent of any kind, but he has washed and combed his hair. When Paula catches him checking his reflection in a car window after work, she says, "Going somewhere special, Jim?" Darren gives a thumbs-up and also such a colossal wink it looks painful. They've made Jim feel like one of them, so he winks and gives a thumbs-up too.

"I'm meeting Eileen," he says. "I have a present for her."

Paula rolls her eyes, but to Jim's surprise she doesn't shout. "Takes all sorts," she says.

"Good for you, mate," Darren laughs.

The crowds jostle along the pavement, making last Christmas Eve purchases. Some of the shops have already started their sales. In the window of the sweet shop, a young assistant sets up a display of Easter eggs. Jim watches her arrange them in order of size. He likes the way she balances the smallest ones at the top, and the way she tucks five yellow fluffy chicks around the boxes. Maybe she is a little like him. Maybe he is not so strange, after all.

Eileen's pens are safe in Jim's jacket pocket. It was Moira who helped wrap them in Christmas paper and then tied the bundle with metallic ribbon. In a separate carrier bag he has stowed the makings of his Christmas lunch as well as extra duct tape. It would be nice not to have to carry duct tape and his Christmas lunch on a date. It would be nice to think of one thing at a time. But he sees that this is another part of being normal, that you have to carry several things in your mind at once, even when they do not feel right together.

The pub is packed with Christmas Eve drinkers. Some of them have clearly been here all afternoon. They wear paper crowns and Father Christmas hats. They shout to be heard. There are flashing lights and plates of free mince pies at the bar, in silver foil cases. One of a group of men in business suits is asking if they do bottles of Côtes du Rhône, and the bargirl is asking is that red or white, that's the only sort of wine they do, she's saying. Threading his way through the crowd, Jim carries a tray with two drinks, only his fingers hurt today, and by the time he reaches the table the beer swims all over the tray. The carpet is spongy beneath his feet.

"I will—I will get more," he says.

Eileen laughs and says bugger that. She lifts both drinks and mops the underside of the glasses. She is wearing her green winter coat, and she has added a colored glass brooch. Jim realizes there is something funny about her face and then that it is lipstick. She has also done a new thing with her hair. It is quite flat and wet around her face. Noticing the direction of his gaze, Eileen lifts her hands and presses both sides of her head. Maybe the thing she has tried to do with her hair is brush it.

Eileen asks about Jim's plans for Christmas. In turn he shows her the turkey supreme in his shopping bag and the ready-prepared potatoes and sprouts, as well as the microwaveable pudding for one.

"Sounds like you have everything you need," she says.

He explains that he doesn't. He has no microwave, for a start. "And I have never c-cooked a Christmas lunch b-before."

This last sentence takes a long time. It is partly because he is nervous, partly because he has to shout. Overhearing him, three young women at the table directly behind Eileen turn to look. This is strange, because they seem to have forgotten clothes. They are wearing underwear, or garments that would once have passed for underwear: tiny strappy tops that reveal soft white flesh and inky coils of tattoos. If anyone should be staring, it is surely Jim.

"I actually hate Christmas," says Eileen. "Everybody has this idea you have to have a good time. Like happiness comes in a ruddy packet." Her face is flushed with heat.

"One time," she goes on, "I stayed in bed all day. That was one of my best Christmases. Another time, I went to the seaside. I got this idea Rea was there. I stayed in a B&B."

"That was nice," says Jim.

"It wasn't. Someone in the next room took an overdose. He had gone away to kill himself at Christmas. See what I mean? It's crap. For loads of people it's crap. It took me and the landlady hours to clear up."

Jim explains that this is his first Christmas in the van. He is looking forward to it, he says. Eileen shrugs and drinks, suggesting it takes all sorts. "I've been thinking," she says. She twiddles her glass around and around on the table.

"What have you been th-thinking?"

Hearing his stutter again, the young women share a smirk, though they have the generosity to do it behind their hands.

"You can say no to this idea," says Eileen.

"I d-don't think anyone s-s-says n-n-no to you, Ei-ei-ei-eileen." The words take forever to emerge from his mouth. It is like throwing up a selection of consonants and vowels. But Eileen does not interrupt. She watches, she waits, as if she has nothing else to do but listen to Jim, and this somehow makes the stupid words even more difficult. He can't think why he is bothering. It isn't even funny. However, when he gets to the end she throws back her head and laughs so hard you would think he had told her a joke, a proper one, like the nurses used to pull from the crackers at Christmas. He can see the creamy folds of Eileen's neck. Even the young women at the table behind her are smiling.

Eileen takes a large swig of her beer. She mops her mouth with the back of her hand. "I'm actually embarrassed," she says. She drags her fingers through her flattened hair, and when she replaces her hands on her hips a wedge of hair is sticking out sideways like an orange flap. "Fuck, this is difficult."

The girls have noticed Eileen's hair. They nudge one another.

"W-w-what is difficult?"

The girls repeat what he has said. "W-w-w-w," they go, and clearly the sound of this in their mouths feels so hilarious they have to laugh.

Eileen says, "I'm going away."

He tries to drink his beer but a splash of it hits his lap.

"Are you listening?" says Eileen. "I'm leaving."

"Leaving?" It is only as he repeats the word that he realizes what it is, what it signifies. Eileen will be an absence, not a presence. "W-w-w-w—?" He is so devastated, already so lonely, that he can't get the word out, he can't ask why. He covers his mouth to show he is all done.

"I'll go in the New Year. I don't know where. I'm going— I'm going to travel again." Now Eileen can't get the words out, and she doesn't even have a stammer. "The thing is, Jim— The thing is— Blimey, why is this so difficult? I want you to come."

"Me?"

"I know I'm a handful. I know I ran you over and everything and that's not exactly a good start. But we've been through stuff, Jim. We've both been through stuff, and the fact is we're still standing. So why not? While we can. Why don't we go away and give ourselves a go? We can help each other try again."

Jim is so bewildered he has to look away to replay what she has just said. She wants to go away with him. From the bar, a businessman stares. He is with the group looking for Côtes du Rhône. Catching Jim's eye, the man mutters something to his friends and breaks free. He is heading straight for Jim and Eileen. He is pointing at Jim. "I know you," he is mouthing.

"Oh," Eileen says, feeling the stranger's presence. She gives a smile, a girlish small one, and it is heartbreaking to see her cowed suddenly by this businessman in his suit.

"Hi, how are you? I'm back to see the folks for Christmas," says the man. He has the loud, confident voice of a Winston House boy, a college chap, a chap who has followed his father into the City. He takes no notice of Eileen. "But I can't stay in the old house for more than five minutes."

Before he can say any more, Jim staggers to his feet. He yanks his jacket from the chair, only the sleeve is caught and he has to pull it so hard the chair is thrown to the ground.

"What's happening?" says Eileen. "Where're you going?"

How can he start again with Eileen? What about the rituals? She says she's a handful. She snores. She sleepwalks. But he is used to all this. He has shared dormitories for years with people who do these things. What she has no idea about is who *he* is, what he did in the past and all that he must continue to do to atone for that. She wants Jim's help? She has no idea. Look at the girls watching him, waiting for him to try to voice what he feels, waiting to laugh.

He can see only Eileen's buttons and her wild red hair. Despite the earlier brushing, it has risen like a cloud from her shocked-white parting. He wants to tell her he loves her. "Goodbye," he says.

Eileen's face drops and she gives a groan. She lowers her head. Even the businessman looks uncomfortable. "Sorry, guys. My mistake." He is already backing away.

Jim's coat is not even on his shoulders, it is caught around his arms as he pushes his way toward the door. He has to knock into customers and they shout things like "Where's the fire?" and "Watch my glass, tosser," but he doesn't stop, he keeps pushing, past the men in party crowns and the girls dressed in underwear. It is only when he is halfway down the street that he realizes his hands are empty. He still has Eileen's present in his pocket, and he has left under the table the carrier bag with his Christmas lunch.

It is too late to go back and fetch it.

19

Jeanie and the Butterfly

It was too late to go back. The summer had acquired an energy of its own. Byron didn't know how much longer it would continue. The heat, the long days, his mother's guilt, Jeanie's leg, and Beverley's visits.

Jeanie sat on her wool rug beneath the fruit trees. Her legs were straight out in front of her, the one with the caliper and the other with its ordinary white sock and sandal. She had the Cindy dolls, or at least she had their torsos in one pile and their heads in another, and she had the coloring books and pens. She had her glass of Sunquick and a biscuit as well as some apple. Every time Byron passed, she was singing gently. From the house he could hear Beverley practicing a new piece on her organ, and he knew that his mother was resting in the armchair down by the pond. It had been a difficult night. Every time he woke, he had heard her playing the record player downstairs. She probably hadn't been to bed again. Lucy was inside the house. She refused to come out of her room.

A pale yellow butterfly landed close to Byron's feet. He tried to touch it, but it flitted up to the white bell of a flower and rested on the petals, fanning its wings. He whispered to the butterfly not to be frightened, and for a moment he thought it had heard because it remained very still as he reached out his finger. Then it skittered into the air again and landed on a buttercup. For a while he followed it, up and down the garden, until Beverley hit a bass chord with her organ and the butterfly flew toward the sky like a little leaf. He kept trying to watch for it, screwing his eyes tighter and tighter, until at last the butterfly grew so slight it was not there. Glancing around him, he realized he had strayed right to the edge of Jeanie's blanket.

"I'm sorry," he said in a rush.

She stared back up at him with round, frightened eyes.

Byron knelt on the edge of her blanket to show he meant no harm. He had not been alone with Jeanie since the visit when he had found her sleeping in Lucy's bed. He didn't know what to say. He gazed at the worn leather of her caliper, the straps and the buckles. It looked painful. Jeanie gave a small sniff and he saw she was crying. He asked if she would like him to play with the dolls. She nodded.

Byron gave hats to the heads and dresses to the bodies. He said it was a shame they were all broken. Again she nodded. "Would you like them to be fixed?"

She didn't nod or speak, but she smiled.

Byron found a head and a body. He pushed one hard over the other, and for a while he thought it couldn't work until with a snap the head suddenly slipped back into place.

"There," he said. "We fixed them."

It wasn't strictly true that she had helped, but somehow his saying it made her smile again, as if she might have fixed them if circumstances were different. Jeanie took the doll in her hands. She touched its head. She touched its arms, its legs. Gently she stroked its hair.

"Oh, but what happened to these poor girls?" he said suddenly, picking up another torso and head. They were covered in felt-tip spots.

Jeanie gave a tiny cry and cowered. It was so nervous and sharp a movement, it made him jump too, as if she expected he would smack her.

"Don't worry. I won't hurt you," he said softly. "I wouldn't do that, Jeanie."

She gave an uneasy smile. He asked if the dolls had measles. She nodded.

"Oh, I see," he said. "Poor things."

She nodded.

"Do they like having the measles?"

Slowly she shook her head. Her eyes were fixed on his.

"Do they wish they were better?"

When she gave another nod his heart began to bang so hard he could feel it in his fingers, but he breathed slowly. It was a shame, he said, that these girls were stuck with measles, and Jeanie nodded to say yes, it was a shame. "Do they need help to get better?" he asked gently.

Jeanie did nothing. She simply looked at Byron with her wide, alarmed eyes.

He picked up a red pen. He drew three spots on his hand. He said nothing about what he was doing, partly because he had no idea, he was just doing it, and partly because he sensed they were better off, he and Jeanie, in a place that had no words. Jeanie remained very still, watching as he drew on his fist, watching the red felt-tip pen and the marks like small berries.

"Do you want to have a go?" he said. He gave her the pen. He offered his hand.

Jeanie reached out with her slight fingers, and he placed his plump hand in hers. Her palm was cold, like stone. She drew one circle on his hand and colored it, then she did another. She didn't press. She did them slowly and carefully.

"You can do spots on my leg, if you like," he said.

She nodded and drew some more spots on his knee, then his thigh, then all the way down to his foot. Overhead the warm breeze rustled the leaves of the fruit tree.

"Would you like some, Jeanie?" he said.

Jeanie glanced up at the house, where her mother was playing the organ. She looked confused or sad, Byron wasn't sure which. She shook her head.

"No one will be angry," he said. "And I will help you wash them off afterward." He held out his spotty arms and his spotty legs. "Look," he laughed. "You can have measles like me."

Jeanie gave him her hand. It was like touching stone again. He gave her four small spots on her knuckles. He did them gently because he was afraid of hurting. When he had finished she drew her hand close to her face. She examined his work carefully.

"Do you like them?" he said.

She nodded.

"Do you want any more?"

She stared back at him, and the look she gave was a strange one, a questioning one. She pointed to her legs.

"This one?" he said.

She shook her head and pointed to the caliper. He glanced

back at the house and then down to the pond. Beverley was play-ing a new piece. She kept stopping and going back to the begin-ning to get it right. There was no sign of his mother.

His hands shook as he undid the buckles. He unfolded the leather, and the skin of her leg was soft and white, and it smelled a little of salt, but it wasn't unpleasant. He didn't want to upset her. There was no plaster. There was no scar on either knee.

"Poor, poor leg," he said.

She nodded.

"Poor Jeanie."

He drew one spot on her knee. It was so faint, so slight, it was like the smallest blemish. She didn't flinch. She watched very carefully.

"Do you want another?"

She pointed to her ankle, then her shin, then her thigh. He drew six more. All the time he drew, she craned her head forward, studying his work intently. Their heads were almost touching. He saw that she was not lying about her legs. She was just waiting for them to be ready to move again.

"We're the same now," he said.

A yellow leaf flittered through the sunlight. It landed on the blanket, and Byron saw it was the butterfly with her yellow wings. He didn't know that it could be a sign, the butterfly, but its reap-pearance was certainly like the joining of two moments that would otherwise be split apart. Beverley's music was building to a finish. She hit the chorus with a crescendo of chords. He even thought he heard his mother calling from the pond. He had a sense that something was coming, another landmark, and that if he didn't capture it quickly it would be gone again.

"The butterfly is looking for a flower," he whispered. He held out his fingers like petals and so did Jeanie. "It thinks our spots are flowers."

He scooped the butterfly gently inside his hands. He could feel its wings, pale as paper, beating against his skin. He lowered it into her hands and told her to be still. It sat in her palm, and somehow the butterfly knew too about keeping still, it didn't flap its wings or get frightened. Jeanie was so still she was not breathing.

"Jeanie!" called Beverley from the terrace.

"Byron!" called his mother, crossing the garden.

The butterfly edged toward Jeanie's fingertips. "Oh no," he said with barely any voice, "it might fall. What can we do, Jeanie?"

In the silence and very slowly she began to lift her knees to make a flowery bridge. As the butterfly crept over her fingernails and down toward her legs, she brought them higher. The women were shouting, they were running toward them, but he kept saying to Jeanie, "Higher, higher, sweetheart." The butterfly tiptoed up and down her small white lifting knees, and at last she laughed.

PART THREE

Besley Hill

Rain Dance

A new moon in early September brought a change in the weather. The heat subsided. The days were warm but no longer fierce. There was a slight chill in the morning air, and a white cloud of condensation at the windows. Already the leaves of the clematis were drying brown twists on the stems, and the ox-eye daisies were almost over. The morning sun peeped at Byron over the hedgerows as if it couldn't quite reach the zenith of the sky.

The new moon brought a change in his mother too. She was happier again. She continued to post small gifts to Beverley and to telephone about Jeanie, but she no longer drove to Digby Road and Beverley no longer came to visit. James greeted the news of Jeanie's recovery with silence. He informed Byron that he was spending the last weekend of the school holidays at the seaside. Maybe he would get to see a concert, Byron suggested. James said awkwardly that it would not be that sort of trip.

Beverley's response was the opposite. It was a miracle, she concluded. That a child should recover when all the doctors had given up. She thanked Byron profusely. She apologized over and over for the anxiety she had caused. Things had got out of hand, she kept saying. She just wanted to be Diana's friend, she never meant her to suffer. Everybody makes mistakes, she cried. She had never guessed that Jeanie's lame leg was imagined. She promised to return the soft toys, the pushchair, the kaftan dress, the borrowed clothes. There were many tears. But Diana reassured her. It had been a strange summer, she said. Maybe the heat had got to them all? She seemed so relieved to have reached a conclusion, she had no space for blame or even understanding. The last time Beverley telephoned, she confided that Walt had asked her to marry him. They were thinking of moving north; they would be like a proper family. She had an idea too for a small import business. She talked about grabbing opportunities and thinking big, but with the threat of strikes, her business idea seemed unlikely to work out. She promised to fetch her organ, but somehow or other she never did.

Meanwhile, Diana retrieved her pencil skirts from where they had been hiding, screwed up beside her shoes, and pressed them. They were a little loose about the waist, but they returned her to that tight way of walking with her clippy steps. She stopped spending hours at the pond, and sleeping under the stars. She retrieved her notebook and baked small butterfly cakes with sponge wings. Byron helped her carry her mother's old furniture back to the garage, and they covered it with the dust sheets. Diana reset the clocks. She began to tidy the house and clean. When Seymour came for his first visit, she did not contradict him. She washed his smalls, and over dinner they talked about his shooting holiday and the weather. Lucy played "Chopsticks" over and over again on her electric organ. And even though Seymour insisted it was an extravagant birthday present for a little girl, when Diana assured him that none of the other families had Wurlitzers he gave his upside-down smile.

The children returned to school. Now that Jeanie was no longer lame, James rarely discussed what had happened and how the boys had planned to save Diana. Once or twice he referred to that business in the summer, but only in a disparaging way, as if they had been childish. He gave Byron the Operation Perfect folder. He did not talk about magic tricks or ask about Brooke Bond tea cards. Maybe he was disappointed in Byron; it was hard to tell.

Besides, it was not simply James who seemed altered. Being in their scholarship year made young men of the boys. Some of them had gained inches. Their voices alternately squeaked and growled. Their faces bore spots like marbles. Their bodies smelled and moved and bulged in new ways that were both confusing and exciting. It was like the heating going on in parts of themselves they were not aware they owned. Samuel Watkins even had a mustache.

One night in mid-September they sat outside, Byron and his mother, beneath a clear sky that was upholstered with stars. He showed her the Plough and the Seven Sisters and she gazed up, with her glass on her lap, her neck tipped back. He pointed out the winged eagle shape of Aquila, Cygnus the Swan, and Capricornus. "Yes, yes," she said. She was obviously listening. She kept nodding at the sky and then turning to gaze at him.

"They're playing with us, aren't they?" she said.

"Who?"

"The gods. We think we understand, we've invented science, but we haven't a clue. Maybe the clever people are not the ones who think they're clever. Maybe the clever people are the ones who accept that they know nothing."

He had no idea what to say. As if reading his thoughts, she reached for his hand and wove his arm through hers. "You're clever, though. You're really clever. And you'll be a good person. That's what counts."

She pointed to a veil of opaque light above their heads. "Now tell me about that."

He told her it was the Milky Way. Then, from nowhere, a star shot through the dark as if it had been hurled, and snapped out of sight. "Did you see that?" He grabbed her arm so hard she almost spilled her drink.

"What? What?" She had clearly missed it, but once he explained she sat very still, watching the sky and waiting. "I know I'm going to see one," she said. "I just feel it in my bones." He went to laugh but she held up her hand as if to silence him. "Don't say anything else or I will want to look at you. And I mustn't because I have to concentrate." She sat so neat and expectant she looked like Lucy.

When at last she found one, she leapt up, her eyes wide, her finger making a tapping movement at the night. "Look! Look!" she told him. "Do you see?"

"That's a beauty," he said.

It was an airplane. He could even see its vapor trail, lit up by the moon and shining through the sky like a stitchwork of silver thread. He kept waiting for her to realize, and when she didn't, when she laughed and squeezed his hand and said, "I made a wish for you, Byron. Everything will be all right now that I've seen that lucky star," he had to nod his head and look away. How could she be so innocent? So stupid? He followed her to the house, and she slipped and he had to hold out a hand to steady her.

"I've forgotten how to wear heels," she laughed.

Seeing the wishing star seemed to lift his mother's spirits further. The following day she worked in the garden while the children were at school. She dug over the rose beds, and as the sun began to slide from the sky, Byron helped her pile the first of the fallen leaves into a wheelbarrow to make a bonfire. They collected windfall apples and watered the flower beds near the house; they needed rain. Then she talked about Halloween, how she had read in a magazine that in America they carved faces into pumpkins. She would like to do that, she said. They stopped to watch the bank of cloud, like pink candyfloss towers over the moor. Diana said that it had been a truly beautiful day. People didn't look enough at the sky.

Maybe it was as simple as believing things were what you wanted them to be? Maybe that was all it took? If there was anything Byron had learned that summer, it was that a thing was capable of being not one thing but many different things, some of them contradictory. Not everything had a label. Or if it did, you had to be prepared to reexamine that label from time to time and paste another alongside it. The truth could be true, but not in a definite way. It could be more or less true, and maybe that was the best a human being could hope for. They returned to the house.

It was almost teatime when Diana announced that she had left a cardigan outside. She called that she was going to fetch it and would only be a few minutes.

Byron began a game with Lucy. It occurred to him that it was getting dark, and he rose to switch on the lamps. He made sandwiches because Lucy was hungry and sliced them into triangles. When he glanced again at the window, the light was green.

Setting out a new game of Snakes and Ladders, he told Lucy

he had to fetch something from the garden. "You have your go first," he told her. "Count very carefully. I'll be back for my turn." When he opened the front door, he was shocked.

The cloud over the moor was dark as a stain. There was a storm coming, no question. He called out to his mother from the threshold but she made no answer. He checked the rose beds and the perennial borders and there was no sign of her. A sudden gust of wind tore at the trees, and as the clouds raced forward, corners of the hills were briefly illuminated in silver shafts of light and then eclipsed. The leaves in the branches began to tremble and rattle. Byron made a dash through the garden and toward the picket gate just as the first drops of rain came.

They were bigger than he expected. The rain was driving down from the upper peaks in thick curtains. There was no way she could be at the pond. He turned back toward the house and tried to hide from the rain, tucking his hands into his armpits, ducking his head, but very quickly water was sliding from his hair and down his collar. It surprised him how quickly he went from dry to wet. Byron dashed back through the garden toward the garage.

The rain hit like peppercorns at the roof, but his mother's furniture was still under its sheets and Diana was not there. Briefly he wondered if she was sitting in the Jaguar, if she was asleep on the seat, but the doors were locked and the car was empty. She must have gone back to the house. Maybe even as he shut the garage doors she was drying her hair and talking to Lucy.

Lucy was waiting for him at the threshold. "Where did you go, Byron? I waited and waited. Why did you be so long?" She looked frightened, and seeing her like that he realized he was frightened too. The rain had leaked all over the hall floor. It was only when

he turned and saw the pools of water behind that he realized they
had come from him.

"Where's Mummy?" he asked.

"I thought she was with you."

Byron began to go over all that had happened, trying to calcu-
late the time his mother had been gone. Stooping to remove his
school shoes, he found they were soft like pulp. His fingers
couldn't manage the laces, and in the end he had to yank them off
without undoing them. He began searching the house, gently at
first and then faster, until he was hurrying from bedroom to bedroom, flinging open doors. At the opened windows the curtains
ballooned like sails, and beyond them the branches of the trees
shook helplessly up and down. He secured the windows, and the
rain shot at the glass in rods and splattered on the roof. All over
the house, he heard the wind throwing doors open and punching
them shut.

"Where is Mummy? What are you doing?" said Lucy. She was
trailing him like a shadow.

He checked his mother's bed, the bathroom, his father's study,
the kitchen, but there was no sign, no hint, of her.

"Why are we rushing everywhere?" wailed Lucy.

It was all right, he kept saying, everything was all right, as he
ran back to the front door. His chest was beginning to hurt. He
fetched the umbrella and his mother's waterproof coat from her
peg.

"It's all right, Luce," he said. "I will have Mummy back in a
minute."

"But I am cold, Byron. I want my blanket." Lucy clung to him
so hard he had to wriggle free.

It was as he was guiding her to the drawing room and fetching her blanket that it struck him. What was he doing? He shouldn't be fussing over the blanket. He should be outside. He couldn't understand why he had even come back to the house. "Just sit and wait," he said, and he led Lucy by the hand to an armchair. After that he tried to run away, but he came back to kiss her because she was crying again. "Just sit still, Luce," he said. Then he suddenly dropped everything, the coat, the umbrella, the blanket, on the drawing room carpet. He fled.

Outside, the hood of sky was darker. The rain shot straight down, as hard as spikes. It smashed against the leaves. It flattened the grass. It pelted at the house as if it meant harm, and poured from the gutters onto the terrace. The noise was deafening.

As he ran he shouted for his mother, but the crashing of rain was so loud he seemed to make no noise. He was still in the garden. He couldn't even see as far as the pond. Shoulders hunched, he threw open the picket gate without stopping to close it. He moved toward the pond, but it was no longer a run. He was sliding and slipping, arms out to steady himself; he could barely lift his head. The land was saturated. The water swelled through the grass. With each footfall, it splashed as high as his face.

The pond came into view, and he couldn't believe what he was seeing. He had to flail at the rain with his arms in order to clear it away.

"Mummy! Mummy!" he shouted, but she didn't hear.

There she was, on the pond. Her hair, her clothes, her skin, were so wet she shone. Only here was the thing: She was not on the turfy hummock in the middle, but balancing on the watery space between the island and the bank. How could this be? Byron had to rub his eyes to check. Glass in hand, she was at a midway point that was no longer earthbound, that was only water. She moved slowly, arms outstretched, as if she were dancing. Occasionally her body seemed to buckle and sway, but she kept her balance and went forward, back straight, chin high, arms wide, through the hard silver lines of rain.

"Over here!" he shouted. "Over here!" He was still at the top of the meadow.

She must have heard, because she suddenly stopped and waved. Byron gasped because he was afraid she would fall, but she didn't. She remained upright and balanced on the surface.

His mother shouted something back at him but he couldn't hear what it was, and then she raised her hand, not the one with the glass but the other, and he saw that she held something white and heavy. It was a goose egg. She was laughing. She was happy she'd got it.

The relief at finding his mother filled Byron like hurt. He didn't know anymore what was crying and what was rain. He tugged his handkerchief from his pocket to blow his nose. The cotton was soaked, but he bowed his face into it, not wanting her to know he had been crying. Just as he folded the handkerchief and returned it to his pocket, he looked up as something seemed to strike at the back of his mother's knees. He thought she was doing it to make him laugh. Then her body gave a sudden downward jolt, her hands flew upward, and both the glass and the egg went spinning out of her grasp. A movement caught her upper body, rippling along one arm, through her torso, and out to the other shoulder. It was like witnessing the gathering of a wave.

She shouted something else to him and then she seemed to fold and go down.

Byron stood a moment, waiting for her to reemerge. He

couldn't move. And then, when she did not reappear, when there was only rain hammering at the pond, he began to shift, slowly at first and then faster and faster, knowing he didn't want to get to the water's edge, but sliding through the mud all the same, his shoes gaining no purchase. Knowing, even as he fell forward, that when he arrived he would not want to see.

The following morning, soft plumes of mist rose from the hills, as if all over the moor small fires were being lit. The air creaked and pattered, although there was no rain now, there was only the memory of it. A frayed moon lingered like a ghost of the sun, and all through the sky swarmed tiny summer flies, or were they seeds? Whatever they were, it was a beautiful beginning.

Byron walked down to the meadow, where the overflow of water lay on the land as huge as silver plates. He climbed the fence and sat at the pond's edge. He gazed at the sky's reflection, like another world, or a different truth, one that was coral-colored and upside down. Already his father was home, talking in his study with the police, and Andrea Lowe was boiling the kettle for visitors.

A flock of gulls flew east, rising and falling, as if they might clean the sky with their wings.

2

Rituals

A mountain of cloud is stacked against the night sky, so solid it is like another horizon. Briefly Jim watches from the opened door of his van. The church clock chimes nine across the hills. It's dark, though. So this must be nighttime. The rituals are back, and they are worse than ever. He cannot stop.

It is over for Jim. There is no escape. He does the rituals all day. And yet they make no difference. It is like being pressed against the bars of a cage. He knows they do not help, he knows they never work, and yet he has to do them. He has not slept or eaten since he fled from Eileen.

The very thought of her makes him move inside the van and shut the door. She was his one hope. She asked his help. How could he have abandoned her like that?

Christmas has come and gone. Days have been nights and he has lost track of how many of them have passed. It could be two, three, he has no idea. He has heard rain, wind, he has noticed the van interior lit by patches of sunlight, but it is only once they are gone that he registers they may have been present. Catching his reflection in the window, he jumps, thinking someone is staring in, someone who intends him harm. His face sails flat and pale against the black square of glass. Stubble pins his jaw. Deep shadows hang beneath his eyes. The pupils are dark and bulging. If he were a stranger, passing himself on the street, he would skirt around. He would pretend he had not seen.

How did he get here? When he first started, all those years ago, the rituals were small. They were his friend. He could say, Hello, Baby Belling, and it felt like a secret between himself and his bedsit. It was something easy to make things right. Even when he realized that he had to say it every time he entered the room, it only took a moment and then he could get on. If he felt a little panicky, if he was frightened, he could say hello quickly in a public place and make it sound like a joke. "Hello, Cup of Tea!" he could laugh, and people might think he was thirsty, or jovial, but not that he was weird. He could hide the words with a little cough.

Time changed the rituals. It was only when wrong thoughts or words swooped into his head that he began to experience new anxieties about them. He began to see that if you wanted everything to be safe, you couldn't expect that to happen simply because you had said hello and moved on to do something else. You had to work for everything to be truly safe, otherwise it would not be strong enough. This was logical.

He is not sure how he got to the number 21. That idea seemed to present itself as a rule to his mind and then get stuck. There was a period when he was terrified if the time did not involve a 2 or a 1. He had to keep doing the rituals, until the hands of the clock reached one of those numbers. His favorite times were two minutes past one. Or one minute past two. Sometimes he set his alarm so that he could wake up and look at them.

Soap, hello. Plug Socket, hello. Teabags, hello.

He thought he was cured. He thought he could be ordinary. But the social worker was wrong and so was the psychic counselor. It is too late for Jim.

There is nothing but him and the rituals.

3

An Ending

James remained absent from school after the news of Diana's death. Her funeral came on a Monday in early October. It was the same day as the accident on Digby Road, and a mere four months later, but so many large things had happened within that small space that time had changed yet again. It was no longer a linear progression from one moment to another. It lacked all regularity, all sense. It was a wild, ragged hole into which things indiscriminately fell and changed shape.

Above the moor, the October sky grew soft with blooms of purple cloud, broken occasionally by a cone of sunlight, or the swooping path of a bird. It was the sort of sky his mother would have loved, and watching it made Byron hurt because he could imagine her pointing at it and telling him to come and look. Sometimes he felt he was offering her perfect opportunities to return, and her not doing so made her absence even more bewildering. She would surely come back soon. He only had to find the right incentive.

And so he kept looking. After all, her coat was on its peg. Her shoes were by the door. Her removal was so sudden it lacked all credibility. He waited every morning at the pond. He even lifted her armchair over the fence. He sat where she had sat at the water's edge, and the cushion still held the shape, the scent, of her. He couldn't understand how it was that in the moments it took for a boy to blow his nose, something so substantial as a mother's life could stop.

All the women were present for the funeral, and most of the fathers too. Some chose to bring their sons, but the little girls were not included. The women had decorated the church with arum lilies and cooked a York ham for the reception. There would be a good spread. So much energy went into the planning that it was like a wedding, except that there would be no photographer and the guests wore only black. Tea would be served and orange squash, though Andrea Lowe had brandy in a flask for emergencies. No one could be expected to survive the morning without a little help.

It was the drink, Byron overheard people say. Toward the end poor Diana had rarely been sober. No one explicitly mentioned Beverley's concert, but it was clear they were thinking of such things. All the same, it was a tragedy. That a mother of two, and a wife of one, should die so young. And then came the autopsy and here was another shock. Diana's stomach contained water and the remains of an apple. Antidepressants were found in her blood. Her lungs were plump with water and loneliness, as were her liver, her spleen, her bladder, and the tiny cavities of her bones. But there was no alcohol. Not a trace.

"I only ever saw her drink it once," Byron had told the policeman who came to interview the family. "She had a glass of champagne in a restaurant. She only took a few sips and then she left the rest. Really what she liked was water. She drank it all the time with ice. I don't know if you need to write this down, but I had tomato soup in the restaurant. She let me have prawn cocktail as well. It wasn't even lunchtime."

This was the most he had spoken about his mother since her death. The room stood very still, as if the air was suspended, waiting for him to continue. He had caught sight of the adult faces and the policeman's notebook and suddenly the gap that was his mother shot open at his feet. He had cried so long and uncontrollably, he forgot to stop. His father cleared his throat. The policeman signaled to Andrea Lowe to do something and she fetched biscuits. It was an accident, the policeman said to Andrea. He didn't even lower his voice, as if grief rendered the bereaved deaf. It was a terrible accident.

A private doctor in Digby Road was interviewed. He confirmed that he had been providing Mrs. Diana Hemmings with the drug Tryptizol for several years. She was a gentle lady, he said. She had come to him when she found she could not cope with her new surroundings. He expressed his sorrow and sent his condolences to the family.

Of course there were other stories as to why Diana had died, the most common being that she had drowned and that this was her intention. How else to explain the stones in her pockets? Some gray, some blue, some banded like humbugs? Byron overheard the stories. He knew they were about his mother by the way people glanced in his direction and then fell silent, smoothing imaginary creases from their sleeves. But they had no idea. They had not been there. They had not seen what he had seen that evening by the pond, as the light dimmed and the rain fell. She had stood on water, swaying as if the air was full of music, and then she had lifted out her arms and dropped. She had returned not to earth but to water.

The town church was so packed, the last mourners had to stand. Despite the autumn sun, most wore winter coats, gloves, and hats. There was a smell cramming the air, and it was so full, so sweet, he couldn't tell if it was happy or sad. Byron sat at the front beside Andrea Lowe. He noticed how the congregation had watched and parted as he approached. They were sorry for his loss, they told him in muted tones, and from the way they looked at their feet, he saw that his loss had made him important, and it was a strange thing but he felt proud. James sat farther back with Mr. Lowe, and even though Byron turned several times to smile and show how brave he was, James kept his head bowed. The boys had not met since before Diana's death.

When the coffin bearers emerged, it was too much for some people. Beverley gasped and Walt had to help her out. They limped down the aisle like a broken crab, crashing into the lily arrangement as they passed, so that a trail of yellow powder clung to their black sleeves. The mourners stood very still, watching the coffin, singing quietly, while outside in the autumn sunshine Beverley screamed. Byron wondered if he should be screaming too because after all it was his mother, not Beverley's, and maybe it would be a relief to make a noise like that, but then he caught sight of his father, standing stiff beside the coffin, and Byron stretched his spine up tall. He heard his own voice singing louder than everyone else's, and it was like showing them the way forward.

The sun was out for the reception at Cranham House. Beverley and Walt made their excuses and went home. It was exactly the sort of party Diana would have liked, except that she wasn't there; they had lowered her into a cavity so deep it had made Byron's head reel to look at it, and then they had scattered it with soil and her favorite roses, as if she would take notice, and hurried away.

"You have to eat," said Andrea Lowe. The new mother fetched Byron a slice of fruitcake and a napkin. He didn't want it, he suddenly didn't think he would ever want to eat again, it was as though his insides had gone, but it would be rude to refuse the cake so he ate it in one go, almost without breathing, just stuffing it into his mouth. When the new mother said "Better now?" he said yes, to be polite. He even asked if he might have another slice.

"Poor children. Poor children," sobbed Deirdre Watkins. She held on to Andrea Lowe and shook like a shrub in wind.

"It has been very hard for James," said Andrea, lowering her voice. "The nights have not been good. My husband and I have decided—" She gave a sideways conspiratorial glance that landed on Byron and made him feel he shouldn't be there. "We have decided steps must be taken." Byron put down his cake plate and slipped away.

He found James down by the pond. On Seymour's orders, it had been drained. A local farmer had taken the geese, and the ducks had either gone with them or flown away. It still shocked Byron how shallow the space looked, how slight, without water or birds. The green tangle of nettles, mint, and cow parsley came to an abrupt halt where the surface of water had previously started. The bare black mud glistened in the sun, strewn only with the remaining logs and stones that Byron had once so carefully placed to make a bridge, and the turfy island in the middle was no more than a hump of earth. It was hard to understand how his mother could lose her balance and drown in something so insignificant.

James must have climbed over the fence and slid down the bank; his church trousers were a mess. He stood in the center of the mud bed, hauling at one of the longest branches and grunting with the effort. He was bowed into it, clutching one end in both hands, but the thing was almost his size and he couldn't shift it. His shoes were caked with mud, as were the sleeves of his grown-up jacket. A column of gnats hung beside him.

"What are you doing?" called Byron.

James didn't look up. He kept heaving and heaving and getting nowhere.

Byron climbed the fence and moved carefully down the bank. He stood on the edge because he didn't want to ruin his funeral shoes. He called James again and this time James paused. James tried to hide his face behind the crook of his elbow, but there was no denying he was upset. His face was so red and swollen it looked mangled.

"It's too big for you," shouted Byron.

There was a grating sound from James's chest, as if the pain inside him was more than he could bear. "Why did she do it? Why? I can't stop thinking—" He went back to yanking at the log and groaning, but his hands were so muddy they kept slipping, and twice he almost dropped it.

Byron didn't understand. "She didn't mean to fall. It was an accident."

James was sobbing so hard he had stringy bits dangling from

his mouth. "Why—why—why was she trying to cross the pond?" he wailed.

"She was fetching an egg. She didn't like the crows to get them. She slipped."

James shook his head. The gesture was wild and it shot through his whole body so that he stumbled beneath the weight of the log, on the verge of losing his balance. "It was because of me."

"You? How could it have been?"

"Didn't she know our bridge was dangerous?"

Byron saw his mother again, waving from the pond. Showing him the goose egg. She wasn't walking on water, of course she wasn't. Despite the heat, his skin prickled with cold.

"I should have checked the load bearing," sobbed James. "I said I would help her and I did all the wrong things. It all came from me."

"But it didn't. It came from the two seconds. That was what started everything."

To Byron's alarm, his words caused James to howl again. He had never seen James like this before, so raw, so desperate, so angry. James was still tugging at the log but with such small, ineffectual movements he looked almost defeated. "Why did you listen to me, Byron? I was wrong. Don't you see? I was even wrong about the two seconds."

Byron didn't know why, but suddenly it was hard to get enough air inside his lungs. "You read it in your newspaper."

"After your mother—" James couldn't say it. He tried again. "After she—" He couldn't say that either. He pulled harder at the log. He looked furious with it. "I did more research. The two seconds didn't happen in June. One was added at the beginning of the year. The other will be at the end." He bared his teeth as he sobbed. "There were no extra seconds when you saw them."

It was like a physical blow. Byron clutched his stomach. He stumbled. He saw in a flash his hand poking in front of his mother's face as he tried to show her the second hand of his watch. He saw the car swerve to the left.

The air was broken with shouts from the lawn. Figures in black were searching the garden, calling for James. They were not calling for Byron. Hearing them, Byron realized that for the first time ever there was a rift, a breakage, between the two friends that could not be healed.

He said quietly, "Your mother's looking for you. You'd better put the log down and go back."

James lowered it toward the mud, as if it were a body. He rubbed hard at his face with his sleeve and moved toward the bank where Byron stood waiting for him, but when Byron offered his handkerchief James did not take it. He couldn't even lift his eyes. He said, "We won't be seeing each other anymore. My health is a concern. I have to move schools." James gave a clunk of a swallow.

"But what about the college?"

"We have to think about my future," said James, sounding increasingly not like himself. "The college is not the best place for my future."

Before he could ask more, Byron was aware of a twitching movement in his left pocket.

"This is for you," said James.

Reaching down, Byron felt something smooth and hard between his fingers, but there was no time to look because his friend was already running away. James scrambled up the bank, almost on hands and knees, clutching at the long grasses to haul himself forward. Sometimes they tore out in his hands and almost sent flying him backward, but he kept hauling himself up. He practically flipped himself over the fence.

Byron watched James tearing through the meadow. His jacket was hanging from one shoulder, and several times he stumbled, as if the grass was trying to pull off his shoes. The space between them grew wider, until James was finally through the picket gate and racing toward the group of parents at the house. His mother rushed across the upper lawn to guide him out of the way while his father drew up in the car. She ushered James into the backseat as if he were on the verge of breaking and slammed his door shut. Byron knew he was being left behind.

In one last effort to stop what he knew was coming, Byron threw himself up the bank and over the fence. He stooped to crawl between the fencing posts, and in the rush maybe he knocked his head, or maybe he caught the nettles, because his legs were fizzing suddenly and his head was pounding. He tore through the thick meadow grass in pursuit of the Lowes' car as it made its steady progress down the drive. "James! James!" he was shouting, and the panting and the words burned like wounds to his chest but he wouldn't stop. He threw open the picket gate and charged past the cutting garden, the stone path slapping at his feet. He ran the length of the beech hedging, sometimes crashing into the leaves he was so dizzy, and across the grass to the drive. The car was almost at the road. "James! James!" He could make out his friend in the backseat, the tall silhouette of Andrea Lowe beside him. But the car did not slow and James did not look back. It turned out of the drive and then it was gone.

4

The End of the Duct Tape

Despite the change in temperature, the unseasonably mild weather, Jim does not go to the moor. He does not go to work. He cannot even walk as far as the phone box to ring and explain to Mr. Meade. He assumes he will be out of a job and hasn't the energy to feel, let alone do, anything about that. He doesn't check his planting. He spends each day in the van. The rituals never stop.

Sometimes he darts a look out of his window and he sees life continue without him. It is like waving goodbye to something that has already gone. The residents of Cranham Village appear with their Christmas gifts. There are children with new snow boots and new bicycles. There are husbands with battery-operated leaf vacuums. One of the foreign students has received a sledge, and despite the absence of snow, they all walk up to the ramps in their hats and Puffa jackets. The man with the dangerous dog has a new sign outside his house that warns intruders he has CCTV cameras. Jim wonders if the dog is dead, and then it occurs to him that he never saw a dog, dangerous or otherwise, and maybe the old sign was only a trick, and not the truth at all. The old man is back at his window. He seems to be wearing a baseball cap.

So this is being ordinary. This is getting by. And it is small, really, but Jim can't do it.

The interior of the van is striped with duct tape. There is only one roll left. Jim doesn't know what he will do when it is finished. And then it occurs to him, like a slow dawning, that he will not last any longer than the duct tape. He has not eaten, he has not slept. He is finishing everything, himself included.

Jim lies on the bed. Above his head the pop-up roof is a crisscross of tape. His head reels, his blood thumps, his fingers sting. He thinks of the doctors at Besley Hill, the people who tried to help. He thinks of Mr. Meade, of Paula and Eileen. He thinks of his mother, his father. Where did this begin? With two seconds? A bridge over the pond? Or was it there from the very beginning, when his parents decided their son's future should be golden?

His body shakes, the van shakes, his heart shakes, the windows shake, all with the waste of it. *Jim, Jim,* it shouts. But he is nothing. He is hello, hello. He is strips of duct tape.

"Jim! Jim!"

He is falling into sleep, into light, into nothing. The doors, the windows, the walls, of the van *thump, thump,* like a heartbeat. And then just as he is nothing, the pop-up roof bursts from its hinges. He feels the slap of cold air. There is sky, there is a face, and maybe it should be a woman, but it isn't, it is frightened, very frightened, and then comes an arm, a hand.

"Jim, Jim. Come on, mate. We're here."

5

Strange in the Head

Seymour employed a middle-aged woman to look after the children. Her name was Mrs. Sussex. She wore tweed skirts and thick tights and had two moles with hairs like spiders. She told the children her husband was an army man.

"Does that mean he is dead like my mummy?" said Lucy.

Mrs. Sussex said it meant he was posted abroad.

When Seymour arrived for weekends, she told him to get a taxi from the station if he didn't want to drive. She made casseroles and pies for the fridge and left heating instructions before going to her sister's. Sometimes Byron wondered if she might invite him and Lucy too, but she didn't. Seymour spent weekends in his study because he had so much work to catch up on. Sometimes he fell over when he went upstairs. He tried to make conversation, but the words smelled sour. And although Seymour never said it as such, all this seemed to be Diana's fault.

What bewildered Byron most about the death of his mother was that, in the weeks following, his father died too. But his was a different kind of death from Diana's. It was a living death, not a buried one, and it shocked Byron in a different way from his mother's removal because he had to keep witnessing it. He discovered that the man he had assumed his father to be, the man who stood remote and upright beside his mother, urging her to get in the left-hand lane now, Diana, and dress in old-fashioned pencil skirts, was no longer the same person once she had slipped away. After her death, Seymour seemed to lose his balance. Some days he said nothing. Some days he raged. He flew through the house, shouting, as if his anger alone was enough to make his wife come back.

He didn't know what to do with the children, Byron overheard him saying another time. He only had to look at them and he saw Diana.

It's only natural, people said.

But it wasn't.

Meanwhile, life went on as if his mother's loss had not touched it in any way. The children returned to school. They dressed in their uniforms. They carried their satchels. In the playground, the mothers crowded around Mrs. Sussex. They invited her for coffee. They asked how the family was coping. She was reserved. Once she said that she was surprised at the state of Cranham House. It was a cold place, not a happy environment for young children. The women shared a glance that seemed to imply that they had had a lucky escape.

Without James, and without his mother, Byron felt marked apart. He waited several weeks, hoping for a letter from James with the address of his new school, but nothing came. Once even telephoned James's home, but hearing Mrs. Lowe's voice he hung up straightaway. At school he spent whole lessons staring at his exercise books and failing to write. He preferred to spend playtime alone. He overheard one of the masters describe his circumstances as difficult. Little should be expected.

When Byron found a dead sparrow at the foot of an ash tree in the garden, he cried because at last there was more death and it seemed a sign that Diana was not alone in it. Really what Byron wanted was not one dead bird, but hundreds. He wanted them dropping from the air like stones. He asked his father at the weekend if they might bury the bird, but Seymour shouted at him not to play with dead things. It was strange in the head, Seymour said.

Byron did not mention that Lucy had buried her Cindy dolls.

It clearly was not true that Byron had worried too much. His mother had been wrong about so many things. Sometimes he pictured her in her coffin and found the idea of her being surrounded by darkness almost impossible to bear. He tried to think of his mother when she was alive, the light in her eyes, her voice, her way of draping a cardigan over her shoulders, and then he missed her even more. He told himself to concentrate on his mother's spirit and not to focus on the thought of her body locked beneath the earth. Often his head got the better of him, though, and he woke in the night, bathed in hot sweat, unable to push away the image of her trying to get back to him, of her beating at the locked coffin lid with her fingers and screaming at him to help.

He did not tell anyone, just as he could not bear to confide that he himself had begun the string of events that led to her death.

The Jaguar remained in the garage until a pickup truck came to take it away. It was replaced with a small Ford. October passed. Leaves that his mother had once looked at loosened from the trees and twisted through the air, gathering in a slippery carpet at Byron's feet. The nights grew longer and brought days of rain. Crows fronted the storm and were scattered by it. In one night alone, the rain was so heavy that the pond began to refill and Seymour had to have it drained again. Hedgerows were bare and black and dripping, but for the ghostly weaving of old man's beard.

In November the winds moved in and the clouds scudded over the moor until at last they joined forces and lay so thick, the sky was a slate roof over the land. The mists returned and they hung over the house all day. When a winter storm felled an ash, the tree lay butchered in pieces across the garden. No one came to clear it. With December came flurries of snow and hail. The Winston House boys spent every day preparing for their scholarship exam. Some had private tutors. The substance of the moor changed from purple to orange to brown.

Time would heal, Mrs. Sussex said. Byron's loss would grow more bearable. But here was the crux. He didn't want to lose his loss. Loss was all he had left of his mother. If time healed the gap, it would be as if she had never been there.

One afternoon, Byron was talking to Mrs. Sussex about evaporation as she was peeling potatoes when the knife slipped and she cut her finger. "Ouch, Byron," she said.

There was no connection between Byron and her injury. She was not blaming him. She merely fetched a plaster and continued to peel potatoes, but he began to have thoughts. Thoughts he didn't want and couldn't stop. They even came when he was asleep. He thought of his mother screaming from her coffin. He thought of Mrs. Sussex rinsing her finger under a tap, and the way the water turned red. He became convinced it would be Lucy next, and that just as the accident had been his fault, and also Mrs. Sussex's cut, Lucy's injury would be his fault too.

To start with, he hid his fears. He found simple ways of leaving the room when Lucy entered, or perhaps if he couldn't leave, if it was dinner, for instance, he would gently hum to distract himself from thinking. He took to placing a ladder outside Lucy's bedroom window at night so that if anything happened she would have a safe escape. Only one morning he forgot to move it in time, and Lucy woke, saw the ladder at her window, ran into the hall screaming, and slipped. She needed three stitches just above her left eye. He was right. He caused injury, even when he didn't want to.

The thoughts that followed were about boys at school, as well as Mrs. Sussex, and the mothers. Even people that he didn't know, people he saw from the window of the bus as he sat behind Mrs. Sussex and Lucy. He saw he was a danger to each and every one of them. What if he had already hurt someone and he didn't realize? Because he had thought the awful thing, about hurting a person, it must be that he had done it. That he was the sort of person who *could*—because otherwise, why would he be having those thoughts? Sometimes he did little things to himself to show people he was not well, maybe bruising his arm, or pinching his nose until it bled, but no one appeared concerned. Ashamed, he pulled his shirt toward his knuckles. He needed something different to keep the thoughts away.

When the truth emerged in the playground about Lucy's stitches, Deirdre Watkins telephoned Andrea Lowe, who in turn suggested to Mrs. Sussex a marvelous chap she knew in town.

When Mrs. Sussex said that all the boy needed was a good cud-
dle, Andrea Lowe rang Seymour. Two days later, Mrs. Sussex resigned.

Byron remembered very little about his visit to the psychiatrist. This was not because he was drugged or mistreated in any
way. Far from it. In order not to be frightened, he hummed, first
gently to himself and then, when the psychiatrist raised his voice,
somewhat louder. The psychiatrist asked Byron to lie down. He
asked if Byron had unnatural thoughts.

"I cause accidents," said Byron. "I am unnatural."

The psychiatrist said he would be writing to Byron's parents.
At this, Byron went so silent and still, the psychiatrist called an
end to the session.

Two days later Byron's father told him he was to be measured
for a new suit.

"Why do I need a new suit?" he said. His father staggered
from the room.

This time it was Deirdre Watkins who accompanied Byron to
the department store. He was measured for new shirts, pullovers,
two ties, socks, and shoes, both indoor and out. He was a big boy,
said Deirdre to the assistant. She also asked for a trunk, full sports
kit, and pajamas. This time Byron didn't question why.

At the cash till, the assistant wrote out a bill. He shook Byron
by the hand and wished him luck at his new school. "Boarding is
marvelous, once you get the hang of the place," he said.

He was sent to a school in the north. He had the impression
no one knew what to do with him and he did not fight that. If
anything, he agreed. He made no friends because he was afraid
of hurting them. He lingered on the edge of things. Sometimes
people jumped because they had no idea he was in the room. He

got ridiculed for being quiet, for being strange. He got beaten up. One night he woke to find himself being carried outside on a sea of hands and laughter, but he simply lay very still and did not fight them. It amazed him sometimes how little he felt. He no longer even knew why he was unhappy. He only knew that he was. Sometimes he remembered his mother, or James, or even the summer of 1972, but thinking of that time was like waking out of a sleep with shards of dreams that made no sense. It was better to think of nothing. School holidays were spent at Cranham House with Lucy and a succession of nannies. Seymour visited rarely. Lucy began to choose to stay with friends. Back at school, Byron failed exams. His reports were poor. No one seemed to mind either way, if he was clever or stupid.

Four years later, he ran away from boarding school. He took several night trains and a bus and returned to Cranham Moor. He went back to the house but it was locked up, of course; there was no way in. So he took himself to the police station and handed himself in. They were at a loss. He hadn't done anything, although he kept insisting he might. He caused accidents, he said. He cried. He begged them to let him stay. He was clearly so distressed, they couldn't send him back to school. They rang Seymour and asked him to fetch his son. Seymour never arrived. It was Andrea Lowe who came instead.

It was several months later that Byron heard about his father's suicide. Things were very different by this time, and Byron had no space left in which to feel. As a precautionary measure, he was given sedatives before and after the news. There was talk of a shotgun and a terrible tragedy as well as most sincere condolences, but by then he had heard words like these so many times, they were sounds that meant nothing. When he was asked if he would like to attend the funeral, he said he wouldn't. He remembered to ask if his sister knew, and was told that she was at boarding school. Didn't he remember that? No, he said, he didn't. He didn't remember very much. Then he saw a fly, a dead one, black and upside down, on the windowsill and he began to shake.

It was all right, they told him. Everything would be all right. They asked Byron if he could be still? If he could not cry, and remove his slippers? And he promised he could do those things. Then the needle pierced his arm, and when he came around they were talking about biscuits.

6

The Meeting

Jim has to keep looking at his trainers. He can't decide if his feet have grown or stayed the same. They feel different inside shoes. He has to wriggle his toes and lift his heels and admire the way they stand, side by side, like a pair of old friends. He is glad they have each other again. It is strange to walk not with a limp but evenly, to be like everyone else. Maybe he is not so irregular after all. Maybe you have to take things away sometimes to see how right they were before.

He knows he owes his rescue to Paula and Darren. Concerned about his absence from work, they took the bus to Cranham Village. They knocked at the door and windows of the van. At first they thought he must be on holiday. It was only when they were walking away, Paula admitted afterward, that other thoughts occurred to them. "We thought you were dead and stuff." It was Darren who had clambered onto the roof of the van and yanked open the pop-up roof. They wanted to take him straight to A&E, but he shivered so hard they made tea instead. With difficulty they removed the tape from the windows, doors, and cupboards.

They fetched blankets and food. They emptied the chemical toilet. They told him he was safe.

It is late afternoon on New Year's Eve. Jim cannot believe he so nearly gave up. It was in him, to surrender. And yet now that he is on the other side of that, now that he is back at work and wearing his orange hat, his orange apron and socks, he sees how wrong it would have been. He almost gave up, but something else happened and he kept going.

Rain clings like beads to the darkened windows of the supermarket café. Soon it will be time to close. Mr. Meade and the staff begin to wrap cling film over pastries. The few customers finish their drinks and put on their coats and prepare to drive home.

Paula has spent the afternoon discussing her fancy dress outfit for the party Darren is taking her to at the Sports and Social Club. He in turn has spent a long time in the lavatories doing something with his hair to make it look as if he hasn't done anything. At five-thirty, Mr. Meade will change into the black suit hired from Moss Bros by Mrs. Meade and meet her downstairs. They will attend a dinner dance, followed by fireworks at midnight. Moira, it turns out, has a date with one of the youth band and will accompany them on the minibus to a New Year's gig. The café will close and everyone will have somewhere to go, except Jim, who will make his way back to the van and perform the rituals.

"You should come with us," says Paula. She clears the empty plates and cans of Coke from a table. Jim takes out his spray and his cloth in order to wipe. "It would be good for you. You might meet someone."

Jim thanks her but says he won't. Since she and Darren found him in the van, he has to keep reassuring Paula that he is happy. Even when he is frightened or sad, and occasionally he is both those things, he has to push his face into a wide smile and give her a thumbs-up.

"By the way, she rang again," says Paula.

He tells Paula he doesn't want Eileen's message. But she has rung three times, Paula insists.

"I thought you said—?" The sentence stabs at the air. "I thought you said—you said—she was t-t-t—"

"She *is* trouble," interrupts Paula. Since there is now only one customer left in the café, she puts down her tray. She tugs a blue wig out of her pocket and yanks it over her hair. She looks like a mermaid. "But she's good trouble. And here's the thing, she likes you."

"It's no—it's no g-good." Jim is so confused by what Paula is telling him, and in turn by what he feels, that he finds himself squirting the table of the single remaining customer. The man sits very still. He has not yet finished his coffee.

"Suit yourself," says Paula. "I'm going to get changed." She walks away.

"Excuse me, do you have the time?"

The question is part of the café. Jim barely hears. It is part of the youth band finishing their limited New Year medley downstairs, part of the flashing fiber-optic tree. It is part of other people going about their lives, but Jim does not consider it as pertinent to him, and so he continues to wipe. The man clears his throat. The question comes again, only this time it is a little louder, a little more placed in the air. "Pardon me for asking. Do you have the time?"

Glancing down, Jim realizes with horror that the stranger is staring straight up at him. The café seems to snap to a standstill, as if someone has turned down the light and the volume. He points at his wrist to show he does not have it, the time. There is not even a mark on his skin for a strap.

"I beg your pardon," says the stranger. He drains the last of his cup and mops his mouth with a festive paper napkin. Jim continues to spray and wipe.

The man is dressed in pressed casual clothes: fawn trousers, checked shirt, rainproof jacket. He looks the sort of person who has to think about relaxing. Like his clothes, his thin hair is a nondescript shade of graying brown, and his skin is soft and pale, suggesting a life spent mostly indoors. Beside his coffee cup, his driving gloves are folded into a bundle. Is he a doctor? It seems unlikely he was ever a patient. He smells clean. It is a smell Jim dimly remembers.

The stranger pushes back his chair. He stands. And then just as he is about to move away he appears to pause. "Byron?" he whispers. "Is it you?" His voice is thicker with age, a little more fluid around the consonants, but unmistakable. "I'm James Lowe. I don't suppose you remember?" He offers his hand. It is palm-open, like an invitation. Years fall away.

Suddenly Jim would like to lose his own, to have no hand, but James waits and there is such kindness in his stillness, such patience, Jim cannot move away. He reaches out. He places his hand on James's. His own is shaking, but James's feels clean and soft, and warm too, like freshly melting candle wax.

It is not a handshake. There is nothing shaken about it. It is a handgrasp. A handhold. For the first time in more than forty years, Jim presses his right palm against the right palm of James Lowe. Their fingers touch, slide together, and lock.

"Dear fellow," says James softly. And because Jim is suddenly shaking his head and blinking his eyes, James removes his hand and offers instead the festive paper napkin. "I am sorry," he says. Though whether he is sorry for gripping Jim's hand, or for offering a used napkin, or for calling him "dear fellow," is unclear.

Jim blows his nose to suggest he has a cold. Meanwhile, James aligns the fastening of the zip on his jacket. Jim continues to dab his nose, and James runs the zip right up to his neck.

James says, "We were passing on our way home. My wife and I. I wanted to show her the moor, and where we grew up. My wife is getting some last-minute shopping done before we head back to Cambridge. Her sister will be with us for New Year." There is something childlike about him, with the zip fastened all the way up to his collar. Maybe he realizes that, because, looking down at it, he frowns and carefully unzips it to a midway point.

There is so much to take in. That James Lowe has become a short, thin-haired man in his fifties. That he is here, in the supermarket café. That he has a home in Cambridge and a wife. A sister-in-law who visits for New Year. A waterproof jacket with a zip.

"Margaret sent me to buy a coffee. I get under her feet. I am afraid I'm still not a practical man. Even after all these years." Since the handshake, James can't seem to look Jim in the eye. "Margaret is my wife," he adds. And then he says, "I am her second husband."

Bereft of words, Jim nods.

"It was a shock," says James. "It was a shock to find Cranham House gone and the gardens too. I didn't intend to drive that way; the satnav must have made a mistake. When I saw the estate, I had no idea where I was. Then I remembered I'd heard about the new village. Only I had somehow imagined they would keep the old house. I had no idea they would flatten it."

Jim listens and keeps nodding as if he is not trembling or holding antibacterial spray or wearing an orange hat. Occasionally James pauses between sentences, offering an opening, but Jim can only muster a few *hm-hm* noises, a few trudges of breath.

James says, "I had no idea, Byron, about the size of Cranham Village. I can't believe the developers got away with it. It must have been so hard to see the old house go. And the garden. It must have been very hard for you, Byron."

The use of his real name is like being repeatedly hit. Byron. Byron. He has not heard it spoken in forty years. It is the ease, the kindness, with which James says it that floors him. Still, Jim, who is not Jim, who is Byron after all but has long been someone else, this other person, this Jim, this man without roots, without a past, can't speak. And sensing this, James continues:

"But maybe you were ready to let the place go? Maybe you wanted them to flatten it. After all, things don't always go the way we think. They never made another landing on the moon, Byron, after 1972. They played golf up there, they collected samples, and then the whole thing stopped." James Lowe pauses with his face in a frown of concentration as if he is rewinding the last sentence and listening again. "I don't have a problem with golf. It just seems a shame they had to play it on the moon."

"Yes." At last. A word.

"But it is easy for me to be sentimental about the moon, just as it is easy for me to be sentimental about Cranham House. The truth is, I haven't come back. Not for many years."

Jim opens his mouth. It gropes and snaps around words that will not come. "They—they s-sold—"

"The house?"

He nods. But James does not appear confused or embarrassed or even surprised by the stutter.

"The trustees sold it?"

"Yes."

"I am sorry. So very sorry, Byron."

"There was no—there was no money left. My father let things—he let things go."

"I heard as much. Such a terrible thing. And what happened to your sister, Lucy? What did she do?"

"London."

"She lives there?"

"She-she-she married a banker."

"Does she have children?"

"We lost—we lost—touch."

James nods sadly as if he understands, as if the rift between brother and sister was inevitable, given the circumstances, but nevertheless to be mourned. He changes the subject. He asks if Byron still hears from any of the old crowd. "My wife and I went to one of those drinks receptions—for old Winstonians. I saw Watkins. Do you remember?"

Jim says yes, he remembers. James tells him that Watkins went into the City after Oxford. He married a nice French lady. James adds that parties are more Margaret's thing. "So what brings you here, Byron?"

He explains it is his job, to squirt tables, but James does not look surprised. He nods eagerly, suggesting this is marvelous news. "I'm retired myself. I took it early. I didn't wish to keep up with new technology. And time is such a precise measurement. One cannot afford to make mistakes."

Jim feels his knees weaken as though someone has just struck them with a blunt instrument. He needs to sit, the room is spinning, but he can't sit, he is at work. "Time?"

"I became an atomic scientist. My wife used to say my job was fixing the clock." James Lowe smiles but not in a way that suggests he thinks he has said anything funny. It is more crumpled, his smile. "It was a difficult job to explain. She found that people looked either tired or busy. Although you would understand, of course. You were always the intelligent one."

James Lowe refers to caesium atoms and minus the twenty-fourth. There is a mention of Greenwich Observatory, as well as phases of the moon, gravitational pull, and Earth wobbles. Jim listens, he hears the words, but they do not register as sounds with meaning. They are more like soft noise drowned by the confusion inside him. He wonders if he heard right, that James Lowe said that he, Jim, was the intelligent one? Maybe he is staring or making a face, because James falters. "It's so good to see you, Byron. I was thinking of you—and then here you are. The older I get, the more I have to admit that life is strange. It is full of surprises."

All the time James has spoken, there has been no café. There has been only the two men, and a bewildering collision of past and present. Then there is a noise from the servery, a whoosh from the coffee machine, and Jim glances up. Paula is staring straight at him. She turns to Mr. Meade, lifts her mouth toward his ear, and then he too stops what he is doing and stares in the direction of the two old friends.

James, however, sees none of this. He is back to his zip. He realigns the pull with the metal teeth. He says, "There is something I need to say to you."

And all the time that Jim is hearing James Lowe, he is also seeing Mr. Meade. The manager pours two cups of coffee and sets them on a tray. James's voice and Mr. Meade's actions blend to become part of the same scene, like a soundtrack matched to the wrong film.

"This is so difficult," says James.

Mr. Meade lifts the plastic tray. He is heading straight toward them. Jim must find a way of excusing himself. He must do it immediately. But Mr. Meade is so close, the coffee cups make a nervous rattle against their china saucers.

"Forgive me, Byron," says James.

Mr. Meade stops at their table with his plastic tray. "Forgive me, Jim," says Mr. Meade.

Jim has no idea what is happening. It is like another accident that seems to make no sense. Mr. Meade sets the tray on the edge of the table. He addresses the hot beverages and also a plate of mince pies. "I have brought refreshment, courtesy of the management. Please, gentlemen, be seated. Sprinkles?"

"I beg your pardon?" says James Lowe.

"On your cappuccinos?"

The gentlemen agree they would both like sprinkles. Mr. Meade produces a small dispenser and applies a liberal coating of powdered chocolate to each drink. He sets the table with knives and forks and clean napkins. He places the condiments in the middle. "Bon appétit," he says and "Enjoy," as well as "Gesundheit." Turning swiftly, he scampers toward the kitchen, only relaxing his pace when he is at a safe distance. "Darren?" he calls out with sudden authority. "Hat."

Jim and James Lowe stare a moment at the gift of coffee and pies as if they have never seen such richness. James pulls out a chair for Jim. Jim in turn passes James his coffee and a fresh paper napkin. He offers him the larger of the two pies. They sit.

For a moment the two childhood friends do nothing but eat and drink. James Lowe carves his mince pie into quarters and tidies each one into his mouth. Their jaws chew, their teeth bite, their tongues lick, as if to draw every shred of goodness from the sustenance provided. They are so insignificant, these middle-aged friends, one tall, the other small, one in orange hat, the other in waterproof jacket, and yet they each wait as if the other holds the answer to a question that for now lacks words. It is only once they have finished that James Lowe begins again. "I was saying." He folds his napkin in half and half again and then into a tiny square. "There is a summer I've never forgotten. We were boys."

Jim tries to drink, but his hands are shaking so hard he has to give up on the coffee.

James leans one hand on the table to steady himself and puts the other over his eyes, as if shielding himself from the present and seeing nothing but the past.

"Things happened. Things neither of us really understood. They were terrible things that changed everything." His face clouds and Jim knows that James is thinking of Diana because all at once he is thinking of her too. She is everything he can see. Her hair like a gold frill, her skin pale as water, her silhouette dancing on the surface of the pond.

"Her loss—" says James. And here his mouth freezes. There is a long moment of silence in which they both sit, saying nothing. James reassembles his face. "Her loss is still with me."

"Yes." Jim fumbles for his antibacterial spray, but even as he picks it up he knows it is redundant and puts it down.

"I tried to tell Margaret—about her. About your mother. But there are some things that can't be said."

Jim nods, or does he shake his head?

"She was like—" And again James falters. All at once, Jim can clearly see the boy, the intense stillness that was always James Lowe. It is so obvious, he can't understand how he initially missed it. "Apart from the newspapers, I was never a big reader. It is only in my retirement that I have discovered books. I like Blake. I hope you don't mind my saying this but—your mother was like a poem."

Jim nods. She was. A poem.

It is clearly too much for James to keep speaking of her. He clears his throat, he rubs his hands. Eventually he lifts his chin, just as Diana used to lift hers, and he says: "And what do you do, Byron, in your spare time? Do you read too?"

"I plant."

James smiles as if to say yes. Yes, of course you plant things. "Your mother's son," he says. And then without explanation the smile slides into an expression of such grief, such sorrow, Jim wonders what has happened. James says with difficulty, "I don't sleep. Not well. I owe you an apology, Byron. I've owed it to you for many years."

James screws his eyes shut, but tears shoot out anyway. He sits with his fists clenched into balls on the tabletop. Jim would like to reach out across the laminated table and take his hand, but there is a plastic tray between them, not to mention more than forty years. And such is the consternation in his heart, his head, he can't remember how to lift his arms.

"When I heard what had happened to you—when I heard

about Besley Hill—and your father's loss—all those awful things that followed—I felt terrible. I tried to write. Many times. I wanted to visit. I couldn't. My best friend, and I did nothing."

Jim looks around helplessly and finds Mr. Meade, Darren, and Paula all staring from the servery. Embarrassed, they try to become busy, but there are no customers, there are only plates of cakes to rearrange, and they are not fooling anyone. Paula mimes a little series of words with her fingers. She has to do it twice because he doesn't respond, he only stares. "Are you two OK?" she mouths.

He nods once.

"Byron, I'm sorry. I've spent my life regretting it. If only— My God, if only I'd never told you about those two seconds."

Jim feels James's words reach him. They slide beneath his orange uniform and touch his bones. Meanwhile, James brushes down his jacket sleeves. He picks up his driving gloves and undoes the buttons and slips his fingers inside.

Jim says, "No." He says, "It wasn't your fault." In a fumbling rush, he plunges his hand into his pocket. He pulls out his key. James Lowe watches in confusion as Jim struggles to unhook the key ring. His fingers are shaking so hard, he wonders if he will ever do it. He catches his nail on the silver ring, but at last it is free and lying in the palm of his hand.

James stares at the brass beetle. He doesn't move. Jim stares too. It is as if both men are seeing it for the first time. The smooth folded wings. The small engraved markings of the thorax. The flattened head.

"Take it," says Jim. "It's yours." He offers it again. He is both desperate to give it back and terrified of what it will mean when he goes to the van and does not have it. Everything will fall apart.

He knows that and yet he also knows the key ring must be returned.

Understanding none of this, however, James Lowe nods. "Thank you," he says softly. He takes up the beetle and twists it between his fingers, unable to believe what he has been given. "My goodness, my goodness," he says, smiling over and over, as if what Byron has returned to him is an intrinsic and long-lost part of himself. And then he says, "I have something of yours."

Now it is James's turn to tremble. He fumbles with his inside jacket pocket, his eyes on the ceiling, his lips parted, as if waiting for his fingers to get it right. Eventually he produces a wallet. It is brushed leather. He opens it, and from a line of pockets he pulls something out. "Here." He places a crumpled card in Jim's palm. It is the Brooke Bond Montgolfier Balloon card. Number one in the series.

It is hard to say how the next things happen. One moment they sit opposite each other, staring at their returned possessions. The next, James stands and something seems to undo him even as his legs straighten. Before he can fall, Jim has leapt up and caught him. They stand a moment like this, two grown men, caught in each other's arms. And finding each other again after all these years, they cannot let go. They hold on tight, knowing even as they do so that the moment they pull away, they will behave as if they have not.

"It was good," says James Lowe into Jim's ear. "To find you again. It was good."

Jim, who is not Jim, who is Byron after all, murmurs yes. It was good.

"Tout va bien," says James bravely. Or rather, his mouth makes the shapes of those words. The two men break apart.

When they say goodbye they shake hands. Unlike the first time, and unlike the embrace, this is both swift and formal. From his wallet, James Lowe produces an old business card. He points to the telephone number and says that the mobile details are still the same. "If you are ever in Cambridge, you must visit." In turn, Jim nods and says yes, he will, knowing all the while that he will never leave Cranham Moor, that he will always be here and his mother will be here too, and now that he has found it again there can be no disconnecting from the past. James Lowe turns and creeps out of Jim's life as unobtrusively as he has just entered it.

"That looked intensive," observes Paula. "You all right?" Darren suggests that Jim might like a nip of something strong. In turn, Jim asks if they would excuse him a moment. He needs fresh air.

There is a tugging at his elbow, and looking down, he finds Mr. Meade. Flushed like a raspberry, Mr. Meade suggests that Jim might be more comfortable if, if—he can't say it, he is so embarrassed—if he removed his orange hat.

7

A Name

Changing his name was not something Byron planned. The thought had never even occurred to him. He assumed that once you had a name that was who you were, you could not move from that. His new name was something that happened in the same way that his mother's death was something that happened, or Besley Hill was something that happened, or the clouds' movement over the moor was something that happened. All these things came in the same moment they passed. There was no warning. It was only afterward that he could look back and put words to what had occurred and thereby began to make order of something fluid, to find a specific context in which to fix it.

When his father failed to collect Byron from the police station, Andrea Lowe came instead. She explained that Seymour had telephoned her from London and asked for her help. Byron sat very still and heard the constable reply that they had the poor kid in a cell because they didn't know what else to do with him. He had traveled three hundred miles in his pajamas, school blazer, and shoes. From the look of him, he hadn't eaten for days.

Byron tried to lie down, and his feet reached the end of the mattress. The scratchy blanket would not cover him.

Andrea Lowe was saying that there were family issues. Her voice was sharp and fast. Byron thought she sounded frightened. The mother was dead. The father was—how could she put it?—not coping. There were no other living relatives, apart from a sister, and she was at boarding school. The problem was, Andrea Lowe said, that he was a problem. He was trouble.

He didn't know why she would say that about him.

The constable pointed out that they couldn't keep the boy in a police cell just because he'd run away from school. He asked Andrea Lowe if she could take him in for the night, but she said she could not. She would not feel safe alone with a young man with a history like his.

"But he's sixteen. And there's nothing wrong with him," said the constable. "He says he's dangerous, but you only have to take one look at him to see he wouldn't hurt a fly. He's in his pajamas, for goodness sake." He actually raised his voice.

Andrea Lowe's voice, however, remained low. Byron had to keep very still in order to hear, so still he was almost not himself. She spoke in a rush as if she didn't want the words in her mouth. Had the police not heard? Byron had been sent away because he was trouble. These were facts, she said. He had stood and done nothing while his mother drowned. He even ate cake at her funeral. "Cake," she repeated. If that was not enough, there had been further trouble. The boy had been responsible for a serious head injury to his sister. The signs were there from the start. When he was ten, he had nearly killed her son in a pond. She had been forced to remove James from the school, she said.

Byron's mouth yawed open in a silent scream. It was too much to hear these things. He had wanted to help his mother. He would never have hurt James. And when he put the ladder outside, he was trying to save his sister. It was as if they were talking about another boy, one who was not him, but who also appeared to be himself. Maybe she was right? Maybe it was all his fault? The bridge and Lucy's accident? Maybe he had wanted to hurt them all along, even though another part of him would never want that? Maybe he was two boys? One who did terrible things and another who needed to stop them? Byron began to shake. He got up, he kicked at the bed, at the bucket beneath. The tin bucket spun around and around, it was dizzying, and then it crashed against the wall. He picked it up. He threw it again at the wall, and then it was too much to keep hurling the bucket at the wall because the bucket had dents in it now. It would fall apart. Instead he knocked the wall with his head to stop hearing, to stop feeling, to meet something solid, and it was like shouting at himself because he didn't want to be rude and shout out loud. The wall was cold and hard against his head and it was a crazy thing to do and maybe that was why he couldn't stop. He heard shouts at the door of the cell. Everything seemed to be going up a notch. To be happening in ways that did not add up.

"All right, all right, son," said the constable, and when Byron still wouldn't stop, the constable slapped him. Andrea Lowe shrieked.

It wasn't to hurt, the constable said. It was just to pull the boy up. He looked appalled that he had done that to Byron. Watching from the door, Andrea Lowe was white. The constable paced up and down. This was too much, he kept saying, as if he couldn't believe what was happening.

"I cause accidents," Byron whispered.

"Are you listening?" shrieked Andrea Lowe.

"I need to go to Besley Hill. I want to go to Besley Hill."

"You heard what he said," said Andrea Lowe. "He wants to go. He's asking to go. He needs our help."

Another phone call was made and Andrea Lowe fetched her car. She was clearly beside herself now. She insisted with a brave voice that she was a close friend of the family; she would see this through. She wouldn't let him sit in the front, however. When he asked where they were going, she wouldn't answer. He tried to say something different, a question about how James was getting along at his school these days, but still she gave no reply. He wanted to tell her she was wrong about the pond, the bridge had not been his idea, it was James's, but the words were too hard. It was easier to sit with his nails digging into his hands and say nothing.

Andrea Lowe's car thumped over the bars of the cattle grid, and the moor opened up around them. It was wild and endless and Byron had no idea what he was doing in her car. He didn't even know why he had run away from school or why he had gone to the police or why he had battered his head against the wall. He was maybe trying to show them that he wasn't coping, that he was unhappy. He could so easily go back to being what he had been before. If only she would stop the car, if only they could pause everything a moment, it wasn't too late, he could get back to what he was. But the car swung into the drive and people were already running down the steps to meet them.

"Thank you, Mrs. Lowe," they said.

She jumped out of the car and rushed toward the entrance. "Just get him out of my car," she was saying. "Get him out."

They moved so fast he had no time to think. They swung open

his car door. They swooped on him as if he might explode at any minute. He dug his nails into the car seat, he grasped tight to the seat belt. Then someone grabbed his feet and someone else pulled at his arms and he was shouting no, no, no, please. More people were coming with jackets and blankets and they were saying mind his head and asking one another if they could find his veins. They were pulling up his sleeves and he didn't know if he was crying or making no noise at all. How old is he? someone was shouting.

"He's sixteen," Andrea Lowe was shouting back. "He's sixteen."

Andrea Lowe was crying, or maybe it was someone else.

All the voices were getting mixed up because his head was not his anymore. They were carrying him toward the building. The sky flew above him, as if pulled, and then he was in a room with chairs, and then he was nothing.

The first day at Besley Hill he was not fit to move. He slept and woke and remembered where he was and felt such pain he returned to sleep again. On the second day he showed more signs of being calm, and this was when one of the nurses said maybe he would like to take a walk.

She was a small, neat woman. Maybe it was the color of her hair—a soft gold bob—but he felt that she was kind. She showed him the dormitory where he would sleep, and the room where he could bathe, and where he could go to the lavatory. She pointed to the garden through the window and said it was a shame that such a lovely place had run to seed. He could hear voices, shouting and sometimes laughter, but they came and went. Mainly there was silence, a silence so profound he could believe the rest of the world had been shorn away. He didn't know if he was happy or sad for that. Since the injections they had given to calm his nerves, he found his emotions stopped at the point before he felt them. It was the same as seeing the black of sadness and being filled with something that did not match sadness, purple maybe, light as a bird that never lands.

The nurse unlocked the door to the television room, and when he asked why they had to keep it behind a glass door, she smiled and said he was not to be frightened. He would be safe at Besley Hill.

"We are going to look after you," she said. Her face was pink and powdered, as if she had been dusted with icing sugar. She reminded Byron of a sugar mouse and he realized in that moment he was hungry. He was so hungry he felt like a hole.

She told him her name was Sandra. "What's yours?" she said.

He was about to answer when something stopped him. It was as if, in hearing her question, he saw a door, like the glass one in front of the television, in a place where previously he had assumed there was nothing but wall.

Byron thought about what his life had become. He thought of all the mistakes he had made, and there were so many his head reeled. Given the shame, the loneliness, the constant sorrow, there was no way Byron could keep being the person he was. It was more than he could endure. The only way to keep going was to become someone else.

The nurse smiled. "I'm only asking your name. You needn't look so worried."

Byron reached inside his pocket. He closed his eyes and thought of the cleverest person he knew. The friend who was like the missing part of himself and whom he adored as much as he had loved his mother. He curled his fingers around the lucky beetle.

"It's James." The name felt soft and raw in his mouth.

"James?" repeated the nurse.

He glanced over his shoulder, waiting for someone to spring out and say, This young man is not James, he is Byron, he is a failure, he is a mess. But no one sprang from anywhere. He nodded his head to show the nurse he was a James.

"My nephew is called James," said the nurse. "It's a nice name. But, do you know? My nephew doesn't like it. He makes us call him Jim." The name sounded funny, like *jam,* and he laughed. The nurse laughed too. It was like sharing something at last, and it was a relief.

He remembered his mother smiling the day they bought presents to take to Digby Road and her strange story about the man who liked champagne. He thought of her different voices, the feathery one for Seymour and the kind one for the children. He thought of her laughing with Beverley and the way she could slip, like a pool of water beneath a door, into being someone else. Maybe it was that easy? Maybe it was simply a question of giving a new name to what you were, and you could become that. After all, James had said you could call a dog a hat and discover, in doing so, that you had been missing something all along.

"Yes," he repeated, a little more boldly. "I am Jim too." Already, now that they had abbreviated it, it didn't seem so much of a lie. It was as if his friend was right there with him at Besley Hill. He wasn't frightened anymore. He wasn't even hungry.

The nurse smiled. "Let's get you comfy, Jim," she said. "Why don't you take off your belt and your shoes?"

A little trail of men passed in pajamas, walking slowly. He

wanted to wave, they looked so tired. Each had two marks stamped on his forehead, red as poppies.

"You see," said the nurse, "lots of gentlemen wear slippers while they are here."

Through the windows, Byron could see the moor rising to touch the winter sky. The clouds were so heavy, there might even be snow. He remembered the way the sun used to spill through the windows at Cranham House in such clean warm squares he could stand in them and feel lit up.

Byron knelt to remove his shoes.

8

A Different Ending

Up on the moor, a veil of rain falls. Even in the dark, Jim is aware of the first traces of spring. Curled leaves prod through the earth, so new that they are thin as grass. He finds a perfect yellow celandine and scraps of leaves that will become cow parsley and nettles. In town, he has already seen cherry blossom, pale catkins, new buds the size of crumbs. Once again, the land is changing.

Jim thinks of James Lowe and Diana; of his sister, Lucy, whom he no longer sees; of his father, whose funeral he did not attend. It made no difference. All the years of duct tape and double-checking and h-hello. He sees it with a clarity that robs him of breath, it hurts so much. He could never be safe. No matter how many times he did the rituals, he would never protect himself, because the thing he most feared had already happened. It happened the day he glanced at his watch and saw that seconds were being added. It happened the day his mother took a walk on the pond and dissolved into rain. The worst is not to come. It is already here. It has been with him for more than forty years.

There is so much to take in. He stands still, taking his breath in short gasps, as if someone is punching him from inside. He doesn't know how he will walk back into the café, how he will resume his old life. The rift between the past and this moment is so huge it is like being marooned on a square of ice, seeing other patches of his life also floating around him, and unable to piece them all together. Sometimes it is easier, he thinks, to live out the mistakes we have made than to summon the energy and imagination required to repair them.

He sees his mother throwing her watch into the pond. He thinks of the years that have come and gone since then, the days, the minutes. Their measurement means nothing.

James Lowe is right. Their meeting has been there all along. It is something the universe requires. But for one person to help another, for one small act of kindness to succeed, a lot must go well, a myriad of things must fall into place. More than forty years have passed, and yet the time in which they have not seen each other has not broken the two friends apart. James Lowe has found a good job, he has a wife and a mortgage; just as Byron has had many jobs, has never married, and does not own a house. They have held on to the hope that some day this moment will arrive. They have waited. He has kept James's lucky beetle; James has kept the Brooke Bond tea card. Tears fill his eyes and stars lance the sky. He sobs, he sobs hard, hard as a child. For the loss, the suffering, the pain. For the waste, the wrong turns, the mistakes. For his friend. For forgiveness.

With a clutter of wings a flock of starlings lifts into the air, unraveling and lengthening like black ribbon. He walks across the moor and further, further into the night.

Byron, says the wind, the grass, the earth. And he tries to say it too: "I am Byron. Byron Hemmings."

He is no longer two people. He is no longer two fractured stories. He is one.

The Subtraction of Time

It is New Year's morning and the air is clear. Giant clouds pass slowly over the stars. The land is spiked with hoarfrost, and each blade of grass sparkles in the moonlight. It is too early to see clearly, but a wind moves through the dead leaves and the sleeves of ivy, and they give the gentlest whishing. Across the hills, the church bell rings six.

Byron sits outside the van in coat and wool hat. Already he has been out to check his planting and cleared back a frozen carpet of leaves. Eileen is still sleeping on the pull-out bed, her hair thick across the pillow. As he got up he tucked the covers around her, and she ground her teeth but did not waken. She was fully dressed. He marveled again at the smallness of her boots, the holly green of her coat on the back of his door. The wrapped pens hang in her pocket. Her sleeve, he noticed, was caught up on the shoulder. He stopped. He took the cuff, where her hand might be, and smoothed the sleeve straight.

He found himself wondering if he should do it twenty-one times. His fingers twitched. He left the coat as it was. He shut the van door quietly behind him.

He had not done the full set of rituals the previous night. He had completed only part. After arriving at Eileen's, and drinking tea, they had driven to the moor and walked to a high point to watch the fireworks. From there the walk extended itself to Cranham Village, from there to the Green, and from there to his van. They didn't even discuss what they were doing. Their boots just kept going. It was only as they reached the cul-de-sac that he realized what was happening and began to tremble.

"Are you all right?" Eileen said. "I could go home."

It took him a long time to say he would like her to stay.

"Maybe one step at a time," she said.

He has told her his real name and the story of James. He has told her about Diana and the accident. He has told her about Cranham House, how it was sold to developers, how he watched the bulldozers knock it to the ground. He has told her about the different treatments over the years, and with difficulty he has explained that he is safe so long as he does the rituals. None of this has come easily. The sentences have been like pieces of glass in his throat and mouth. They have taken hours. All the time, Eileen has listened, waiting, with her head very still, her blue eyes wide. She has not said, I can't believe this. She has not said, I must get some sleep now. She has said none of these things. The only thing she has mentioned is that she likes Cambridge. She would like to visit one day. He has shown her the Brooke Bond tea card.

Next to the van he sets up a picnic table and two Zip Dee chairs, along with a pot of tea, milk, sugar, mugs, and a packet of custard cream biscuits. The chair opposite his is for Eileen, and it sits there, looking back at him, open as a question.

He arranges her mug so that the handle will be facing her when she sits.

If she sits.

He arranges the mug handle so that it faces himself.

He turns it to a noncommittal midway point.

He says Eileen's Cup, hello.

Her name in his mouth is like touching a small part of her, a part she might not notice, like the soft cuff of her coat. He thinks of lying beside her in the night, their clothes creaking. The close-up smell of her skin. Her breathing alongside his breathing. He wonders if they will ever sleep naked, but the thought is so big he has to shoo it away with a biscuit. His head spins.

The truth is, he hasn't slept. It was past four when he finally realized that Eileen was staying. He explained that he had not said Jubilee Tea Towel, hello, Mattress, hello, and she shrugged and said he was not to mind her. She would wait, she said. And after ten rounds of his unlocking the door and stepping inside, each time jumping at the shock of the solid shape of her by his two-ring hob, she said, at last:

"You haven't said anything to me."

"I beg your pardon?"

"You haven't said, Eileen, hello."

"But you are not part of my van."

"I might be," she said.

"You are not an inanimate object."

"I'm not saying you have to. I'm just saying it might be nice."

After that he lost heart. He pulled down the foldout bed and fetched blankets, hoping to finish when she was asleep. She lay down and asked if he wanted to lie next to her. He sat first in a casual way, somewhere near her knees, and then gently he lifted his feet, and after that he made a sighing noise as if he had not noticed he was lying down. She rested her head on his arm and was asleep within minutes.

Pressed close to Eileen, he screwed his eyes shut, waiting for something terrible to happen. Without the duct tape the space felt vulnerable and terrifying—if anyone was unclothed, it was the van—but nothing happened. She did not sleepwalk. She quickly snored. He felt he would cut off his arm rather than disturb her.

He eats a second custard cream. He is so hungry that one at a time does not seem enough.

When Eileen comes out to join him, one side of her face is red and creased from the pillow. She has put on her coat—the buttons are done up wrong—and the fabric is concertinaed around her waist. Her hair lifts out in two giant wings. She sits in the chair opposite his, saying nothing, looking out where he is looking. She takes the mug as if it is hers and pours tea. She helps herself to custard creams.

"It's nice," she says.

That's all.

Already the dawn is growing. To the east, a crack of gold splits the night just above the horizon. The leaves of ivy rustle, rustle, and there is no need for words. Suddenly Eileen stands, hugging her torso. She stamps her feet on the ground.

"Are you going?" he says, trying to sound like someone who doesn't mind.

"I need a blanket if you want to sit out here."

Stepping up to the van, she turns. Her hands rest on the doorframe as if she has done this many times. As if she will continue to do so hundreds more.

He says, "There's something I would like to show you, Eileen."

"Give me two secs, love," she says. She disappears into the van.

Byron guides Eileen toward the Green. The moon is still up, but the sky belongs to the dawn now, and the circle of white is losing its shine. Beneath their boots the frosted grass snaps. The blades twinkle as if they are sugarcoated. He remembers that Eileen likes frost better than snow, and he is happy she has a day like this. They are not holding hands, but once or twice their shoulders or their hips find each other. They do not jump away.

Eileen and Byron come to a standstill beside the first of the houses on the cul-de-sac. "Look," he says. He tries not to laugh, but his heart is vaulting with excitement.

He points at the home of the foreign students. No one is up, though a box of empty bottles and beer cans has been left on the doormat along with several trainers. Eileen looks confused. "I don't get it," she says. "What am I looking at?"

"Look there." He points.

"I still can't see anything."

He guides her closer. They are standing right by the ground-floor window; there is no sound coming from inside. Gently he reaches into the plastic window box and parts a layer of leaves. Eileen peers to look closer. There are two unfolded purple crocuses.

"Flowers?"

He nods. Putting his finger to his mouth, he whispers: "I did this."

She looks confused. "Why?" she says.

"I don't know. Maybe it was a bit for you."

"For me?"

"Maybe."

"But you didn't know me then."

"Well, I don't know." He laughs.

Eileen reaches down and takes his hand in hers. She is warm as a glove. It does not frighten him. He does not flinch.

"Would you have preferred pens?"

"No," she says. "I like this."

He leads her to the next window box. This one is hidden by the washing line and the laundry that is never taken down. They stoop beneath the frozen tea towels and creep toward the window. Again, there is no sign of life inside the house. Beneath the layer of frozen leaves poke two slim green stalks. They are too slight yet to bear flowers but they smell clean, like pine. "These too?" says Eileen. Again, he says yes. These too.

And finally Eileen gets the whole picture. She looks not simply at the two small houses in front of her, with their plastic window boxes. Hands over her eyes, as if she is creating a tunnel, she scans the whitened length of the cul-de-sac. Every house is the same. Beneath the surface of frosted leaves, there will be small signs of new life, poking through the earth.

"When?" she asks at last. "When did you do this?"

"When people were sleeping."

She stares at him. For a moment he wonders if he has something stuck in his teeth, like spinach, except that he hasn't eaten any.

"Good for you," she says.

Hand in hand, they cross the patch of mud that residents call the Green and head toward the enclosed ditch in the middle. This time he doesn't need to point or speak. Instinctively, Eileen seems to know what she is going to find. The leaves he swept away earlier remain in glittering piles at the edge.

Inside the fencing, the pocket of land glows with many colors. There are tiny crocuses, aconites, snowdrops, Star-of-Bethlehem. Not all of them are in flower. Some are still tight buds.

"This is where my mother died."

"Yes." She wipes her eyes.

"Nothing would grow here. The water kept coming back. Not much. Just enough to make a ditch. Water doesn't always do what people want it to."

"No." She nods, though.

"Maybe that is the thing we have to accept about water. It comes and goes."

Eileen wriggles a paper tissue out of her sleeve and blows her nose with a rattle.

He says, "So I brought soil. I carried manure. I planted bulbs. Every night I checked that they were all right."

"Yes," she whispers. "Yes."

Eileen breaks free and moves toward the fence. She gazes down at the pool of winter flowers, where once there was a pond. Watching her, it is as if something wakens inside him. He sees his mother all over again, balancing on water. He feels the heat of that summer in 1972 when she slept under the stars and the air was drugged with the sweetness of night-scented stocks and white nicotiana. He finds his mother's furniture: the frilled lamp, the occasional tables, the chintz armchair. All this is so clear, it is hard to keep remembering that more than forty years have passed.

James Lowe was right. History is an inaccurate thing. Byron hardly dares blink in case he loses what his eyes are giving him.

But it is all around. To his left he no longer finds the rows of affordable two-bedroom homes wearing satellite dishes like hats. There is a Georgian house that stands square and alone against the moor. Where there are children's swings he sees his mother's rose beds. He finds the patio terrace and hears her dance music. He sees the bench where they sat on a hot September night and watched for shooting stars.

Eileen turns. Suddenly, out of the frost-filled air, a cloud of summer flies converge and hover around her hair like tiny lights. She bats at them with her hand. He smiles—and in that moment his mother, the house, the summer flies, are gone. They were all once here, these things, they were once his, and now they are over.

Slowly the sun rises over the horizon, like an old helium balloon, spilling color over the sky. The clouds flame, and so does the land. The moor, the trees, the frozen grass, the houses, they all blaze red, as if everything has decided it would like to be the shade of Eileen's hair. Already cars are passing. Walkers and their dogs. There are calls of Happy New Year. People pause to look at the sunrise, the towers of saffron cloud, the ghost of a moon. Some notice the flowers. A mist rises over the land, and it is so soft it looks like breathing.

"Shall we go back to yours?" says Eileen.

Byron walks to the pond and meets her.

From inside the house, the old man studies his window box. He frowns, his face pressed to the glass. Then, disappearing for a few minutes, he reappears at the front door. He wears slippers and a tartan dressing gown, tied at the waist, and his new baseball cap.

The old man sets one foot outside, testing the air, the ground. He picks his way toward the window box, slight as an old sparrow, and peers down.

The old man touches the two purple flowers, one and then the other, cupping them between his fingertips. He smiles as if this is what he has been waiting for all along.

And in other rooms, in other houses, there is Paula with Darren, there are Mr. and Mrs. Meade, there is Moira with the boy who plays cymbals. There is James Lowe with his wife, Margaret; Lucy with her banker. Somewhere, yes, there must even be Jeanie, married three times now and running her mother's lucrative import business. The foreign students; the man with or without his dangerous dog; all the residents of Cranham Village. Each of them believing on this New Year's morning that life can change a little for the better. Their hope is slight, pale as a new shoot. It is midwinter, and God knows the frost will probably get it. But for a moment at least, there it is.

The sun climbs higher and higher, losing color, until the moor is blue as dust.

Acknowledgments

My thanks to Susanna Wadeson, Kendra Harpster, Clare Conville, Benjamin Dreyer, Alison Barrow, Larry Finlay, Claire Ward, Andrew Davidson, Hope, Kezia, Jo and Nell, Amy and Em. But most of all, Paul Venables, because he knows this story as well as I do.